P9-CAL-450

RANDOM HOUSE
CHILDREN'S BOOKS

Dear Educator:

I am honored to share with you the Teachers Edition of *Moon Over Manifest*, the 2011 Newbery Medal Winner by Clare Vanderpool.

Parts mystery, adventure, and historical fiction, *Moon Over Manifest* stars twelve-year-old Abilene Tucker who is sent to live with an old friend of her father's in Manifest, Kansas, during the Great Depression. There she searches to find her father's footprint in the town and in doing so uncovers the stories at the core of a truly unique cast of characters in both 1918 and 1936 Manifest.

"The absolute necessity of story as a way to redemption and healing past wounds is at the heart of this beautiful debut," said *Kirkus Reviews* in a starred review. It is this that makes *Moon Over Manifest* a timeless classic with appeal to both boys and girls.

I hope you share this gem with your class and let it spark discussion about community, friendship, acceptance and belonging, and prejudice. Beginning on page G1 you will find an extensive teachers guide as well as an interview with the author.

Best wishes,

Lisa Nadel

Lisa Nadel
Senior Manager, Educational Marketing

MOON
OVER
MANIFEST

CLARE VANDERPOOL

A YEARLING BOOK

Sale of this book without a front cover may be unauthorized. If the book is coverless, it may have been reported to the publisher as "unsold or destroyed" and neither the author nor the publisher may have received payment for it.

This is a work of fiction. Names, characters, places, and incidents either are the product of the author's imagination or are used fictitiously. Any resemblance to actual persons, living or dead, events, or locales is entirely coincidental.

Text copyright © 2010 by Clare Vanderpool
Cover art copyright © 2010 by Richard Tuschman

All rights reserved. Published in the United States by Yearling, an imprint of Random House Children's Books, a division of Random House, Inc., New York. Originally published in hardcover in the United States by Delacorte Press, an imprint of Random House Children's Books, New York, in 2010.

Yearling and the jumping horse design are registered trademarks of Random House, Inc.

Visit us on the Web! randomhouse.com/kids

Educators and librarians, for a variety of teaching tools, visit us at randomhouse.com/teachers

The Library of Congress has cataloged the hardcover edition of this work as follows:
Vanderpool, Clare.
Moon over Manifest / Clare Vanderpool. — 1st ed.
p.   cm.
Summary: Twelve-year-old Abilene Tucker is the daughter of a drifter who, in the summer of 1936, sends her to stay with an old friend in Manifest, Kansas, where he grew up, and where she hopes to find out some things about his past.
ISBN 978-0-385-73883-5 (hc : alk. paper) — ISBN 978-0-385-90750-7 (glb : alk. paper) — ISBN 978-0-375-89616-3 (ebook) [1. Secrets—Fiction. 2. Fathers—Fiction. 3. Depressions—1929—Fiction. 4. Kansas—Fiction.]
I. Title.
PZ7.P28393Mo 2010
[Fic]—dc22
2009040042

ISBN 978-0-307-97665-9

Printed in the United States of America

10 9 8 7 6 5 4 3 2 1

First Yearling Edition 2011

Random House Children's Books supports the First Amendment and celebrates the right to read.

To Mother and Daddy,
for loving a good story, and a good laugh,
and for giving me a good life

CHARACTERS

Manifest townspeople of 1918

SHADY HOWARD: saloon owner and bootlegger

JINX: con artist extraordinaire

NED GILLEN: Manifest High School track star

HATTIE MAE HARPER: up-and-coming journalist for the *Manifest Herald*

THE HUNGARIAN WOMAN: owner and operator of Miss Sadie's Divining Parlor

SISTER REDEMPTA: nun, not a universal

IVAN DEVORE: postmaster

VELMA T. HARKRADER: chemistry teacher and maker of home remedies

MR. UNDERHILL: undertaker

HADLEY GILLEN: Ned's father and owner of the hardware store

EUDORA LARKIN: president of the Daughters of the American Revolution (Manifest chapter)

PEARL ANN LARKIN: daughter of Mrs. Larkin, and Ned's girl

ARTHUR DEVLIN: mine owner

LESTER BURTON: pit boss

FINN: Jinx's uncle

Additional townspeople and their countries of origin

DONAL MACGREGOR: Scotland

CALLISTO MATENOPOULOS: Greece

CASIMIR AND ETTA (AND LITTLE EVA) CYBULSKIS: Poland

OLAF AND GRETA AKKERSON: Norway

MAMA SANTONI: Italy

HERMANN KEUFER: Germany

NIKOLAI YEZIERSKA: Russia

Manifest townspeople of 1936

ABILENE TUCKER: new girl in town

GIDEON TUCKER: Abilene's father

LETTIE AND RUTHANNE: friends of Abilene

PASTOR SHADY HOWARD: still a little shady

HATTIE MAE MACKE: still writing "Hattie Mae's News Auxiliary"

IVAN DEVORE: still postmaster

VELMA T.: still the chemistry teacher

SISTER REDEMPTA: still a nun

MISS SADIE: still a diviner

MR. UNDERHILL: still the undertaker

MR. COOPER: the barber

MRS. DAWKINS: owner of Dawkins Drug and Dime

MRS. EVANS: woman who sits on her porch and stares

MOON
OVER
MANIFEST

Santa Fe Railway

SOUTHEAST KANSAS
MAY 27, 1936

The movement of the train rocked me like a lullaby. I closed my eyes to the dusty countryside and imagined the sign I knew only from stories. The one just outside of town with big blue letters: MANIFEST: A TOWN WITH A RICH PAST AND A BRIGHT FUTURE.

I thought about my daddy, Gideon Tucker. He does his best talking in stories, but in recent weeks, those had become few and far between. So on the occasion when he'd say to me, "Abilene, did I ever tell you 'bout the time . . . ?" I'd get all quiet and listen real hard. Mostly he'd tell stories about Manifest, the town where he'd lived once upon a time.

His words drew pictures of brightly painted storefronts and bustling townsfolk. Hearing Gideon tell about it was like sucking on butterscotch. Smooth and sweet. And when he'd go back to not saying much, I'd try recalling what it tasted like. Maybe that was how I found comfort just then, even with him being so far away. By remembering the flavor of his words. But mostly, I could taste the sadness in his voice when he told me I couldn't stay with him for the summer while he worked a railroad job back in Iowa. Something had changed in him. It started the day I got a cut on my knee. It got bad and I got real sick with infection. The doctors said I was lucky to come out of it. But it was like Gideon had gotten a wound in him too. Only he didn't come out of it. And it was painful enough to make him send me away.

I reached into my satchel for the flour sack that held my few special things. A blue dress, two shiny dimes I'd earned collecting pop bottles, a letter from Gideon telling folks that I would be received by Pastor Howard at the Manifest depot, and my most special something, kept in a box lined with an old 1917 *Manifest Herald* newspaper: my daddy's compass.

In a gold case, it wore like a pocket watch, but inside was a compass showing every direction. Only problem was, a working compass always points north. This one, the arrow dangled and jiggled every which way. It wasn't even that old. It had the compass maker's name and the date it was made on the inside. *St. Dizier, October 8, 1918.* Gideon had always planned to get it fixed, but when I was leaving, he said he didn't need it anyway, what with train tracks to guide him. Still, I liked imagining that the chain of that broken compass was long enough to stretch all the way back into his pocket, with him at one end and me at the other.

Smoothing out the yellowed newspaper for the thousandth time, I scanned the page, hoping to find some bit of news about or insight into my daddy. But there was only the same old "Hogs and Cattle" report on one side and a "Hattie Mae's News Auxiliary: Charter Edition" on the other, plus a couple of advertisements for Liberty Bonds and Billy Bump's Hair Tonic. I didn't know anything about Hattie Mae Harper, except what she wrote in her article, but I figured her newspaper column had protected Gideon's compass for some time, and for that I felt a sense of gratitude. I carefully placed the newspaper back in the box and stored the box in the satchel, but held on to the compass. I guess I just needed to hold on to something.

The conductor came into the car. "Manifest, next stop."

The seven-forty-five evening train was going to be right on time. Conductors only gave a few minutes' notice, so I had to hurry. I shoved the compass into a side pocket of the satchel, then made my way to the back of the last car. Being a paying customer this time, with a full-fledged ticket, I didn't *have* to jump off, and I knew that the preacher would be waiting for me. But as anyone worth his salt knows, it's best to get a look at a place before it gets a look at you. I'd worn my overalls just for the occasion. Besides, it wouldn't be dark for another hour, so I'd have time to find my way around.

At the last car, I waited, listening the way I'd been taught—wait till the clack of the train wheels slows to the rhythm of your heartbeat. The trouble is my heart speeds up when I'm looking at the ground rushing by. Finally, I saw a grassy spot and jumped. The ground came quick and hard, but I landed and rolled as the train lumbered on without a thank-you or goodbye.

As I stood and brushed myself off, there was the sign not five feet in front of me. It was so weathered there was hardly a chip of blue paint to be found. And it looked to have been shot up so bad most of the words were gone. All that was left read MANIFEST: A TOWN WITH A PAST.

HATTIE MAE'S NEWS AUXILIARY
CHARTER EDITION

MAY 27, 1917

I am pleased as punch to be commencing this groundbreaking column in the *Manifest Herald*. My experience last year as assistant copy editor of the Manifest High School newspaper (Huzzah, huzzah for the Grizzlies!) has provided me with an eye for the interesting and a nose for news.

After Uncle Henry talked it over with his people at the paper, he decided to give me a column anyway. What with our nation involved in a great war and our young men leaving our sweet land of liberty, we must be vigilant on the home front. President Wilson has asked all of us to do our patriotic duty in supporting the war effort, and already many are answering the call. Hadley Gillen says Liberty Bonds are selling quicker than half-inch nails at the hardware store. Mrs. Eudora Larkin and the Daughters of the American Revolution are sewing victory quilts.

Even Miss Velma T. Harkrader generously devoted our last week of senior chemistry class to making relief parcels for our lads in arms. Despite a minor explosion while we mixed her dyspepsia elixir, the parcels turned out beautifully, each wrapped in red-white-and-blue gingham, and I am sure they will be received with great appreciation.

Now, it is time for me to hang up my crown as Manifest Huckleberry Queen of 1917 and trade it for the hardscrabble life of a journalist. And here is my pledge to you, faithful reader: you can count on me to be truthful and certifiable in giving the honest-to-goodness scoop each and every week.

So, for all the whos, whats, whys, whens, and wheres, look at the backside of "Hogs and Cattle" every Sunday.

HATTIE MAE HARPER
Reporter About Town

BILLY BUMP'S HAIR TONIC

Listen up, fellas. Do you have a dry, itchy scalp? Wish you had more hair on your head? Is your hair turning the color of the old gray goat? Then Billy Bump's Hair Tonic is for you. Just rub a little on your hair and scalp before bedtime, and when you wake up, you'll already notice a clean, tingly feeling. This means your hair is growing back, and in the same color you remember from your high school days. That's right, men. The ladies will notice the hair on your head and the spring in your step. Get your Billy Bump's Hair Tonic today at your local barbershop. Tell them Billy sent you and get a free comb. Works on mustaches and sideburns too. But avoid contact with ears and noses.

**Buy a Liberty Bond
and save American liberty!**

Path to Perdition

MAY 27, 1936

First things first after jumping from a train: you needed to check and make sure you still had what you jumped with. That was always easy for me, because I never had much. Gideon said all you needed was your traveling pack and a good head on your shoulders. I had both, so I figured I was in good shape.

Heading for a grove of trees that looked half alive, I found a creek. It was only a trickle but it felt cool and clean on my face and hands. Now I could face the preacher I was to stay with for the summer. How my daddy ever got hooked up with a preacher, I can't say, as he's not a churchgoing man. Apparently the preacher had taken in a wandering soul now and again, and Gideon had been one of them. In any case, Pastor Howard was expecting me and no amount of dillydallying would change that fact.

I hunted up a good fence-running stick and rattled it along the first fence I came to. Gideon and I found that sounds filled up an empty quiet. When I was younger, we spent many a walking hour singing, making up rhymes, playing kick the can. Now the sound of stick on fence carried off into the trees, but it didn't fill the emptiness. For the first time I could recall, I was alone. Maybe I'd try the rhyming. Gideon would start with a line and I'd come up with another that rhymed. The clatter of the stick provided a nice rhythm for the rhyme running in my head. *I wish I had a penny and I wish I had a nickel. I'd trade 'em both in for a coffee and a pickle. I wish I had a quarter and I wish I had a dime. I'd buy a stick of gum before you could tell the time. I wish I had an apple and I wish I had an orange—*

I realized I'd rhymed myself into a corner with *orange* when my stick came to a gate. A wide wrought iron gate that had every manner of doodads welded right into it. Forks, kettles, horseshoes, even the grate off an old potbelly stove. Looking closer, I ran my fingers over the black iron letters sitting along the top of the gate. The letters were kind of crooked and a little uneven but they looked to read PERDI-TION. Now, Gideon and I had been to enough church services, hoping to get a hot meal afterward, that I'd heard the word a time or ten. Preachers used it. They told people to give up their evil ways or follow the devil straight down the path to perdition.

Why somebody would want that word welded on their gate, I can't say. But there it was. And weeds wrapped their way up through the ironwork, daring you to enter. And there was an actual path. Beyond the gate, leaves and dandelions lined a long grassless swatch of ground all the way to a di-lapidated old house. The paint was worn off and the porch swing hung crooked, like it was plumb out of swing.

Surely no one lived there. A train car or a shantytown by the railroad tracks seemed a more welcoming place. But one of the front curtains fluttered. Was someone watching? My heart beat like a bat's wings. For the time being, I was content to stay off that Path to Perdition. The town wasn't far ahead, so I put my stick to the fence and continued walking.

This time I did my rhyme in a quiet voice. *"I had a little cat and it had a little kitten. I'd put it in my lap wherever I'd be sittin'."*

There was a break in the fence but another started up again around a cemetery. Gravestones stood in the wispy grass, seeming to watch me go by. The hair at the back of my neck prickled as the ground crunched behind me. I stopped and looked back. There was nothing but blowing leaves. I moved on, clattering my stick as the trees grew thick around me. *"I had a little dog and his name was Mike. I always let him sit wherever he'd like."* The branches clawed at me and I stumbled on a tree root, landing hard on my knee. It was the knee that had gotten cut a couple of months back. It had scarred over, but the stretched skin felt like it was still working at keeping things together. I massaged it a little and brushed the dirt off.

There it was again. Maybe not a sound, but a move-ment. I held my breath, listening to the quiet, then contin-ued toward lights at the edge of the trees. *"I once had a horse and his name was Fred. He ran all day, then—"*

Another loud crunch behind me, then a man's voice.

"He dropped dead."

Shady's Place

MAY 27, 1936

I swung around in the dimming light. A man stood holding a pitchfork as tall as he was and only slightly thinner. Everything about the man was thin. His clothes, his hair. Even his scruffy whiskers were sparse on his face.

"Is this yours?" he asked.

At first I thought he meant the pitchfork. Then I saw the compass dangling from his fingers. I checked my satchel in a panic. The outside pocket had torn open when I'd fallen.

"I'm Shady Howard. You must be Gideon's girl." I let out the breath I didn't know I'd been holding. He handed me the gold compass. I hung it around my neck and tucked it into my shirt. "When you didn't get off the train, I thought you might be making your own way into town."

He said it like he had jumped from a train or two himself. With his worn plaid shirt and brown pants that had been stitched and patched, he looked the part.

"Are you related to Pastor Howard? The preacher at the First Baptist Church?"

"There's folks that call me Pastor Howard. But you can call me Shady."

I kept my distance, not knowing exactly what he meant. "Do they call you that because you *are* the preacher at the First Baptist Church?"

"Well, that's a kind of interesting story." He started walking, using his pitchfork as a walking stick. "You see, I'm what's called an interim pastor. Meaning the old one left and I'm just filling in till they can get a new one."

"How long you been filling in?" I asked, thinking maybe he hadn't had time to order his preacher clothes yet. Or shave.

"Fourteen years."

"Oh." I worked to put on some manners. "So you weren't in the church business when my daddy was here?"

"No, I wasn't."

"Well, I'm Abilene. I'm twelve years old and a hard worker," I said, like I had a hundred other times in as many towns. "So, I guess you got the letter my daddy sent telling y'all I was coming."

Mind you, I don't really say *y'all*, but it's usually best to try to sound a bit like the folks whose town you're moving into. Never being in Kansas before, I wouldn't know for sure, but I imagined they said things like *y'all* and *up the road a piece* and *weather's coming on.*

"Are you hungry?" Shady asked. "My place is just up the road a piece."

There it was. Funny how people who know exactly where they are can talk so much about directions. I guess those who don't, just keep moving straight ahead. You don't need much direction for that.

"No, sir." I'd had only a hard-boiled egg on the train, but I was here under his hospitality and I didn't feel right asking for food so soon.

"We'll just head into town, then, as I need to pick up a letter."

There would still be daylight enough to take a look around town. As we began to walk, Gideon's stories came back to me in flashes, like views between the trees from a train window. People bustling in and out of colorful storefronts with bright awnings over the windows. Unusual-sounding names painted on the doors. MATENOPOULOS MEAT. SANTONI'S BAKERY. AKKERSON FEED & SEED.

Walking in step with Shady, I tried to conjure up something smooth and sweet from those stories, but looking around, all I could muster was dry and stale. Up and down Main Street, the stores were dingy. Gray. Every third one was boarded up. The only awnings left were torn and saggy. There wasn't an ounce of bustling to be had. Just a few tired souls holding up a doorway here and there.

But then, hard times are a penny for plenty. They call it a Depression, but I'd say it's a downright rut and the whole country's in it.

There was a big gingerbread-like house sorely lacking in paint. A proper-looking lady sat quietly in a rocking chair on the porch, not having the life in her to rock. The barber, leaning against his shop door, stared as I passed. A lady in the grocery store fanned herself as a little dog yapped through the screen door. From some of the glares I got walking up the board sidewalk, I figured these folks would rather suffer through hard times on their own than have a stranger come in to witness their misery.

We didn't slow down at the post office. "I thought we were picking up the mail."

"Not mail. A letter. From Hattie Mae at the newspaper."

"Hattie Mae Harper? Huckleberry Queen of 1917?"

"She's Hattie Mae Macke now, but that's her."

At least there was something familiar in this town. I wondered if Hattie Mae had kept up her "News Auxiliary."

The *Manifest Herald* newspaper office was about centered on Main Street and we walked into a holy mess. Newspapers were stacked two and three feet tall. A typewriter sat on a cluttered desk, its keys splayed open with some scattered on the desk like it tried to spell *explosion* and the explosion happened.

"Shady? That you?" a woman's voice hollered from the back. "I'm just getting ready to close up. Thanks so much for coming by to pick up—"

A large woman came out from the back room, her hair in a frazzled bun. She caught sight of me and her hands went to her face. "Well, aren't you a little darling? You must be Abilene."

"Yes, ma'am."

"My, but you do look like your daddy." She pressed me to her warm bosom and I felt her catch her breath. When I looked up at her again, her eyes were wet. "Would you like a soda pop? Of course you would. You go right on back and get yourself a nice cold bottle. We've got Coca-Cola and Orange Crush. Take your pick. And there's a couple of sandwiches in there. One's cheese and one's meat loaf. You help yourself, now, and don't tell me you're not hungry."

14

"Okay," I said. I started to make my way through the maze of newspapers. Those sandwiches sounded good.

"You'll have to excuse the mess. Uncle Henry insists on saving all these old papers but my husband, Fred, is finally going to build a storage shed out back, so I'm trying to get them organized."

"I've had your very first 'News Auxiliary' my whole life," I blurted out.

"Oh, my heavens. How'd you get ahold of that piece of antiquity?" She laughed and her body jiggled.

"Have you been writing that column all this time?"

"You mean all the whos, whats, whys, whens, and wheres? Yes, I suppose I have. And thanks to the Depression, I've also been promoted to copy editor, typesetter, and coffee maker extraordinaire." She laughed. "Say, if you find yourself with any spare time, you could come and help me if you'd like. As you can see, there are plenty of old newspapers that need to get put in order. If you like reading ancient history, you might find it kind of interesting."

I nodded, thinking that I *would* find that interesting.

"Now go get your pop and a sandwich, sweet pea. And help yourself to whatever newspapers you want. Uncle Henry won't mind giving them away to someone who actually wants to read them. And that'll be all the fewer I'll need to sort through later."

I found the pop chest easy enough and picked out an Orange Crush and the meat loaf sandwich. There was a built-in opener right on the side of the chest. Shady and Hattie Mae were talking about how hot it had been and how there wasn't even a hint of rain. I gobbled down half the sandwich and let my hand run over one stack of newspapers after

15

another. I felt like I was floating in a cloud that was passing from one year to another in no particular order. 1929—STOCK MARKET CRASHES. 1927—BABE RUTH HITS 60 HOME RUNS IN ONE SEASON. 1927—CHARLES LINDBERGH FLIES SOLO ACROSS ATLANTIC IN 33½ HOURS.

Then a particular year caught my eye. 1917—BONE DRY BILL MAKES ALCOHOL ILLEGAL IN KANSAS. That was the same year as Hattie Mae's first "News Auxiliary." That was when Gideon had been in Manifest. My heart picked up speed. I didn't really expect to find Gideon's name in the headlines, or anywhere else in the paper, for that matter. But I might come to know this town a little better through the articles and stories. This town where he had spent time as a boy. This town where he'd chosen to send me.

"You find yourself a soda pop, sweet pea?" Hattie Mae called. "Do I need to come and rescue you from that bottomless pit of newspapers?"

"Coming," I called. "You sure it's okay if I take a couple papers? Something to read while I'm here?"

"Go right ahead."

I thumbed through a stack of papers and chose the only two I found from 1917. July 16 and October 11. I tucked the papers into my satchel and went back to the front room.

Hattie Mae was talking in a hushed voice to Shady. Her face looked a little drawn and worried as she whispered, "Shady, she needs to know—" but she perked up when she saw me.

"Just listen to me, yammering on. You've had a long day, sweet pea, and you need to get refreshed for the last day of school tomorrow."

That must've been what I needed to know.

"School?" I sputtered on my last swallow of orange pop. "But it's summertime." I looked pleadingly at Shady. "Don't folks around here have to be bringing in the sheaves or something?" He gave me an apologetic look, as if he thought the same.

"We just figured you might like to meet some of the kids before they scatter to the four winds for the summer," Hattie Mae said.

I wondered who "we" was and how many of them I was up against. "But my daddy will be coming to get me before school starts up again," I said.

Then I saw Hattie Mae and Shady glance at each other kind of uneasy. They exchanged a look that made me feel a little wobbly and off balance, like I was standing in a train that took an unexpected curve. But I was probably just tired from my travel.

Hattie Mae put her arm around me. "Now, don't you worry. You'll be just fine." As she squeezed me tight, the phone rang. "That'll be Fred. His sciatica is acting up and he's home with the boys. You know how men are. When they don't feel good, the world comes to a standstill. Here's the letter that needs fixing." She handed Shady a key from the typewriter. "The *R* won't type at all, and the *L* keeps getting stuck. You can take the whole thing if you want. I've got tomorrow's column done, so I won't be needing it for the time being."

The phone kept ringing. "I've got to get that, Shady. It's so good to meet you, Abilene. You let me know if you need anything, you hear?"

"Yes, ma'am."

She picked up the phone. "Hello? Yes, I'm coming. Oh, for heaven's sake. Just leave it there. I'll clean it up when I get home."

Shady picked up the discombobulated typewriter and we got while the getting was good. By then it was dark and Shady led the way down an alley off Main Street. We headed back toward the tracks and ended up at a weathered establishment that appeared to be a safe distance from the respectable part of town.

I've lived in a lot of places. Barns, abandoned railroad cars, even Hoovervilles, the shack towns for folks with no money, named for the president before the one we got now, who didn't seem to know that the country was in hard times. So I was prepared for anything. Except Shady's place.

A cowbell clanged above the door as we went inside. Pastor Howard lit a kerosene lamp and set it on a long bar top. There was a mirror behind it, a sawhorse in front with some wood clamped in a vise, and an abundance of sawdust all over the floor. To top it off, there were what looked to be pews shoved up against the wall, and the two windows had honest-to-goodness stained glass.

"Well, this is it," Shady announced, as if that explained everything.

I looked around, not wanting to ask. It was like a jigsaw puzzle I had to piece together myself. Shady's place appeared to be one part saloon, one part carpenter's shop, and—could it be?—one part church.

I must have been staring at the windows, because Shady said, "The First Baptist Church burned down some years back. The windows and a couple pews were salvaged. They're being kept here temporarily, until a Second Baptist Church is built."

"That why the pastor left?"

"Yup," Shady answered. "I think his nerves were about shot by then." He tried to gather up some papers and scraps of wood, as if there were traces of his mismatched life that he hadn't wanted me to see. I looked at the floor. Footprints went every which way, probably from years of drinkers and churchgoers. I felt an ache in my heart that rose like a lump to my throat as I caught myself searching for a less busy part of the room. A small, still place where there might be one or two of my daddy's footprints left.

Shady tossed a block of scrap wood into an empty waste can, causing a big clang that echoed. He looked at me kind of awkward, as if he knew what I'd been searching for, but couldn't help me. "The outhouse is . . . well . . . outside. And there's some cold cuts in the icebox. Would you like me to heat up some water so you can take a proper bath?"

"No thank you. I'm just kind of tired."

"Your room's upstairs. I hope you like it," he said with a quiet politeness.

I wondered about Shady's jigsaw life, but decided not to pry. Not yet, anyway. My daddy, Gideon, had a healthy distrust of most people but he trusted Shady. And so did I. "Good night," I said, and climbed the stairs with my satchel.

There was a kerosene lamp on the nightstand but no matches. With the full moon beaming through the open window, it didn't matter. There was a dresser with a pitcher of water and a bowl. Usually a wash required a trip to a nearby stream or watering trough, so I felt like royalty to be able to pour myself some water and wash the dust from my face and hands. I kicked off my shoes and felt the cool floorboards shift and groan beneath my feet as if the room was adjusting to sudden occupation after being long empty. Yawning at least three times, I put on my pajamas and slipped into bed. It was cozy and soft. I flapped the sheet up and down, letting it fall gently on me like a cloud.

I was drifting off to sleep when I remembered my keepsake bag. Having already come too close to losing something that day, I decided to do what my daddy always did. Anything special and important, he'd hide in an out-of-the-way place that nobody'd find.

In a sleepy scramble I fished the flour sack, my keepsake bag, out of my satchel and checked the contents. It was too dark to read the return address on the letter, but I had it memorized. Santa Fe Railroad Office, Fourth and Main, Des Moines, Iowa. It was the closest thing Gideon had to a place of residence. I rattled the two dimes, making sure they were still there. Finally, I took out the compass box. It was empty except for "Hattie Mae's News Auxiliary," as the compass still hung from my neck. Deciding to keep the compass on me, I put everything else back into the sack.

Now where to put it? It was usually best to find a place that was either high or low. Since I couldn't reach too high, I decided to look low. Putting my feet back on the floor, I again felt the floorboards creak and bow. Maybe one was loose enough to pull up. I took tentative steps around the room until I felt one that had a little more bounce than the others. I knelt on the floor, and with a fairly easy push and pull, the floorboard popped up enough for me to get my fingers under it and pull it up. It would have been the perfect hiding spot but for one thing. There was already something there.

I pulled the something out, slow and gentle, and held it up to the moonlight. It was a Lucky Bill cigar box and inside were papers and odds and ends. There wasn't light for reading, but I could tell that the papers were letters, thin and folded neat. One bigger page looked like a map. The odds and ends clanked inside the box.

"You find what you need?" Shady called from the bottom of the stairs.

"Yes, sir." I slipped the papers into the cigar box and shoved it back into the floor space. My flour sack keepsake bag fit snugly beside it. Then I replaced the floorboard and crawled into bed.

"Good night, then."

I didn't answer right away but I could tell he was still standing there. "Pastor Shady? How far do you think it is to Des Moines?"

There was a pause and I wondered if maybe I'd been wrong and he'd walked away.

"I can't say for sure. But you see that moon out your window?"

"Yes, sir. Plain as day."

"Well, Des Moines is a lot closer than that moon. Fact is, I bet a fella in Des Moines can see the same moon you're looking at right now. Doesn't that just beat all?" His voice was shy and tender. "I'll be right down here if you need anything. Will that be all right?" he asked.

"Yes, sir. That'll be all right."

The pillow was cool against my cheek. It felt good giving

in to sleep. Still, I brought to mind what I'd seen: the cigar box, the letters. Since Gideon had stayed with Shady, maybe this had been his room. Maybe I'd found Gideon's footprints after all.

The breeze died down. But in the calm of the night, my body still felt the movement of the train.

First Morning

MAY 28, 1936

What kind of addlepate starts school on the last day? I'd been asking myself that question since waking to the sound of pans clanking downstairs and the smell of bacon and coffee rising upstairs. My stomach growled, reminding me that Hattie Mae's meat loaf sandwich had become a too-distant memory.

Then I remembered the Lucky Bill cigar box. With a buzz of anticipation, I sprung out of bed and found the loose board, only to have Shady call upstairs.

"Miss Abilene, you're burnin' daylight. Breakfast is ready."

As much as I was itching to get more than a moonlit look at what was in the box, I knew better than to keep a cook waiting. I left the box under the floorboard for safekeeping and checked to make sure the compass was still around my neck. I put on my one change of clothes, a blue dress with yellow daisies. The daisies were a little faded but not so bad you couldn't see them. Then I splashed some water on my face and ran my fingers through my hair. It felt like straw but was the color of a rusty nail. Wearing it short, I never fussed with it much, but I did look forward to that "proper bath" Shady had mentioned the night before.

The stairs emptied into a small back room. More of a porch, really, with a black cookstove, a washtub, and a cot. It appeared Shady could do his eating, bathing, and sleeping all in one place. There was a plate of biscuits, slightly burnt, and bacon, just as warm and pleasant as you please, on the cookstove. Having someone cook my meals made me feel like I was at a fancy hotel.

"There's some of Velma T.'s blackberry jam in the cupboard," Shady called from the big room with the bar top and pews. I spread on a modest amount and set it on a pink glass plate, the kind that came free in bags of sugar or flour or laundry soap.

Since there was no table, I took my pink plate into the big front room. With the light of day shining through those stained-glass windows onto the gleaming bar top, I didn't know whether to kneel down or belly up. Shady was tinkering at his workbench as I ate my breakfast. He was looking real close at a tiny something, cleaning it off with a wire bristle brush. "What're you working on?"

"The letter *L*," he said, squinting at his task at hand. "Hattie Mae's been writing her column for almost twenty years; it's no wonder that typewriter's about give out." He blew on the metal key and eyeballed it from a distance. Wiping off the piece with a cloth, he placed it beside the typewriter.

"Now she can get back to her whos, whats, and wheres and I can get the *L* out of here."

Gideon hadn't told me that Pastor Howard had a sense of humor. Seemed nobody had told Pastor Howard either, as he didn't let on like he thought it was funny.

I finished off the last of my biscuit. It was hard going down, as my mouth had gone dry. Maybe if I made myself useful, I wouldn't have to go to school. I'd been in and out of schools before, but I'd always been in the protective shade of my daddy. Here I was alone and exposed to the heat and clamor of the day.

A bell started clanging from a distance, jarring me out of my thoughts.

"Better get on over to school. You don't want to be late." He studied the splayed-out typewriter in front of him. "Here's a couple things for you to mind while you're there." He handed me the letters *P* and *Q*.

I studied them. "If I took these, it'd sure leave Hattie Mae in a pickle and a quandary and she wouldn't be able to type either one."

Shady smiled a half smile. As I put the letters back on the table, I noticed that day's newspaper lying off to the side. It was folded open to "Hattie Mae's News Auxiliary." I picked it up and read the line at the bottom. *All the whos, whats, whys, whens, and wheres you never knew you needed to know.*

I headed out, giving the cowbell above the door a mournful clang as I left.

Sacred Heart
of the Holy Redeemer
Elementary School

MAY 28, 1936

You'd have thought I'd be used to this by now. Being the new kid and all. I'd been through this umpteen times before but it never gets any easier. Still, there's certain things every school's got, same as any other. Universals, I call them. Walking into the schoolhouse, I smelled the familiar chalky air. Heard fidgety feet rustling under desks. Felt the stares. I took a seat near the back.

My one consolation was that I knew these kids. Even if they didn't know me. Kids are universals too, in a way. Every school has the ones who think they're a little better than everybody else and the ones who are a little poorer than everybody else. And somewhere in the mix there's usually ones who are pretty decent. Those were the ones who made it hard to leave when the time came. And sooner or later, it always came.

I guessed I'd never find out who was who around there,

it being the last day of school and all. The books were already stacked on shelves for the summer. The blackboard was just that: black. No math problems. No spelling words. Then a girl with a rosy round face spoke up.

"I bet you're an orphan."

"Soletta Taylor!" a skinny, red-haired girl scolded. "Why would you say such a thing?"

"She came in on the train without a mama or a daddy, didn't she? It was all the talk at the five-and-dime."

"Well, maybe you shouldn't be listening to 'all the talk.' Besides, that doesn't mean she's an orphan." The girl twisted one of her red braids and looked at me. "Does it?"

My face was hot and probably red, but I squared my shoulders. "My mother's gone to that sweet by and by." I said it loud enough for everybody to hear, since they were all ear cocked anyway. Some gave kind of sympathetic looks for my loss. I didn't figure it was a lie, since who knew for certain what the sweet by and by was? Most folks seemed to think it meant she had died and gone to a better place. But in my book it just meant she had decided that being a wife and mother wasn't all it was cracked up to be, and when I was two, she joined a dance troupe in New Orleans. But since I had no memory of my mother, it was hard to miss her.

"But," I continued, answering their next question before they could ask it, "I got a daddy." I'd often been asked about my mother, but until now, I'd never had to explain the whereabouts of Gideon. It wasn't fair, him putting me in this predicament. "He's working a railroad job back in Iowa. He says it's not fit living for a girl my age, so I'm here for the summer." I didn't say that the railroad had been fit living for

27

me pretty near my whole life and I didn't see why this summer was any different. "But he's coming back for me the end of the summer." For some reason my words rang a little hollow. I wasn't sure if it was the look Hattie Mae and Shady had exchanged the day before or the look of pity on some of those kids' faces just then. Maybe they knew of someone else who got left for good, but Gideon *was* coming back for me and I'd have a few choice words for him when he arrived.

"See, Lettie? I told you she's not an orphan," said the red-haired girl. I figured Lettie must be short for Soletta.

"They're cousins," said a freckle-faced boy in overalls, as if that explained everything. "Your daddy ever seen anyone get flattened by a train?"

"Now what kind of question is that?" It was Lettie who said it. "Come on, Ruthanne, you jumped on me for asking a dumb question. What about Billy's?"

"It ain't a dumb question," Billy said. "My granddad used to work at the depot and he tells a story about how a fella got hit by a train in Kansas City and, dead as he was, he stayed on that engine car all the way to the Manifest depot. Nobody wanted to peel him off and since he had a round-trip ticket, they left him there all the way back to Kansas City."

"I heard a story like that," Lettie said, "only it was about a boy who rode a three-legged horse all the way to Springfield and—"

"Would you two hush up with your stories and let the poor girl tell her own?" Ruthanne scolded.

All eyes were back on me. "I don't suppose I have any story to tell. But my name's Abilene."

"That ain't a name. That's a place," said Billy. "You from the one in Kansas or Texas?"

"Neither."

"It doesn't matter where she's from," said a girl with fancy curls that looked like they were done in a beauty parlor. She raised her eyebrows and looked down her nose at me. "The fact is she's living in a saloon and a stone's throw from that spooky Miss Sadie's Divining Parlor. My mother says that place is nothing but a den of iniquity."

The only places I'd seen within a stone's throw from Shady's place were the cemetery and that broken-down shack of a house with PERDITION written on the gate. Truth was I didn't know what a divining parlor or a den of iniquity was but you can bet I planned to find out.

"Shut up, Charlotte, and give the girl a chance to talk," Ruthanne said again. "Well, where *are* you from? Where's your home?"

That question always came up real quick. It was a universal. And I was ready for it. "All over. My daddy says it's not down in any map. True places never are."

Another voice, an older voice, spoke from the back of the room. "I see your father is well versed in the works of Herman Melville."

Suddenly, chairs scooted back and the whole class stood. "Good morning, Sister Redempta."

"*Moby Dick,* to be precise. Good morning, class. I see you've had ample time to meet your new classmate and welcome her with tales of dead bodies and dens of iniquity." She raised an eyebrow to the class.

I gathered it was a woman, since they called her Sister, but since she was covered in black with only her face peeking out of what looked like a little white box, it was hard telling.

Gideon says a rose is a rose. But when it comes down to

it, there's some more rosy and some more thorny. I didn't know yet if she was rose or thorn, but one thing I knew for sure. She wasn't any universal.

She was a towering figure, gliding solemnly to the front of the room. Her posture was straight and formal; the only movement about her was the swaying of a long strand of wooden beads wrapped around her waist and extending down to her knees. I caught the scent of lye soap as she walked past. Strong as it was, she must be a believer in cleanliness being next to godliness and she wasn't taking any chances.

It did occur to me to find it strange for a Baptist minister to send me to a Catholic school. Sometimes religious folks draw pretty deep lines in the sand. But having seen Shady's place, which was also part church, saloon, and workshop, I could tell his lines were a bit fuzzy.

Sister Redempta placed a stack of papers on her desk. "I'm sure you are eagerly awaiting your final report cards." There was a good amount of moaning and shuffling. "Rest assured you have all received marks that are fair and representative of your work throughout the past year." She picked up the first paper in the stack. "Billy Clayton."

Billy walked to the front. "Sister." He nodded, accepting the paper. As he shuffled back, those freckles got lost in the red rising in his cheeks.

"Charlotte Hamilton."

Miss Beauty Parlor pranced to the front of the room. "Thank you, Sister." She smiled at everyone on her way back, but hearing the yelp she let out afterward, I thought she'd sat on a tack. Her hand shot up. "Sister Redempta, I'm afraid there's been a mistake. There is a B marked beside catechism."

"I am aware of that, Charlotte. I graded your final exam,

and among other things, I do not believe that wearing black to a funeral or giving last year's feather bonnet to your sister can be classified as corporal works of mercy. Mae Hughes," she continued. "Ruthanne McIntyre . . . Noah Rousseau . . . Soletta Taylor."

It was almost worth having to go to school just to see everybody itching and squirming. After looking at her report card, Lettie Taylor slouched in her seat and whispered to Ruthanne, "Charlotte better air out her black dress for a funeral, because my mama's gonna kill me."

I was sitting pretty as each name was called, knowing mine would not be among them.

"Abilene Tucker."

I must have been smiling for a while, because all of a sudden my mouth hurt from changing positions so fast.

"You *are* Abilene Tucker." Sister Redempta said it as if I'd been wondering about that for some time. "I understand that you have just arrived, and unfortunately, that leaves me with no basis on which to give you a grade for this term."

"Yes, ma'am," I said. *Ain't it a shame?* I thought.

"Therefore, you will have a special assignment to complete during the summer."

"Assignment? Summer?" A rose is a rose, but she was sprouting thorns, all right.

"I am pleased that your ears are in such able condition. Let us put your mind to the test as well. It seems everyone is fond of a good story, dead bodies on trains notwithstanding. Therefore, your assignment will be to write a story of your own. You may select the topic and it will be graded for grammar, spelling, punctuation, and creativity. It will be due September first."

She didn't wait for any ifs, ands, or buts from me. Good thing, too, as I couldn't think of a thing to say. But I didn't have any plans of still being in Manifest come September.

"If you need help getting started"—she peered out of her white box at the class—"I am quite certain there are some students who would be happy to offer their assistance."

There was a god-awful quiet as nobody even looked my way. Then Lettie Taylor chanced to shoo a fly off, and quicker than an auctioneer, that woman pegged her.

"Thank you, Soletta. Perhaps your mother will allow you a stay of execution for a few months."

Ruthanne laughed behind her hand.

"And, Ruthanne, a kind gesture on your part. As for the rest of you"—she shot an evil eye at the class—"it would do you well to remember for next term that acts of charity and kindness are also taken into consideration in one's overall grade."

Charlotte's hand shot up again. "I'd be happy to help the poor girl, Sister." She gave me a pitiful look. "I'll even help her find some more suitable clothes. Something a little less traveled."

"That won't be necessary, Charlotte. I'm sure Abilene will have quite enough help. Now let us stand for prayer."

The class stood and Charlotte flipped her hair around. "No matter," she whispered over her shoulder. "I'm spending most of the summer with relatives in Charleston. You know, South Carolina." She was suddenly talking with a Southern accent. "Pity, though. I would have thought clothing the poor in taste would have been a fine corporal work of mercy."

Snooty rich girl. A universal.

Fort Treeconderoga

MAY 28, 1936

Fortunately, the last day of school was brief. Just long enough to hand out report cards and clean out desks. After lunch, when Shady said I could use the old tree house out back for having friends over, he was off on two counts. First, I didn't have any friends. Second, that conglomeration of half-nailed boards could hardly be called a tree house. Oh, it was in a tree, all right. Thirty feet up with nothing to climb on except skinny branches and a rope ladder that looked to be holding on for dear life.

But I'd spent part of the afternoon helping tidy up around Shady's place and now I wanted to be alone to look through the Lucky Bill cigar box I'd found under the floorboards. That tree house looked to be as alone as I could get. So I stuffed the box in my satchel and climbed, one creaky step at a time.

The daylight coming through the floorboards was enough

to make me wish I had a little fat on me so I wouldn't slide right through to the ground. Inside, I looked out a jagged hole that was pretending to be a window. I could see everything from up there. The *Manifest Herald* on one side of the hardware store, Koski's Diner and the Better Days Funeral Parlor on the other. Across the street were the bank, the post office, Dawkins Drug and Dime Store, Cooper's Barbershop, and the Curly Q Beauty Emporium. And those train tracks that Gideon was at the other end of.

Then I saw Lettie and Ruthanne run into Dawkins Drug and Dime. I'd stood on the outside, looking in, on my way home from school. It had a soda fountain and jars of lemon drops, licorice whips, and candy buttons. I must have been steaming up the window, because a stern-looking woman, probably Mrs. Dawkins herself, had shooed me off. I wondered what treats those girls were getting. Maybe Gideon'd take me there when he came to get me. Again I felt a little off balance, like I'd felt in the newspaper office the day before. But who wouldn't feel a little wobbly in a rickety tree house so high above the ground?

Enough goosenecking. I had a look around the tree house, figuring what I'd haul up with me next time. Food, for one thing. I'd skipped lunch and the afternoon was heading from mid to late.

There wasn't much left in the tree fort from previous dwellers. Just an old hammer and a few rusted tin cans holding some even rustier nails. A couple of wood crates with the salt girl holding her umbrella painted on top. And a shabby plaque dangling sideways on one nail. FORT TREECONDEROGA. Probably named after the famous fort from Revolutionary

War days. Anything else that might have been left behind had probably been weathered to bits and fallen through the cracks.

No matter. I'd have this place whipped into shape lickety-split. First off, I picked out the straightest nail I could find and fixed that sign up right. Fort Treeconderoga was open for business.

Kneeling in front of one of the crates like it was an altar, I opened the cigar box and let the contents tumble out. There was the map. Not a folded-up road map, but a homemade one on faded paper with worn edges. It was a hand-drawn picture of places around the town, labeled with names. Up top in a youthful hand were the words *The Home Front*.

Then there were the keepsakes. Little things kept for the sake of something. Or someone. A cork, a fishhook, a silver dollar, a fancy key, and a tiny wooden baby doll, no bigger than a thimble, painted in bright colors, with a face and everything. To me they were like treasures from a museum, things a person could study to learn about another time and the people who lived back then.

Then there were the letters. I selected one and held the thin paper to my nose, wondering, hoping that I'd smell something of Gideon as a boy. Maybe smells like dog, or wood, or pond water. I felt like I was floating in my daddy's world of summer, and hide-and-seek, and fishing when I opened the paper and read the greeting. *Dear Jinx,* it said in an unfamiliar penmanship.

My heart sank like a five-gallon bucket full of disappointment. The cigar box and letters didn't belong to Gideon. But I kept reading.

Dear Jinx,

If my penmanship is a bit jiggly, it's because I'm writing to you from the train. I know you're sore at me for leaving but when you're older, you'll understand. Besides, I won't be gone long. Check in on Pop for me. He might need a little help at the hardware store.

In the meantime, somebody's got to keep watch on the home front. With a war going on, you can't be too careful about spies. You've heard some of the fellas talking about someone rattling around in the woods at all hours. Just last month, Stucky Cybulskis and Danny McIntyre said they were out night fishing when they heard a rattling that sent their dogs into a tizzy. Stucky says his dog, Bumper, can sniff out spies just as well as raccoons, but after sniffing around the woods, both dogs came back with nothing but a shank bone to show for their effort. Well, that rattling spy, he's probably digging up all kinds of secret information to give to the Germans, like what's the best time to catch night crawlers or which boys are sneaking out at night to go skinny-dipping.

I wrote up a map for you so you'll know what's important, what you're protecting. Plus I left some mementos I know you've been eyeballing. My Liberty Head silver dollar, fishing lure, and skeleton key. But don't get any ideas. When I get back, which will probably be by the end of the summer, they are to be returned to their right-ful owner. Me.

So, remember, be on the alert. Keep your eyes and ears open. THE RATTLER is watching.

Ned

The yellowed paper felt brittle in my hands. *Home front? Spies? Skinny-dipping?* I didn't know Ned or Jinx, but the words in the letter thrilled me. Their lives seemed full of adventure and mystery.

A girl's voice jolted me from my thoughts.

"Abilene. Yoo-hoo, Abilene. You up there?" someone called. "Shady said we'd find you in that tree house, but from the looks of it, you're likely to fall out at any minute."

I peeked out of the tree house, then pulled my head back quick. It was Lettie and Ruthanne. I had wanted them to come. I should have been glad they did. But I was still filled with disappointment about the letter's not being to Gideon and curiosity about Ned and Jinx and the spy known as the Rattler.

"I can't work on that assignment just now," I hollered back without looking out.

"Assignment? It's the last day of school, for crying out loud," Lettie called. "The assignment can wait. After all, everyone's on vacation."

"That's right. We just saw Sister Redempta wearing her wading habit down at the river," Ruthanne yelled.

I poked my head out. "You did?"

"No. But I bet that'd get you down from that tree house in a hurry." Lettie laughed.

I pulled my head back in, feeling a little foolish. Even if Sister Redempta had a wading habit, there probably was no water in the riverbed. "I'm busy right now."

"Okay. I guess we'll come up. You first, Soletta?"

"After you, Ruthanne."

I was sure they were just teasing me again, until I heard the creak and pull of the rope ladder. I tried to fold the map before they pulled themselves up. They were fast climbers.

"What're you doing up here?" Ruthanne poked her head up first and scrambled onto the platform.

I slipped the map and keepsakes back into the Lucky Bill box. "Nothing much. What are y'all doing up here? I really don't need help with that assignment. Nope, I'll be long gone before Sister Redempta can lasso me with that rope around her waist. Besides, y'all probably have better things to do, like run off to the dime store or something." I didn't know why I was being so snippy. I guessed it was because Gideon had taught me not to be anybody's charity case.

"Well, as a matter of fact, that's where we just came from," Lettie said, reaching up for Ruthanne's hand. With her short curly hair, she looked like the salt girl on the crates, and she carried a red bandana knapsack on her back.

"We brought you something." She opened the pack and pulled out three lovely sandwiches wrapped in wax paper, three apples, and, my goodness me, three ice-cold Coca-Colas. At the same time, Ruthanne saw me clutching the letters.

"What are you hiding?" She snatched them out of my hand.

"Give them back," I said.

"Are these letters from your boyfriend?"

My pride welled up like a blister ready to pop. I grabbed the letters. "I know why you're here. Y'all are the ones hoping to get noticed by the teacher or your parents for doing a good deed to the new girl. Well, I don't need no corpus works of mercy," I said, slipping into my new-girl-in-town way of talking. "So y'all can just find someone else to get your extra credit from this summer."

Seeing the looks on their faces, I almost busted out crying to be so mean.

They looked at each other as if silently agreeing which one would speak to me.

"That's just fine." It was Ruthanne. "But I'd like to point out that they're the *corporal* works of mercy. You know, doing things like clothe the naked and feed the hungry. And we weren't doing them in the first place. But I think even Sister Redempta would agree there isn't one among them says anything about sitting in a tree house with the pigheaded. Isn't that right, Lettie?"

"That's right." Lettie was quietly putting the food and drinks back into the bandana.

"Nor one about running all over town collecting empty pop bottles for trading in to bring Coca-Colas to the ungrateful. We came up here to pay a visit and get acquainted. But it looks like you've got your own self to keep you company. Or y'all self or whatever it is you keep saying. Come on, Lettie. Let's go."

They both stood.

I wasn't sure what to say but knew it had better be something good and quick.

"You mean y'all don't say 'y'all'?"

They paused; then Ruthanne answered, sounding kind of

disgusted. "No, we all don't say 'y'all.' That's two words. 'You all.' You might as well get that straight right now."

I cleared some dust off the floor with my foot. "Anything else I need to know? For while I'm here, that is?"

Lettie and Ruthanne looked at each other again, probably deciding if they could tolerate me another minute. They must've figured they could, because they sat back down and opened their parcel of sandwiches.

"Well," Lettie said while Ruthanne popped the bottle tops off with the hammer claw, "there's a river that when it's in Arkansas, you can say it like that. The *Ar-kan-saw* River. But once it hits Kansas, it's called the Ar-*kansas* River. That's kind of important."

"And there's a woman up the way who sits on her porch and stares. Don't let her look you in the eye or you'll turn to stone," Lettie said, as if that was on the same level of importance as how to pronounce *Arkansas*.

"And you might want to work on your grammar," Ruthanne added with a mouthful of egg salad sandwich. "It doesn't bother us any. Fact is, during the summer we all talk however we want. But come fall, Sister Redempta's kinda picky when it comes to 'don't need nos' and 'might couldas.' And as for that *lasso* around her waist, it's not a lasso. It's a rosary and it's for praying on."

I could tell it would take a while to learn the lay of the land. But that was okay. Those girls were real friendly, the Coca-Cola was going down good, and come fall I'd be long gone, I told myself, pushing aside the wobbly feeling I'd been having off and on.

I opened the cigar box. "You ever seen a spy map?" I asked.

Main Street, Manifest

MAY 28, 1936

"An honest-to-goodness spy!" cried Lettie as the three of us crouched behind the wooden Indian in front of the hardware store. "Right here in Manifest! Why, I've never heard anything so exciting."

I kept the mementos hidden away in the cigar box, but showed them the first letter and the spy map. It might've been a little selfish of me, but I wanted to read the other letters by myself before letting Lettie and Ruthanne see them. Maybe there would be some mention of Gideon in those.

"The Rattler. That sounds as mysterious as the Shadow." Lettie took on the deep, dramatic voice everyone knew from the Sunday-night radio broadcast. "Who knows what evil lurks in the hearts of men? The Shadow knows."

Ruthanne rolled her eyes.

"In fact," Lettie continued, "it's just like that episode a few months ago. A lady, she gets mysterious letters from her dead husband—well, they're not letters really, they're more like notes, because they don't come in the mail, they're just left under her pillow, and right before she goes insane—"

"Not now, Lettie," Ruthanne said. "The Rattler, whoever it was, could still be here, spying on us at this very minute."

"After all this time? The letter was written"—Lettie did the calculating in her head—"eighteen years ago. And I don't see how this map is going to help us." She looked over the paper. "It's just a map of Manifest, or at least Manifest as it was back in 1918. See here, that Matenopoulos Meat closed down forever ago."

The cousins' debate continued. Ruthanne said, "So, maybe it's a map of likely suspects and places the spy might frequent."

"Maybe he's dead by now. The Matenopoulos place is on there and Mr. Matenopoulos is dead."

"Maybe you shouldn't be such a stick-in-the-mud. Come on, let's scout around."

As we all got up, I figured Ruthanne had won. And from Lettie's skipping along beside us, I gathered she didn't mind.

We looked up and down Main Street, taking in store owners and passersby.

There was the butcher, hanging up a big hunk of meat to cure outside his store. He pulled the fleshy meat hook and wiped it on his already bloody apron. The iceman whacked his spiky tongs into a block of ice and hoisted it out of his truck. The barber shook out his apron and wiped his razor blade clean. Thinking of spies and people going insane made everyone seem a little frightening.

They were like nameless men in a scary nursery rhyme—

the butcher, the iceman, and the barber—until Lettie identified them as Mr. Simon, Mr. Pickerton, and Mr. Cooper.

We made our way into and out of a few stores, asking if anyone had heard of the Rattler. No one seemed inclined to shed any light on the matter.

"The Rattler could be any one of them," Lettie breathed. "But I still say the Rattler could be dead and buried by now."

"Or maybe not," Ruthanne said with authority. "Look."

It was the undertaker, all dressed in black, hauling a slab of granite into the Better Days Funeral Parlor.

"Maybe it's Mr. Underhill," Ruthanne whispered. "He's always itching to carve somebody a grave marker. Maybe he even killed a few bodies himself."

"The letter didn't say anything about murder. We're just looking for a spy, right, Abilene?" Lettie asked.

"Yes, but . . ."

"But what?" Ruthanne asked.

"Well, say there *was* a spy. What do you think he was spying on?"

Lettie and I looked at Ruthanne. She rolled her eyes and gave a sigh, like she was disgusted to have to explain something so simple. I figured she was just stalling till she could think up an answer.

"There *was* a war going on, you know," Ruthanne said.

We kept staring.

"And in wartimes there's always secrets that need keeping from the enemy."

Still staring.

"So what makes you think Manifest didn't have a few secrets of its own that some spy might want to find out about?" Ruthanne asked.

Since Lettie and I couldn't come up with a better explanation, we shrugged and turned our eyes back to Mr. Underhill, who'd come outside. He wiped the sweat off his forehead and looked up at the cloudless sky.

"Look at him," Ruthanne said. "He's sniffing for death in the air."

A breeze picked up and when Mr. Underhill crossed the street, walking in our direction, I thought for sure he'd pluck one of us for that new grave marker. We backed into an alley and watched as he passed by. He hunched forward and his arms didn't move as he walked. They just hung stiff by his side.

"Come on," Ruthanne whispered, and we all three took off after Mr. Underhill. He headed to the edge of town and skirted around the trees near Shady's place. Lettie stepped on a twig, snapping it in two, and Mr. Underhill turned around. We stayed still in the darkness of a tree until he moved on.

"Where's he going?" I asked.

"Where else would an undertaker go?" Ruthanne pointed ahead to the wrought iron fence that surrounded hundreds or maybe fifty or so graves. "Come on, there's an opening on the other side."

This was one of the universals I had so far avoided. In other places, I'd seen kids who followed their leader like blind mice, right into the carving hands of the farmer's wife. Being an outsider, I didn't usually fall under the leader's spell. But I'd never been on a spy hunt before. So here I was, traipsing after Ruthanne, enjoying the excited, scared feeling that made my spine shiver.

Ruthanne went first, squeezing through the fence where there was a missing iron rod. Then Lettie, then me.

"Over here," Ruthanne said, crouching behind a tall tombstone. We followed, then waited. And peeked.

Mr. Underhill plodded over to a grassy spot between two graves and stretched his arms between the markers. His fingertips barely brushed the stones on both sides. I'll be hung if he didn't lie flat on his back then, like he was ready to die himself. From our hiding spot, we could only see his knees poking up as his long legs butted against another grave marker in front.

He lay there, seeming a little too comfortable. Then he got up and made some notes on a pad of paper and, arms hanging down again, walked out of the cemetery.

We waited for the gate to quit squeaking before we gave up our hiding spot.

"He's measuring for somebody's grave," Lettie said.

Ruthanne looked over the grassy space Mr. Underhill had recently occupied. "The way his legs were bunched up, looks like there's not enough room for a full-grown adult." She stretched out her arms, measuring length, as the undertaker had done. Then, with one hand about the same height in the air, she turned real slow. "In fact, I'd say there's probably just enough room for someone about the size of . . . one . . . Soletta Taylor!" She placed her hand on Lettie's head.

"You stop that right now, Ruthanne McIntyre! Or I'll tell your mother that you used her colander for catching tadpoles."

Ruthanne laughed. "Oh, don't get your knickers in a knot."

"Let's go home, Ruthanne," Lettie said. "I'm thirsty and Mama will be awful upset if she finds out I was clear out in the woods. It must be near midnight."

"For heaven's sakes, Lettie, it's barely dark."

"Still . . ." Lettie whined just a little.

"Oh, you're probably right. Supper will be waiting at my house too," said Ruthanne.

I hated to see them go. "Maybe we can find a creek to fill our pop bottles," I suggested.

"There's nothing more than a trickle within a hundred miles of here. Everyone knows that," said Ruthanne, kicking up dust as we walked.

"My daddy said he'd heard the drought hadn't taken hold here like it had in other parts."

"Bad enough," she answered, stuffing a wad of grass in her lip like tobacco as we made our way back to Shady's place.

"Still," said Lettie, "Uncle Louver says folks around here are lucky. Least there's underground wells to draw from to keep people watered. He says places not that far west of here are so dry people shrivel up like November leaves and blow all the way to California."

We started back toward the tree house to get Ruthanne's pack.

"I'm tired," Lettie groaned.

"Nice to meet you, Tired. I'm Hungry," Ruthanne answered, pulling a half-eaten apple from the pack.

Truth was we all seemed to be getting a little tired of the spy hunt and probably would have dropped the whole thing right then if it hadn't been for what happened next.

When we got back to Shady's property, we saw that there was a note nailed to the trunk of Fort Treeconderoga. At eye level, right on the knobby bark. Someone didn't want us to miss it.

"What's it say?" Lettie asked.

I tore it off the nail and adjusted the paper to read it in the dimming light. There were only four words written on it, each one capitalized. I read it out loud.

"Leave Well Enough Alone."

It was more jarring than scary. But it was scary too. To think that somebody not only knew we were on the trail of the Rattler but had taken the time to write a note to three girls. What had we stirred up? What was the writer of the note afraid of?

"That means the Rattler is still here," Ruthanne said, "alive and kicking." She took a bite of apple.

"How can you eat at a time like this?" Lettie said with a shiver. "He knows we're looking for him."

Ruthanne continued munching, pondering the situation. "Maybe we shouldn't have come right out and asked about the Rattler."

It was a little late for that revelation, I thought. "What are we going to do now?"

"What are we going to do now?" Lettie repeated. "Aren't we going to leave well enough alone?"

Ruthanne looked at Lettie like she'd given the wrong answer to two plus two. "Of course we're not going to leave well enough alone. We're going to start up our spy hunt again first thing tomorrow."

I put the note into my pocket for safekeeping. We made plans for Lettie and Ruthanne to come back the next morning and said our goodbyes.

The saloon-church looked warm and inviting with its light glowing through the stained-glass windows. But I wished Gideon was there waiting for me. To say good night to me. I reached for the compass to hold, but it was gone. My heart pounded, and even though I hadn't moved, I felt like I'd lost my bearings. The compass was my most valued possession and I'd lost it twice in two days! I must have snagged it when I'd squeezed through the cemetery fence.

The cemetery. Now, no human being wants to be in a cemetery at night—no normal one, anyway—but I had to find Gideon's compass.

"Ruthanne. Lettie," I called, hoping they'd go back with me. They were already out of earshot.

I couldn't ask Shady. I wasn't sure how he'd feel about us following Mr. Underhill into the cemetery in the first place. I didn't plan to show him the note either. That would surely end our spy hunt. So I did the only thing I could. I turned my feet back toward that cemetery and made them walk, one in front of the other.

The moon was on the rise and shed some light for me to look around by, but also made strange shadows on the tombstones. I searched near the fence but found no compass. I slipped back through it to look. Wandering around the markers, I couldn't help noticing the dates, wondering if Gideon had known some of these folks while they were still among the living.

Some stones had sweet little verses. Others said something

about the person who was six feet under. Some of them spoke volumes about the deceased's life and times.

HERE LIES JOHN FOSTER—EXEMPLARY HUMANITARIAN,
DISTINGUISHED BUSINESSMAN, CIVIC LEADER,
GENEROUS PHILANTHROPIST,
AND DEVOTED FATHER OF TEN.

And next to John Foster:

HERE LIES MARY FOSTER—WIFE OF JOHN.

The wind was picking up, blowing a warm, dry air over me. I was about to give up my hunt until morning when I heard a faint sound, something akin to church bells beckoning in the distance. I squeezed back through the fence and let the breeze take me just a little farther toward the sound.

I knew I was nearing the gate marked PERDITION, and sure enough, there was what Charlotte had called Miss Sadie's Divining Parlor. That den of iniquity. Preachers used the word *iniquity* when talking about the strange and wicked. That divining parlor looked to fit the bill.

Wind chimes of all shapes and sizes lined the porch, making their lonely music in the breeze. And hanging among them was my compass, glinting in the moonlight. How it had got there, I couldn't be sure. But I knew the wind hadn't carried it. Someone had hung it there.

The house was dark and a rocking chair added an unharmonious sound to the delicate tinkling of the chimes. It creaked back and forth in the dark shadows of the porch. I opened the wrought iron gate, with all its welded forks and pans, and tender-footed my way to the porch. The compass hung far from the stairs, and the porch was too high to reach from the ground. But beside the uneven steps was a large clay pot. Going up onto the porch seemed like it would be asking for trouble, so I scooted the pot over. It was so heavy I could barely move it. I hoped I'd scooted it within reach of the compass.

My balance was good enough. I stepped up on the lip of the pot, holding on to the porch rail to steady myself, and reached for the compass. Just another inch. If the breeze would just catch the compass and nudge it my way . . . The breeze had died down. But the rocking chair still moved. I stood motionless, realizing that it wasn't the wind rocking the chair but a large dark form sitting in it. I caught my breath with a tiny cry and tumbled to the ground, breaking the pot in two.

The figure heaved itself from its chair, and I confess, I didn't stay long enough to see what happened next. I ran home, made an excuse to Shady about not being hungry, and was in bed before you could say boo. Even as my heart was still thumping loud, it didn't drown out the sound of those chimes in my head.

Miss Sadie's Divining Parlor

MAY 29, 1936

After tossing and turning most of the night, I imagine I looked a bit puny the next morning. Shady gave me a sideways look as he doled out a hot bowl of Cream of Wheat at the far end of the bar. I skimmed off a spoonful and blew on it, waiting for it to cool.

I glanced behind him and noticed a bottle of amber liquid tucked up on a shelf. Having been raised around men who were down on their luck, I was no stranger to the sight of alcohol. There was only the one bottle and it was full. I guessed it made sense to have a little hooch in a saloon, even if it was part church.

"You had a couple of callers yesterday. Did they find you in the tree house?"

"Oh, Lettie and Ruthanne?" I tried to sound casual. "Yes, they stopped to visit awhile." I didn't think he'd take too kindly to the nighttime activities, and judging from

Ruthanne's and Lettie's talk, I figured their folks would be even less receptive.

"Let's see, they're cousins. They'd be Nora's and Bette's girls. Those Wallace girls, their mothers, used to get into all kinds of mischief when they were young. I guess they're getting their comeuppances now," Shady said with a grin.

I wondered if he knew about the mischief that had gone on the night before.

"There's an old shed that's falling down behind the MacGregor place. I'm going over to gather up some scrap wood. You're welcome to come along."

"Thank you, but I'll stay here and clean up the breakfast dishes. Gideon says I'm supposed to be a help, not a burden."

"Never you mind about that. But all right, then. I'll be back around noon. We're having church services here tonight, followed by a potluck dinner. Be sure to invite your friends. Tell them we'd be pleased to have them." It was flattering, but Shady was highly overestimating my circle of friends. "It looks to be a hot one today." Putting on a hat that seemed to have long ago lost its shape, he stepped outside and peered into the cloudless sky. He lifted the handles of a wheelbarrow and started off.

That put an idea into my head, and I mulled it over while washing the dishes and wiping down the bar top. If he was trying to get his outside chores done early, maybe that Miss Sadie would be off doing the same and wouldn't come back till noon. This was my chance to get my compass back without risking loss of limb or soul.

My rag caught on a crack in the bar top. At first I thought it was just a split in the wood, but looking closer, I could see that the top of the bar was a movable panel. I pulled on it, and with hardly any effort, the whole section moved forward and then down, another panel taking its place on the top like the first one had never been there. My washcloth had disappeared underneath without a trace.

Well, the word *speakeasy* sprung to mind, I can tell you. Those are the places all over the country where folks sell and drink bootlegged alcohol and hope to not get caught by the law. I've heard tell they have secret entryways with passwords to get in. And once you're inside, they've got all kinds of hidden panels and quick hiding spots so they can stash their liquor in case there's a raid by the police.

Still, I thought it strange that in Shady's whole establishment, I hadn't seen but one bottle of liquor, and it was sitting right out in the open. This was something to ponder, but for now, I was wasting the cool of the morning.

I hung the dish towel on its hook and headed down the Path to Perdition. Miss Sadie's place wasn't quite as scary in the daylight. It had gone from being a full-fledged den of iniquity to a sorry excuse for a house. Grass and weeds snuck their way up through the saggy porch and all around the sides of the house, giving it the scruffy look of a week-old beard. If this was a ghost house, it looked like that ghost had lost his job and all his savings along with the rest of the country.

With not a breath of wind to be had, the chimes hung in silent disregard. I gauged I could be up and down those porch steps, compass in hand, in five seconds. That is, I could have if the compass had still been hanging there. But it was gone.

Maybe she'd moved it. As I tiptoed up the rotting stairs,

they creaked and groaned, cussing me for stepping on their aching backs. In the dusty window a faded sign read INSIGHTS FROM THE BEYOND—MISS SADIE REDIZON, MEDIUM. There was no compass to be found outside and the house looked deserted. The screen door had a yellowed index card stuck in the wire mesh that said, ENTER. I reached into my pocket, felt my two dimes, and tried to decide which one would give me the best answer. I chose one and flipped it. Heads, I'd go home. Tails, I'd go in. Tails. That dime was a dud. I switched to the other one. Tails again. Darn it all.

The air in Miss Sadie's parlor was hot and thick. I thought sitting on one of those red velvety couches chock-full of fringy pillows was probably akin to suffocating. Still, I had to find my compass. I took a deep breath and ventured around the room.

Suddenly, the double doors of the parlor whooshed open. A large fleshy woman stood before me in full regalia. Her eyes were all made up, earrings and bracelets jangling. The sign in the window said Miss Sadie was a medium. From the look of her, I'd say that was a bit wishful. The heavy red dress she wore brushed across the floor, tossing up dust as she hobbled to an ornate chair behind a round table. She seemed to have a bad leg and took some time squeezing herself between the arms of the chair.

Thinking she hadn't seen me, I turned to make a clean getaway.

"Sit down," she said, her voice thick and savory, like goulash. She put her hands flat on the table. "Let us see if today the spirits are willing to speak." Suddenly, it became clear. A diviner. A Medium. This woman was a fortune-teller and a spirit conjurer. If you believed in that sort of thing.

I stood near the front door. "I'm not here for—"

"Silence!" She held out a hand, motioning me to the chair across from her. I sat.

She slid a cigar box across the table. I almost told her, "No thank you," but then I saw a little slot cut into the lid. Now, I didn't usually have two coins to rub together, and when I did, I was real slow to part with them. But if this was the only way to get my compass back, I guessed I'd have to go along with it. I dropped in a dime. Miss Sadie peered inside the box and slid it back to me.

She tapped her fingers on the table. "Today is hot. The spirits are reluctant."

I wondered if her divining abilities allowed her to see the other coin in my pocket. I might be wanton enough to risk eternal damnation on Miss Sadie's spiritualism, but I'd be hung if I'd waste another dime.

"You can tell the spirits it ain't getting any cooler." I pushed that cigar box back.

She heaved a sigh so heavy it might've been mistaken for a dying breath. "Very well. What is it you want? Your fortune? Your future?"

I squirmed, not knowing what to say. She peered at me hard and asked again. "What do you seek?"

Maybe it was the way she studied me so hard that made me feel like she could see right through me to the brocade wallpaper behind me. I didn't know what made me say what I said next, and I wasn't quite sure what I meant by it. It just came out.

"I'm looking for my daddy."

Her eyebrows went up. "I see. Now we get somewhere. Do you have a bauble?"

"Bauble?"

"A totem. Trinket. Something your father may have touched?" She puckered her lips, and her already wrinkled face drew into more wrinkles.

She probably knew darn good and well I was missing Gideon's compass. And I wasn't parting with any more money. Besides, she was just an old woman full of beans anyway, so I decided to call her bluff. I pulled out the letter from Ned to Jinx that was folded in my back pocket. If Miss Sadie came up with some cock-and-bull story about my daddy from something that wasn't his, I'd know she was as phony as a two-headed nickel. I slid the paper over to her.

Miss Sadie opened it, smoothing the yellowed paper beneath her fleshy palms. As she looked at the words, her hands began to tremble. She held them to her face, and her breath came out in short, shuddering gasps. For a minute, I couldn't decide if she was crying or dying, but then figured this must be part of her divining preparations.

Finally, she lifted her head and touched the letter again, gently stroking the page with her palm, as if she was trying to draw the words into herself. "The letter," she said, without looking at me. "It mentions certain *mementos*. You have these?" There was something deep and old in her voice. It sounded like need.

I remembered that the letter mentioned the silver dollar, fishing lure, and skeleton key. "I found them in a Lucky Bill cigar box under a loose floorboard," I answered a little too quickly, and it made me sound guilty. "There was other stuff, too," I continued, overexplaining. "An old cork and a tiny wooden baby doll, no bigger than a thimble and all painted up in bright colors." I wished I could shut myself up.

56

After a long pause she rested her gaze on me, puckering her lips again in thought. She seemed to be weighing whether to go on, as if deciding if I was worthy of receiving her divination. "Very well. Place your hands on the table. I will build a bridge between the world of living and dead."

"But my daddy is alive," I said, figuring she'd just given herself away as a fake.

"The lines between the living and dead are not always clear." She closed her eyes and breathed slow and deep.

I closed one eye and peeked out of the other.

"It is time to reveal secrets of future and past. I see a boy from long ago," she began. "He is on a train."

So far I wasn't impressed.

"The boy, he is a stranger to Manifest."

"Where is he now?" I asked, cutting to the chase.

"Silence. The spirits will not be rushed."

Miss Sadie was working up a sweat. I'd had no idea it took such effort being a spirit conjurer. I stared, wide-eyed, as the diviner began.

"The boy, he is tired and hungry. He must act now. He must make a leap of faith. . . ."

Triple Toe Creek

CRAWFORD COUNTY, KANSAS
OCTOBER 6, 1917

Jinx watched the ground rush by in the late-afternoon light. He'd jumped from enough boxcars to know that the jumping was easy. It was the landing that could present a problem. Figuring that the cottonwoods along the creek would be as good a place as any to hide out for a while, he grabbed his pack and leaped.

Unfortunately, he saw the ravine from midair. Rolling and tumbling, he tried to keep his pack up so it wouldn't bang on the ground like every other part of him. Finally, he stopped, then listened. He heard a girl's voice just ahead.

"Ned Gillen, you have only one thing on your mind. If I'd known why you brought me out here . . . Why, I am a lady and I'll have no part of it! And maybe you should find someone else to take to the homecoming dance."

Jinx peered over the bush in front of him just in time to see a young woman raise her parasol and march off. A boy—a young man, really—with olive skin and dark wavy hair was left holding a catfish hooked on a line.

After a moment, the boy stared into the catfish's bulgy eyes and cleared his throat. "Pearl Ann, I apologize for compromising your femininity by exposing you to the rugged world of fishing. Would you please reconsider and do me the honor of accompanying me to the homecoming dance?" The fish stared back, unmoved.

Jinx was intrigued by the romantic scene developing before him, but was even more enamored with the catfish wriggling on the hook. He knew he should hop another train to put more distance between him and the events from the night before. The sound of the sheriff's dogs barking and growling still rang in his ears. But his stomach was the one growling now. Jinx hadn't eaten since the day before and could already smell that catfish sizzling on a spit.

"You're going to have to do more than sweet-talk a fish," Jinx said, emerging from the bushes.

Ned Gillen spun around, then relaxed when he saw that it was just a boy. "Is that right? And I suppose you would know in your, what, twelve years of experience with women?"

"Thirteen, and it's not what I know, it's what I have." Jinx took a brown bottle, which had miraculously remained unbroken, from his pack. "You got all the right words to go after her, but you can't go smelling like catfish and creek water, can you?"

Ned sniffed the fish and grimaced. "I suppose not."

"What I have here will solve all your problems. It's a cologne, aftershave, and mouthwash all in one. It comes from the arctic glacial waters off the coast of Alaska. I got it from a hundred-year-old Eskimo medicine man."

"And where did you happen to run into a hundred-year-old Eskimo?"

"I did some work at the docks in Juneau. At any rate, if it can make a polar bear smell good, just think what it can do for you." Jinx jiggled the bottle. "Time is of the essence, my friend."

"I suppose a little fresher-up wouldn't hurt. But something tells me you're not in the business of giving away arctic glacial water for free."

Jinx pursed his lips. "I suppose we could make a trade. Say, that catfish for this bottle. That is, unless you're getting kind of sweet on her."

Ned grinned and unhooked the fish, revealing a green and yellow spotted fishing hook. He held up the lure. "It's brand-new. They call it a Wiggle King. So colorful it'll catch a blind fish. Anyway, I doubt that concoction is worth the fish and the lure." He handed over the fish and took the bottle.

"I'll take good care of her," Jinx said as Ned left.

The October night was still and mild as Jinx stretched out by the fire in his shorts, his belly full of catfish. He'd rinsed out his clothes earlier to lessen their scent and hung them from a tree to dry. Jinx was exhausted, but knew he should get moving. He'd hop the next train and head wherever it took him. Still, he reasoned, it might be a while before the next train came by. And he was close enough to the tracks to listen for the chug of an engine. So he eased himself into the cool creek, letting the dust and grime from there to here wash away.

His uncle Finn had suggested they split up in Joplin. They'd be harder to track if they were separate. Maybe that was the best thing to come out of the whole mess. Even on the run, Jinx felt a sense of freedom, and for the first time, he felt like he could make a fresh start. Still, it was hard to make a fresh start when there was a dead body in your past. It had been an accident. But Finn had said no sheriff would believe that, and his dogs wouldn't care.

Jinx leaned back in the water, letting the creek flow through his hair and between his fingers. The current gently pulled him and he gave in to it. Maybe he'd go to Denver or San Francisco. Someplace where no one would notice a kid on the run. Someplace even his uncle Finn couldn't find him. But the blissful thought vanished as a figure splashed nearby. Cussing and muttering, someone was frantically scrubbing his hair and face.

It was that fellow Ned. Uh-oh, Jinx thought, noticing that Ned's build was strong and tall compared to his own shorter, wiry one. Jinx knew he should have moved on long before then. Unfortunately, Ned spotted him.

"Why, you little . . . Arctic glacial water, you said. Makes a polar bear smell good, does it? It smells, all right, and I'm sure Pearl Ann would agree."

Before Jinx could retreat, Ned had him by the arm and looked about to drown him or punch him, or both. Then a gunshot went off. Both boys froze.

"Get your clothes and come with me," Ned said.

To his own surprise, Jinx obeyed. But when he went

back to the tree where he'd hung his clothes, they were gone. Only his shoes and the socks stuffed in them were left. He ran back to catch up with Ned, who was also dressed in dripping shorts and holding only his shoes.

"They must've taken our clothes," said Ned. "Come on."

Whoops and hollers filled the night air. Jinx followed Ned about thirty yards up the creek. The two crouched low to the creek bed, still dripping and bare. As they peeked over the bank, heat from a bonfire struck them like a train. They saw greetings being passed from one man to the next. Hands were shaken and backs were slapped. Everything was Brother this and Brother that. It could have been a church meeting if not for the white hoods and cloaks. The scene made Jinx shiver.

"They're using our clothes for kindling." Ned pointed to the bonfire. A hooded figure tossed their shirts into the crackling blaze while another laughed.

"Why would they want to burn our clothes?"

"They're drunk and they're mean. That's a dangerous combination." Ned pulled Jinx away from the bank. "Let's get out of here. Besides, I still have a debt to settle with you."

"But who are they? And why do they wear sheets and hoods?" Jinx whispered. He'd already caught a whiff of Ned's glacial scent and was in no hurry to settle that debt. The so-called glacier water smelled one way in the bottle and a lot different once it hit a person's skin. But usually, Jinx was long gone by then.

Ned looked at Jinx like he was born yesterday. "Geez, kid. You've been in Alaska too long. They call themselves the Ku Klux Klan and they hate pretty much everyone who isn't like them. If you have the wrong color, religion, or birthplace, they don't like you. Around here it's mostly foreigners they hate." Ned's face flushed with anger.

"They wear hoods because they don't want anyone to know who they are. Like that one with the crooked arm who threw the clothes in the fire. That's Buster Holt. He's a knacker. A fella who carts off dead animals. He hates foreigners, but he doesn't mind taking their money to pick up their dead cows and horses. The other one, laughing like a girl, that's Elroy Knabb. He's one of the bosses at the mine, but if his wife found out he was here drinking and carousing—well, let's just say Mrs. Knabb is wicked with a rolling pin."

Just then, two other men stepped away from the fire and took off their hoods.

"Who are those two?" Jinx asked, his eyes wide. "And how come they took their hoods off?"

"The big one's Arthur Devlin. He's the grand knight. And he owns the mine. The other one is his pit boss, Lester Burton," Ned answered, his voice charged with anger. "Devlin doesn't care who sees him, because he doesn't have to answer to anybody. They all answer to him. Around here, whoever owns the mine pretty much owns the town. Everybody has to come crawling to him, his mine, his company store. And believe me, with his wages and his prices, he makes sure you stay on your knees." Ned took a slow breath and whispered, "Come on. Let's get out of here."

Ned moved away and Jinx followed. "Be careful, kid. There's poison ivy along the bank. Let's wade downstream and get out at that clearing."

They glided quietly through the shallow water, holding

their shoes in the air. Sounds of tree frogs and cicadas filled the still night.

"Listen," Jinx said, "maybe we can work out a deal. . . ."

"Shhh." Ned held up his hand. They heard voices several yards ahead. Two men splashed water from the creek onto their faces.

"Must be a hundred degrees up there," a big man said, kicking off his shoes.

"Hotter than Hades, I'll say," the other agreed, his bald head shining in the moonlight. "This ain't much of a rally. I went to one in Arkansas that makes this one look like a marshmally roast."

"Yeah, well, what do you expect from a place that's made up of a bunch of foreigners? They come here and can't even speak good English."

"I hear there's enough Irish, French, and I-talians around these parts to have us some fun tonight." The big man staggered out of the water. "That chili's kicking in. I gotta see a man about a dog first." He plopped down on the muddy bank, trying to get his shoes back on.

"Who's he talking about?" Jinx asked.

"Foreigners, kid. Immigrants. People who come from another country. That's most of the people in Manifest. The whole town is made up of immigrants who came here to work the mines."

Jinx detected a note of personal injury in Ned's voice. "Where are you from? I mean, where were you born?"

Ned paused before answering. "Truth is, kid, I don't know. Darnedest thing, right? Seems like a person should know where he was born. Where he's from and who his people are. But I came here on a train when I was real young. Hadley Gillen adopted me and this is the only home I can remember." He squinted, as if trying to peer into his past. His vision must have been too fuzzy and he shook it off. "The way I see it, those two fellas are the foreigners and I'd like to put a burr in their britches before they get too comfortable around here."

Jinx saw a chance at redeeming himself. "I'll be right back."

Ned shook his head but Jinx slipped noiselessly out of the water. A couple of tense moments passed before he returned.

"Here, put this on." Jinx held out a white cloak to Ned, then put one on himself.

"Where'd you get these?"

"Those two guys in the creek. They won't miss them for a while. Besides, you said you wanted to put a burr in some britches. Well, here's your chance." Jinx held out a handkerchief full of three-pronged leaves.

Ned shook his head but couldn't help grinning. He looked at the large man still trying to put his shoes on. "You're crazy, kid," Ned said to Jinx, "but I like your way of thinking."

They put on their shoes, donned the white hoods, and hoisted themselves over the bank. Like flies in a Venus flytrap, they were immediately swallowed up by the crowd of more than fifty men. The point on Jinx's hood fell short of those around him and the bottom of his robe brushed the ground.

Ned and Jinx maneuvered their way casually through

the sea of white. They peeked through the eyeholes in their hoods, trying to see over shoulders and around big bodies, moving toward the far side of the camp. Suddenly, a wiry man stood hoodless in front of them, wagging his cigar. It was Lester Burton, the mine pit boss. Their path was blocked.

"Well, lookie what we got here," he said in a gravelly voice.

Jinx took a step to the right but Burton grasped his shoulder. Ned, a few years taller, stepped closer to Jinx. Whatever happened now, they were in this together.

"Got us a babe in the woods," Burton said as a few hooded figures gathered around.

Jinx's hands were sweating. If they could just get around these men . . . He straightened up tall. "Yeah, this is only our second rally. Our dad took us to one all the way down in Arkansas, ain't that right, Cletus?"

"Arkansas?" Ned repeated, a little slow on the uptake.

"Yeah, they sure know how to do things down there, ain't that right, Cletus?" Jinx was more insistent this time, hoping Ned would catch on.

"Uh, that's right, Emmett. That was quite a rally down in Arkansas. 'Bout twice the size of this one, don't you reckon?"

"I'd say that's about right. Course that wouldn't be counting the women."

"Women?" This seemed to rile one of the hooded men. "They got women in the Klan down in Arkansas?"

"Why, sure they do," Jinx said. "Who do you think puts the hems in all their white sheets?"

All eyes descended to the bottoms of the men's cloaks.

"See there?" Jinx pointed. "You got raggedy bottoms. I'd say you boys could learn a thing or two from the folks down in Arkansas. Wouldn't you say, Brother Cletus?"

"I'd say so, Brother Emmett. Come on. I think I hear Pa calling us. Coming, Pa."

They left the men gazing downward and made a bee-line to the far side of the camp.

"Over there." Jinx nudged Ned toward a dilapidated cabin that looked long abandoned. The nearby outhouse apparently stood in good stead, since six or seven men waited in single file.

The boys fell in line and Jinx hopped around enough that three men let him move ahead. It was dark inside, but he easily found the leaves wrapped in his handkerchief. Making appropriate grunts and sighs, he grabbed a stack of newspaper scraps and dropped them into the open hole. Careful not to touch the leaves, he left them in place of the paper, remembering a well-known rhyme:

Ivy on the vine, two leaves on a stem are fine,
Pick up one with three, and itching you will be.

"Come on, son. We're backed up out here," came a holler from outside.

"Yeah, we're backed up something fierce," Ned yelled.

Jinx opened the door. "I guess leaves'll do in a pinch, but can't you boys afford any newspaper or something? Let's go, Cletus."

The boys sauntered away, Jinx yelling over his shoulder, "They got toilet paper In Arkansas."

A Bargain Is Struck

MAY 29, 1936

Miss Sadie looked to be done for the day. Her voice had gotten raspy toward the end of her fortune-telling and she breathed like she'd been carrying something heavy.

I wanted my dime back. "I said I wanted to know about my daddy. That was just some old story from twenty years ago about two people I don't even know."

Her eyes narrowed a bit and she raised her chin as if she had just figured me out. "You show me a letter. I tell you what the letter shows me." She wagged a finger. "Next time you should be more specific about what it is you are seeking."

I didn't plan on there being a next time. So she'd told a story about Ned and Jinx. A made-up story about two names she read in the letter. I pictured the yellow and green fishing lure in the Lucky Bill cigar box. She knew the mementos I had and she'd zeroed in on the fishing lure mentioned in the letter to conjure her story. Anybody could do that.

I looked at Miss Sadie sitting there, her leg propped up. She was a pathetic sight. What kind of purveyor of the future could only tell stories from the past?

"Go home," she said. "Communing with the spirits is a privilege. I have ointment on the top shelf, just behind the baking soda, above the icebox. But I will get it myself."

She sure gave good directions if she was planning on getting it herself.

"I'll get it," I said with no small amount of reluctance. "Long as you don't charge me another dime for the *privilege.*"

I maneuvered my way through the maze of velvet and fringe into her pantry and retrieved the nearly empty jar of salve. I gave it a whiff and nearly singed my nostrils.

"What is this stuff?"

"Hawthorn root," she said, scooping out the remainder and rubbing it onto her leg. "It helps to increase circulation." She moaned a little, massaging her swollen leg. It was then that I could see the wound that was causing her so much distress.

"What happened to your leg?" I asked with a grimace.

"I catch it on barbed wire. It is slow to heal."

That was putting it mildly. That sore, with its scabbing and yellow pus, looked to have gone from bad to worse and about another mile past that.

"If you tell me where another jar is, I'll fetch that for you and then I'll be on my way."

"There is no more. I gather the last of the hawthorn root

near the cemetery last night. But I am sure there is more to be found elsewhere."

I looked outside at the scorching sun. "Maybe you haven't been outside lately, but there's not much growing around here. There's not enough water to fill a thimble."

"There is water. It remains deep and hidden, but there is always water."

"How do you know?"

"Because I know what my father knew. And his father before him. It is what diviners know."

"Your people are all fortune-tellers?" I hoped they were better at it than she was but I didn't say so.

"No. We are a family of diviners. We see and understand things most people overlook. We read the signs of the land."

"You mean like those hill people who walk around with a jiggly stick, thinking they can find underground wells?"

She made a guttural, scoffing sound. "Pah, what does one need with a stick? All one needs is eyes and ears. The earth speaks loud enough when it wants to be heard."

I was beginning to have no doubt that she heard things. The woman wasn't right in the head.

"All right, then. You have a nice day," I said, backing toward the door.

"I believe there is still a matter to be settled about my broken pot. It survives a boat ride all the way from Hungary and now it is in pieces." Hungary. That explained the accent.

I stood my ground. "Well, it wouldn't be broken if you hadn't taken my compass."

"Take your compass? I am out to gather hawthorn root

70

and find something on my property. How am I to know it is yours?"

She had a point, I thought as she winced, rubbing her leg. I was surprised she could make it to the cemetery and back, but figured that was why her leg had swelled up so bad today.

"I'd offer to pay for the pot but I don't have that kind of money."

"Yes, it is worth much more than the coin you have remaining in your pocket."

The hair on the back of my neck prickled. I didn't believe in fortune-tellers, but how had she pulled that one off?

"So," Miss Sadie said, knitting her fingers together, "it appears you have something I want and I have something you want." She said her *w*'s like *v*'s. *You have something I vant and I have something you vant.*

"You have my compass. But what could I have that you vant . . . I mean, want?"

"Two. Good. Legs," she said, punctuating each word.

I wasn't sure where this was going but I knew I wasn't going to like it.

"You will come here to do a few odd jobs."

Any job for her would be odd, I thought. But she had me over a barrel. I did break something of hers and I wanted my compass back.

"For how long?" I asked.

"You will know when you have finished."

She handed back the letter I'd given her, and suddenly, I found myself heading toward the front door. I stopped short. There, just inside, was my compass, hanging on a single

71

nail, daring me to take it. I gave it a strong look but knew I'd broken her pot and needed to make restitution. I marched down her rickety steps, a bead of sweat already trickling its way down my back. Curiosity had set in.

I ran back to Shady's place, clomped up the wooden steps to my room, and reached under the floorboard for the Lucky Bill cigar box. Dumping the contents onto the bed, I found the fishing lure I hadn't paid much attention to. The words from Miss Sadie's story came back to me as I looked at the fancy green and yellow spotted lure. The underside of the lure, in pretty gold lettering, read WIGGLE KING—SO COLORFUL IT'LL CATCH A BLIND FISH.

At that moment I wished I'd never set foot on the Path to Perdition.

Likely Suspects

MAY 30, 1936

I lay in bed the next morning, feeling mightily burdened. Something had been gnawing at me all night. It was Gideon. Where did he fit into all this? How was he connected to this town? To these people? Manifest was the place he'd chosen to send me to, and yet it didn't seem like he'd even been there. Did he know Ned or Jinx? Did anyone know him? I wasn't even sure that I did.

Now, there was a thought. What did I know about Gideon? What did I think people should know about him? I started a list in my head. He always walked like he knew where he was going. He was a better cook than Shady. He tucked the blanket up under my chin when he thought I was asleep.

I stretched out in the warmth of my bed and pulled the blanket up to my chin. *Let's see,* I thought. He was smart. Not so much book smart, even though he did know all forty-eight states and capitals *and* all the presidents from Washington to Roosevelt. No, Gideon was more "living by your wits" smart. He had once turned a bunch of wildflowers into a twenty-dollar bill. Some might have said that wasn't smart, that was magic. Not the way Gideon had done it.

He'd gathered up a nice bunch of wildflowers and traded them for a sewing kit in Decatur, then, in Fort Wayne, swapped that for a camera, which he raffled off at a church picnic in South Bend. Chances were twenty-five cents apiece or five for a dollar. He ended up with seven dollars and fifty cents and bought us a tandem bicycle. But our behinds were so sore by Kalamazoo that he sold it for a twenty-dollar bill to a man with twin grandkids.

I remembered all these things about Gideon, but I couldn't remember if he'd said the words or if I'd only imagined them. Those words *I'm coming back for you.*

Memories were like sunshine. They warmed you up and left a pleasant glow, but you couldn't hold them.

I'd have to do some divining of my own, I thought as I rolled over. There was the Wiggle King fishing lure, sitting on the windowsill, where I'd left it the night before. I should have put it back in the cigar box, but somehow it had separated itself from the rest of the items. It had become different. Special. And it needed a special place.

There was a welcome breeze blowing through the open window. I was no stranger to hard work, but the thought of being cooped up in Miss Sadie's Divining Parlor left me feeling a bit short of breath. Maybe I could busy myself helping Shady and wouldn't have to go.

There was a plan. I'd saunter downstairs and make myself so useful Shady couldn't possibly see fit to allow me to walk out the door, let alone to do someone else's bidding. I figured Shady might be feeling a little down in the mouth that day. He'd held his church service the night before, followed by a potluck, but it turned out to be more of a "down on your luck," as only one person showed up. A fellow with a week-old beard and a hole in his hat brought a can of beans.

I hopped out of bed, put on my overalls, and headed down the narrow wooden stairs.

"Good morning, Shady," I said, ready to sit down to a plate of his usual warm, slightly burnt biscuits and molasses. Shady stashed something under the bar and mumbled words I didn't catch. When he looked up, I could see that his eyes were kind of bloodshot and his whiskers hadn't been shaved since the day before. The bottle on the shelf behind the bar was still full, but I supposed it was like any craving. If a person liked cookies, he was going to keep more than one at hand. When Shady went back to the stove for my breakfast, I leaned across the counter and peered behind it, but there was only a chipped coffee cup holding a couple of nickels and a button. Was it Shady's drink money? Alcohol was against the law then as much as it was in 1917, but folks could usually get a bottle of the stuff here or there. I didn't know if bootleggers would take buttons for payment along with nickels.

I scooted back to my barstool as Shady came in, presenting me with a plate of cold, more than slightly burnt biscuits and half a leathery pork chop. I knew that times were hard, so I didn't complain, but my stomach couldn't help its moaning and groaning. Hattie Mae had brought by some delicious fried chicken the day before, but that was a distant memory. I bit into a hard biscuit, hoping I had enough spit to soften it up. But just then, Shady brought me a cold glass of milk. I nearly drank it down in one gulp and he poured me another glass. It filled my stomach nicely, but in my head I made plans to go by the newspaper office later to see if Hattie Mae had any leftovers.

"I thought maybe you could use some help around here," I said to Shady, wiping off my milk mustache. "I do laundering and mending. I'm even good with a hammer and nail."

He scratched his whiskery face, making a sound like sandpaper on rough wood. "Well, that's awful nice of you to offer. But I'm feeling a little spent this morning and need a bit of a lie down. Besides, Miss Sadie'll be expecting you," he said.

I choked a little on the biscuit brick, wondering how Shady knew of my ill-conceived agreement with the diviner, when he went over to a box in the corner of the room and pulled out a wire-bristle brush, one glove, a half-full bag of chewing tobacco, and a cracked mirror.

Then his eyes lit up and he said, "There you are." He pulled out a long coil of rope and proceeded to tie a large knot at each end. He gave the rope a good tug, testing its worth, and presented it to me. "Every little girl needs a skipping rope," he said with a smile as he replaced the odds and ends and hauled the junk box out back.

I held the rope in my hands and felt a stinging in my eyes. I didn't really think of myself as a little girl anymore, but I smiled. "I had a skipping rope once," I said when he returned. "It was in Tennessee, and I was using it to pull a wagon full of firewood. I guess I loaded too much wood in it, because the rope broke in two. I've always wished I could do that over. I wouldn't have carried such a heavy load."

"Seems to me you've been carrying a heavy load for some time." Shady's eyes looked like deep watery pools. "Besides, everyone deserves a do-over. Now you've got yours." He smiled.

I smiled back, feeling the rough and bristly rope. It was like Shady. He had his rough edges but he was strong and steady. I guessed I'd better fess up about the diviner, since that cat was out of the bag anyway.

"About last night . . . I lost my compass again the other day, and had to go see about getting it back."

"Mm-hmm. Miss Sadie told me. I take a little milk over to her on my way back from town a couple times a week. Did you two have a nice visit?"

"If you mean did she tell my fortune, no, she did not. She just carried on a bit, jingling and jangling, telling me an old story about a couple boys who lived here a long time ago." I kind of liked having the letters and mementos mostly to myself, so I decided to keep those a secret. "But I broke her pot and now I have to go back to work it off."

Shady had perked up a bit. "She told you about a couple of boys?"

"Yeah, and some trouble they got into with the Klan with some poison ivy and such. Ned and Jinx. Did you know them?"

Shady occupied himself by scrubbing down the bar top. "I did."

That gnawing feeling came back to me and I worked up my nerve. "Shady?"

"Yes, Abilene."

"Do you think Gideon knew those two boys? Did he have many friends when he was here? Did he ever go fishing with anyone or swimming in the creek?" My questions and my need to know came out in a rush.

"Well, now." Shady rubbed the back of his neck. "Let me see. I'm sure your daddy did most things boys do. Swim, fish, cause havoc." He worked at a stubborn spot on the counter but I caught him catching a glimpse of me. "Didn't he tell you much about when he was here?"

"Yes, he told me lots of things. He said there was a man who drove a cart around town and brought fresh milk to people's doorsteps. And ladies who'd walk down the street in white gloves and fancy hats with big feathers sticking way up. But it's like he was telling things you'd notice from the tree house. Storefronts and activity, people going here and there, but only what you could see from a distance. Nothing up close. Why, I only heard about you a few weeks ago. Did he write to you at all?"

Shady paused and his shoulders looked heavy. "A post-card now and then. Sometimes, when folks move on, it's hard to look back. It's not their fault. We knew he wandered a bit after he left here, but then we got word that he had a little girl, and we knew he'd take good care of you."

I did warm a little at that but I wasn't ready to be done grumbling. I stuck my chin on my fists. "Well, Gideon's telling of Manifest was nothing like Miss Sadie's. Her story was full of names and faces and who did what where. I learned more about Manifest in one sitting with her than from all of Gideon's stories put together," I grumped. But I still hadn't learned anything about Gideon.

Shady looked up, and with the sun gleaming in through the stained glass, he looked like he was having a revelation.

"Yes, that Miss Sadie sure can weave a story. I bet she could fill in some of the missing pieces."

I don't know if Shady would've said more, but he looked relieved to hear a jingle at the door.

Lettie and Ruthanne poked their heads in. "Hey, Abilene?" Then, remembering their manners, they added, "Good morning, Shady."

"Good morning," he answered. "Would you girls care for a glass of buttermilk?"

"Yes, please," Lettie and Ruthanne answered together.

Shady went into the back room and Lettie whispered, "First we have to sell some eggs in town. Then we can work on the Rattler mystery. We've made a list of suspects. Mr. Cooper, the barber. Mr. Koski at the diner. Hattie Mae."

"Hattie Mae?" I whispered back. *The nice newspaper lady?* "Surely you don't think she's the Rattler?"

"Well, not really, but she's got a sweet tooth and she'll probably give us a licorice whip or some jelly beans if we stop by. But we'll start with Mr. DeVore, the postmaster."

Mention of Hattie Mae made me think of something. "Wait a minute. I need to run back upstairs." I went up and thumbed through the newspapers I'd selected from Hattie Mae's office. I found her column in both and gave each a quick look-see. It was the one from October 11 that rang a bell. I carefully tore it out and made a point to take another look through Hattie Mae's old newspapers later.

As I went back downstairs, Shady was pouring the buttermilk. "What are you girls up to today?"

"Uh, we're doing some corporal works of mercy. Mr. DeVore needs visiting."

"Oh, he does? Is he sick?"

"Sick?" Ruthanne pondered the question. "I guess you could say that. If you consider loneliness a sickness. Who wouldn't be? Spending all day sorting everybody else's letters from dear ones far and near and never having a loving word sent your way."

Shady looked like he'd been given more answer than he'd asked for. "Well, you be sure to give him my regards. Tell him we missed him at last night's service and we'd be pleased to have him come next week at the same time." He reached behind the bar, where he'd stashed something earlier, and took out that something wrapped in a brown paper bag. "Good day, girls," he said as he left.

There was an awkward silence as I thought about what might be in that bag. Then Ruthanne said, "Come on, Abilene. Finish up and let's go."

"Can't," I said before washing down the last of my biscuit with some buttermilk.

"Why not?" asked Lettie.

I handed her the October 11 "Hattie Mae News Auxiliary." The paper was a little wet from my sweaty hand. "I got a debt to work off."

HATTIE MAE'S NEWS AUXILIARY

OCTOBER 11, 1917

I hope all of you are having a festive and convivial fall. With the autumnal surrogation to winter and the Thanksgiving holiday quickly ascending upon us, I find myself reminiscing to mind the many blessings and bestowments of the past.

I suppose having matriculated to my nineteenth year has provided me with a depth of insight which I am only beginning to excavate.

My ruminations were particularly profound at church last Sunday when Pastor Mankins illuminated us all. His words of purging our souls of anger and hatred were so taken to heart by some that they rose out of their seats, just itching to praise the Lord. Buster Holt and Elroy Knabb were so moved they fairly fled the service afterward to spread the Word. In my rovings about town, I've learned that the same two gentlemen have been frequent patrons at the drugstore. They didn't say so, but I gathered they were putting together supplies for the missions. I had no idea there was such a need for calamine lotion among the indigent, but that selfless act of charity will be forever embalmed on my mind.

I regret there will be no "Hattie Mae's News Auxiliary" next week, as I will be visiting my aunt Mavis. I was tickled pink last week with the birthday gift she sent all the way from Jefferson City. A thesaurus is a commodious tool for any reporter.

So, for all the whos, whats, whys, whens, and wheres, refer to the penultimate page every Sunday (except Sunday next).

HATTIE MAE HARPER
Reporter About Town

BURT'S BOTTOMS UP

Got bumps in your bottom? Those itchy, sore hemorrhoids that make sitting uncomfortable? Well, Burt's Bottoms Up is the elixir for you. Just drink a vial of Burt's Bottoms Up and you'll be sitting pretty in no time. No more worries about those hard kitchen chairs. You can eat your meals in peace and comfort with Burt's Bottoms Up. On sale today at the drugstore elixir aisle—bottom shelf.

Miss Sadie's Divining Parlor

MAY 30, 1936

"You can't be serious," Lettie said as the three of us peered through the wrought iron gate in front of Miss Sadie's house. Ruthanne and Lettie thought I was crazy to be going to work for her. I'd told them all about Ned and Jinx and the poison ivy as we'd kicked up parched leaves on the way over from Shady's place, and they'd read Hattie Mae's column.

"Read it again, if you want. Buster Holt and Elroy Knabb. Calamine lotion? Those were the two guys at the Klan rally in Miss Sadie's story. They used poison ivy for toilet paper. At least that much of her story was true," I argued.

"You don't know that for sure. And for crying out loud, don't you know what 'perdition' means?" Lettie pointed to the sign on the iron gate.

I nodded. "I know what it means," I said. I recalled a preacher in Des Moines who had warned folks who had come for a soup supper to give up their evil ways and stay off the path to perdition. My stomach had been a little upset after that.

"What if she's a witch and casts a spell over you?" asked Lettie.

"She's not a witch. More than likely she's just crazy," I said, even though I didn't believe that either.

"Like a fox," Ruthanne said, chewing on a blade of grass. "Be careful, Abilene. That old woman might have more up her sleeves than jangly bracelets."

My confidence was seeping out of me like water through a bucket full of holes. I wished Lettie and Ruthanne could go with me, but they had eggs to sell. Besides, it was my debt to work off. "I broke her pot and I want to get my compass back. It's as simple as that. I'll meet you at Hattie Mae's later on."

I took my leave with all kinds of frightful images rolling around in my head. Miss Sadie's house seemed lifeless, as there was no breeze to give breath to her wind chimes. So I was glad when I found her out back and she said she'd have me working in the garden that day, although calling it a garden required a whole lot of imagination. Mostly what I did was break up clods of dirt. Miss Sadie sat in a metal patio chair, smoking a corncob pipe and giving me instructions on how to put my weight into that shovel to turn up the dirt.

Just what she figured on planting in that parched earth, I couldn't reckon. It reminded me of sermons I'd heard from priests and preachers about planting in dry soil. Those seeds would just wither up and blow away, never taking root.

"Deeper. Dig deeper," Miss Sadie said in her rich voice. "The ground should not merely cover the seed. It must embrace it."

"What kinds of things do you plan on growing here, if you don't mind my asking?"

Miss Sadie closed her eyes and took a deep breath. She sniffed the air around her, as if it would give her the answer. "It is not yet clear."

I took a whiff too, but all I smelled was dirt. Dry, dusty dirt. Seemed like that was all there'd ever been. Oh, I had a vague notion of green grass, soft and wavy. Before Gideon and I were on the road, he'd worked as a groundskeeper at the Maple Grove Park in Chicago. I was three or four and we'd lived at a boardinghouse across the street. I thought there had been swings, but I had been so young and the memories were so distant that it could have been a dream.

"I wonder what it was like before the world went dry," I said, looking up into the sun.

"The world? Pah. What is it you know of the world?"

"I know that any place I've been to is dead dry."

"I suppose. But what appears to be dead can still hold life." Her voice sounded small and far away. That day she wore a light housedress instead of her velvety fortune-teller garb, but it seemed like she was fixing to go into another one of her trances anyway. And since my back was aching for a chance to stretch out, I decided to help her along.

"So, what about that Klan rally?" I asked. I'd heard of really bad things Klan folks did to Negroes. Mean, hateful, deadly things. I didn't know they were hateful toward white folks too.

"They think they hide their hate behind a mask," she said, her accent thick, "but it is there for all to see."

"And the boy whose girl got sore at him over the fish? And his friend?" I asked, pretending to be disinterested enough not to remember their names. "What happened to them?"

"Ned and Jinx," she answered. "They are a match from the start. Jinx is cocky and streetwise. He knows a con for every day of the week. But he knows little of friendship and home. Ned provides both. He takes Jinx to Shady's place, where many a wayward soul is welcome and no questions are asked."

So Jinx must've been the one who'd hidden the letters and mementos under the floorboards at Shady's house. "I'll say. My money's betting that Shady ran a speakeasy. He's got the perfect setup to have run one of those secret saloons with the hidden cabinets and movable bar top for hiding illegal alcohol away when the law would come calling." I spoke of it as if it was only in the past, but from what I'd gleaned of Shady, I wasn't so sure. I waited for Miss Sadie to confirm or deny.

"Shady and Jinx share something in common. They both have dealings they are reluctant to reveal," Miss Sadie said, not telling me if I'd win my bet. "It is clear Jinx runs from something, but Shady asks for no explanation." I figured that was about as much answer as I was going to get. "It is not the first time he takes in a stranger in need. But, he says, Jinx must attend school. Sister Redempta takes him into her classroom."

"I bet she plopped an assignment on him right off the bat too."

"It is possible. In a town of immigrants, new students come all the time."

"Is that how Ned got here?" I asked, wanting to stretch out my stretching out.

Miss Sadie breathed in again. "He comes to America on a boat, yes. But to Manifest, he comes by train. A train for orphans. He stays with the Sisters for a time. Sister Redempta cares for him. But he is a little boy, five years old, of undetermined nationality, so he belongs to all the people. Of course, it is Hadley Gillen, the widower hardware store owner, who adopts him as his own. But the town grows to love the boy and imagine that his future can be theirs as well."

It got quiet as Miss Sadie lingered in the past. The heat took over me like a dream. A hot breeze seemed to conjure up exotic smells and faces of colorful people. People who had come from their various parts of the world to build a better life.

I stretched out my body under the willow tree, my face feeling cooler in its shade. Somehow, I felt like I was one of those people. Someone taken out of one place and put into another. A place where I didn't belong. *Why did my daddy really send me here?* I wondered. "Why here?"

"The coal mines." Miss Sadie answered my question that I didn't realize I'd asked out loud. "People need work and the mines need workers. It sounds like a good match, but most do not realize the mines will consume them." It took me a minute to realize she wasn't talking about Gideon or me but about the people of Manifest years ago. She was heading into another story and I hadn't even paid her a dime. Miss Sadie must have figured that since she wasn't getting paid, she wouldn't put on quite as much of a show as before. This time she left off all the divining gyrations and jingle-jangle antics and just started her story, plain and simple.

"The mine whistle was the sound that brought us together. And kept us apart at the same time. . . ."

The Art of Distraction

OCTOBER 27, 1917

The shrill whistle of the Devlin Coal Mine signaled the end of one shift and the beginning of another. Jinx gripped the handlebars of a dilapidated bicycle and shuddered in the midmorning breeze as he waited for Ned to emerge from the mine shaft.

Three weeks had passed since Jinx had jumped the train near Manifest, but for him, it seemed a lifetime. He had come to a community where strangers arrived every day, from places farther away than the next state over. He knew he might be fooling himself into thinking that he could stay. That he could leave his past behind. But he'd met Ned and was living with Shady. He was going to school. Leading a normal life. And for now, he felt safe.

The shaft elevator strained and heaved its way slowly out of the ground. A tall wooden shack housed the cage elevator, which carried miners one to two hundred feet underground, where they would disperse into various dugouts called rooms, each supported by a single wooden pillar. Here the miners worked their eight-hour shifts, picking out the coal, loading it into a cart, and hauling it back out.

That day, as the rickety cage elevator surfaced, a group of soot-covered faces emerged, only to be replaced by a waiting group of men ready to go below.

As one looked at them, all carrying their metal lunch boxes and wearing their denim overalls and miner's helmets with gas lamps attached, it was difficult to distinguish one man from the next, one group from another. However, when they spoke, it became clear the Italians were ending their shift and the Austrians were beginning.

That was the way Devlin preferred it. Keep each to his own kind, speaking his own language, and everyone would stay in his place. The men coming out of the ground, squinting against the daylight, were like dead men rising out of a grave. They walked in somber formation to the water pump to wash.

That day was unusual in that Mr. Devlin himself stood near the mine elevator. Jinx hadn't seen him since the night of the Klan rally and felt himself draw back a bit at the sight of the grand knight. Of course now there was no white hood or cloak. Mr. Devlin was dressed in a large pinstripe suit and an immaculate celluloid collar. His slicked-back hair glistened in the sun as he appeared to be having a heated discussion with the mine geologist.

Jinx was relieved when Ned finally emerged from the elevator cage with the Italian crew. He walked his bike over to join Ned in line at the water pump. Ned removed his miner's hat, revealing his sweaty hair and white forehead against his otherwise soot-blackened face. He eyed the two men arguing. "What are they going at it about?"

"Something about the direction of the vein," Jinx answered. "Seems the coal vein took a turn it shouldn't have and now it's going the wrong way. I think the geologist is about to get the boot."

"Oh, well," Ned said. "Let 'em argue. Where'd you get that contraption?" he asked, motioning toward the bicycle.

"Shady won it in last night's poker game. Want to take it for a spin?"

"Can't." Ned pumped fresh water and washed his face and hands. "My legs are aching to be stretched after being cooped up for eight hours. I might just run from here to Erie and back."

Several other mine workers stood around, waiting for their weekly pay.

"Benedetto. You working too much," Mr. Borelli said, using his Italian nickname for Ned. "Study. Learn. You go to college."

"Yes, sir. I hope to go on a track scholarship next year."

"Good, good." He patted Ned on the back. "You run hard and study harder. Then you'll not have to go work underground to feed your family. Man was not meant to spend his days in the dark, eh, Vincenze?"

Mr. Vincenze wiped his face with a handkerchief. *"C'è un inferno oggi!"* he answered.

"Sì, sì. It is a hot one today," Mr. Borelli answered. He patted Mr. Vincenze along, then whispered to Ned and Jinx.

"He speaks no English. These mines. They keep us in the dark in more ways than one."

Just then, Lester Burton, the pit boss, stepped among them and nailed a notice to a post near the water pump. The letters were big and bold enough to be read from several feet away.

BY WAY OF PUBLIC NOTICE

AMERICAN DEFENSE SOCIETY WARNING

Every German or Austrian in the United States, unless known by years of association to be absolutely loyal, should be treated as a potential spy.

Be on the alert. Keep your eyes and ears open. Take nothing for granted. Energy and alertness may save the life of your son, your husband, or your brother.

The enemy is engaged in making war in this country, transmitting news to Berlin, and spreading propaganda and lies about the condition and morale of American military forces.

Whenever any suspicious act or disloyal word comes to your notice, communicate at once with Fred Robertson, United States district attorney, Kansas City, Kansas, or the American Defense Society, 44 East Twenty-third Street, New York City.

Burton turned his sun-splotched face to the men. "In wartime, that spy could be your neighbor. The chump sitting next to you at the pool hall or even at church." He looked straight at Ned. "Could be anyone of unknown or questionable background. Be alert and trust no one. Got it?"

There was a stir among the crowd. Mostly men asking for a translation from the few who could speak some English.

"Good." Burton fanned a stack of envelopes. "Borelli," he called out. "Servieto. Vincenze."

One by one, the men took their pay and drifted away like shadows.

"Gillen." Ned stepped forward to receive the last envelope.

Burton held out the envelope only to pull it back as Ned reached for it. "So you plan to go to college, eh?"

"That's right."

"Looks like studying's going to be a tight squeeze working double shifts."

"Sir?"

"That's right. There's been a bit of a mix-up. We need to dig out a new room and Weintraub's out with a broken leg. You'll go in for him."

"But I just worked a full shift."

"Strong kid like you, shouldn't be a problem. I suppose we could call in your old man. I recall seeing an unpaid balance on the Hadley Gillen account at the Devlin Mercantile. He might want some extra work in case a 'payment in full' notice comes due. Think about it."

Burton handed Ned his pay envelope and walked off.

"That's not fair," Jinx said. "There's lots of folks who could fill in for Weintraub. Why does he want you so bad?"

"I've beaten Devlin's son too many times at track meets."

"So what? His son has everything else going for him. Money, privilege, family name."

"Yeah, and that kind of person doesn't like to get beat by a person of questionable background." Ned's voice shook with emotion.

"Forget about him," Jinx said. "Let's go down to the fairgrounds later on. I hear there's a fella selling all kinds of fireworks."

"Selling," Ned said, opening his envelope, "as in money, of which you have none." He stared at the contents in disgust. "And, I guess, neither do I. They work us like pack mules for seventy-eight cents a ton of coal and then pay us in vouchers for the company store. It's no wonder we can't get out from under their thumb." He crumpled up the envelope. "So unless they're selling fireworks at the Devlin Mercantile, we're out of luck."

"I didn't say we were going to buy any. We're just going to look. Once we see what goes in one, we can make our own. We'll have fellas all over Crawford County buying our fireworks."

"Not in the mood."

"C'mon. Where's your spirit of adventure?"

Ned slowly buckled his belt and pick around his waist. "It's buried a hundred and fifty feet underground. Maybe I'll start working triple shifts. Then I can buy a piece of that coal vein and somebody might have a little leverage against Devlin."

"Suit yourself. But I did see Pearl Ann Larkin trying on a fetching hat at the millinery today. Big pink thing with feathers. She waved at me through the window."

Ned shrugged, opening the lower chamber of his miner's lamp and dropping in a small handful of little white cubes. He turned the knob to the chamber above, allowing a few drops of water to hit the cubes, creating a gas that rose to the top. Ned flicked the flint, sparking a flame. Donning the hat, he said with a smirk, "Big pink thing with feathers, huh? If it doesn't come with a carbide gas light, I'm not interested."

"She said something about looking forward to sharing some popcorn with you tonight at the carnival and taking a ride on the carousel. But I guess that doesn't interest you either."

Ned adjusted the flame and shined it in Jinx's squinting eyes. "She said that?"

"Sure as I'm standing here. And I happen to know you've got forty cents at home."

Ned sighed. "This shift doesn't end until six o'clock."

Jinx smiled, knowing he had won. "I'll meet you at the fireworks booth at six-thirty."

Ned studied Jinx under the light of his helmet lamp. "What are you cooking up, Jinx? The last time you were this interested in my courting Pearl Ann, I ended up smelling like a glacial skunk."

Jinx straddled his bike. "By the time you're done working two shifts, you'll smell plenty without any help from me. So be sure to wash up," he called as he pedaled off.

The autumn night was cool. Hensen's field just outside of town was aglow with hanging lanterns strung from one booth to the next. The county fair was a welcome time for all. Farmers had finished harvesting their soybeans, milo, and alfalfa and had planted their winter wheat. The kids had a break from school. Folks from neighboring towns stopped in to sample the variety of foods.

The Italians baked everything from cannelloni to ziti. The Swedes served up braided bread and hard baked pretzels, while the Germans and Austrians touted their strudels and bierochs.

Jinx spotted Ned and handed him a calzone. "Compliments of Mama Santoni. She heard you had to work two shifts."

"Grazie," Ned called to the large woman, his mouth already full of bread and cheese.

"Eat, eat," she insisted, her arms deep in dough. "Come back, I have biscuits baking. I keep them warm for you, yes?"

"We'll be back," Jinx said, leading Ned away by the elbow.

A few booths over, a placard read JASPER HINKLEY, PYROTECTIC. The exuberant Mr. Hinkley worked a crowd of young boys who apparently had plenty of money to spend. "There you go, lads. And remember, be careful with fire. Once you start it, *fire works!*"

The boys ran off, leaving Mr. Hinkley to laugh alone. He smoothed the handlebar mustache covering his upper lip. "Just a little pyrotectic humor, gentlemen. What can I do you for today? See here, you've got your Shanghai Sizzlers, Sparkling Marys, Chinese Color Changers."

Jinx picked up a red cylinder behind the rest. "What's this one?"

"Easy there, son!" Mr. Hinkley took it from Jinx and gently replaced it with several matching red cylinders. "That little fella's not for sale. He's a Manchurian Fire Thrower. They're ones that shoot upwards of three hundred feet in the air and explode in two different colors."

Jinx hooked his thumbs in his pockets. "What do you take us for, mister? A couple of them schoolboys? You expect us to believe these here cans shoot up in the air and explode in color?"

Mr. Hinkley looked bewildered. "That's exactly what I'm telling you. Haven't you ever seen fireworks, boy?"

Jinx stuck out his bottom lip and spoke with a feigned country-bumpkin accent. "Well, mister, we may look stupid, but that's as far as it goes. I bet there's nothing more than beans in them cans."

Mr. Hinkley took a medium-sized canister and cranked off the lid. "You see that there powder? That's pure T-N-T. Mix that with a little potassium nitrate, sulfur, and charcoal and you got the beginnings of a first-class shell."

Jinx looked sideways at Ned. "Sounds like quite a recipe. But even if you can get it off the ground, and I'm not saying I believe you can, how you going to get it to explode in the air?"

"Now, that's the trick." Mr. Hinkley gently reached into the canister and exposed a thin fuse. "This little fella, he starts to burning when the shell goes up. When he's all used up, kapow! You got yourself a mighty fine pyrotectic display. That's fireworks in layman's terms." He put the lid back on the canister. "Course, you got to be a bona fide pyrotectic to handle these little darlings. I apprenticed with a full-fledged Chinaman up in Omaha."

Jinx nodded and crossed his arms. "Well, you do seem to know your trade."

"Fine. Now, which one of these quality specimens would you be interested in? Keeping in mind, I don't sell the Manchurian Fire Throwers. Those are only for official pyrotectic displays."

Jinx looked over his shoulder. "Uh-oh. Isn't that Mama Santoni calling, Ned?"

Ned took his cue. "Uh, yeah. She's keeping those biscuits warm for us in the oven."

"Sorry, Mr. Hinkley. If we don't hurry up, those biscuits are going to turn into *fire crackers*. Just a little humor from one pyrotectic to another," Jinx called as he and Ned walked off. Mr. Hinkley smoothed his mustache as a new group of boys crowded around the stand.

Jinx and Ned wandered past the next few booths of carnival games, where vendors tried to attract the attention of passersby. "Step right up! Toss three balls in the hole and win a prize. Or try your luck in the shell game. Win a Liberty Head silver dollar."

"So much for your big con, Jinx," Ned teased.

"A con is merely the art of distraction." Jinx studied the booths. "Come here."

Jinx grabbed Ned by the elbow and led him to the shell game. A man in a striped shirt and bow tie smiled a crocodile smile. A tiny monkey perched on his shoulder. "Ready to try your luck and win yourself this here Liberty Head silver dollar? It's an easy game. I'm practically giving away money today. Right, Nikki?" The monkey twittered his agreement.

Ned shook his head. "I'm not into wasting money. No thanks."

"Come on," Jinx said. "It only takes a dime and you can win a dollar. Then you can buy Pearl Ann a bag of popcorn and a lemonade with change to spare."

Ned grimaced and placed a dime on the counter.

The man lined up three walnut shells and placed a pumpkin seed under one. He shuffled them around. Ned kept his eyes on the shell with the seed, and when the man stopped, Ned tapped it.

The man uncovered the seed. "You've got a good eye."

Ned was jubilant. "So, hand over my Liberty Head silver dollar."

"You don't get that on the first try. It takes three chances. And each chance costs a dime."

"Go ahead, give him another dime. You're good at it," Jinx coaxed.

"Oh, all right," Ned grumbled, reaching for another coin.

Again, the man revealed which shell held the seed and shuffled them back and forth. Again, Ned tapped the correct shell.

"Woo-hoo," Ned shouted. This time, he didn't need any coaxing. Pleased with his success, he already had his third dime on the table and waited for one last game to claim his silver dollar.

Again, the man shuffled and Ned watched as the shell with the seed went left, then right, then around and ended up in the middle. The monkey hopped onto Ned's shoulder and twittered with excitement. "Hey, little fella. You know a winner when you see one, don't you?"

Ned reached to tap the middle shell but Jinx stopped his hand. "Not that one. This one." Jinx moved his hand to the shell on the right.

"But I was watching. It's not—"

"This one," Jinx said firmly.

"Now, don't let him sway you, son. You're a natural at this game," the man said without his usual smile.

There was something so definite in Jinx's voice that Ned uncovered the shell on the right. There was the pumpkin seed.

The monkey jumped from Ned's shoulder, snatched up the seed, and popped it into his mouth.

"Now, look here," growled the shell man. "This is not a two-player game. If you want to play, put up your own dime." The monkey chattered more and more loudly in agitation.

Just then, Judge Carlson approached the booth, patting Ned on the back. "Keeping those legs warmed up, son?"

"Yes, sir," Ned replied. "I'll have my work cut out for me staying ahead of Heck and Holler," he said, referring to the Judge's sons, who were also star runners on the Manifest track team.

"That's right, Judge," Jinx said, emphasizing the word *Judge*. "He might even get a new pair of shoes with the dollar he just won. That is, if this gentleman will give Ned his rightful winnings."

Judge Carlson looked at the shell man. "Is there a problem here?"

The man grimaced. "Nope." He pulled the silver dollar from his pocket and shoved it across the counter. Judge

Carlson picked it up. "May I?" he asked Ned. He held up the coin, studying the woman's profile, with her wavy hair and crown. "Lady Liberty. She's a beauty." He flipped it into the air to Ned. "Don't spend her all in one place."

The judge moved on and Ned and Jinx walked away from the scowling man and his monkey.

"I never took my eyes off that shell. I knew it was in the middle," Ned said.

"Just like I told you. The art of distraction. You took your eye off the shells when the monkey jumped on your shoulder. Nikki did his part and the shell guy switched the shells."

"You mean that monkey is trained to do that?"

"Sure. Most people aren't willing to make a thirty-cent bet, so they let you win a couple of easy rounds to get you to put down a couple more dimes. Then Nikki makes his move and you lose."

"The art of distraction," Ned mused.

"Yup. All kinds of things can be accomplished when someone's looking the wrong way." From behind his back, Jinx revealed the large red canister from Jasper Hinkley's fireworks booth.

Ned's eyes got big. "Nice trick. But you can't just steal his Manchurian Fire Thrower."

"It's not stealing. It's like the library. You check out a book, look at what's inside, and take it back. We'll use this canister as our model. We make our own and return this one."

"Then what?"

"Then we set up shop and sell them to every kid around."

Ned caught sight of Pearl Ann standing in a pretty pink

dress. He headed for the popcorn wagon. "Count me out."

Jinx caught sight of Sheriff Dean near the popcorn wagon, and as he always did when he saw the sheriff—or any sheriff, for that matter—he turned the other way. This time he ducked into the diviner's tent.

Frog Hunting

JUNE 5, 1936

In bare feet and overalls, I looked out my bedroom window. It had been several days since Miss Sadie had left me hanging with her last story, about Jinx and Ned at the county fair, and that day I had the afternoon off. The Liberty Head silver dollar mentioned in Ned's letter had taken its place on the sill, next to the Wiggle King fishing lure. I had to admit, it was exciting and mysterious how the diviner could draw a whole story out of these little somethings. I could see why people would come to visit her.

And they did come. I'd been going to Miss Sadie's for a week and sometimes I'd be there only an hour or two and she'd call it quits for the day, which was fine by me. She wouldn't say why, but then a visitor would come calling just as I was leaving. The day before, an old woman who'd seemed anxious and fretful had come. She said her mind wasn't what it used to be.

This morning it was a young, pretty woman. I recognized her. It was Betty Lou, the beautician from the beauty emporium, and I could tell she was close to crying. I wasn't exactly eavesdropping, but before I got all the way out the door and past the porch window, I heard her say something about being afraid she was barren. I knew that meant she couldn't have a baby, and wondered why she thought Miss Sadie would have anything to say about that. But maybe she just wanted someone to listen to her troubles. Miss Sadie said she'd show her how to make tea with some special herbs, and the two got quieter. I went on my way after that.

I was glad to have the afternoon off, but I was sort of hankering to know what was going to happen with the Manchurian Fire Thrower. And had Jinx managed to avoid the sheriff? And was it Miss Sadie's tent he'd ducked into? Had he unburdened himself to her? Had he seen her more than that one time and was that how she knew about events she wasn't present to witness? I touched the raised face of Lady Liberty on the silver dollar. Miss Sadie was an awful purveyor of the future, but she sure knew how to spin a tale from the past.

Ruthanne and Lettie hollered to the window from outside. "Yoo-hoo, Abilene. You up there?"

In my free time from Miss Sadie's, I'd helped Hattie Mae at the newspaper office some, and helped myself to a few more old editions. But mostly, Lettie, Ruthanne, and I had been spying on people all over town, peeking in windows and eavesdropping on conversations, figuring we'd come upon the Rattler sooner or later. But so far, nobody had given himself up. And we were all ready for a break from spy hunting.

"Come on, lazybones," called Ruthanne. "The frogs are waiting."

I lumbered my way down the stairs and outside. "Lazybones," I moaned. "My back's so sore from digging in Miss Sadie's dry dirt I could spit. Except my mouth's too parched."

"Well, we can remedy that." Lettie produced a jar of cold water. "Mrs. Dawkins gave me some ice from her cellar. She's got enough down there to last all summer."

"You got a frog sack?" Ruthanne asked, swinging her own burlap sack.

Truth was I'd never been frog hunting. But as I didn't want to seem inexperienced, I said, "I just use my pockets."

"How do you get 'em to stay put?" Lettie asked.

"I tie their legs in a knot, how else?" I tried to keep a straight face, but Lettie was looking at me so serious I couldn't help grinning.

She wagged a finger at me. "You are a hoot, Abilene Tucker. Let's get going. Mama's going to have the frying pan ready to fry up some frog legs for supper."

Frog legs, huh? When you were hungry most of the time, you learned to eat what you could get. Still, frog legs sounded a bit exotic even to me. But the three of us set off into the woods on my first frog-hunting expedition.

We could hear them croaking all around. But finding them seemed to be a different story.

"Once you spot one, work him into a corner somewhere," Ruthanne instructed.

"A corner? In the woods."

"Yeah, there's rocks and trees, and logs all over."

I crouched low to the ground, listening and watching,

when suddenly a fat green frog hopped in front of me. "There's one!"

"I got one too," Lettie yelled.

Before I knew it, the three of us had taken off in three different directions. My frog hopped this way and that, always staying just out of reach. I chased him into a clearing, where he hopped into a prickly bush. He sat there, calm as could be, knowing I couldn't reach in and get him.

I thought about waiting him out, but then something caught my eye. It was a gravestone beside an old craggy sycamore tree. Just a simple arched marker, nothing special about it, except it was the only one. *Whose could it be out here in the middle of nowhere?* I wondered. My curiosity got the best of me and I moved closer to read the name.

But just as I reached to brush the years of dirt from the marker, I heard a scream. It came from just up the way, through the trees. I ran through the bushes toward the sound, my face and arms getting scratched as I went. Then I stopped short. The scream had come from a little house tucked back in the woods.

It was a tidy house with a neat stack of firewood piled up against the side. Straight and sturdy stairs led up to a little porch and I could see red and white gingham curtains in the windows. This was a nice house that probably housed nice people. But right now, there was an air of distress all around.

Lettie and Ruthanne tumbled into me, out of breath and similarly scratched.

"What's happened? We heard a scream."

"Shhh."

Billy Clayton came around the corner of the house, his

face drawn with worry and fear. He steadied a log upright on a tree stump, and with an ax that looked bigger than he was, he gave it a whack and chopped it in half. He tossed the two pieces into a pile and reached for another log. Lettie, Ruthanne, and I kept hidden among the trees when the door to the house opened.

"Holy Moses," Ruthanne whispered in disbelief.

Sister Redempta came out of the house and walked over to the well. She still wore her long black dress and rosary beads, but had no veil on her head. Her hair was cropped short, her face red with exertion. She hoisted a bucket from the well, rolled up her sleeves, and splashed water on her face and neck. Then, with her hands in the small of her back, she stretched and let out a deep breath, probably as deep as that well.

She closed her eyes.

"What's she doing?" Lettie asked.

"You think she's praying?" I asked.

Billy stopped chopping and waited for Sister Redempta to open her eyes.

When she did, she seemed surprised to see him standing there, as if she'd been away for a spell. "Billy Clayton, we're going to need some of that wood now. Your mother is resting and your new baby brother is in need of a warm bath."

"So everything's all right? I mean, Mama? She's gonna be all right?"

"Yes, Billy. She had a tough go of it, but she's a strong woman. She must be to keep an ornery boy like you in line."

Billy smiled. "Yes, Sister. Thank you, Sister," he said, his voice shaky with relief.

Sister Redempta went back inside and Billy gathered up a few wood splits and followed her.

Lettie, Ruthanne, and I dropped to the ground in exhaustion, as if we'd delivered that baby ourselves.

"Thunderation," Lettie whispered.

"You said it," Ruthanne agreed.

"I can't believe it either. A nun delivering a baby?" I said, shaking my head.

"Oh, Sister Redempta does that all the time," Lettie said. "When any baby is being born upside down or a mother is too small for her baby, Sister Redempta is called in."

"That's right," Ruthanne said. "Why, she's birthed lots of folks around here for years. My mama says my oldest brother wouldn't be here at all if it wasn't for Sister Redempta."

"Well, if it's so common, what are you two all 'thunderation' about?"

"We've never seen Sister Redempta without her veil on," Lettie said. "There've been stories that she has hair the color of a tomato. Others said she had no hair at all."

"Come on," Ruthanne said, hoisting herself up. "We'd better get home and tell our mamas that we didn't catch any frogs and that Mrs. Clayton could use some tending to."

As we began the walk home, I kept my eyes open for the grave marker, still curious about what lonely soul might be buried alone, but we never passed it.

Miss Sadie's Divining Parlor

JUNE 6, 1936

A warm wind blew as I headed for Miss Sadie's house the next day. I was still wondering about the grave marker beside the craggy sycamore tree near Billy Clayton's house. With Miss Sadie's stories floating around in my head, I came up with any number of folks who might be buried there. Maybe it was a lonely immigrant with no family. Or it could be a drifter who had come through town and they'd buried him where he'd dropped dead. Either way, I wondered if the lanky Mr. Underhill had measured out the grave.

Maybe it was just thinking about spooky Mr. Underhill that made me feel a little uneasy. Like someone was watching me, following my footsteps. I was nearing Miss Sadie's but wasn't close enough to make a dash through the gate. I kept walking, looking back over my shoulder. I expected to see Mr. Underhill's long legs and hunched shoulders right behind me.

My game of rhyming started up. *"Horse is in his stable and Pig is in his pen. Dog is in his doghouse and Farmer's in the den. Cow is in the field and Cat is on the stoop, but where is Chicken? Fox is in the coop!"*

I was not comforted by my rhyme, and feeling a little too out in the open, I veered off the path and into the hedge for some cover. I took another long look behind me, through leafy branches swaying and bowing in the wind, to convince myself that my imagination had run away with me. I could swear I'd even heard a rattling sound echo in the woods. But there was no Mr. Underhill. No one was there. Finally, I let out a long breath and vowed to stop thinking about graves, and undertakers, and dead people. I tried to start up what I hoped would be a happier rhyme. *"Johnny likes sunshine, I like rain. Johnny likes to ride his bike—"* I bolted from the bushes and ran headlong into a tall figure dressed in black.

"Thunderation!" I yelped. My heart was pounding to beat the band when I saw that it was Sister Redempta.

"Thunderation, indeed." She raised her chin at me.

I hoped *thunderation* wasn't on a list of forbidden words. It must not have been, as she'd said it herself.

"I, uh, I didn't see you. Sorry for running into you." For the life of me, I couldn't figure where she had come from, but scary as she was, I was relieved it was her.

"That happens when one comes sprinting out of bushes." She tucked her hands up into her sleeves, studying me. "Well, go on. Finish it. If Johnny likes to ride his bike . . ."

"I ride the train?" I hadn't meant for it to come out as a question.

"I see. I think it's best that I assigned you a story to write

110

over the summer and not a poem. Still, I know a good rhyme can calm the soul." She looked a ways past me. "When the sisters ran an orphanage here, some children would sing themselves to sleep, often in their native language, as many were immigrant children."

For some reason, I felt tears creeping up in my eyes. I felt like one of those orphan children. "Did it help? Did their rhyming make them feel better?" I asked, knowing that I'd get a truthful answer from Sister Redempta.

"For some, their rhymes would make them smile; others would cry. But eventually they would all fall asleep." She seemed to sense I needed one that ended in a smile. "I remember one boy who used to play a sort of peekaboo game. He would cover his face with his hands, just barely peeking out. Of course, his didn't actually rhyme, because it was half in English and half in his own language. It started with 'Where is little boy hiding? Where did little boy go?' Then he'd finish the verse and take his hands away from his face as if he'd been found."

"That's a nice story," I said, afraid to ask if he ever had been found, or taken in by somebody.

"Are you making good use of your summer?" Sister Redempta asked, back to business.

I thought she stole a glance at Miss Sadie's Divining Parlor, and figured she would have something to say about my going down the Path to Perdition, so I didn't mention my visits with the diviner. Searching for the Rattler probably wouldn't go over too well either. I was glad I didn't run into Sister Redempta very often, as it seemed there wasn't much to talk about.

"Lettie, Ruthanne, and me went frog hunting," I said.

"Lettie, Ruthanne, and *I* went frog hunting."

The thought of Sister Redempta and anybody going frog hunting was a hoot, but I knew she was just correcting my grammar.

"Well, I'm sure you will have much to write about for your end-of-the-summer assignment," she said.

I'd almost forgotten about that. "Yes, Sister." She must have heard the hesitation in my voice.

"You might want to start with a dictionary."

"A dictionary?" Even I knew that a dictionary didn't have stories.

"Yes. Start with the word *manifest*. It's a verb as well as a noun. Look it up." Sister Redempta started to take her leave, then called back over her shoulder, "And remember, Abilene Tucker: to write a good story, one must watch and listen."

Lord-a-mighty, if she didn't sound like a diviner herself.

I was still wondering where Sister Redempta had come from and what the dictionary might have to say about what *manifest* meant when I opened Miss Sadie's gate and plodded up the creaky stairs.

As I walked through the divining parlor, I was hopeful that maybe I'd mostly worked off my debt. My aching back and blistered hands were equally optimistic. But Miss Sadie was sitting out back on her metal patio chair, smoking her corncob pipe, like she hadn't budged since the day before.

Her intentions of making me work on her garden hadn't budged either.

"Your rows must be straight. Some plants must be kept apart. Otherwise neither will thrive."

I didn't say anything, as I was still pondering my run-in

with Sister Redempta. Besides, dry as it was, those seeds were never going to sprout, let alone thrive.

"When you are finished today, I have herbs to be ground into paste for Mrs. Clayton. They go in her tea and will help her milk come in."

I looked up, surprised that she knew about Mrs. Clayton and the new baby, and wondered if some visitor had given her the news. For someone who didn't get around much, Miss Sadie never seemed to be short on information. And there were all those people and events in her stories. I'd pretty much put aside the notion of Miss Sadie's being a fortune-teller, but how *did* she know everything?

"We were out near the Clayton place yesterday, Lettie, Ruthanne, and me. I think that new baby had a hard time being born." This didn't register any sort of amazement from Miss Sadie. "Sister Redempta looked nearly worn out. We saw her without her veil on and her sleeves all rolled up. She's almost like a regular woman," I said.

It occurred to me that maybe Sister Redempta had come by and told Miss Sadie about the baby, but Miss Sadie's silence gave no clue. I remembered the way Sister Redempta had raised an eyebrow that last day of school when referring to Miss Sadie's den of iniquity. It seemed there was something between those two, but I couldn't put my finger on it. Maybe these were two women who lived far enough off the beaten path that there was some strange common ground between them.

"*Elam bouzshda gramen ze.*"

I poked my head up from the dust. "Say again?"

"It is Gypsy. It means the person you encounter is often more than the person you see."

113

The last person I'd mentioned was Sister Redempta. Was that who she was talking about? I knew better than to lock her in to only one explanation. Something I was beginning to learn about Miss Sadie was that whatever she said could mean more than one thing at a time. And it usually led straight to the past.

Miss Sadie continued in her Hungarian accent.

"There was much churning in Manifest those many years ago. A war. A quilt. And a curse . . ."

The Victory Quilt

OCTOBER 27, 1917

That evening at the fairgrounds, Ned paid for a bag of popcorn. He walked past the army recruitment booth and the Liberty Bond table, over to the Daughters of the American Revolution. Pearl Ann stood with a bevy of women bragging about their sons and nephews in the army and all a-twitter over the coming New Year's festivities.

Mrs. Larkin seemed to be holding court as she passed out flyers.

VICTORY QUILT AUCTION

Sponsored by
the Daughters of the American Revolution
Manifest Chapter
Mrs. Eugene Larkin, President

The ladies of each fraternal order are invited to
submit squares for a special victory quilt to be

signed by President Woodrow Wilson himself on his tour of the Midwest.

The Manifest Victory Quilt will be auctioned off to the highest bidder during the New Year's festivities at the Manifest depot following the president's quilt signing.

Quilt squares should be the standard six-inch block and must be submitted for approval by December 1 to Mrs. Eugene Larkin, president.

Proceeds will go toward the purchase of Liberty Bonds to support our young men in arms.

Mrs. Eugene Larkin, President

"Now, ladies, everyone take a quilt square and flyer." Mrs. Larkin clucked. "My husband, the late Eugene Larkin, who, as you know, was the county appraiser for twenty-five years, was a strong supporter of President Wilson. I'm sure that is in large part why Manifest is one of the stops on the presidential tour of the Midwest. Of course, my nephew, my sister's boy, works in the governor's office. He's an assistant to the assistant. . . ."

Ned sidled up to Pearl Ann. "So the president's coming to town. He must have heard we have the prettiest girls in the state." Pearl Ann smiled as Ned handed her the bag of popcorn. "You going to enter a quilt square?"

"Every girl's got to do her part in supporting our boys in arms," she said, waving a swatch of paisley fabric. "But with my quilting, I think I'd set the war effort back a few Liberty Bonds." She tucked the fabric into Ned's shirt pocket like a handkerchief.

"Care to take a ride on the carousel?" Ned asked.

Before she could answer, a high-pitched voice called from the bevy of quilter women: "Pearl Ann." It was Pearl Ann's mother, Mrs. Larkin. "Come along, dear." Mrs. Larkin spoke with pursed lips and looked at Ned as if he was not fit to carry Pearl Ann's luggage, let alone share popcorn with her.

"I don't think your mother is too fond of me," Ned said.

"She just doesn't know you yet."

"Yet? I've lived in Manifest most of my life."

"To someone whose people have lived here for generations, that's not that long."

"Oh, so I have to have a pedigree going back to the time of George Washington."

"I didn't say that. It's just that Mother doesn't feel she *knows* a person until she knows their aunts, uncles, and second cousins twice removed. She just likes to have her ducks in a row."

Ned's shoulders stiffened. It was this whole notion of lineage and background that had sent him back into the mines for a second shift. He shoved his hands into his pockets. "Yeah, well, you'd have to row quite a ways to find my ducks somewhere in Italy, or France, or maybe Czechoslovakia, so that presents a problem, doesn't it?"

"That's not what I meant. *I* don't care where you're from," she said softly.

"Pearl Ann!" Mrs. Larkin called again, this time with one eyebrow raised.

Just then, Arthur Devlin, wearing a dapper pin-striped suit and sporting a sleek black cane, approached Mrs. Larkin. He bowed and took her hand. "Good evening,

Mrs. Larkin," he said in a booming voice. "Or may I call you Eudora, as in our school days?" He winked as he kissed her hand. "Would you be so gracious as to accompany me on a stroll?"

"I'm afraid as president of the DAR, I really must distribute these quilt squares—"

"Come now, surely that can wait. My dear departed Esther always said, 'Don't do today what you can put off until tomorrow.'" He chuckled, turning Mrs. Larkin away from Pearl Ann and Ned, his large build cutting her off from view.

"It's pretty clear that your mother cares about where a person is from," Ned said.

Pearl Ann grimaced. "Who is it you want to take on the carousel? Me or my mother?"

Ned dug in his heels and didn't answer.

"I see. Well, be careful going round and round on the carousel. Mother is prone to nausea." Pearl Ann marched away from Ned *and* her mother.

"Hey, *Benedetto*." A young man snatched the paisley fabric from Ned's pocket. "You getting your quilt square ready for the victory quilt?" It was Lance Devlin, the mine owner's son, with a couple of his buddies. "Well, it's good to see you're doing your part for the war effort." The boys, who normally sported their high school letter sweaters, were dressed in smart brown military uniforms and jaunty hats. They formed a half circle around Ned.

"Going to a costume ball?" Ned said, still smoldering.

"You didn't hear? We signed up to do our bit. After all, somebody's got to go over and fix the mess your folks got themselves into over there."

"I didn't know the army was so desperate that they've lowered their requirements in intelligence as well as age."

"You mean because I haven't had my eighteenth birthday yet?" Lance asked. "Yeah, well, it's amazing how twenty-five dollars can help a recruitment officer overlook a thing or two. Maybe you should try it, Ned old boy, but then, company vouchers might not do the trick."

"You're right about that. The Devlin vouchers aren't worth the paper they're written on."

"Tut-tut, Ned. You should be relieved that you won't see me on the track this spring."

"Oh, I am relieved." Ned rubbed his neck. "I strained my neck last year running against you in the mile."

"Really?" Lance looked a little pleased as well as surprised.

"Yeah, from craning my neck to see how far behind you were."

The other boys in uniform snickered behind their hands. Lance Devlin got his face up close to Ned's and tucked the paisley fabric back into Ned's pocket. "Well, for now you'd better just stitch up your little quilt square and leave the fighting to us. Then again, maybe we should check to make sure you're not stitching in some kind of spy message. You can never be too careful around those of *unknown* heritage. And your heritage is about as unknown as it gets, isn't that right, *Benedetto*?" Lance stepped back and spoke loudly. "For all we know, that might not even be your real name. Maybe it's Fritz or Hans. C'mon, fellas." He bumped Ned's shoulder in passing.

Jinx walked up with some warm biscuits. "What was that all about?"

"Nothing." Ned stole a glance at the army recruitment stand. "So a con is the art of distraction, huh?"

"Yes. Are you reconsidering my little pyrotectic plan?"

Ned squared his shoulders. "Sign me up."

The first of December rolled around and all the quilt squares had been turned in—except one.

"But the deadline is today." The Hungarian woman shook her quilt square, her bracelets jangling.

"I'm sure you must have misread." Eudora Larkin peered through the screen door of her home. "The deadline has passed and the quilt is full. Besides, as president of the DAR, it is my responsibility to ensure the suitability of anything going before the president of the United States. Involvement of someone of your profession would be inappropriate, to say the least."

"My profession?" the woman said, challenging her.

"Well, yes, you know, a fortune-teller. A caster of spells and curses."

"Curses?" the woman repeated, her eyes blazing. "Keep your victory quilt. I give you a curse." She pulled open the screen door. *"Ava grautz budel nocha mole."*

Mrs. Larkin stepped back, cowering, as the screen door slammed shut. Then, trying to regain her composure, she said, "Oh, for heaven's sake. It's all poppycock." She watched the woman walk away. "Poppycock, I tell you."

Mrs. Larkin was so distressed by the woman's curse that by New Year's Eve she had dark circles under her eyes and was of an overall irritable disposition.

• • •

During the weeks leading up to the New Year's festivities, Jinx and Ned were busy collecting empty cans and filling them with ingredients gathered from sources as varied as the hardware store, bakery, and mine supply.

After word had gotten out that the coveted Manchurian Fire Throwers were for sale, Jinx and Ned knew they could sell as many as they could make. The abandoned mine shaft Shady used for mixing hooch became a convenient hideout for a new shady endeavor. It was located on the long narrow stretch of land, owned by the Widow Cane, that ran alongside the mine. The shaft had been abandoned years before, when Devlin's geologists had figured that the heart of the coal vein would be found farther west. For Jinx and Ned, it was a secluded area perfect for making fireworks.

Jinx carefully emptied black powder from his pockets into a large can.

"Whoa. Hungarian olives." Ned read the label on the oversized canister. "Those must be some olives."

"Yeah, I've been helping the Hungarian woman with some fence work and she gave me this one. It'll be just the right size for the last of the TNT. Otis, at the mine, said even though a bottle of Shady's hooch for two pockets of TNT is a bargain, he can't risk Burton finding out."

Ned shrugged. "I wouldn't worry about it. Burton, Devlin, the whole mine has no trouble blasting through anything or anyone who gets in their way."

Jinx looked sideways at Ned. He'd been awful moody of late. Ned must have noticed Jinx looking at him, because he said, "How'd you learn all this stuff? The shell game, the art of distraction? *Arctic glacial water?* And don't tell me you picked it up from a hundred-year-old medicine man."

Jinx shrugged without looking up. "I guess it started a couple of years ago when my mom got sick. My dad took off when I was little, so it was just my mom and me living in a one-room apartment in Chicago. We did okay for a while. She took in sewing and laundry. But when she got sick, my uncle Finn, my dad's brother, said he could help me make some money for food and medicine. He taught me all kinds of tricks of the trade. Then, when my mom died, it was either end up in an orphanage or go with Finn. He took me on with him, kind of as his assistant."

"And . . . ?" Ned wasn't dumb. He knew that Jinx had come to Manifest on the run, but until now, he had never pressed him for an explanation.

Jinx was tired. The canister felt heavy in his hands. He set it down, wanting to unburden himself.

"It was a mediocre con at best. Usually it was missions and tent revivals that worked like a charm, because people came looking for something and we'd provide it. But you had to have a mole, someone not known to be associated with Finn."

Jinx took a breath. "I was the mole. I'd have some malady and Finn was the person with the cure for what ailed me. Sometimes I'd be blind. Other times crippled. But it was always something that would be visible to everyone there. Then, when Finn came along, he'd tell the folks about his elixir or balm that was a time-honored remedy from the natives of the Zambezi jungle or a special mixture prepared by a hundred-year-old Indian medicine man. He'd ask for a volunteer to try the stuff. I'd hold back and wait for someone to volunteer me. It was always best if they came up with the idea themselves."

"A hundred-year-old medicine man, huh?" Ned said. "I knew it."

Jinx grinned. "Yeah, so I'd drink it, or rub it on, depending what my ailment was. Then, with no small bit of drama, I'd be healed. Folks couldn't get their wallets out fast enough to buy a bottle or two."

"But isn't that nothing more than lying, cheating, and stealing?" Ned asked.

"I guess I never looked at it that way. That's what Finn did and I was with Finn." Jinx grew silent, knowing that his answer had fallen flat.

"Go on," said Ned.

"Well, there was a tent revival in Joplin. They were usually loud and raucous, with lots of shouting and arm waving in one part praise and two parts damnation. But this one was different. The preacher was quiet and gentle. He spoke like a neighbor chatting over the fence. He talked of how he'd done things in his life he wasn't proud of. Said he'd had sadness and hardship that had left him wandering. Then he'd decided he didn't want to wander anymore. He started singing and others joined in." Jinx rested his hands on his knees.

"That song was about green pastures and restful waters. The preacher talked about walking in the valley of the shadow of death and not being afraid." Jinx grew quiet, reliving the memory. "I'd never heard anything so nice. All Finn ever told me was that if it wasn't for him, I'd be dead or in an orphanage someplace where they feed the kids rat soup and make them scrub toilets day and night. So I let that preacher's words linger in my head and found myself wishing I could be in those green pastures instead of always sneaking into one town and hightailin' it out of another.

"But pretty soon the service was over and Finn had to do his act and I had to get healed. Everything went off like usual until Finn and me were in the woods outside of town."

The abandoned mine shaft seemed to fade away as Jinx revealed his story.

Finn was counting the money by the fire when a man sauntered into our campsite. "Hey there, Finn," he said through buckteeth. "Long time no see."

I sat up, thinking Finn would be surprised. But he didn't act like it. "Hey, Junior," he said without looking up. Finn just counted the rest of his money and stuffed it into his pocket.

"I've been living just up the road with my aunt Louise. Got my eye on a girl in town."

Finn didn't answer.

"I saw you at the revival," Junior said, sitting down at the fire.

"Yeah, I saw you too."

"Boy, we had some times, didn't we, Finn? Remember that job we did in St. Louis down at the freight house? We left those boys knowing who was boss, didn't we, Finn?"

"That was a two-bit hack job, Junior. It didn't take any brains to clonk a couple guys on the head and steal their hat and shoes. No, sir. I'm a confidence man now. Playing

124

for higher stakes these days. Nothing you'd be capable of."

Junior nodded. "This your new partner?" He motioned to me.

"Yup. He's younger than you, but smarter."

Junior just smiled a goofy smile. "Maybe you're right, Finn. But I've kind of fallen on hard times lately, and I could use a little hand up, if you know what I mean."

"More like a handout. That's what you mean, isn't it, Junior?" Finn's voice was hard and mean. "Well, you can forget it. Now go on. Get out of here."

Junior stood and walked over behind Finn. "Folks around here wouldn't be too happy to know you cheated them out of their church money."

Finn stood up. "You threatening me, Junior?" Finn's face cracked into a strange smile. "Go on. Tell the sheriff you've captured the notorious outlaw who sells fake elixir. He'll laugh in your face. Besides, by the time you get back to town, I'll be halfway to who knows where."

Junior pulled a knife from his vest pocket, his hands shaking. "Maybe so, but if I take you into town and I tell them I've got the man who killed that banker's son in Kansas City, I think they might be real interested."

Finn froze. "So much for honor among thieves, eh, Jinx?"

It happened not long after my mother died. Finn and me were living in a fleabag apartment in Kansas City. He'd been out all night, drinking and gambling, when he stormed in and told me to grab my things. We were leaving. I never knew why until Junior shed some light on what had sent us packing.

I remember thinking two things as I sat by the fire, watching this scene play out. One was that I felt sorry for Junior, and two, I didn't want to be like him. Wandering in the valley of the shadow of death. Because that was what I'd be doing with Finn.

In one move, Finn wrenched the knife from Junior's hand and twisted his arm behind his back.

Finn winced in pain. "I was just funning with you, Finn. I wouldn't have turned you in."

"Jinx, get a rope."

"Just let him go and let's get out of here," I said.

"What's your hurry, boy? You afraid of me now?" Finn said.

I didn't answer.

Finn threw the knife, planting it in the ground right in front of my feet.

"I'll give you something to be afraid of." His eyes were like smoldering coals as he held on to Junior. "Now go cut a piece of rope in the bag over there."

I pulled a long rope from the bag and cut off a section.

Finn shoved Junior to the ground. "Tie him up."

Junior cowered on the ground. "Come on, Finn. I didn't mean nothing."

I walked toward Junior, still carrying the knife and rope, trying to figure out what to do. Finn was rustling around the campsite, grabbing his belongings. Maybe he wouldn't notice if I did a haphazard job on the tying.

I wrapped the rope loosely around Junior's hands and tied it off in a slipknot that could be easily undone. Then I picked up the knife and stood facing Junior. I whispered, "Get your hands free while we're packing and go."

Junior didn't answer. He just looked past me with fear in his eyes. I knew that Finn was behind me and I knew he'd heard. I turned just in time to meet Finn's fist as it came crashing into my face. The last thing I remember was the gleaming knife in my hand.

I couldn't have been out long, but when I came to, I was lying beside Junior with blood all over me. The knife had gotten him right in the stomach.

Finn knelt to examine Junior, then looked at me. "You killed him." He shook his head. "Boy, you are some kind of jinx. I was just going to tie up Junior here and leave him in the woods until we was gone. Now look what you done."

I did look. Long and hard.

"Yes, sir, there's a shadow of bad luck all over you. First your daddy leaves; then your mama dies. Now poor, stupid Junior." He took the knife. "I must be the only one free of your hoodoo bad luck." He looked at me with a combination of disgust and pity. "I guess you'll have to stick with me," he said, wiping the blade with his handkerchief. "Otherwise, you might end up bringing bad luck to your own self."

I was scared.

Jinx accidentally kicked over the canister of TNT, bringing the abandoned mine shaft and disassembled canisters and fuses back into focus.

"Go on," Ned said.

"Within a couple days, word got out that the sheriff of Joplin was looking for a pair that was responsible for killing Junior Haskell. Junior had told some of his pals that he was

127

meeting up with a couple of fellas from his glory days. That he'd seen us at the tent revival. His aunt Louise told the sheriff about the revival and there was a whole town full of witnesses who knew what we looked like. Finn said since they were looking for a pair, we'd better split up. That's when I hopped a train heading one direction and he hopped one heading the other way."

Ned locked his eyes on Jinx, giving him his full attention. "That can hardly be considered murder. It was an accident. If anything, it was your uncle's fault."

"But I was the one holding the knife. I must have swung around when Finn hit me, and, well, the knife went where it went. But try explaining that to an angry crowd or a jury of Junior Haskell's peers." Jinx's face flushed and his hands were shaking. "Here, help me put Mr. Hinkley's shell back together." He handed Ned the original Manchurian Fire Thrower, ending the conversation. "He's setting up his big fireworks show down by the depot. They're pulling out all the stops for President Wilson's big visit."

"Where's the fuse?"

"We must have used his fuse in one of our canisters. Just cut me a piece off that roll. Better make it good and long. Three hundred feet in the air is pretty high."

The following days held a thriving business for Jinx and Ned. Boys from all over found excuses to frequent Shady's place. When the last canister was sold, the boys had taken in a grand total of fifty dollars and seventy-five cents. Ned took his half and insisted that since Jinx was the idea man, he should have the extra seventy-five cents.

The whole enterprise would have gone off without a

hitch if little Danny McIntyre, Joey Fipps, Froggy Sikes, and a dozen other freckle-faced ne'er-do-wells hadn't taken to setting off Manchurian Fire Throwers all over town. One angry mother after another confronted Shady on the street or in a store. Sometimes one was even bold enough to enter his saloon, pulling on a youngster's ear, demanding that Shady deal with the hoodlum under his own roof.

Shady let the first few incidents slide. After all, Donal MacGregor's pig, Stanley, wasn't killed. Fortunately for him, he was wallowing in the mud pen when his lean-to had a hole blasted through the roof boards. But then Greta Akkerson arrived, claiming that her son had gotten hold of a can of Hungarian olives and *somehow* her chicken coop had its roof blown off and chickens went squawking everywhere. Well, then Shady knew he had to take action.

Jinx had been the face of the whole operation, and not one to pass blame, he took full responsibility and promised to make amends. He wasn't sure what those amends would be until Shady made it clear to him at the New Year's quilt auction.

New Year's Day was cold and clear. The special festivities held enough distractions, with so many people milling around the train depot, that no one noticed Ned Gillen at the army recruitment station, signing his name on the dotted line. Even the recruitment officer was so busy counting out the twenty-five one-dollar bills Ned handed him that he neglected to ask for proof of age.

HATTIE MAE'S NEWS AUXILIARY

JANUARY 2, 1918

The 1918 New Year's celebration was a rousing success, if a bit unpredictable. Many townsfolk gathered in the train depot, drinking eggnog and wishing cheers to each other's health. A few verses of "Auld Lang Syne" were sung and some had imbibed enough brandy that much of the event will be "never brought to mind."

Of course, the utmost anticipation was centered on the arrival of the 7:45 train and President Woodrow Wilson. The Manifest High School band was out in full force and played the most inspiring rendition of "Hail to the Chief."

The unfortunate explosion of fireworks in the water tower—and subsequent dousing of the president and the newly signed victory quilt—was a somewhat surprising turn of events. While shock among the onlookers was widespread, the range of glee and dismay was split mostly along party lines. Although, it seemed the ruffling of feathers at the president's "pond jumpers" comment (referring to our foreign-born citizens who crossed the ocean) permeated throughout.

After the departure of the 7:45 train at 8:07, the day culminated with the much-anticipated Daughters of the American Revolution auction. Enthusiasm for the victory quilt waned, what with the president's signature being blurred beyond recognition, but all were pleased to see it bring such a high bid. Although, this reporter has not quite figured out the strategy of members of the same household bidding against each other. It was neck and neck between Shady Howard and the boy Jinx until the youngster won out, taking home the 1918 victory quilt for a bid of $25.75.

The mayor wishes to extend his thanks to all the volunteers for their participation in the day's festivities and is soliciting help with the construction of the new water tower, to be built "not within fifty feet of the depot" by order of the president.

Also, if anyone has information regarding the whereabouts of the fireworks salesman, a five-dollar reward is being offered by the Daughters of the American Revolution. See Mrs. Eudora Larkin, president. For all the whos, whats, whys, whens, and wheres in the modern township of Manifest, containing 1,524 registered voters, refer to the Sunday edition.

HATTIE MAE HARPER
Reporter About Town

VELMA T.'S VITAMIN REVITALIZER

Need a pick-me-up? Try this chemist's solution to low energy and waning stamina. With a carefully tested combination of iron, potassium, and calcium, it will give you a new spring in your step and you'll be able to accomplish the many tasks asked of you throughout the day. Just one teaspoon at morning and night and you will have the wherewithal of your youth. See Velma T. at the high school to get your Vitamin Revitalizer today.

PVT. NED GILLEN

CAMP FUNSTON, KANSAS
FEBRUARY 10, 1918

Dear Jinx,

I am settled in here at Camp Funston at almost 2100 hours. (That's military jargon for nine p.m.) It'll be lights-out pretty soon. It seems early for that, but reveille sneaks up faster than Pop's wake-up call of scorched eggs and charred bacon. Sarge says we'll be here a few weeks before shipping out, so that doesn't leave us much time for training. Most fellows here are in pretty good shape from football, basketball, or track and we're raring to go.

Hope you're not still mad at me for leaving. After all, I couldn't have done it without you. Without the money from the fireworks sale, I could never have convinced the recruitment officer to sign me up underage. So I owe you, buddy.

Don't know if I'm supposed to say where we're going but I'll have to parley vous *a little on my* vichy swaz, *if you know what I mean. Looks like this Manifest boy is going to shake the coal dust from his shoes and see the world.*

Got our uniforms already. Went into town with Heck and Holler to get our pictures made. The man behind the camera was confounded by their outlandish names. Said their mama and daddy must have drunk too much hooch before naming those boys. Don't tell that to Judge and Mrs. Carlson. A house that dry is liable to go up in flames. I'm sending a big photograph to Pop for the mantel, but here's one for you. Think I'll be able to kill a few Huns with my charm and dashing good looks?

How are things coming in your search for the Rattler? At least now there's one person you can eliminate as a suspect. Moi. *(Another clue to my destination.)*

Oh, river (that's how Heck says au revoir),
Ned

Under the Stars

JUNE 12, 1936

I'd told and retold Miss Sadie's last story and what I'd learned from Hattie Mae's news auxiliary to Lettie and Ruthanne. I'd told them all about the Manchurian Fire Thrower, the untimely demise of Junior Haskell, the explosion at the water tower, and the unfortunate dousing of the victory quilt. I tried to remember every detail, even down to the Hungarian woman's not being allowed to contribute a quilt square. But there were still things that needed pondering.

"So the Hungarian woman was Miss Sadie!" Lettie's words broke the stillness of the dark woods. "So why does she call herself the Hungarian woman? Why doesn't she just say 'me' or call herself Miss Sadie?"

"When she tells the stories, she's sort of removed from them. She's the storyteller."

"Okay," Ruthanne said, "but how does she know certain

things that happened when she wasn't there to see for herself?"

"I wondered about that too," I answered. "But remember the Hungarian olives? Jinx had ducked into her tent at the fairgrounds and later he was doing fence work for her. That must be how she knows some of the things she knows. He had to have told her."

"Well, she's got to have some kind of hoodoo. After all, the curse on Mrs. Larkin and the quilt worked!" Lettie said.

Lettie still got excited even though she and Ruthanne had made me tell them the story umpteen times in the past week. And we'd all read Ned's letters so many times we practically knew them by heart. It was always interesting when Miss Sadie's stories overlapped with something in Ned's letters.

Lettie marveled at various parts of the story as Ruthanne and I walked alongside, our feet crunching through twigs and leaves in the moonlight. I was on another one of Miss Sadie's nature errands. She'd had me do all manner of *divining*, as she called it. Things like venturing out at dusk to collect blue moss from under a fallen sycamore tree, and getting up at sunrise to gather a handful of dandelions before the morning dew burned off. The tasks were always unusual and she'd mash whatever I'd brought back into a paste or a powder. To what end, I didn't know. But that night was a bit more mysterious, as I wasn't sure exactly what I was looking for. Miss Sadie said a good diviner needed to watch, and listen, and wait.

"What do you think the curse was?" Lettie continued. "I mean, what curse causes a water tower to explode?"

Truth was I'd been afraid to ask Miss Sadie about the

curse she'd placed on Mrs. Larkin. The words seemed so ancient and full of bad omen I didn't want her saying them in English and accidentally directing them toward me.

"And I still don't understand why Shady was bidding against Jinx for the quilt," Lettie said.

Ruthanne rolled her eyes. "How you ever got a better grade than me in math, I'll never know. Now listen and I'll explain it again." Ruthanne always spoke about the stories as if she had witnessed the events herself. "At the auction nobody wanted the quilt, because it got wet and the president's signature was all smudged, right?"

"Right," Lettie said, concentrating.

"But Shady knew that Jinx had made a bundle of money selling his homemade fireworks."

"Right. His share was twenty-five dollars and seventy-five cents."

"Right. Since it was Jinx's fireworks that caused the water tower to burst all over the place, Shady wanted him to make restitution and made him buy it. Jinx probably started with a lowball bid, so Shady kept bidding against him until the quilt finally sold to Jinx for twenty-five dollars—"

"And seventy-five cents!" Lettie's eyes lit up. "The same amount he'd made off the fireworks."

"Yes," Ruthanne said with a sigh. "But it was probably Miss Sadie's curse that doomed the quilt in the first place, don't you think, Abilene?" She didn't wait for me to answer. "She must be a witch. Even Mrs. Larkin called her a sorceress. A caster of spells."

"Then why does she call herself a diviner?" I asked. "How come her sign doesn't say, 'Miss Sadie: Sorceress and Caster of Spells'?"

"Because people in her line of work like to be mysterious. Just like whatever it is we're traipsing through the woods for in the dark right now. There's a mystery." Ruthanne looked at me for an explanation.

"Miss Sadie gave me this bucket and told me to find a young cottonwood tree in the moonlight."

"But what's the bucket for?"

"She said to just keep my eyes open."

"What kind of crazy instructions are those?" Ruthanne grumbled.

"It is kind of adventurous, though," said Lettie. "It's like that song 'Riding the Rails in the Moonlit Night.' " Unbidden, Lettie broke into song.

> *"I lit out on a dark and dreary night, life had dealt me*
> *a heavy blow.*
> *First my boss gave me the knee, then it up and rained*
> *on me,*
> *And I had no earthly place to go.*
> *Yodel-ay-hee. Yodel-ay-hee. Yodel-ay-hee."*

"For the love of Pete, Lettie, if you don't sing something a little more cheerful, Abilene and me are going to throw you on a train and not wave goodbye."

"Don't worry. It gets better," Lettie said reassuringly.

> *"My soul and my shoes were all wore through, no money*
> *or job in sight,*
> *But once I hit the tracks, my burdens at my back,*
> *I hopped that train in the pale moonlight."*

I couldn't help but join in.

"Yodel-ay-hee. Yodel-ay-hee. Yodel-ay-hee."

We reached a clearing at the creek bed and studied the rocky, parched ground, and I imagined a time when this had been a lively stream that one could wade in for a swim. "There's cottonwoods all along here," Ruthanne said.

I touched the rough, heavy bark. "They look too old. She said a *young* cottonwood."

"Then let's look for some volunteers that have sprouted up more recently. Besides, the moon isn't very bright yet. Come on. I'm getting hungry." She steered us toward a clearing in a grove of cottonwoods and elms, some not much bigger than saplings.

Ruthanne sat down, her back against a rotted tree trunk, and opened a knapsack. "I guess if we have to wait for the eye of newt and heart of toad to present themselves, we might as well get comfortable. What'd you bring?"

We had agreed that we would each bring some food to share during our outing. Ruthanne pulled out three liverwurst sandwiches. I produced a dusty jar of pickled beets I'd found in Shady's pantry. They wouldn't have been out of the running next to the liverwurst sandwiches, but then Lettie produced a tin with two cookies in it. She handed one to me and one to Ruthanne.

"Gingersnap!" I said, biting into one, its sweet spiciness giving me a thrill. "Where's yours?"

"I already had my fill. It was my sister Susie's birthday on Tuesday, and as a surprise we all agreed to go without eggs for breakfast this week so Mama could exchange them for sugar at the grocer's," Lettie explained. "She made a dozen gingersnaps."

"Here, have half of mine," I offered. Lettie took the half with some reluctance, I thought.

Ruthanne took one bite of her cookie, and then another. "Your mama sure makes a fine gingersnap. My mama always says she was born to manhandle a cast iron skillet but your mama was blessed with the lighter touch of a baker." Ruthanne ate the last of the cookie. "Sing us a song, Lettie."

Lettie beamed. *"I lit out on a dark and dreary night. . . ."*

We were in no hurry, since Lettie and Ruthanne had gotten permission to spend the night with me at Shady's place. I hadn't been sure if they'd be allowed to stay over, what with Shady being . . . Shady. But it seemed their mothers had known Shady their whole lives and they said it was fine as long as we could stomach his burnt biscuits in the morning.

Lettie's song lulled us for a time. Then all grew still. We'd talked so much about Ned's letters and who the Rattler might be. It seemed like a good time to set our minds on other things.

"How's your story coming, Abilene?" Lettie asked. "The one Sister Redempta assigned you?"

"I don't know. I don't really have a story to tell."

"Telling a story ain't hard," Lettie said. "All you need is a beginning, middle, and end."

"Hmm," I answered, wondering if it was that simple.

"It's so quiet out here," Lettie said, changing the subject.

I listened for sounds of birds or cicadas . . . or rattlers.

Both the rattly spy kind and the slithery snake kind. "Do you think maybe there are snakes in these woods?" I asked.

"Snakes?" Ruthanne pondered the notion. "Uncle Louver says there's critters of all shapes and sizes out here. He tells quite the tale about goings-on in the woods."

I wasn't really up for hearing it, but judging by the way she stretched back and put her hands behind her head, I knew she was waiting to be asked.

"Maybe now's not the best time for that story, Ruthanne," Lettie said. "It's already kind of spooky out here."

"Go on," I said, pretending to stifle a yawn. "Let's hear it."

Ruthanne looked sideways at me, I guess gauging if my level of enthusiasm deserved her tale.

"Well," she began, "he was setting some traps—Uncle Louver, that is—when he hears a god-awful noise. He thinks it's a raccoon or maybe a possum, so he goes to check it out. By the time he realizes it's no critter, it's too late."

"Mm-hmm. Too late," Lettie echoed.

Ruthanne leaned forward. "He sees a man looking all afraid at something. His face all pale and eyes wide. That man was petrified."

"Pet-ri-fied," Lettie said.

"Of what?" I asked, my interest on the rise.

"The ghost. A big black ghost floating and rattling right towards that man. The fella's backing up, backing up. Then Uncle Louver hears one of his traps snap." Ruthanne clapped her hands together. "And things get quiet."

"What'd he do?" I asked. "Uncle Louver, I mean."

"He ran away. Fast as he could."

"Mama says Uncle Louver always was a bit skittish," Lettie added.

"Who was it? Who was caught in the trap?"

"That's just it." Ruthanne leaned back again, leaving a sufficient pause for the night sounds of the forest to fill in. "Never was a body found. He brought his brothers back to find it and there sat the trap, still snapped shut. All that was left was an old boot."

"That's right. An old, beat-up boot," Lettie said.

Then both girls said together, "And the foot was still in it."

I wasn't sure if they were fooling, but right then, in the darkness of those same woods, that image hung before me like the ghost itself.

"So the boot, the foot, what'd they do with 'em?" I asked.

Ruthanne continued. "Uncle Louver wanted nothing to do with it, in case the ghost came looking for it, so he buried it."

"Did anyone ever see the ghost again?"

"Oh, some would see a passing shadow now and again, but they could hear it rattling around in the woods."

"Rattling?" I said. "What if that ghost and the Rattler were one and the same?"

"I suppose that's a thought." Ruthanne considered the possibility. "Uncle Louver says that sometimes, even now, he catches a shadowy glimpse of that figure going hither and yon, especially during a full moon."

As she said it, we realized the moon was full and brilliant above us.

"Look," I said.

"What? Did you find the eye of newt and heart of toad?" Ruthanne asked.

"Close." I pointed. Glistening in the soft ground around the saplings were hundreds of big fleshy worms. "Miss Sadie knew we'd find worms here for her garden."

"Or her witch's brew."

"Either way, let's put them in the bucket. Then we can get out of these creepy woods."

We worked quickly, scooping up handfuls of dirt before the worms could wiggle their way deep into the ground. Then, with two of us at a time sharing the weight of the bucket, we started back to Shady's place, looking hither and yon for any ghostly movement.

All three of us crawled into bed, one beside the other, listening to the sound of a harmonica in the distance. It was probably just a folk tune being played, but after Ruthanne's story, it sounded like a mournful wail.

When Lettie and Ruthanne were quiet, I reached for the not-so-shiny Liberty Head silver dollar in my windowsill collection of mementos. I tilted it slightly to catch the glimmer of moonlight. It no longer surprised me to find connections between the articles in the box and Miss Sadie's stories. Still, some things were a mystery. I thought of our stash of worms outside. The life churning in the bucket was a mystery. How did Miss Sadie know things like where to find worms in the moonlight? What happened to the man who lost his foot in Uncle Louver's trap? Who or what was haunting the woods? Was it the Rattler? I put the silver dollar back in its place beside the Wiggle King lure.

These many questions swarmed in my head, leaving me restless and uneasy. But it was the look on Lettie's face that night in the growing moonlight that made me wonder the most. The way she'd beamed when Ruthanne had asked her to sing us a song. I thought I knew a thing or two about people. Even had my list of universals. But I wondered. Maybe the world wasn't made of universals that could be summed up in neat little packages. Maybe there were just people. People who were tired and hurt and lonely and kind in their own way and their own time.

Once again, I felt off balance, as if I was playing tug-of-war and the person I was tugging against let go.

Lettie, half asleep, sang, *"Once I hit the tracks, my burdens at my back, I hopped that train in the pale moonlight."* I admired how Ruthanne knew what I did not. That Lettie hadn't had her fill of gingersnaps. With six kids in her family, she had more than likely given up her own cookie and traded something for an extra one to share with us.

The moonlight shone on the silver dollar and I thought of Miss Sadie's story of Jinx and Ned. Of Uncle Louver's ghost story. Of Lettie's story about having had her fill. Of Ned's letters and Hattie Mae's "News Auxiliaries," that I read like bedtime stories. And of Gideon's story I was struggling to learn. If there is such a thing as a universal—and I wasn't ready to throw all of mine out the window—it's that there is power in a story. And if someone pays you such a kindness as to make up a tale so you'll enjoy a gingersnap, you go along with that story and enjoy every last bite.

Yodel-ay-hee. Yodel-ay-hee. Yodel-ay-hee.

PVT. NED GILLEN

CAMP FUNSTON, KANSAS
MARCH 14, 1918

Dear Jinx,

Thanks for your letter. We're shipping out soon. Troops already over there will be whooping and hollering to see us replacements show up. Heck, Holler, and me are in the same regiment. Guess they figured the Manifest championship track team should stay together. Soon as we send old Heine back to Germany, the other guys from the Manifest High class of '18 plan to meet up at the Eiffel Tower with us to drink a toast. Tell Pearl Ann and the other girls not to be jealous of the mademoiselles. Their bonne *boys in uniform will be home in time to take them to the homecoming dance in the fall.*

And tell Velma T. thanks for the relief parcels she sent. There's some kind of bug going around that's waylaid half the camp with aches, fever, and chills. It started a few days ago, when one guy reported to the infirmary before breakfast, and today there are five hundred in makeshift beds all over the place. I've been taking an assortment of Velma T.'s home remedies. After my umpteenth trip to the latrine, I figured most of her elixirs are laxatives, but so far I'm holding up better than most.

All for now. Next time you hear from me, it'll be on some of that fancy perfumed paper from "over there."

Ich habe widerlich footen *(I have stinky feet)*,
Ned

P.S. We told Heck that means "Put down your weapon."

HATTIE MAE'S NEWS AUXILIARY

MAY 30, 1918

The recent commencement ceremony for the senior class of 1918 was a momentous occasion and certainly brought back fond memories of my own graduation last year. However, by all accounts, this year's event was bittersweet, as some of the class members were not present. You all recall the recent bon voyage celebration for the army recruits from the Manifest class of 1918. It was a moving event as we said goodbye, though only for a time, to our brave lads. I thought it fitting to name them here, along with some of their activities.

LUTHER (HECK) CARLSON
Track and Field, Glee Club

IVAN (HOLLER) CARLSON
Track and Field, Class Treasurer

LANCE DEVLIN
Track and Field, Football

NED GILLEN
Track and Field, Senior Play

DOUGLAS HAMILTON
Booster Staff

Having bid a fond farewell to our boys in arms, now is the time for all good men to come to the aid of their country. That means you, ladies! The Daughters of the American Revolution will be sponsoring a blanket drive, a bake sale, a letter-writing campaign, and much more. Thanks to Pearl Ann Larkin for organizing the effort before she heads off to college. Miss Velma T. Harkrader was going to enlist the aid of her chemistry class in mixing up some of her "good for what ails you" elixir. (It seems the need is great at Camp Funston, as many of the soldiers are still battling the flu.) Unfortunately, she is having to produce her elixir at home, due to another freak mishap, which resulted in her classroom windows being blown out. But thanks to everyone for your support. And for those of you who requested a printing of the special send-off cheer, it is as follows.

Off to war and don't be late!
Here come the boys of
one-nine-one-eight!

(Special thanks to Margaret Evans, senior class president, for writing the class cheer, which I have adapted here. Permission granted for printing.)

For all the whos, whats, whys, whens,

and wheres, both here and abroad, refer to the *Manifest Herald*. We've got sources we don't even know about.

HATTIE MAE HARPER
Reporter About Town

OLD ST. JACK'S LUMBAGO LINIMENT

**Don't Moan About
the Ache in Your Back.
Rub It Out
with Old St. Jack.**

Back hurt you? Can't straighten up without feeling sudden pains, sharp aches, and twinges? That's lumbago or sciatica, or maybe you're just getting old. But whatever the case, Old St. Jack's is the liniment for you. Just have the little missus rub the ointment on your back and blessed relief will come your way. The ointment leaves a slight discoloration of the skin, but this gives a hearty glow, and it can be used on the face as well. Don't wait. Get your trial bottle of Old St. Jack's at your local hardware store, next to the varnish.

Miss Sadie's Divining Parlor

JUNE 13, 1936

The next day was hot. I wasn't sure those worms were going to be happy with their new place, but they wiggled their way into that dry dirt like it was home sweet home. I figured they'd have to go down so deep to reach water that they'd come up on the other side of the world.

Miss Sadie seemed in a dark mood that morning. "Today you make rows. Not too deep. Not too wide. Dig." Her leg was red and swollen, so even her rocking on the back porch made her grit her teeth. And her bark made me grit mine.

Still, I'd been working up the nerve to ask her what the curse she'd laid on Mrs. Larkin was. The one that had left the county appraiser's wife in a tizzy. Lettie and Ruthanne weren't going to let it go until I found out.

"Um, m-ma'am?" I stuttered, not sure if she'd mind my having figured out she was the Hungarian woman in the story. Miss Sadie kept rocking. "That curse you popped on Mrs. Larkin?"

"Curse," she scoffed. "You believe everything that is told to you. Curses? Spies?" I jumped at her mention of spies. How did she know about that? I'd never even mentioned the Rattler to her. She may not have a bead on the future, but Miss Sadie surely had second sight when it came to the present.

"The only curse that woman bore was her own ignorance," Miss Sadie huffed.

"Well, what exactly did you say to her?"

"Ava grautz budel nocha mole."

I cringed as she repeated the phrase.

"It is Gypsy. It means 'May your life be as long as the hair on your chin.' And if you do not get busy, I will put an equally devastating curse on you."

I couldn't help grinning as I took up a shovel. Digging a square of dirt, then pitching it to the side, I hoped Miss Sadie's mood had lightened. It hadn't.

"No," she scolded. "You shovel like a *disznó*. A pig. You cannot toss the ground aside like an old rag. Then it will not help you later. Use a hoe, there by the shed."

What kind of demon woman is she? I wondered as I gripped the hoe, scooping the dirt to one side and then the other, making a gully in the middle. That made me a bit cantankerous, because crazy as she was, I could see the sense in making a neat row of ground piled on each side to keep the moisture from running off. If ever the rain came.

But time wore on, and as the dirt mingled with the sweat on my body, I felt strangely comforted by the *chunk, chunk, chunk* of the hoe digging into the ground. I let the rhythm of it take me back to many a dusty ride in a freight car with Gideon. The two of us, listening to the *chunk, chunk, chunk* of the track joints, lost in our own thoughts.

I continued with my list of what I knew about Gideon. He could start a campfire quicker than most. He always let out a contented breath after a first sip of coffee. And he liked to flip flapjacks high into the air.

I smiled at the thought, but a worried frown took over as I wondered what Gideon was doing right then. Maybe unloading twenty-pound sacks of flour from a boxcar. What if he'd been let go from his railroad job? Was he sidling his way into a diner, offering to work for food? He'd know that the man behind the cash box would turn him down, but on a good day, a man eating at the counter might buy him a sandwich and a cup of coffee. It always helped to have a little girl in tow. He needed me.

Or so I thought. What had changed? If there was ever a part of Gideon's life that needed divining, it was this. Why had he sent me away? As Miss Sadie liked to say, I'd have to dig deeper.

It had only been a scratch on my leg the day Gideon had started turning in on himself. It was April 12. I remembered because it was Easter and the day after my twelfth birthday, just two months earlier. We were in Shreveport, Louisiana. The Shreveport Gospel Mission Church was having an Easter supper for anyone who would come and listen to the preacher's sermon. The way he went on for two hours about sitting down to the Lord's great banquet and eating manna from heaven, we had our hopes set a little on the high side. So when they ran us through the chow line for a bowl of watery onion soup and stale bread, it was a disappointment. One weathered old hobo told the preacher that if he wanted more pilgrims on that road to heaven, they should pave it with pork and beans instead of onion soup.

That night we hopped the Southern bound for St. Louis. We were both in a mood. Hungry and tired, I sat with my legs dangling out the boxcar, catching a breeze, when a tree branch caught me on the leg. It nearly flung me from the car but I managed to stay on. Still, it gave me a good gash on the leg and we had to find a doctor.

Chunking up the dirt in Miss Sadie's yard, I could feel it grinding into the scar above my knee. The infection and fever had lasted three days. I didn't remember much other than frightful dreams and sweating clear through my night-gown and sheets. And Gideon's worried face beside my bed. When I finally came out of it, he looked at me like I was a different person from the little girl he'd known before. He kept saying I was growing up. I was becoming a young lady and other nonsense. I told him I hadn't seen the branch coming and it was just a scratch, but I guess he figured it would be easier traveling without me along to get into trouble.

"He thinks it is his fault," Miss Sadie said in her out-of-the-blue way.

The hoe nearly struck my foot. "Why would he think that?" I asked, not even bothering to wonder how Miss Sadie could know the thoughts swimming in my head.

"To see Ned get on the train and leave Manifest and the people who love him. Jinx thinks it is his fault."

"Oh," I said. "Yeah, I suppose it was Jinx's fireworks

scheme that got Ned the twenty-five dollars he used to bribe that recruitment officer into letting him enlist underage. But Ned's the one who was so anxious to leave."

"When there is suffering, we look for a reason. That reason is easiest found within oneself." Miss Sadie held up her hand, shielding herself from the stark light of day.

I thought of Jinx saying goodbye to Ned at the train station. Watching him until he was out of sight, then watching some more. Wondering why one had to leave while the other stayed behind.

For some reason, my face flushed, and it wasn't from the heat. "So let me guess. Jinx skipped town. He ran away. Isn't that what people do when things get tough? They move on to the next town and leave all their troubles behind? And everyone they care about?" My words came out in such a rush I wasn't sure if I was talking about Gideon or Jinx.

"You speak of a town of immigrants. People who already left everything behind." Miss Sadie spat. "Yes, there is plenty of blame to go around and much of it ended up in Manifest." Her words trailed off and she fixed her stare ahead.

Somehow, I felt we weren't talking about Gideon *or* Jinx anymore, but about Miss Sadie. It was in that moment, when I saw the weight of age and pain weighing down on her, every creak of the rocking chair sounding as if it was coming from her very bones, that I had a revelation. As much as I had a need to hear her story, she had a need to tell it. It was as if the story was the only balm that provided any comfort.

"So what happened after Ned left?"

Miss Sadie drew a breath and seemed to hold it forever. Finally, she exhaled and her breath carried the words.

"After Ned left, the troubles we had all run away from came and found us. . . ."

Elixir of Life

JULY 12, 1918

Ned had been gone for months, and for Jinx the warm summer days dragged. After Ned had enlisted, he'd been able to come home once or twice a month on leave from Camp Funston, but now that he'd shipped out overseas, there would be no more visits until he came home for good. Most of the troops were figuring they'd be home before Christmas. Jinx wasn't so sure.

He occupied his time doing odd jobs. Shady thought Jinx needed to learn a trade, so he set about doing some welding. He was even commissioned to make a wrought iron gate. With helmet down and torch blazing, he practiced to his heart's content, welding all manner of metal objects— forks, shovels, horseshoes, even the grate off a potbelly stove—right into the gate. His highly unusual work did not spark any great demand and that was his one and only paying job.

His next assignment was working chemistry boot camp at Velma T.'s house to make up for blowing out the chemistry room windows during science class. And, of course, Sister Redempta kept after him about his studies, assigning him extra reading to do over the summer to get him caught up with the rest of his class. Still, fishing was his favorite pastime and he had great luck with Ned's Wiggle King fishing lure. In these long summer days, his uncle Finn, Junior Haskell, and Joplin, Missouri, all seemed like a faint memory that was no longer nipping at his heels.

"You think it's a ten-pounder, Shady?" Jinx stood in the doorway of Shady's place, holding up a catfish still dripping from the creek.

Shady wiped a wet rag across the bar top. "If he's not, he ought to be. There's a scale in back."

Jinx made his way through a cramped maze of tables, chairs, and empty whiskey glasses, past a frayed curtain. He found the scale, filled with stubbed-out cigar butts, in the back room.

"Did you have a good crowd last night?"

"It was kind of slow," Shady said, following Jinx to the back room. "All the Germans were having a miners' meeting at the German Fraternal Hall."

"Miners' meeting? I'd think they'd have enough of mining when they're working. Why do they want to meet about it?"

"They're trying to get organized enough that they can have some say in their working conditions. You know, when they work, how long their shifts are. Anyhow, it's kind of empty here without them. And the ones that were here seemed kind of puny. Lots of aches and coughs." He dumped the cigars onto the floor and flopped the fish onto the tray. The arrow teetered, then stopped just under ten pounds.

"Not quite." Jinx frowned, looking at the scale.

Shady rubbed his whiskers. "What time is it?"

"I went fishing at sunup. It's probably around eight by now."

"Well, you caught this feller before he could even have breakfast." Shady shoved a half-eaten apple into the fish's mouth, sending the arrow over the ten-pound mark. "Even a condemned man gets a last meal. I'd say that fish deserves nothing less."

Jinx grinned. "I'm pretty hungry myself."

"You'd better get to scaling if we're going to have us some fish for breakfast."

A voice called from the front, "Anybody here?"

Shady peeked out from behind the curtain. "It's Sheriff Dean," he whispered to Jinx.

Jinx looked toward the back door, ready to bolt. He'd been able to avoid Sheriff Dean all these months, and even though he seemed to have evaded his past, he didn't want a face-to-face encounter now. Jinx's reaction did not slip past Shady. "Be right with you," Shady called. Then he whispered to Jinx, "He's coming for his complimentary libations." That meant his illegal alcohol.

Jinx stood still. Shady had never asked any questions about Jinx's dealings before he'd come to Manifest. But Shady wasn't blind and it was painfully obvious that Jinx got nervous anytime Sheriff Dean was within a stone's throw.

"Son, if I was you, I'd stay here and keep that catfish out of sight or he's liable to requisition all ten pounds of it."

Jinx nodded. He stayed behind the curtain and peeked out.

"How do, Sheriff Dean?" Shady hoisted up four jugs full of whiskey and placed them on the bar. "There you go. Your twice-monthly requisition, right on schedule."

"That it?" Sheriff Dean inquired skeptically.

"Every last drop," Shady answered, his eyes not meeting the sheriff's.

Jinx had seen Shady play enough poker hands to know that his friend had no knack for bluffing. There was more alcohol somewhere.

Sheriff Dean poured himself a shot and took a drink. It hit him like a fireball and he gave a wheezy cough. "What'd you put in that? Gasoline?"

"The corn was a little green," Shady said apologetically.

"Truth is," Sheriff Dean said, his eyes still watering from the whiskey, "I already got a fire in my belly. There was some trouble over at the Missionary Baptist Tent Revival in Joplin back in October. One fellow ended up dead."

Jinx caught his breath and felt his knees get weak.

"That must've been some revival," Shady said over his shoulder as he took the jugs two at a time out to the sheriff's truck.

"Yeah, well, he didn't die of praying," Sheriff Dean said when Shady resumed his place at the bar. "He was stabbed. There's two fellas they're looking for. One older, one younger."

"Is that right? Well, October was some time ago. I'm sure those fellas are long gone. I'll bet you're relieved that's out of your jurisdiction." Shady took up his rag and

159

wiped the bar top to a shine. "I guess the Missouri boys'll have to deal with it."

The sheriff hoisted his belly sideways to show off his gun. "If only that were true, Shady. Thing is, one of those Missouri boys, the one that's sheriff in Joplin, also happens to be my wife's brother, Leonard Nagelman. Seems as though the whole affair had died down but now he's got it in his head those fugitives stayed around here. Somebody thinks he saw the older one a few miles from here, near Scammon or Weir. Recognized him from the revival. 'Keep an eye out,' he says. Knowing Leonard, he'll be sniffing around here till he finds someone he can string up, if you know what I mean." He raised an eyebrow. "I'd prefer that he stay on his side of the state line."

The sheriff started opening cabinets. "Man like yourself, with such a fine establishment, I bet you hear a lot of talk in a place like this," he said, stepping past the curtain into the back room. His gaze went past the coat hook holding Shady's raincoat, not noticing the two bare feet sticking out below.

He poked and prodded a bit around the back room, looking in the cookstove and under the table. Just as he was leaving, his foot bumped against the washtub, which gave a not-so-hollow sound. He kicked it over, revealing a jug of whiskey.

Sheriff Dean heaved a sigh. "You been holding out on me, Shady. And I thought we had an agreement. Now, I'm going to need double the amount by tomorrow, or I'll shut you down."

"Be reasonable, Sheriff. I can't make that kind of liquor

by tomorrow. It takes over a week to make a quality batch of deep shaft."

Sheriff Dean caught sight of Jinx's trout still tipping the scale at ten pounds. He yanked the apple from the fish's mouth and tossed it to Shady. The scale pointer sagged below the ten-pound mark. "Looks like liquor's not the only thing you been cheating on." He slapped the fish onto the table and, in one clean stroke of the hatchet, lopped off its head. "There's one thing I'd think you'd know about me by now, Shady." He wrapped the catfish in a piece of newspaper and tucked it under his arm. "I always find what I'm looking for." He hefted up the jug in the crook of his finger. "I'll be by tomorrow. And you'll keep an ear out for any news on those two runaways?"

"Will do."

Sheriff Dean lumbered out of the place, leaving the screen door open. He cranked up his automobile and sped off, sending a plume of dust to settle on Shady's clean bar top.

Jinx came out from his hiding spot, still a bit shaken. "Shady, I—"

Shady held up his hand and for a moment said nothing. Then he began again mopping off the dusty bar top. "Some fish get caught for biting and some fish just get caught for being in the wrong part of the pond." Shady studied Jinx, letting his words find their mark. Then he leaned over the bar top, staring into the sheriff's half-empty glass of whiskey. "I'm no diviner, but having been in the wrong part of the pond most of my life, I can usually tell which fish bite and which fish don't. I suspect you may have found yourself in the wrong part of the pond a time or two."

Jinx felt himself relax a little. "That man's got you over a barrel," he sighed.

Shady peered questioningly into the whiskey glass, seeming to look for an answer. "We're living in drastic times, Jinx. War's going on and a man trying to make a living gets his legs knocked out from under him by a crooked lawman. Where's the justice?" Shady's hand shook as he swallowed the last of the liquor. "Hand me that cork," he said. "At least I can smell the stuff."

Jinx picked up the damp cork and sniffed the strong whiskey aroma. He rolled it back and forth in his fingers and sniffed it again. There was something familiar about that smell.

"Give it here. A boy your age has better things to do than sniff hooch. I'd offer you breakfast, but seeing's how all that's left of it is an apple core . . ."

Jinx eyed the cork as if it was gold, then slipped it into his pocket. He hopped off the stool. "Drastic times call for drastic measures, Shady."

"What's that supposed to mean?"

"It means meet me in the alley behind Velma T.'s tonight at midnight," Jinx called over his shoulder as he let the screen door slam behind him.

The night was dark, lit only by a quarter moon. Shady looked around but could barely see the shed behind Velma T.'s house. He heard a twig snap.

"Hooo, hooo," he called out, sounding like an owl who'd smoked a few too many stogies.

"Shady, over here, in the shed."

Shady banged his head on the low doorway. He held his forehead, letting loose a string of oaths. "What's this all about, Jinx? I'm surprised Velma T. lets you near her place after that explosion in her chemistry class." Shady stooped to step inside, accidentally kicking one five-gallon jug against another. A dog barked.

"Shhh." Jinx pulled the rickety door shut. "It wasn't an explosion. It was more of a strong disagreement between some carbolic acid and nitrous oxide. Besides, I guess Miss Velma T. figures if I'm going to be in chemistry boot camp as punishment, she might as well put me to good use. She had me filling these jugs the other day. She'd just made up a new batch of one of her 'good for what ails you' elixirs."

"I don't think this stuff's going to fix what's ailing me. Sheriff Dean is still going to shut me down when I don't have his whiskey ready by tomorrow."

Jinx wiggled one of the corks out of a jug. "Smell this."

Shady took a slight whiff, then a deeper one.

"Smell familiar? She used the same green corn you did in your last batch of whiskey."

Shady sniffed again. "So?"

"So if it smells like whiskey, maybe it'll taste enough like it to get Sheriff Dean off your back."

Shady looked up as if seeing the light at the end of a long tunnel, but shook his head. "No can do. Velma T.'s not going to hand these jugs over. And I won't abide stealing."

"It wouldn't be stealing. She said her elixir has to

163

oxidize for two weeks. We'd just borrow some of hers now and replace it with some of yours later."

"You don't think she'll be able to tell the difference?"

"She probably never drinks the stuff, but we can save some of hers and mix it with yours."

Shady considered the prospect. "It'd sure make her concoction go down a little easier. Maybe we'd be doing her a favor. More people might drink the stuff."

Jinx handed Shady a hose. "We'll siphon out a couple gallons from each jug and pour it in those empties." A dog barked again as the two began work in silence.

Several nights later, the scene was identical except that the moon had waned to a sliver and the siphon was pouring liquid back into the jugs left half full of Velma T.'s elixir.

"Hand me that stick, Jinx." Shady stirred each jug to blend the two elixirs.

"Everything go down all right with Sheriff Dean?" Jinx asked.

"Without a hitch. Said he was going to save it for a poker game he had coming up next Saturday. Said his brother-in-law was breathing down his neck to find those two runaways from the revival in Joplin. They'd been seen having an argument with the deceased before he come up dead. One older, one younger, he said." Shady glanced sideways at Jinx. "Whoever it is better lay low or they're going to find themselves in more than chemistry boot camp."

Jinx jerked and nearly upset a half-filled jug.

"Take it easy there, Jinx. No sense getting the jitters now, we're almost done." He set the jug upright. "There now. Still plenty left. Besides, it's not like this stuff's going to save lives or anything." Shady filled up the jug and replaced the cork.

Even after Shady's comment about Sheriff Dean and his sheriff brother-in-law in Joplin, Jinx felt strangely at ease and comforted as they made their way back to Shady's place. Never before had Jinx felt this safe. Manifest had been a refuge for him and he'd allowed himself to be lulled into thinking that bad things didn't happen there. Not in Manifest.

But as they neared the German Fraternal Hall, he noticed that the area around it was strangely lit up. Shady put a hand firmly on Jinx's elbow and they both stood motionless, staring at the sight before them. The men in their white hooded robes were nowhere to be found, but there in front of the small building stood a large cross set ablaze.

HATTIE MAE'S NEWS AUXILIARY

JULY 20, 1918

Since the recent unfortunate happenings at the German Fraternal Hall, everyone has been on edge and the mood of the town has been somber. It is unclear if the motive was the Germans' nationality or their attempt to organize at the mine. Mr. Keufer says future meetings of the order have been postponed until further notice.

It is in times like these that this news column cannot provide the needed comfort and solace. But as I was instructed in my journalism correspondence course through *Harper's Magazine,* a good reporter must continue to do her job, even in the most trying of times. These are certainly trying times.

It has been one year since the first "Yanks" went overseas, and the country hoped they would be home by Christmas past. However, our boys rally on. The American Defense Society continues to push for abolishing Hun names in

America. For example, changing *sauer-kraut* to *liberty cabbage* and *frankfurters* to *patriotic pups*. However, many folks in Manifest seem to think that a bit unnecessary. Especially Mr. Hermann Keufer, who rather likes his name and does not consider himself or his sauerkraut to be a threat to national security.

Many of the soldiers from Camp Funston had a rough boat ride overseas and are still feeling indisposed with flu symptoms. The army doctor says he's never seen such a fast-spreading outbreak but it should soon be under control. The troops will be pleased to know that Velma T. has sent off more relief parcels with her newly concocted elixir.

For Mrs. Larkin, who hasn't been feeling herself of late, the elixir went down fairly easy the day of the Women's Temperance League meeting. After consuming nearly an entire bottle, she appeared to be feeling better, and although her rendition of "How Dry I Am" was a little off tune and a somewhat surprising selection for the gathering, she did seem to have a healthy glow about her.

On a sad note, the Widow Cane passed away in her home on July 1. A foremost authority on prairie flora and fauna, she could discuss at length the thirty-seven varieties of hydrangea in Crawford County. Mrs. Cane was blessed with ninety-three years of healthy living, and several people who attended the funeral commented, "She didn't look a day over ninety." For all the whos, whats, whys, whens, and wheres both here and abroad, turn to "Hattie Mae's News Auxiliary."

HATTIE MAE HARPER
Reporter About Town

SOUR STOMACH? TRY SIZER'S STOMACH TABLETS

Is your stomach continually kicking up a disturbance? Do you feel bloated and distressed? Do you belch gas and sour food into the mouth? Then you need Sizer's Stomach Tablets. Take five tablets before bedtime and experience instant relief. They force out the poisonous gases that cause fermentation of food and thoroughly clean, renovate, and restore the stomach so that it can digest food without all that excess gas. You will be amazed as your load is lightened and relief surrounds you like a cloud. Get your Sizer's Stomach Tablets today and expel your troubles tonight.

Dead or Alive

JUNE 17, 1936

I folded Hattie Mae's article and found myself in the same somber mood the town of Manifest had been in after that cross had been set on fire in front of the German Fraternal Hall. It usually didn't take me long to find a "News Auxiliary" that related to Miss Sadie's stories. The events she'd told me about so far had taken place over the course of several months and Hattie Mae's articles were all dated and ready for reading. Plus I had time on my hands.

Lettie and Ruthanne were away for a couple of days at their great-aunt Bert's second funeral. Her first, they said, had been on Aunt Bert's seventy-fourth birthday. She'd wanted to hear all the nice things folks would say about her, so they went ahead and held the services early.

But this time was for real and Lettie said everyone was trying to come up with new nice things to say. Unfortunately, as Great-Aunt Bert could be a bit cantankerous, they were having to be creative. According to Lettie, most of the family agreed that in the future, family members would be allowed only one funeral and they'd have to pick if it would be when they were dead or alive.

With Lettie and Ruthanne gone and no new prospects on who the Rattler might be, I was left with nothing to do but hunt down more roots, weeds, herbs, and bugs for Miss Sadie. One morning she had me traipsing out at the crack of dawn for prickly poppy, toadflax, spiderwort, and skeleton weed. If that doesn't sound like the makings of a witch's brew, then I'm the queen of England.

I made a pass into town, hoping to stop by the newspaper office for a glance through some of Hattie Mae's old newspapers. She was just pouring herself a cup of coffee.

"Well, good morning, Abilene." She greeted me with a smile. "I'm fresh out of lemonade this morning. I've got a little milk if you'd like some."

The smell of her fresh pot of coffee took me back to many a chilled morning with Gideon. "Could I have coffee, please?"

"Well, sure, if you think you'll like it. There's a little cream. Help yourself, sweet pea."

I liked it when she called me sweet pea. "Thank you," I said, pouring in more cream than coffee. I thumbed through a stack of papers, enjoying the smell of ink and newsprint. Those old newspapers were full of stories about all kinds of people in good times and bad. Mainly, I looked for "Hattie Mae's News Auxiliary." It was in her whos, whats, whys, whens, and wheres that I found the most colorful and interesting news.

"Hattie Mae," I said, working up my nerve. "How come nobody seems to know much about my daddy?"

"Why, what do you mean?" she said, not looking at me. "I can tell you your daddy was sure one to fish—"

"I know, he fished, swam, and caused havoc. That's what Shady said." I remembered the look of revelation Shady'd had when I told him about Miss Sadie's story. He'd been pretty tight-lipped about Gideon ever since. It seemed Hattie Mae had a case of lockjaw herself. I wondered if Miss Sadie had cast a spell over both of them. Maybe I could undo her hex. "There has to be something more. I mean, he lived here. If a person lived and breathed in a place, shouldn't he have left some kind of mark? Shouldn't there be some kind of whos, whats, whys, and wheres that he left behind?"

Hattie Mae put down her mug. "You miss your daddy, don't you?"

I nodded, thinking that I had started missing him before we'd ever said goodbye.

"Well," she said thoughtfully, "maybe what you're looking for is not so much the mark your daddy made on this town, but the mark the town made on your daddy." Hattie Mae stared into her coffee as if she was looking for the right words to say. "This town left its imprint on your daddy, probably more than even he knows. And sometimes it's the marks that go the deepest that hurt the most."

"Like a scar," I said, touching my leg. It was that scar on my leg that marked me and had marked a change in Gideon.

Hattie Mae patted my arm. "That's right, sweet pea."

I cupped my hands around the coffee mug, trying to feel any warmth that might be left. It had gone cold. "Shady said to tell you he's holding church services this Sunday night and he'd be pleased to have you." Hattie Mae looked at me with a kind of sad smile. "Thanks for the coffee," I said.

Billy Clayton rode up on his bike just as I was leaving. He had half a bag of newspapers left to deliver.

"Hey, Abilene," he said. His freckles stood out even against his tan face.

"Hey, Billy," I said, still distracted by my talk with Hattie Mae. "How's your mama and that new baby brother of yours?" I remembered how relieved Billy had looked when Sister Redempta had told him his mother and the new baby were all right.

"They're fine. Little Buster—that's what I call him—he's been pretty colicky. But Sister Redempta brought over some of Miss Sadie's ginger tea. You just soak the tip of a rag in it and let him suck on it. Calms him right down."

"Sister Redempta brought it over?" I asked.

"Yup, just yesterday."

So Sister Redempta *had* been at Miss Sadie's place. She must have just come out when I'd run into her. I had a hard time imagining the two in the same town, let alone in the same room at the Divining Parlor. Miss Sadie in all her jangly regalia and Sister Redempta with her stark habit. They seemed like a mismatched set of bookends in their flowing gowns, beads, and veils.

What could have prompted Sister Redempta to venture down the path to Miss Sadie's? PERDITION, it said on her gate. According to Miss Sadie's story, Jinx himself had welded that on the gate. Had it been at her request or had he deemed it an appropriate name for the diviner's den of iniquity?

172

The questions swirled and remained unanswered when Billy said, "Well, I'd better get these newspapers delivered or Hattie Mae'll be after me."

"All right. See you later, Billy," I called, still lost in thought.

On my way out of town, I chanced to pass by the faded gingerbread house I'd seen when I'd first come to Manifest. The one with the proper lady sitting in her rocker. There she was again, like she'd been there this whole time without moving. Like her life was standing still. If she *was* alive.

Lettie and Ruthanne had told me that her name was Mrs. Evans. She was the lady who could turn you into stone if she looked you in the eye. They said she never talked to anyone. Just sat on her porch and stared. I stopped at her paint-chipped fence, looking at her from the side of the porch so she wouldn't see me. It was like she wasn't really seeing anything. Just staring.

Then, still without looking at me, she raised her hand ever so slightly and her fingers waved at me like she was tinkling one of Miss Sadie's wind chimes, making music that only she could hear.

Miss Sadie had given me directions. The prickly poppy had white petals with orange and red in the middle. She said to look for them along the railroad tracks. Skeleton weed was purple with no leaves. I was to look near the grazing pasture at the old Cybulskis place. And so on.

I'd already found the skeleton weed, spiderwort, and toadflax right where she'd said, but the prickly poppy was nowhere to be found. With my flour sack stuffed with plants and weeds, I wandered along the railroad tracks, letting my footsteps fall evenly on each tie. There was a comfort in those tracks and my being on them. I closed my eyes and let them guide me. One foot after the other.

I imagined Gideon at the other end of the line, working his way toward me. One foot after the other. It was like one of those story problems in school. If Gideon leaves Des Moines, Iowa, at 6:45 a.m., traveling one railroad tie at a time, and I leave Manifest, doing the same, how long will it take us to meet? I was figuring the problem in my head but started imagining him on a train, getting here faster.

It must have been the growing heat, but I could feel the tracks vibrate beneath my feet. I kept my eyes closed, trying to recall the sound and movement of train on track that could make you feel lonely sometimes and peaceful at others.

Without my willing it, a rhyme formed in my head. *Walking, walking, gotta keep walking, gotta keep walking all the way back. Looking, looking, gotta keep looking, miles to go on this railroad track.*

I heard a mournful whistle off in the distance. Heard the rattle of the boxcars as they worked across the joints.

A train'll be coming, coming, coming, train'll be coming to take me back.

That train seemed so close I could smell the soot and steam. If I stayed on the tracks, maybe it would just sweep me up and take me away.

I opened my eyes just in time to see the black grille of a real train staring me down. It wasn't going to sweep me away; it was planning to run me over. I hopped off the tracks, my heart pounding as the wind from the train nearly knocked me over. As it went past, I could tell it was slowing down, beckoning me to hop on. For a lot of rail riders there is a powerful urge to keep moving. Even if you don't know where you're moving to, it's better than staying still.

Jump on, jump on, jump on, the boxcars taunted. I reached out my hand. Reaching for the only home I'd known—tracks and trains. Reaching for Gideon. Then the sound died down and the train moved on. I stood mourning the silence. I'd missed my chance.

And then Shady was there. He placed a steady hand on my shoulder, and together we watched the caboose disappear around the bend.

Shady handed me two bags of flour to carry while he toted two bags of coffee. We walked in silence for a time; then he said, "Kind of like a hot-air balloon."

I looked at him, puzzled. He shook the bags hanging at his sides.

"Ballast. Like the sandbags that hang off the basket of a hot-air balloon to keep it weighted and steady. I rode in one a long time ago. Fella was giving rides for fifteen cents. Going up it felt so light and thrilling-like. You could see everywhere in the world a person might want to go. But after a time, a body just wants to be back in a place where it belongs." He shook the bags hanging at his side. "Ballast."

His eyes were red again, his face unshaven. He'd been out all night. I'd heard a harmonica playing again the night before and wondered if that was the sound that lured him out. Like the ocean sirens Gideon told me about. They were kind of like mermaids, and their song lured seamen to crash their ships into the rocks. I didn't think poorly of Shady. I'd seen my share of folks who looked to a bottle of whiskey for whatever they'd lost. I believe Gideon himself might have looked there if he hadn't been trying to raise a daughter on the road.

We stopped near Miss Sadie's place and Shady took my bags. "Will I see you tonight for supper?" he asked, seeming to acknowledge that I could still take off if I pleased.

I wanted to ask him a hundred questions. Why had Gideon closed himself to me? Why had he sent me away, and when would he come back? I wanted to tell Shady I had an old cork of his on my windowsill. A cork that had become special because it was part of a story. And I knew that story wasn't finished. But I also knew that Shady wasn't the one to tell me the rest of it.

"Depends," I said. "What's for supper?"

"Oh, I'm fixing something special."

"Let me guess. Beans and corn bread."

"You peeked at my menu," he said, pretending to be hurt, even though it didn't take a diviner to figure that out.

"I'll be there. It sounds better than what I've got." I showed him my sack of skeleton weed, spiderwort, and toad-flax. "Now, can you point me in the direction of some prickly poppy?"

Miss Sadie's Divining Parlor

JUNE 17, 1936

Late that afternoon I returned to Miss Sadie's place in a mood. Having crawled through a bramble bush for the prickly poppy, I was feeling a bit prickly myself just then. Why Miss Sadie had call to send me all over God's creation to dig up plants never intended for human use, I can't say. Her Divining Highness was not in sight when I arrived, so I busied myself with trying to find a pot or a vase to put the flowers in. There was nothing on the back porch but a metal watering can and piles of dried-up leaves that had been pushed into a corner.

The gardening shed looked to be the likely place for a pot, but it was locked. I peeked through the dirty windows, trying to make out what was inside, when—

"Get away from there!" Miss Sadie hobbled from the side of the house. "There's nothing in there that you need," she said, breathing heavy from the effort.

I held up my flour sack full of plants. "I got most of the ones you asked for. I was just looking for a planting pot." I noticed the wound on her leg. It was worse, all red and festering. "I can lance that for you. To let out the infection."

Miss Sadie settled herself in her metal rocking chair and her breathing slowed as if a crisis had passed. "No."

I didn't know what she was waiting for, but it was *her* leg.

"Let me see." Her breathing was still heavy as she motioned toward the plants in my hand. She ran her fingertips all over them, feeling the stems, leaves, petals, smelling them like a blind person wanting to know what she could not see.

"Aren't those the ones you wanted?" I asked.

"They are. But they do not tell me what I wish to know." She gazed up into the cloudless sky. "The earth, it holds back secrets it is not yet willing to part with."

Then, as if she'd seen enough, she started taking the plants apart, expertly sorting leaves from stems from seeds, creating small piles of each in her lap.

"I went all over tarnation to get those and all you wanted were some dead flowers?"

"They are only dead to what they once were. Now they become something else. Go." Without looking up, she motioned to the dry ground of the garden. "Back to work."

I looked at the rows of tilled-up soil splayed out like open wounds and did as I was told. My already blistered hands and scraped knees rebelled as the dust took over me like a swarm of bees. I went to the far end of the yard so I could grumble to myself without being heard. *The earth, it holds back secrets it is not willing to part with,* "I mimicked. "What a bunch of hooey," I said under my breath, tossing a dirt clod over my shoulder against the locked-up garden shed. I studied the little outpost, and feeling the diviner's eyes on me, I came to the only reasonable conclusion. Miss Sadie was holding back a few secrets of her own.

As the afternoon wore on, I began feeling like the miners from years ago, covered in grime. Tasting the dirt in my mouth, I imagined it to be the soot of the mines. Had their families recognized them when they'd emerged from their desolate work? Would anyone recognize me? Would anyone care? I was enjoying my pitiful thoughts. What if I died right there in that dirt? Would anyone notice?

"Death is like an explosion," Miss Sadie said, her accent thick, like the humid air that hovered heavy around me. "It makes people take notice of things they might have over-looked."

I sat back on my haunches, annoyed that my sorrowful thoughts had been not only interrupted but seemingly over-heard. What was Miss Sadie talking about this time? Whose death?

"This is the way with the Widow Cane. Her death causes people to notice things they have overlooked," she contin-ued.

My mind had to work backward. I recalled the name. The abandoned mine shaft where Ned and Jinx had made their fireworks—it had been on the Widow Cane's property near the mine. I tried to shut out the story I knew was com-ing, but Miss Sadie's words pulled at me. It was like being drawn out of the dark mine, only to emerge squinting into the bright light of day. I preferred to stay lost in the darkness of my dismal thoughts.

Unbidden, Miss Sadie went on. "Mr. Devlin and his mine people have a sudden interest in that little stretch of land near the edge of the woods that before had only been a pleasant spring and a shady place to sit between Manifest and the mine."

I could hear it coming like a freight train and there was no stopping it. I kept my back to her.

"Lester Burton, he goes back and forth across that stretch of land. He observes it from this way and that. They even call a new geologist to make a report. The townspeople keep a watchful eye, but ask questions only among themselves."

Keep talking. I'm not listening.

"Before long Mr. Devlin himself pays a visit to the public land office to inquire about purchasing the land now that the Widow Cane is dead. This is his mistake. Mrs. Larkin's neighbor works in that office. Mr. Devlin, he barely leaves his seat before half the town knows he wants to buy this land."

I turned around, but only because I was at the end of one row and starting on another.

"He says he will use it as a picnic area for his miners to eat their lunch. It does not take a diviner to see this is a lie. He barely gives the men time to eat and they do that underground. Too much time is wasted coming up and going down for a few minutes of fresh air. The news spreads and Hadley Gillen calls a meeting. They piece together what I could have told them all along."

She let off for a long pause, and I swear the words came without my willing them to.

"What? What could you tell them?"

Miss Sadie almost smiled. "Where the grass grows thick and animals refuse to burrow, there is ore below."

I remembered something from an early part of Miss Sadie's story. Jinx had seen Mr. Devlin arguing with the

180

mine geologist. It had been something about the coal vein taking a turn and going the wrong direction. Was that what she was talking about?

Miss Sadie picked up where my thoughts left off.

"The vein, it zigs where it should have zagged and runs right under the patch of ground between Devlin's mine and the town of Manifest—the Widow Cane's property. Unfortunately, after her death, it was the only patch of ground that neither side could claim as their own. . . ."

No-Man's-Land

JULY 20, 1918

Jinx rushed headlong into Shady's place. "Hey, Shady, you're not going to believe how many bottles I sold." He fanned a wad of money.

Shady looked furtively toward the front door as dusk set in. "Now's probably not a good time."

Jinx continued, not noticing Shady's uneasiness. "Your hooch and Velma T.'s elixir are a match made in heaven. It's been less than two weeks and just about everybody in town—"

"Quite a few of those folks are going to be showing up here any minute for Hadley's meeting."

"Why here?"

"Because Hadley only invited one or two people from each fraternal order and he doesn't want Burton knowing about it. After the cross burning in front of the German hall, folks are a little on edge. But they're coming, and the way

Eudora Larkin's been doggin' me all week after that episode at the Women's Temperance League meeting, I have a feeling she'll be not far behind them. Your elixir made a lasting impression on her."

Jinx's mouth dropped open. "She bought a bottle from Velma T., not me. Besides, who told her to drink a whole bottle in one sitting?" He hesitated. "Do you think she knows we did a little tampering with it?"

"You've been selling it all over town, so I think she might have a pretty good idea."

Jinx grimaced. "Well, there was extra and I figured I was doing Velma T. a favor to get her elixir out among the ailing public."

"I'm sure that was your utmost priority," Shady said with a sideways glance.

They heard footsteps crunching on the gravel outside.

"Quick," Shady whispered. He hoisted up a movable panel behind the bar that revealed a hidden stash of whiskey bottles.

"What's that for?" Jinx asked in astonishment.

"It's for hiding things. What's it look like? Get in and stay there." Jinx barely had time to stuff his wad of money into his overalls and crawl inside before the front door opened.

The space was dark and cramped. Jinx shifted to find a more comfortable position and noticed a pinhole of light. He strained to reach it and placed his eye against a perfect peephole, through which he could see most of the bar's seating area of small wooden tables and chairs.

It was Chester Thornhill who entered. Chester was a regular customer, who knew nothing of any meeting. "Evening, Shady. I'll have a shot."

Jinx heard Shady behind the bar. "Evening, Chester. Going to have a quick one tonight? I'll bet the missus is waiting for you."

"I'm in no hurry," Chester said.

The front door opened again and more people arrived. Jinx watched from his hiding space.

Chairs shifted and scraped against the dusty floor as people took their seats and eyed each other without speaking. There had never been a town meeting before. Normally, each fraternal order would gather in their own hall and discuss their own business. On occasion there might be an awkward encounter in the mercantile or the hardware store, in which members of one nationality might exchange a halted word of greeting with those of another.

Even in church, folks kept to their own. Among the Catholics, the Austrians went to Mass at eight o'clock, Italians at nine o'clock, and Irish at ten o'clock. Services were divided up similarly among the Lutherans and Methodists.

But in light of the recent goings-on at the mine, the cross burning at the German Fraternal Hall, and the Widow Cane's death, the whole town was abuzz. With everyone's wanting to talk and a more than usual desire not to be noticed by Burton and his pit boys, representatives of each nationality and a few others had been asked to the secret meeting at Shady's place. Chester Thornhill, one of Burton's crew, had not been invited. But here he was, smack in the middle of it.

Wide-eyed, Chester sipped his drink as Velma T. Harkrader arrived. Soon after, Olaf and Greta Akkerson of Norway took their seats. The Akkersons were the driest couple in town. When they started munching on a few beer nuts, it was too much for Chester to swallow.

"What's going on here, Shady?" Chester blustered as Casimir and Etta Cybulskis from Poland joined the growing crowd, their four-year-old daughter, Eva, in tow.

"Why, we're having a discussion on prairie flora and fauna, in honor of the late Widow Cane." Shady whipped out five glasses and filled them with sarsaparilla.

"Flora and who?"

"Fauna," Shady replied without apology. "Did you know there are thirty-seven varieties of hydrangea in Crawford County alone?"

Little Eva stared at Chester as she took her first sip of the bubbly sarsaparilla. Then, being eye level with Jinx's peephole, she peered right at him and giggled.

Chester banged his glass down on the table. "This is a bar, Shady, not a ladies' tearoom." He tossed a coin onto the table, nearly running into the Hungarian woman as he stormed out.

Jinx's hiding spot was getting stuffy and his feet tingled from lack of circulation. But even after being spotted by Eva, he couldn't take his eye away from the drama unfolding before him.

The Hungarian woman, her bracelets and beads jangling, took her place alone at the bar. Shady filled a shot glass for her and couldn't help smiling. Never had there been such an array of people in his establishment. Some were regulars, unbeknownst to their wives, while others would normally sooner be caught dead than set foot across his threshold. But here they all were.

Sitting on the floor, Eva played with her set of colorful nesting dolls, removing one hollowed-out and brightly painted doll from inside the other, while everyone waited for someone to speak. Jinx breathed a sigh of relief. It looked like Mrs. Larkin wasn't going to make it after all, but then the door burst open and Mrs. Larkin came in, wagging her finger. She hadn't been invited either.

"Shady, I've a bone to pick with you. That hooligan you've got staying here—" She stopped, realizing that Shady's saloon was full of people who she was fairly certain were not his usual crowd. "What's going on here?"

Shady just whistled nervously and wiped out a few more whiskey glasses.

"Come on in, Eudora." Hadley pulled up a chair for her at the Cybulskis' table. "We're just having a little town meeting, so I guess this pertains to you too."

Mrs. Larkin was apparently too stunned to speak and quietly took her seat, clutching her handbag in her lap.

"Thank you all for coming," Hadley continued. "I think we all know why we're here, except for maybe Mrs. Larkin. My apologies, Eudora. In a nutshell, Arthur Devlin needs the piece of land belonging to the late Widow Cane, and for once, there's something he can't get his hands on. That land could be a big bargaining tool for all of us. He has to get to his vein of coal, and if we owned the Widow Cane's land, he'd have to go through us to get it."

There was a silence while all present considered what this meant.

"But the Widow Cane, she is dead, no?" said Callisto Matenopoulos. "Who owns the land now?"

"Legally, no one," said Haley. "The Widow Cane passed

away July first and left no heirs. Therefore, her estate is considered in probate, or in holding."

Those assembled stared at him, not sure what he was telling them.

"Effectively, the land, and the vein of coal that runs beneath it, belongs to no one at this time. For all practical purposes, it's—"

"No-man's-land." The words were spoken in a deep voice filled with salt water and brogue. Jinx knew who had spoken without even looking. Donal MacGregor stood just inside the doorway, arms folded across his broad chest, waiting for the image conjured by his words to sink in.

Everyone was painfully aware of the term used to describe the open ground between opposing trenches in the fields of France, Belgium, and Germany and of the deadly struggle for that land.

"Aptly put, Donal." Hadley continued. "The property can be purchased by the township of Manifest along with payment of back taxes within ninety days. If the township does not have the necessary funds, or simply does not want the land, as of October first, it will revert to the county and then be open for public auction."

Donal moved to the bar and poured himself a drink. "And the mine will outbid us all and the property will be theirs. They'll have what they need to keep us under their thumb. Aye, it'll be a right bloody battle to keep that land away from Devlin." He swallowed the whiskey in one gulp.

Even without Mr. Underwood present, everyone could practically hear the final nail being hammered into a coffin.

"What is for us to do?" asked Nikolai Yezierska. "The

mine—it owns us. It says you must work more hours in a day for same pay. They say here is voucher to buy what costs double at the company store. So it is Sunday? First, you work. Then you can go to church. Look at the Germans. They have a few meetings and the men in the hooded robes burn a cross to warn them."

Everyone nodded.

"How much would it cost to buy the land, Hadley?" asked Hermann Keufer, who had been a man of some means in his homeland of Germany until he had spoken out against the Kaiser. He stroked his handlebar mustache, waiting for an answer.

"To buy the land and pay the back taxes, it will cost one thousand dollars."

Callisto Matenopoulos expressed the shock of everyone present. "None of us have money. All we have to sell are store vouchers and perhaps a few silver spoons and thimbles brought over from our homelands."

"What about the skills that we bring?" asked Casimir Cybulskis. "I was a tailor in Poland. I can make suits. Surely there are others who can make goods or provide services for money."

"And who would pay for these?" asked Nikolai. "Yes, I make shoes. But who here will buy my shoes? As you say, we have no money."

"Besides," argued Olaf Akkerson, "Burton and his pit boys, they will know what we do. And they will take action against us. Remember Sean McQuade? He lost his job at the mine for merely suggesting that the men should not work on Sundays."

"We have children to feed." Etta Cybulskis rested a hand on her swollen belly, carrying her sixth child.

"They are right," Callisto said. "We cannot risk opposing the mine. There will be consequences."

There was a fearful rumble of assenting and the room grew quiet. There seemed to be no more to say. Little Eva continued playing with her nesting dolls, opening a larger doll to take out a smaller one and holding it in front of the peephole for Jinx to see. Fortunately, no one took notice of her. Jinx carefully reached down to rub his left foot, hoping the meeting would end soon.

The Hungarian woman plunked her shot glass down onto the bar top and wiped her mouth with the back of her hand. "Do you forget where you come from?" She stared them down. "What about the others who depend on us? Those who are left behind?" Her breathing was heavy. "Casimir Cybulskis." She raised her chin at him. "When your village was attacked, did your grandmother not hide you in a barn? Did she not give you her life savings to send you to America?

"Callisto Matenopoulos. Your mother. Did she not work three jobs to provide you with the chance to make the same voyage?

"And, Nikolai Yezierska? What about your family? They had to make a choice. Which son will go to America and which son will be forced to join the army? Your older brother. He insists you go and he will stay, no?" There was a stunned silence. They hadn't realized she knew so much about them.

"They sacrifice to send us here." she continued. "And

189

for what? To live a dream of freedom and prosperity? Pah. They would be ashamed of us. What is it to defy the Devlin mine to those who have risked everything?"

Her words lingered. Those in the room who had remained unnamed looked into their own pasts—their own stories of coming to America.

Until a moment before, these people in Shady's bar had thought they knew little of each other as they hunkered with their own kind in their own trenches. But with the Hungarian woman's words, they suddenly recognized something in each other. They shared the same blood. Immigrant blood.

There was a long silence finally broken by Donal MacGregor.

"She's right. They've pushed us 'round long enough. I say it's time to do summat about it."

Hadley observed the nods of agreement. "Okay. The question is, what?"

"Aye." Donal rubbed his weathered chin. "They've got us over a barrel and they know it."

"And what do the Scots do when they're over a barrel?" asked Mr. Matenopoulos.

Donal's face broke into a wide grin. "Before or after we drink what's in it?"

There was relief in the laughter. Even Olaf and Greta Akkerson gave a chuckle.

"Well, even if we wanted to," Hadley said, "I don't think we're going to be able to drink our way out of this one. We need money, and lots of it. Unfortunately, the only ones making any money are the mine owners and the bootleggers. No offense, Shady."

"None taken."

Jinx's entire body was becoming one contorted knot. He stretched his leg ever so slightly and accidentally knocked over one of the whiskey bottles with a crash.

Everyone sat rigid and tension filled the room.

"What was that?" Mr. Matenopoulos asked.

Shady grabbed an empty glass. "Anyone want another round? Another cup of tea?"

Hadley Gillen stepped behind the bar, and after a quick examination, he removed the panel and hoisted Jinx from his hiding place, dislodging the wad of bills at the same time and sending them fluttering all over the bar top.

"You!" Mrs. Larkin cried out. "Velma, is this the hooligan who had access to your so-called elixir? More like the devil's brew if you ask me. Is that the kind of thing you concoct in your chemistry class?"

"Calm down, Eudora," Velma T. urged. "I admit there was a bit more kick in it than usual, but even you said it helped your fever and chills."

"Helped me look a fool! The way those Temperance League ladies carry on, I'll never hear the end of it."

Jinx gathered up his money and inched his way toward the door, mistakenly thinking he could slip out while the two women argued it out.

"Call the sheriff. Arrest that boy," Mrs. Larkin ordered.

Donal MacGregor stuck out his foot to block Jinx's escape. "Not so fast, lad."

"He's been a source of conniving and cajolery in this community long enough," Mrs. Larkin continued. "Just look at his loot. Who knows how many other innocent people he's hoodwinked into buying that snake oil. I insist that he be put under arrest."

"Now hold on, Eudora," said Hadley. He looked at Jinx, who had his money in hand. "You'd better have a seat, son, until we get this sorted out. And why don't you hand over that money to Shady for the time being?"

Jinx placed the money on the bar and took a seat behind the counter next to Shady, his one sure ally in the room.

"We have bigger problems at hand," Casimir Cybulskis said, resuming the discussion. "How to raise a thousand dollars without being noticed by Burton. It is impossible."

The room erupted in a din of agreement. Then Shady had an idea. "From the look of things, the mine owners and bootleggers aren't the only ones making money after all." He fanned the stack of bills in front of him.

"What are you saying, Shady?" asked Hadley.

"I'm saying that this young man may have an idea that we would do well to listen to."

"You're not suggesting we take advice from a con artist?" Mrs. Larkin asked in horror.

"All I'm saying is drastic times call for drastic measures."

All eyes looked to Jinx, and Jinx looked to Shady with a horror to match Mrs. Larkin's.

"Hadley Gillen!" Mrs. Larkin protested.

The hardware store owner jumped, wondering how he'd been put in the position of judge and jury. "Well, now . . ." He scratched his head, straining for a solution to this predicament. Then Velma T. came to his rescue.

"It's true that Jinx tampered with the elixir that caused Mrs. Larkin to be a little more . . . well, animated than usual. So it does appear that some restitution is in order.

Might I suggest that he do some manual labor for Mrs. Larkin? He can be quite industrious under the proper supervision."

"That sounds like a fine idea. What say you, Eudora? Will a little restitution do the trick?"

"Well, Your Honor, I hardly think—"

"Settled." Hadley tapped his glass on the table like a gavel. "Now, if we could get back to the subject at hand . . ."

All eyes returned to Jinx.

"Shady, I don't think these folks want to hear from me," Jinx whispered.

"Well, I'm sure Sheriff Dean would be more than eager to ask you a few questions," Shady whispered back. "These folks are desperate. There's no telling what they might do."

Hadley Gillen looked at the worn faces all looking at Jinx. "Young man, this town is at a bit of an impasse. If you have any suggestion that might help, now would be the time to voice it."

Jinx squirmed to his very core. He looked pleadingly at Shady to be relieved of this fix.

Little Eva, who had continued to carefully take apart each doll to remove a smaller one from inside, finally removed the tiniest doll, and tottered over to Jinx. "Matryoshka," she said, naming the nesting doll. She handed the smiling doll to him as if this tiny memento embodied the hopes and fears of everyone in the room.

Jinx accepted the gift and the burden. He cleared his throat. "So," he began haltingly, "you want to keep Devlin and Burton out of town for a month and make a thousand dollars?"

"That's right," Hadley answered for the group.

"Would that include keeping Sheriff Dean out of town?"

Hadley paused, studying Jinx. He seemed to sense the bargaining that was taking place. "I suppose it would."

"Then I have an idea."

There was a solidarity among the people in Shady's bar that night, as one by one they emerged from their trenches and ventured into no-man's-land.

FULL
ASSOCIATION
PRESS

An Excellent Investment
and a Patriotic Duty

MANIFEST HERALD

MANIFEST, KANSAS   SUNDAY—JULY 21, 1918   PAGE 1

SPANISH INFLUENZA— NO OCCASION FOR PANIC

Dr. Alfred Gregory, Mine Medical Staff

The Spanish influenza is nothing more than the old grip or la grippe, which circulates from time to time. Symptoms include chills, aching, fever, and sometimes nausea and dizziness. The germs attack the lining of the air passages, nose, throat, and bronchial tubes, which results in a deep cough and sore throat.

At the first symptoms, go to bed, stay quiet, and don't worry. Take a laxative, such as prunes, and eat nourishing food. One may also apply menthol and camphor rub to the chest, back, and neck. However, prevention is the best medicine. Evidence seems to prove that this is a germ disease spread principally by human contact,

195

chiefly through coughing, sneezing, or spitting. So avoid persons who are likely to do those things. And remember: hard work and healthy living will keep one free of sickness.

HEALING SPRING WATERS HOT SPRINGS, ARKANSAS

Come to the healing springs of Hot Springs, Arkansas. Who needs Colorado Springs when you can find healing and comfort in the moderate climate of Hot Springs, Arkansas? Take a walk on the promenade of Bathhouse Row and choose from one of our many bathhouses. You can bathe in our natural thermal mineral springs, which are known for their therapeutic value in the relief of common ailments such as arthritis, bursitis, rheumatism, and gout. Come visit the springs of Hot Springs, Arkansas.

HATTIE MAE'S
NEWS AUXILIARY

JULY 21, 1918

I regret that there will be no "Hattie Mae's News Auxiliary" this week due to my feeling puny these last couple of days. I will keep my chin up and hopefully resume writing all the whos, whats, whys, whens, and wheres by next week.

HATTIE MAE HARPER
Reporter About Town

PVT. NED GILLEN

IN AN OPEN FIELD
JUNE 28, 1918

Dear Jinx,

How's the spy hunt going? Uncovered any subterfuge? If President Wilson comes to visit again, which he probably won't, tell him Ned Gillen says hey and us boys overseas could use some warm blankets and better food.

We're all tired and hungry right now. After a long ride in boxcars with soldiers jammed shoulder to shoulder, we had an even longer march in the pouring rain. We were heading one direction, watching lines of old-timers trudging the other way. A sad-looking lot with their scraggly beards and muddy uniforms, they seemed like they'd been through it. We'd see sixty, seventy soldiers in a row, Frenchmen, in horizon blue uniforms, all with eyes bandaged, walking with their hands touching the shoulder of the guy in front for direction. Poor chumps got gassed and couldn't even see the Yanks coming to end this war.

We're finally settled in for the night, if that's what you call being wedged into the muddy wall of a six-foot trench. I'm so hungry right now all I can think of is taking out the belly wrinkles, as the fellas say. We're eating in shifts, because there aren't enough chow kits for everyone. We're so short on everything I'm lucky to have a gun.

Beans and bread tonight. I wish I could say Pop's cooking is better, but we both know that'd be a lie. Don't tell him I said that. We're using army forks. That means our fingers, if you're wondering why there are food smears on this letter. So much for fancy perfumed paper. I sure am missing Mama Santoni's home-cooked lasagna. Tell her to keep a pot of sauce simmering for when I get home.

From the sounds of things, we're a ways off from the zone of advance. It sounds like a thunderstorm in the distance, with the rumble of cannons, and every so often the sky lights up like lightning. If I close my eyes, I can almost picture being in Manifest under a stormy June sky. Almost.

Sarge says we're moving out first thing tomorrow morning. Zero hour, he called it. Guess this is what we came here for, so we might as well get it over with. Now I know why they kept Heck, Holler, and me together. We were the fastest guys at camp, along with a chap named Eddie Lawson. Sarge asked us to be runners—guys who sprint back and forth from regiment to base camp, getting orders and supplies. He said it was voluntary, but we weren't about to turn it down. Eddie won the toss, so he's

*out on his first run right now. He's fast as the dickens.
Plus he's an ace of a guy. Can't wait to hear if he saw any
action.*

From the trenches next to Holler's widerlich footen,

*Ned
Hero Abroad*

JUNE 29, 1918

*Eddie was killed last night. Shot just a mile from here. A
mile. He could run that in a little over four minutes.*

One Short, One Long

JULY 3, 1936

I'd read through so many news articles about the influenza that I'd started to feel achy and chilled myself. And in this July heat there was not a chill to be found. Then Ned's letter went from sunny to sad so fast. That was when I knew I needed a break from looking at the past.

Lettie, Ruthanne, and me took turns jumping rope, the heat from the summer sun making sweat run down our backs. We all agreed we'd outgrown jumping rope, but Shady'd given me such a nice gift of a skipping rope, and when there's nothing better to do, I guess you go back to what once felt good. Plus we were in no hurry to become ladies if that meant not getting to go frog hunting or wear overalls, or having to act all proper, like Charlotte Hamilton.

Besides, it was the day before the Fourth of July and we had to think of something to do. The only fireworks on people's minds were possible sparks from an outdoor fire that might make the whole dry town go up in smoke.

The playground was empty except for us and the dirt we churned up with our rhyming.

> *"I had a little teddy bear, his name was Tim.*
> *I put him in the bathtub, to see if he could swim.*
> *He drank up all the water, and he ate up all the soap,*
> *And the next day he died with a bubble in his throat."*

I said the rhymes but wasn't really paying attention. Little Eva's nesting doll nested itself in my mind and had taken its place on my bedside windowsill. I marveled at how each memento had made its way into Miss Sadie's story. After all this time of working at her house, there was a comfort in knowing that I was connected to her stories. By those mementos I'd found under the floorboard—the Wiggle King lure, the Liberty Head silver dollar, Shady's cork, and the tiny nesting doll—I was connected to this place and those people. The places and names on Ned's map were familiar to me now.

And there was Jinx. I felt like I understood this boy who had lived life from one place to the next. This boy who was full of adventure. I held out hope that Gideon would be mentioned in one of Miss Sadie's stories. But there was only one memento left. The skeleton key. I wished it would somehow lead me to Gideon. It was probably in this kind of wishing and hoping that I'd started imagining maybe I *had* found him. I imagined that Jinx and Gideon were the same person. That maybe it was my own daddy who had landed in this town and found a friend in Ned and made fireworks and blew up a water tower and had people who cared about him. Maybe that was who Jinx was. It was in this imagining of him that I'd grown to love that boy from long ago.

Ruthanne and I turned the rope as Lettie jumped out. It was Ruthanne's turn.

"I've got a new one." Lettie and I turned the rope as Ruthanne jumped in.

"In the town of Manifest there was a spy.
They called him the Rattler but who knows why?
Was he slimy like a snake, was he dirty like a rat?
What we really want to know is where he's at.

"Is he the butcher, the baker, or the undertaker?
A miner, shoe shiner, or a railroad liner?
The milkman, the mailman, or the railroad brakeman?
Is the man on the loose, riding in the caboose?"

Just then, we saw Sister Redempta walking over to school. Lettie and I instinctively dropped the rope, figuring we'd better not be singing about spies on school property. Why a teddy bear choking on a bubble seemed appropriate subject matter, I can't say.

Anyway, it was a nice chance to sit, each of us on a swing, letting our toes draw lines in the dirt.

"Sure is hot," I said.

"Sure is," Lettie echoed. "I bet Charlotte Hamilton is romping in some cool beach water down in South Carolina."

"Oh, who cares?" Ruthanne piped up. "We've got a whole spy hunt all to ourselves right here in Manifest."

That was looking on the bright side. I'd been keeping Lettie and Ruthanne apprised of the latest goings-on in Miss

Sadie's stories, and our conversation generally revolved around Manifest in its earlier and more exciting times. I think it helped distract us from the dry, humdrum, and heat of the here and now. For us, part of that excitement was, of course, the Rattler.

"He'd have to be someone with some connections to the world outside of Manifest," I mused. "Someone who could pass along secret information to the enemy."

Ruthanne perked up. "I've got it. Who's in contact with people outside of Manifest every day?"

Lettie snapped her fingers. "Cousin Turk. He delivers fertilizer to folks all over the county."

Ruthanne glared at her and I couldn't help giving her a look of half pity, half consternation. "Cousin Turk is barely eighteen years old."

Lettie recovered, saying, "Who'd you have in mind, Ruthanne?"

"I had in mind someone who was actually *alive* when the Rattler was going about his business." Ruthanne drew her lips in like she was getting ready to spit a seed.

Just then, Mr. Cooper, the barber, stepped outside his shop across the street to shake out his apron.

"What about him?" Lettie whispered. "Maybe he's like the Barber of Seville."

"Who's the Barber of Seville?" I asked. We jumped from our swings and snuck toward the side of the barbershop for a better look.

"I don't know exactly, but I think he had long, wild hair, because he was the only barber in town and had no one to cut his hair. And he probably spent day after day cutting one head of hair after another, until one day, he just snapped."

Mr. Cooper took out his razor and wiped it clean with his apron. He examined it in the sunlight, then wiped it again and went inside.

"And on that day," Lettie continued, "the Barber of Seville took out his razor and waited for the next sorry soul to come darken his doorway and occupy his chair. He got the man all lathered up for a shave, but left his throat clean, then—"

"My word, Lettie! You have some imagination," Ruthanne said. "I think he's just a barber. Let's go check out the post office."

But something caught my eye in the shop window. It was a picture. I crept around to the front of the store. An old picture of a group of men wearing overalls and miner's hats. Each looking into the camera. Looking at me with—what was it? Hope, desperation, defeat? I couldn't tell.

I looked up to see Mr. Cooper staring at me through the store window.

Suddenly, I realized that Lettie and Ruthanne were gone and I was alone. I ran to find them, my heart pounding like a drum. Mr. Cooper didn't seem like a cold-blooded killer, but then, I didn't know any cold-blooded killers, did I? And he'd seen me looking in his store.

I crouched my way through a couple of backyards, getting scratched and scraped by fences and bushes. Then I heard a low growl. It was a bulldog, his slobbery mouth and bared fangs not two feet behind me. I made a beeline for a porch railing and jumped just in time to keep my pant leg away from his snapping jowls. I clung to the railing, not taking my eyes off the angry bulldog.

"Go on," I said in a hushed voice. "Go on, get." He stood his ground and growled, like he'd rather wait me out.

I let my breathing slow a bit and straddled the railing only to have my heart speed up again. I noticed the faded porch with its ornate woodwork and realized I was at the worn-out gingerbread house that belonged to the stony lady who always sat on the porch. What if she was across the porch? Looking at me? I brought my other leg around and there she was, right where I'd seen her before. In her rocking chair, staring off into nothing.

I'd either have to climb over the railing and get down the way I'd come or walk past her to the steps. I peeked back over the porch. The bulldog flapped his jowls and barked. I'd try the steps. I tender-footed across the porch to the steps; then her chair creaked, and without my willing it to do so, my body turned around, and my eyes looked straight at Mrs. Evans. And Mrs. Evans was looking straight at me.

Not knowing what to do, I checked my arms and legs. They still moved, so I hadn't been turned into a statue. For a time, neither one of us said anything. Then I said the only words that came to mind. The ones Shady'd been telling me to say to anyone I met for the last few weeks.

"Shady's having a service at his place this Sunday night. He'd be pleased to have you."

I didn't wait for a response. I just took her porch steps in one leap and was off, not stopping till I ended up with skinned knees and elbows in the alley beside the post office.

"Abilene." It was Lettie. "Over here," she whispered loudly.

"What took you so long?" Ruthanne scolded. "I thought you were right behind us; then you were gone."

I was breathing too hard to answer but crept around to the side of the post office. Ruthanne used her forearm to wipe the dusty window, only to find that there was a cabinet blocking the view on the inside.

"Come on," she whispered. "We'll have to go around front to get a better look."

"At who?" I asked.

Ruthanne placed a finger to her lips. She peered around the corner of the building like she was waiting for some incoming artillery. Then she made a break for it and ended up with Lettie and me beside her, peeking in the front door.

"Him," she answered, pointing to the very tall, very thin man behind the mail counter. He wore suspenders over his white shirt and, even without long sideburns, bore a remarkable resemblance to Ichabod Crane of the Sleepy Hollow legend.

"Ivan DeVore?" Lettie said as if considering him the Rattler was akin to suspecting Santa Claus. Ruthanne had mentioned him before, but we'd never gotten around to spying on him.

"Think about it," Ruthanne replied, not taking her eyes off the man. "He'd have known of all the mail that came in and out. He was the telephone operator *and* he ran the telegraph machine. So he could click, clickity, click whatever information he wanted to whoever he wanted and no one would be the wiser."

We watched Mr. DeVore move efficiently about the room, placing one letter in this box and another in that. Then he tapped on the counter, like he was debating something. Finally, he removed a key from his pocket, unlocked the top drawer of his desk, and took out a single sheet of yellow stationery and a matching envelope. Then, with a half smile, he penned a brief note, placed it in the envelope, and, after a suspicious look this way and that, quickly stuffed the note into one of the boxes on the wall.

"That's Velma T.'s mailbox," Lettie said. "I know because that time she went to visit her cousin in Oklahoma—remember that, Ruthanne, when her cousin had the shingles? Velma T. had me pick up her mail for her." Lettie paused in thought. "Come to think of it, she had one of those same yellow envelopes once a week. Now, why would Ivan DeVore put a letter in her mailbox when he sees her all the time? He could just say what he wants to say. Unless, do you think they're both spies and they have to talk in code or secret notes?"

We studied Mr. DeVore as he whistled and moved about the room. "Spies don't write spy notes on pretty yellow paper. I think he's sweet on her," I said.

"Then why doesn't he just tell her?" Ruthanne asked.

"He's probably scared to. I bet he doesn't even sign those notes."

Just then the telegraph machine began clicking and Mr. DeVore sat to take down the message. One long click, followed by two short. One short. One short, one long. Short, long, short.

Gideon had worked for a time in a freight yard in Springfield, Illinois, and Miss Leeds, the lady in the office, had taken me under her wing. She could work a telegraph machine like nobody's business. She said that over time, she could tell a woman operator from a man, as each operator developed a style, or a voice, so to speak. The operator in Decatur was a woman who displayed a precise staccato touch. Each letter came across the wire sharp and pointed. "She probably has a pointed nose, too," Miss Leeds would say. The operator in Peoria had a harsh, hammering quality.

Miss Leeds imagined him to be a gruff man who would pound his fists on the table when demanding his dinner. But the operator in Quincy, he had a firm, steady touch. One that indicated a fair hand and well-mannered demeanor. Truth be told, I thought she was real fond of him even though she'd never laid eyes on him.

Now, as we sat hunched just outside the door, listening to those first four letters, I felt my insides ball up. D-E-A-R. Someone was being addressed. Someone who was dear to the person sending the telegram.

I slumped down, not wanting to decipher the rest of the message. What did I care what sweet words this someone away had to say to their "dear" someone here. My eyes stung a little. I tried to let the clicks, long and short, blend into each other so I wouldn't make out the words. But they kept clicking into my head. M-I-S-S Y-O-U.

I knew Gideon was busy. He was probably working hard to make enough money to send for me. Why, here it was July already. He'd be coming to get me himself in a few weeks. Sometime in August, probably. H-O-M-E S-O-O-N. I didn't want to hear any more. I started running, my feet pounding as loud as my heart.

Gideon's sending me a telegram wouldn't speed things along anyway. Still, my heart ached like it was being squeezed in two.

I kept running, knowing that eventually I'd find myself at Miss Sadie's.

Miss Sadie's Divining Parlor

JULY 3, 1936

I made it to Miss Sadie's house but all I found was hot dirt and a cranky old woman. Miss Sadie was in a mood and she was not going to be coaxed, cajoled, or otherwise budged from it.

All day I slaved away, scrubbing down her porch, sorting buttons, picking dead flies from her screen door. Why, she even had me pull the big Persian rug out of her divining room and beat the dust out of it with a broom. I can tell you that was a pure waste of time, as the dust kicked up in the air like someone kicking a bad habit, only to settle into its old ways, right back on that rug.

She kept me busy doing anything but working in the garden. And *anywhere* but near the garden shed.

When I first started working off my debt to Miss Sadie for breaking her Hungarian pot, she said I'd know when I was done. I knew I'd worked off more hours than was needed to square my debt. But I also knew I wasn't done. I wasn't done hearing her story of Manifest.

I could have asked Shady to fill in the rest and saved myself some work. But somehow I knew he would know only his piece of it, like Hattie Mae would know just her piece of it. Only Miss Sadie knew the whole story. She was the one who'd watched and listened all these years. Even now the people who came by her place, they talked and talked, unburdening themselves of all manner of tales and stories. And she listened to them all.

I was also becoming more interested in Miss Sadie's own story. What had brought her to America? Why did she stay in Manifest if she was such an outcast? There was more to Miss Sadie than baubles and beads.

Her mood was putting me in a mood. I was working and she wasn't talking. I tried to find a way to bait her into a story, and I figured there's no better bait for a storyteller than to get part of the story wrong.

"I saw some lilacs down by Ruthanne's place," I said. It was miserable hot that afternoon on Miss Sadie's porch. My hands were deep in a tub of soapy water, cleaning out one dusty mason jar after another, while Miss Sadie rocked steadily in her porch rocker.

"Hmm," she murmured with little interest as she blew some tobacco ash from her pipe.

"I bet the Widow Cane could say which of the thirty-seven varieties of lilac it was. I'm sure a bunch would look nice in one of these jars."

"Hydrangea," Miss Sadie said, tamping down a wad of new tobacco into the pipe.

"What's that?"

"There are thirty-seven varieties of hydrangea, not lilac—and I plan to use the jars for canning fruits and vegetables."

Fruits and vegetables from her parched garden, no doubt. "Hydrangeas, lilacs. Probably didn't make much difference in the long run. I don't imagine anyone could raise a thousand dollars in four weeks."

She stopped rocking. "So that is what you think?"

"That's what I think," I answered, swishing suds in and out of the umpteenth mason jar that would probably collect another year's worth of dust before there'd be any fruit fit for canning.

"Pah," Miss Sadie grunted. "One who cannot tell the difference between lilac and hydrangea can hardly speculate about such things."

I was close but not quite there.

"Well, at least Shady stayed out of it. He'd never be involved in something . . . well . . . shady."

Miss Sadie heaved a heavy sigh.

"Shady was in it . . . How do you say? Up to his neck. We all were. . . ."

The Walls Go Up

AUGUST 15, 1918

It started with a few coughs and body aches. Then it moved to fever, chills, and dizziness. Everyone had read of the symptoms that were not supposed to cause any concern— the same symptoms that were spreading from town to town throughout the country.

All over Manifest, people were showing signs of this influenza. In church, the library, the mines, a few coughs that turned into a wheeze. Rubbing of the neck and shoulders. Even in the August heat, you might see a woman draw on her shawl to calm her shivers.

There was a tension that permeated Manifest, as if one shoe had fallen on it and the whole town was waiting for the other to drop. But where, when, and on whom it would fall was still unknown.

Many were the times Jinx thought he'd better get while the getting was good. But every time he thought he'd light out, he'd see Sheriff Dean hovering about, watching him. No, for now, he just had to hope that the town had some luck that was better than his.

Once the telltale signs of sickness had been exhibited, it didn't take long for Lester Burton, Arthur Devlin, and their wives and associates to start feeling a bit puny. Or if they weren't actually feeling sick yet, it was clear to them that with everyone coughing, sneezing, and wheezing all around them, it was only a matter of time. So anyone with means, including Burton, Devlin, and their lot, used the opportunity to take a holiday—elsewhere. Even Sheriff Dean stayed close to his home, which was down by the river and safely outside of town.

The county medical examiner was called in, and within thirty minutes he declared that until the influenza ran its course, the entire town of Manifest would be under official quarantine. Nobody goes in. Nobody gets out.

After the last train had pulled out and the smoke from the last Model T had settled, there was an unearthly quiet, as if death had won out. Then, after a minute or two that seemed to last for hours, the mine whistle blew.

A few curtains were pulled aside by people peeking out to make sure that all was clear. Mr. Keufer, still wearing his pajamas, was the first to venture into the street. Then Mrs. Cybulskis stepped onto her porch, washing from her face the powder that had given her a deathly pallor.

Soon everyone was smiling and shaking hands, patting one another on the back. It was as if a miracle had happened and all were healed, but the real miracle was that Burton and Devlin had fallen for their ruse. With the mine included in the quarantine, there would be no whistles calling the men to work. No long hours of labor that did little but line the pockets of Devlin and Burton.

The children were particularly excited. The start of school would be postponed. Food and supplies would be brought by train and left just outside of town. Word spread quickly, and soon Stucky Cybulskis, the McIntyre boys—Danny, Michael, Patrick, and Sean—the Santoni brothers, and even nine-year-old Rosa Santoni, who was as pretty as pie but as rough and tumble as the big boys, all climbed trees or perched themselves on rooftops, appointing themselves sentries of Manifest. They would stand guard to keep a careful eye on anyone approaching from the outside. Among them all, Jinx was hailed as a local hero for coming up with the greatest scheme ever.

But the greatest scheme ever would involve a lot of work. While the trees were lined with young sentinels keeping watch, the adults would be busy making the one thing that had brought in any money of late: the combined concoction of Shady's hooch and Velma T.'s elixir.

Mama Santoni donned an apron and led the women in shucking corn. Greta Akkerson and Etta Cybulskis rolled up their sleeves and joined in. Their many hands made light work as they shared stories of home and family.

They talked of their common experiences of traveling to America on ships filled with immigrants, tears of emotion welling up as they recounted their first sightings of the Statue of Liberty, and the joy and fear of arriving at Ellis Island.

"I was so afraid I would be turned back," said Mrs. Cybulskis, wiping her brow with the back of her hand. "The way they examined everyone for disease and malady." The women nodded in agreement. They had all experienced the fear of being labeled unfit to enter America. A simple chalk mark drawn by the medical examiner on one's clothes could have a person barred from entering his newly adopted country. An *E* for eye problems, an *L* for lameness, an *H* for heart problems. They would have to board another boat and go back to wherever they'd come from no matter how long a journey they had just traveled.

"In Poland," Mrs. Cybulskis continued, "I have no shoes, so my neighbor, he is a cobbler, he makes me a new pair. Beautiful shoes with fancy heels. Never had I walked in heels. The inspectors detain me, because they think I have a problem with balance and maybe am sick." Mrs. Cybulskis shrugged, raising her hands, which were full of corn husks. "I have to take off my shoes to show I can walk straight!" The women laughed together as they filled bucket after bucket with corn.

Callisto Matenopoulos and Hermann Keufer loaded the corn onto a wagon and hauled it over to Shady's place. "Ma-ten-o-pou-los," Mr. Matenopoulos said, sounding out his name. He laughed as Mr. Keufer stumbled over the pronunciation. "You think my name is difficult. At Ellis Island, the inspector asks my friend Milo, 'What is your last name?' 'Zoutsaghianopoulous,' he says. The inspector asks him if he wants to change it to make it easier to pronounce. My friend gives this much thought. After all, this is his family name. Finally, after much consideration, he agrees. 'Take out the *h*.'" Mr. Keufer chuckled loudly.

Of course, the real excitement was at Shady's place, and

Jinx was right in the thick of it. This was the first time Shady's whiskey still had seen the light of day. The whiskey-making machine had been retrieved from the darkness of the abandoned mine shaft on the Widow Cane's property, where it had been in constant activity since the start of Prohibition. But one wouldn't be enough for the operation they hoped to have up and running. So Donal MacGregor, Hadley Gillen, and Nikolai Yezierska assembled four more stills out of spare tanks and copper tubing and set them up in a run-down barn near the natural spring. This gave them an easy supply of water and an out-of-the-way location to run their operation.

But it was as if Shady himself was also thrust into the light of day and he was left stunned and unsteady. He reached for a bottle of whiskey stashed under the eaves overhanging the back steps. Just a sip to stop the shakes and give him a little liquid courage. He uncorked the bottle and moved back into the shadows of the eaves.

The back screen squeaked open and Jinx stood beside him. "Come on, Shady, you can do it. Just show 'em what you know."

Shady ran the back of his hand over his whiskery face. "I don't know anything."

Jinx's voice was calm and steady. "Right now there's only one thing these folks need to know and you're the only one who can teach them."

Shady stood still a full minute before placing the cork back in the bottle. He returned it to its hiding spot above and stepped into the warm daylight as Jinx held open the screen door. Then Shady oversaw the process with the watchful eye of a master craftsman, wanting each of his apprentices to learn the art of his trade. He seemed grateful to have Jinx nearby for moral support.

"That's right, keep that burner low, Mr. Keufer. We don't want to scorch the mash. Casimir, why don't you get another batch going in that tank over there? Corn, water, yeast, and sugar," he said, rattling off the contents of a time-honored recipe used by bootleggers throughout many a dry region.

"I knew a guy in Chicago," Jinx said, "he scorched the sugar to make a richer color."

Shady shook his head. "It may be wrong to make whiskey, but there's a right way to do it."

The first batches of mash fermented day after day, with any number of men standing by, like children in Mama Santoni's kitchen. Stirring, smelling, eyeing, wondering.

On the ninth day, Donal MacGregor stood at a simmering tank. "Give it a whiff, Shady. I think it's ready."

Shady smelled the brew. "Cap it off and Jinx'll hook up that copper tubing. When the liquid separates from the mash, it goes through the tubing and ends up in this barrel." He lifted the spigot at the base of the oak barrel and captured a few ounces of amber liquid in a glass jelly jar.

Shady's hand showed only a slight tremor of need as he held the jar to the light to check the color, and smelled the liquid's aroma. Folks who knew Shady knew he struggled with the drink. So when he poured the whiskey back into the barrel and said, "It's ready for Velma T.'s elixir," everyone understood that was to be the code of conduct. Not a drop would be had by any man there.

• • •

Jinx and Shady hauled the first barrel over to the high school. Mrs. Larkin caught sight of them on the front steps. "Shady," she called in a shrill voice. "Shady Howard."

They pretended they didn't hear her, and walked into the high school and down the hall to the chemistry room. Mrs. Larkin had been working Jinx pretty hard, making him weed her garden and clean out closets of her husband's old papers. Worst of all was sitting down for afternoon tea, carrying on what she called polite conversation, which, in her estimation, was something every gentleman should be capable of doing. So it was understandable that Jinx would wish to keep his distance.

But as Mrs. Larkin stormed in behind Shady and Jinx, all three stopped dead in their tracks.

"What's that smell?" Jinx rubbed his neck as the pungent odor practically singed through his nose, clear to the back of his head.

Hattie Mae looked up through safety goggles while Velma T. stood sentry over several beakers of clear liquid warming over Bunsen burners. "A fermented mixture of corn, castor oil, eucalyptus extract, menthol, iron, potassium, and calcium," Hattie Mae answered.

"Nothing that wasn't in it when you two ne'er-do-wells took it upon yourselves to play hanky-panky with my elixir," said Velma T., jotting some notes on a clipboard. Her safety goggles looked like bulgy fly eyes against her narrow face.

Shady and Jinx both knew they'd have to tread lightly, as Velma T. was not completely on board with their endeavor.

"How do you make so much with just those little beakers?" Jinx asked.

"This is what is called the base mixture," Velma T. answered, "which you would know if you ever showed up to my chemistry class. This syrup combined with Manifest springwater in an exact four-to-one ratio makes up a palatable and restorative elixir."

"Velma," Mrs. Larkin interrupted, "surely you are not going to participate in this"—she struggled for the right word—"this . . . charade. My husband, the late county appraiser, would be rolling over in his grave at this exercise in depravity. Why, I've a mind to telegraph my sister's boy in Topeka. He works in the governor's office. He's the assistant to the assistant, you know."

Most folks were surprised and more than a little curious when Mrs. Larkin stayed behind for the quarantine instead of leaving town with the rest of the people of means. She'd certainly made her objection to Jinx's plan clear the night of the town meeting. Her daughter, Pearl Ann, was already away at the university, and some speculated that Mrs. Larkin was less a person of means than she liked others to believe and maybe couldn't afford to leave town. At any rate, since she was still here, there was nothing they could do but hope that she wouldn't ruin everything.

Ignoring Mrs. Larkin, Velma T. lifted her safety goggles onto her head and glared at Shady and Jinx through narrowed eyes. "You know, I should have let Sheriff Dean arrest both of you for tampering with a medicinal product and endangering the public health. My elixirs are carefully synthesized compounds of potentially dangerous elements." She poured the syrupy liquid into a measuring glass and tested the volume and density. "They are meticulously prepared remedies that deserve a little respect."

"Yes, ma'am." Neither Jinx nor Shady pointed out that her elixir had never remedied anybody until it was mixed with Shady's whiskey. However, the following silence said it all.

"Still, I suppose serendipity is a force to be reckoned with," Velma T. said with a sigh.

Hattie Mae came to the rescue. "Now, don't you underestimate yourself, Miss Velma. Of course there are discoveries made by unexpected occurrences. But it takes the right someone to make sense of it all. You told us yourself, 'An apple is just an apple until it falls on Sir Isaac Newton.' "

"Then what is it?" Jinx asked.

"Gravity," Velma T. said. "I suppose you're right. Even Louis Pasteur, the father of modern medicine, said that 'chance favors the prepared mind.' "

Mrs. Larkin was beside herself. "Velma, really! You can't be serious about this so-called miracle medicine."

"I'm not prepared to say that there is anything miraculous about this combined elixir. But it seems to have put you right, Eudora."

"Yes, right out of the Women's Temperance League. Besides, I'm sure I was already well on the road to recovery."

"Still," Velma T. continued, "I hear there have been outbreaks of the influenza as nearby as Pittsburg and Baxter Springs. If my medicine will help, then—"

"Now, dear," Mrs. Larkin interrupted. "I'm sure your elixir is fine for keeping a body regular, but I think it can hardly be classified as medicine."

Velma T.'s back stiffened; her lips pursed; even her nose seemed to get a little pointier.

Everyone in the room knew that Mrs. Larkin had said the wrong thing.

"Very well, Shady. I will be happy to make my elixir available to anyone who is in need. So we had better get busy. As word spreads about Mrs. Larkin's recovery, I'd imagine bottles of the Manifest elixir will be in greater demand than before."

Shady muttered to Jinx, "Certainly won't hurt that it tastes better than before."

"I heard that, Shady." Velma T. patted her pockets. "Who took my safety goggles?"

Shady pointed to his head, indicating that the spectacles rested above her forehead. Velma T. recovered the goggles, breathed on them, and wiped them with her white lab coat. "All right, then, where exactly are we going to mix up the stuff? Between my elixir and your . . . contribution, there will be a lot of liquid to be combined."

Shady cleared his throat. "There has been considerable discussion about that. It needs to be something big, like a horse trough, but clean."

"That goes without saying," said Velma T.

"There's a horse trough over at the Baptist church."

"I don't recall seeing a horse trough outside."

"It's not outside. It's inside." Shady was counting on Velma T.'s being more a woman of science than religion.

"Surely you're not suggesting using the baptistry," said Mrs. Larkin, a staunch Baptist and lifelong member of the First Baptist Church. "What did Pastor Mankins say?"

"He's not around to ask. He hightailed it out of town before the quarantine."

"Well, then," Velma T. said, "I guess it serves him right. Besides, it is, after all, three parts elixir to only one part alcohol."

"More like half and half," Jinx piped up before Shady could shush him.

"But why can't you do it at the Catholic church? Or the Methodist church?" Mrs. Larkin asked.

Shady answered. "Their little fonts wouldn't do much good. They're just for sprinkling. It's the Baptists who enjoy a good full-body dunking."

The Baptist church, normally home to only the purest of Manifest citizens—meaning the ones who had parents and grandparents and even great-grandparents born in this country—was suddenly filled with strangers. Each held his or her own jar or jug of either Velma T.'s elixir or Shady's whiskey.

Casimir Cybulskis spoke first. "This seems such a solemn moment. I think it calls for a prayer."

Everyone looked to Shady, as, standing at the head of the baptistry, he seemed to be in the place of the minister.

Shady held his hat in his hands, rotating it in a slow circle. "I don't spend much time in church, but I do recall a story my mother used to tell me. Some folks had a wedding and they ran out of wine. The bartenders brought out big jugs of water. But lo and behold, out poured wine, the best they ever tasted." He looked at the faces around him. "I reckon that's something akin to what we're doing here."

Everyone nodded, waiting for the prayer.

Shady shifted from one foot to the other. Jinx nudged him in encouragement.

"All right, then." Shady cleared his throat and began what sounded more like a toast than a prayer. "Lord, here's hopin' that what lies ahead is the best we ever tasted."

"Amen," they said in unison, these citizens of the world, and they held their breath as the many and varied ingredients that had been simmered and stewed, distilled and chilled, were combined to make something new. Something greater than the sum of its parts.

FULL
ASSOCIATION
PRESS

An Excellent Investment
and a Patriotic Duty

MANIFEST HERALD

DEADLY INFLUENZA EPIDEMIC MOVING WEST

Philadelphia health officials have issued a warning bulletin about the influenza epidemic. Hundreds of cases of the sickness are being reported every day. Boston and New York have already been ravaged by the disease, with hospitals being filled to beyond capacity, and the deadly disease is moving west across the United States.

Troop ships returning from France and Belgium are reporting to sick bay at the Commonwealth Pier in Boston with the usual symptoms of the grippe. However, these cases have gotten progressively worse, developing into a deadly pneumonia. Commonwealth Pier is currently overwhelmed with the disease, and new cases are being transferred to Chelsea Naval Hospital.

Dr. Victor Vaughn, acting surgeon general of the army, has witnessed firsthand the effects of the influenza at Camp Devens, a military camp near Boston. "I saw hundreds of young stalwart men in uniform coming into the wards of the hospital. Every bed was full, yet others crowded in. The faces wore a bluish cast; a cough brought up the bloodstained sputum. In the morning, the dead bodies are stacked about the morgue like cordwood." Sixty-three men died at Camp Devens in a single day.

PVT. NED GILLEN

Dear Jinx,

Thanks for the newsy letter. It was dated before I even left the States, so I guess the army's still using the Pony Express. How's doins in Manifest? Folks back home are probably having a Fourth of July parade and a picnic. I can picture everyone having the best dog-robbin' time. That's good. Us lumps over here feel a little better knowing that our families and friends are doing the things we remember. Like Stucky Cybulskis writing his "Ode to the Rattler" in the classroom and somehow not getting caught. Mrs. Dawkins trying to get Hadley to throw in fifteen nails for the price of a dozen. Velma T. working on the cure-all for whatever ails you. And Pearl Ann picking out a pretty new hat.

Gives a body hope that maybe we're fighting for something. Got to admit something to you, buddy. Sometimes

I lose track of exactly what we're fighting for. But then, I've been losing track of a lot of things here lately. Like I can't quite recall the last time I ate. Two days. Maybe three.

I've run back several times to where our supplies and rations are supposed to be but they haven't shown up yet. So we sit and wait. The days are scorchers but I almost prefer them to the nights. It cools off some, but the sounds don't stop.

I try to imagine they're normal sounds. Like angry hornets are zipping past my ears instead of bullets. Or that the ack-ack-ack of the German machine gun is really just a woodpecker getting his nose out of joint.

Then I remember the last mail call. The names of the guys who got letters from family, girlfriends, kid brothers. I remember hearing those names go unanswered, one, then another and another and another. So many letters sent back home, unreceived and unopened. Gets hard to listen anymore.

Sorry, buddy. You've got better things to do than read my rambling. Been fishing lately? Try Echo Cove down at Triple Toe Creek. The waters run a little deeper, so it's not as hot for the fish. You can even use my green and yellow sparkle lure. Gets one every time.

                                                                    Ned

P.S. Catch one for me, will you?

Ode to the Rattler

JULY 4, 1936

It was cloudy as Ruthanne reread Ned's July Fourth letter out loud. We didn't hold our breath for rain, but a hot breeze blew through the tree house.

"Did you bring 'em?" Ruthanne asked.

"Yeah, I brought 'em." Lettie showed her stash of four scraggly firecrackers she'd found in her brother's tackle box. We'd decided to set them off in honor of Ned's Fourth of July letter on our own Fourth of July. Sort of a tribute by doing the normal things Ned mentioned.

"But this letter always makes me sad," said Lettie.

It was interesting how Ned's letters struck us differently from one reading to the next. Lettie might get teary one time at the thought of all those unopened letters, and another she might smile at his fishing advice for Jinx. We had read them so often they almost started to feel the way I'd heard folks talk about scripture, like the words were alive and speaking straight to us.

That day my thoughts lingered on the ending and Ned's mention of the green and yellow sparkle lure. I still hadn't told Lettie and Ruthanne about the mementos I'd found under the floorboard in my room. Never having had much to call my own I guess I liked having those few treasures all to myself.

Ruthanne's thoughts were somewhere else altogether. "I wonder if it's still there."

"If what's still where?" Lettie and I asked together.

Ruthanne sat up as if she'd been jerked out of a dream. "What Stucky Cybulskis wrote in their classroom. His 'Ode to the Rattler.' Ned said he didn't get caught, so he must have written it somewhere he wasn't supposed to. I wonder if it's still there."

Lettie brushed a strand of sweaty hair off her face. "After all these years? Surely it would've been washed off, painted over, or just thrown away by now. Why don't we just set off our firecrackers and go see Hattie Mae about some lemonade?"

"Maybe he wrote it in an out-of-the-way place," Ruthanne continued, "or stashed a note somewhere . . . someplace where his classmates might see it but the teacher wouldn't."

"What if it is still there?" I asked. "Do you think it might tell us something about who the Rattler was . . . or is?"

"Only one way to find out," Ruthanne answered, already shinnying down the rope ladder. Lettie and I shrugged at each other and followed.

Another of life's universals is there's always those things in a town that "everybody knows," except for the person who's new. So when we got to the high school and I asked Ruthanne how she planned to get in, I wasn't surprised when she said, "Everybody knows the storage room window doesn't shut all the way."

We skirted around the back of the building and Ruthanne laced her fingers together to give me a leg up. Casting a last nervous glance around the school yard, I hoisted myself through the window. With an unexpected shove from below, I ended up tumbling into the storage room, overturning a galvanized bucket with a god-awful clamor.

Lettie was next to make her way through the window. She was much more graceful in her landing. Lettie and I used the upturned bucket to stand on so we could reach out the window and grab hold of Ruthanne.

"I'm surprised they don't fix that window," I said now that we were all safe inside.

Ruthanne rubbed her stomach where she'd scratched herself on the windowsill. " 'They' would be Mr. Foster, the janitor. And he'd probably be delighted to spin a little web to catch some kids sneaking in."

Lettie nodded. "My brothers say he can sniff out mischief and shenanigans before they even happen. And when he's not chewing his tobacco, he loves to grab a kid by the scruff of the neck and march him into the principal's office, and before you know it, he's turned a little mischief into cause for big trouble."

"Besides," Ruthanne added, "kids spend nine months of the year trying to get out of school. I guess they don't figure anyone's going to sneak back in."

That made sense. And yet here we were.

"Come on." Lettie led the way out of the storage closet. "The senior classroom is down the main floor." I didn't doubt that Lettie, who had six older siblings, knew her way around this school.

We tiptoed down the hall to the second classroom on the right. The heavy wooden door opened easily and we stepped in. There is an eerie, expectant feeling to a schoolroom in the summer. The normal classroom items were there: desks, chalkboards, a set of encyclopedias. The American flag with accompanying pictures of Presidents Washington and Lincoln. But without students occupying those desks and their home-work tacked on the wall, that empty summer classroom seemed laden with the memory of past students and past learning that took place within those walls. I strained to listen, as if I might hear the whisperings and stirrings of the past. Maybe Ruthanne was right. Maybe there was more here than met the eye.

"We're not going to find anything just standing here," she said.

We spied around, in the cloakroom, behind the teacher's desk, on all the walls.

Ruthanne checked by the pencil sharpener and flipped through the dusty pages of a large dictionary atop a book-shelf. "Too bad we can't just look it up. That would make things simple."

"It would have to be somewhere that wouldn't get painted over," Lettie said, for some reason looking in the trash can.

The room was still and the desks looked familiar and inviting. Ned's letter was fresh in my mind, so sitting in one of the desks and running my hands over the grainy wooden top, I could imagine this room full of past students: Ned Gillen, Stucky Cybulskis, Danny McIntyre. Tracing my fingers along the ornate cast iron legs, I could picture Heck and Holler Carlson, Pearl Ann Larkin, even Hattie Mae Harper.

"So where would Stucky have written his 'Ode to the Rattler' ?" Lettie interrupted my thoughts. "Where would a teacher not look?"

I tapped my fingers on the desktop, preferring to fall back into my daydream of an earlier time filled with raised hands, muffled giggles, lessons yet to be learned, and lives yet to be lived.

And then came the questions I could never seem to keep at bay. Did Gideon ever sit in this classroom? Did he ever raise his hand to answer a question? Or write a hidden message that had not been erased?

That was when it dawned on me. "Where *would* a student write a secret message?" I was thinking the words, but I must have said them out loud, because Lettie and Ruthanne abandoned their own search and stood beside me as my drumming fingers suddenly went still.

I lifted the desktop and laid it back on its hinges to reveal the space where each student would store his or her books and slate or tablet of paper. Where one might keep a secret note or a drawing passed from a friend or an admirer.

The desk was empty except for an old pencil whittled down to a nub. There were no messages from admirers, no hidden notes that had been passed behind the teacher's back. My shoulders slumped like I'd just flunked a final exam.

Then Lettie saw it. "Look." She pointed at the underside of the desktop. There, in a handwritten scrawl, were the words

Here I sit, my eyelids sagging,
While teacher's tongue just won't quit
    wagging.
                              Louver Thompson

"Uncle Louver?" Lettie said, sounding shocked. And proud.

"Well, I'll be dipped in sugar," Ruthanne breathed. We all stared as if we had discovered some ancient Egyptian hieroglyphics. "He graduated high school years before even our mothers. This must've been here over twenty years."

"I can't believe it's still here," I said. "It's only in pencil. Somebody could've erased it long ago."

"What kid would want to erase fine poetry like that?" Lettie smiled. "You'd be considered the lucky one to have this desk."

"Let's see if there's any more that have writing," I said, moving to the next desk over. "Here's one. It's unsigned.

"My mind wanders, my attention
    drifts—
Outside it looks like heaven
    Till Mr. Epson calls on me and says,
'Do problems one through seven.' "

Ruthanne read another.

"I hear an explosion. What could it be?
It's chemistry class, with Miss Velma T.
                              Frankie Santoni."

234

Then, suddenly, Lettie screamed from the desk in the far back corner. "Here it is! 'Ode to the Rattler by Stucky Cybulskis.'"

Ruthanne and I hurdled chairs to reach the back. We looked at Lettie in anticipation, but she said, "Ruthanne, I think you should get to read it. After all, it was your idea to look."

"Okay." Ruthanne grinned and raised an eyebrow. "But don't blame me if it's scary. 'Ode to the Rattler,'" she began, making her voice sound spooky like Count Dracula.

"He roams through the woods, prowling the night,
Rattling to wake the dead.
The dogs sniff and bark, chasing this ghost,
But only come back well fed.

What is he up to? Where does he go?
Is he a skeleton clattering alone?
The Rattler is watching, he knows who you are,
Maybe he'll throw you a bone!"

Ruthanne did such a fine rendition that we were pleasantly spooked—until we heard a clattering noise in the hallway. After several seconds of us pointing to each other, determining who should look out the window of the door, it seemed that with Lettie and Ruthanne both pointing to me, I was the chosen one.

Without a word, Lettie got down on her hands and knees next to the door and I stepped up on her back. I saw a man in sweat-stained clothes. A cigar hung from his mouth. He dunked a large scrub brush into a bucket of water and commenced halfheartedly scrubbing the floor.

Lettie fidgeted a little under my weight. "What do you see?" she grunted.

"It's the janitor."

"The janitor?" Ruthanne smacked her hand against her forehead. "Oh, Lord, mean Mr. Foster."

"He's scrubbing the hallway. And from the looks of the tin canister next to him, I think he's fixing to do some waxing."

"That man barely lifts a finger all year long and he picks now to wax floors?"

Lettie shifted again and I bumped up against the door. The noise startled Mr. Foster and he dropped his cigar right into the soapy water. He let fly with a string of curses that would make a sailor blush, and stomped down the hallway and out of sight.

"He left!" I said, jumping down from Lettie's back. "I think he's just going to get another cigar. If we hurry, we can sneak back out the same way we came in."

The three of us scampered out of the classroom and back to the open closet window. Ruthanne and I gave Lettie a boost up. Then I laced my fingers together to give Ruthanne a foothold. She looked at me. "Wait a minute. He's got the bucket. If you give me a leg up, how will you get out?"

I confessed I hadn't thought that far ahead. "I'll find an open door."

"But—"

"Hurry up, or he'll come back and I'll be stuck in here. I'll be fine," I assured her.

"Okay. We'll meet you in the alley behind the schoolyard."

She wiggled out the window and was gone.

I chanced a look into the hallway. He still wasn't there. But as soon as I ventured into the open, his swear words announced his return. The closest place to go was back into the senior classroom. I ducked in and leaned my back against the chalkboard with my heart pounding and sweat trickling down my neck.

By then the shadows in the classroom had grown long. My breathing seemed so loud I was sure Mr. Foster could hear me through the classroom wall. It was the same feeling I had when getting ready to jump from a train. Only this train wasn't slowing down.

I could hear the sound of the janitor's lackadaisical scrubbing against the wooden floor. It looked like I might be stuck there for a while. As I slowly inched along the wall and away from the door, my hand brushed across the pages of the still open dictionary. It was open to the *H*s.

This was the only dictionary I'd seen since coming to Manifest, and I remembered Sister Redempta's instructions. "Manifest," she'd said, "look it up." I thumbed through the pages. *Hobble, hobby, hobnail. What's a hobnail?* I wondered. I flipped ahead to the *M*s. *Magi, magpie, manicure . . . manifest.*

I listened to make sure I could hear scrubbing in the hall. Mr. Foster was still at it.

Manifest—noun. A list of passengers on a ship.

That was interesting, since most of the people who had lived in Manifest years before were immigrants who had come to this country on ships. So their names would have been listed on a ship's manifest. But Sister Redempta had said that the word was a verb as well as a noun.

Manifest—verb. To reveal, to make known.

I admit I was stumped. She had said to start my story with the dictionary and this definition in particular. How was this supposed to help me start a story? What was I supposed to make known? The room was hot and stuffy. I lifted my foot to give my leg a scratch and managed to knock a book off the bottom shelf. It hit the floor with a thump.

Quietly picking it up, all I heard was my own breathing. That was it. No scrubbing noise from the hallway. I scooted quickly back to the door, only to smell the stale odor of old cigar. Then somebody on the other side slowly turned the doorknob. I couldn't move and there was no place to hide anyway. This was just an empty summertime classroom. I squeezed the book to my chest, waiting to be discovered, when there was a loud *kapow, kapang, kapang, kapow* farther down the hallway. It sounded like Al Capone had arrived in Manifest with tommy guns blazing.

Mr. Foster issued forth with another exuberant round of oaths, yelling his way down the hall. I took my chance, sprinting the opposite way down the hall and bursting out a side door that had been left propped open by a can of nails.

I rushed to the alley, not knowing what I feared more, Mr. Foster or the gun-firing gangsters, then ran headlong into Lettie and Ruthanne.

"Quick! Over here!" Ruthanne shoved me behind a rose trellis that didn't provide much coverage, as there were no blooms to boast of.

Ruthanne and Lettie giggled.

"What's so funny? I was nearly caught by Mr. Foster. And then gunshots went off from who knows where. I could have been killed in there!"

They giggled even louder.

"Those weren't gunshots."

"They were firecrackers!"

"We busted you out."

"So happy Independence Day!"

Lettie's firecrackers. I was relieved and a little embarrassed at getting into such a flurry. I smiled a shaky smile.

"Wait!" I said, realizing I still held the book in my hand. "I have to put this back."

But they were already pulling me toward the newspaper office for some of Hattie Mae's lemonade.

"There's no going back in there now," Lettie said. "My brother, Teddy, is going to be a senior this year. He can take it back the first day of school, and no one will be the wiser."

"Are you sure?" I hesitated.

"Sure I'm sure. Just put it somewhere safe until then and Teddy will put it back in its place."

Back in its place. The first day of school. Where would I be then? What was my place?

Where would Gideon be? I had so many questions that had no answers. I recalled the definition in the dictionary.

Manifest—verb. To reveal, to make known.

The way I saw it, that was the wrong name for this town.

Drawing Straws

JULY 11, 1936

In our hunt for the Rattler, Ruthanne, Lettie, and I must not have been as secret as we thought. One day, I was walking up Main Street, caught up in my own little contest of tossing a hedge apple into the air and catching it, hoping to count to two hundred catches without dropping. I was on one hundred and fifty-eight when Mr. Cooper, the barber, stepped out of his shop, blocking my way.

He flapped his haircutting cape to shake off the clippings and said, "Hey, kid."

I looked around to make sure he was talking to me.

"You one of them girls that's been looking for a spy?" he asked, kind of half looking at me.

I wasn't quite sure how to answer that. "Um." I shrugged. I admit it wasn't the best I could come up with, but it kept him talking.

"Yeah, well, my father came here from Germany.

240

Hermann Keufer. We lived at 224 Easy Street. Can you believe that? A street called Easy and a German living on it during the war? I was fifteen when the war started, and I can tell you, it was far from easy." Mr. Cooper took out his razor and wiped it clean with his apron.

I wasn't sure why he was telling me all this, but he kept on. "He worked in the mines and sang baritone in a barbershop quartet. After he died, my mother changed our last name. She thought it would make things easier on us." The sun glinting off the razor made his eyes water. "Somehow, I always felt like we were turning our backs on the old man." He folded the razor on itself and put it into his pocket. "So if there was a spy here, good luck finding him, but it wasn't my dad. All right?"

I nodded, relieved to watch him and his razor go back into the barber shop. My gaze went to the old picture in his store window of the group of men in overalls and miner's hats. It was easy to spot Hermann Keufer with his handlebar mustache. Slowly, thoughtfully, I took up catching the hedge apple again, *One, two, three . . .* , but I wasn't really paying attention to my counting anymore.

A couple of days later it happened again. This time it was the elderly Mrs. Dawkins. She saw me walking by the beauty shop while she was getting her curls done. She rapped on the window and motioned me in. Then she pulled me so close to her that the sharp-smelling concoction for her permanent wave nearly singed my nostrils.

"I know what you girls are up to," she hissed, then looked over her shoulder at Betty Lou, the beautician, who was rinsing out strips of cloth across the room. "Be careful. You might uncover more than you bargained for." With the curlers rolled up tight, her face seemed strangely misshapen, and I wanted to pull away, but she held me with her eyes. "Those were *unusual* times," she said, lowering her voice and raising her eyebrows.

Betty Lou was coming back and Mrs. Dawkins released me. "Go on, now," she whispered, "and remember what I told you."

I hadn't said a word to the woman, but she talked as if she was revealing some long-buried secret. If there was one thing I was learning about the town of Manifest, it was that Secret was its middle name. And if someone had a secret, I seemed to be the one to tell. One thing was clear. Those *were* unusual times.

At Sunday night's church service, the crowd at Shady's place—if eight people could be called a crowd—got settled into their seats. Hattie Mae had been coming regularly, along with Velma T. Harkrader. It was interesting that some people looked just how I imagined them from Miss Sadie's stories, while others looked different. Velma T. was just what I'd imagined. Tall and skinny, a little on the homely side, but smarter than any woman I'd ever known.

Then there was Mrs. Dawkins, who didn't look nearly as scary with her hair done up nice instead of pulled back in curlers. Ivan DeVore, Mr. Cooper, Mr. Koski from the diner, Shady, me. Of course, there were many people from Miss Sadie's stories I hadn't seen yet and wondered if they just kept to themselves or had moved away.

That Sunday night we had a surprise guest. Mrs. Evans. The stone lady from the porch. I didn't think Shady knew she was coming or he'd have mentioned it, but he didn't act the least surprised. He just welcomed her in and found her a seat next to Hattie Mae. I must have been staring and lost in shock, because Shady had to ask me three times to take my seat. I pulled up a chair.

Finally, Shady started the service with a reading from the Bible. It was about two men walking along a road. Then, all of a sudden Jesus was walking with them, only they didn't know it was him. After they talked awhile, they "broke bread"—that was what they called eating—and somehow, just by eating with him, they recognized who Jesus was.

It was a good story, and I wouldn't have minded hearing what Shady had to say about it. After all, he was a preacher, if only a temporary one. But at the First Baptist Church and Bar, as I had come to call it, there never was much of a sermon. Shady figured everyone had been preached to enough in their own churches that morning.

Even though Shady was the interim Baptist minister, I think he was more of a Quaker at heart. One of those people who called themselves Friends. Gideon and I had gone to a Quaker meeting once, because they were having roast beef and sweet potatoes afterward. It was real nice the way they came together in what their preacher called silent, expectant waiting. Of course, eventually, those Friends started talking and sharing about the Lord.

Well, the folks in Manifest weren't really Friends; they were more like acquaintances. And they didn't often get past the silent part to the sharing-about-the-Lord part. I supposed some were coming for the food following the service, just like Gideon and I had, and if that was the case, they were probably glad they hadn't wasted many words on what food was provided. Sometimes beans, sometimes crackers and canned sardines.

But there seemed to be a different mood in the group this Sunday night. Like they wanted to say something but couldn't quite get up the nerve.

After an awkward few minutes went by without anyone saying a word, Hattie Mae ended the silence, saying, "Well, I think it's time to serve up the refreshments."

I was all ready to help parcel out the smidgeon of food when, lo and behold, Hattie Mae uncovered a huge angel food cake. It must have been twelve inches high. She cut it up into nice big wedges while I poured the coffee.

There was a new kind of hush as folks took their first bites and savored the sweet fluffiness of it. For a moment they all seemed lost in their own private enjoyment of the cake. Then I opened my big mouth. "Hattie Mae," I said, "this here angel food cake is so good it could've won first prize in a baking contest." If I'd stopped there, everything would've been fine. But I went on. "I went to a county fair one time where they had a baking contest. They gave big blue ribbons for first prize. Did they ever have a fair like that in Manifest?"

Everyone stopped eating and stared at me. I put my fork down and tried to swallow the too-big a bite I'd taken. "I mean, doesn't every town have a fair like that?" There was another pause, during which the only sounds were forks being placed on plates while glances passed back and forth.

"Yes, honey," Hattie Mae said, rescuing me. "We had a fair like that once. It was a long time ago."

There followed a most painful silence that hovered like hot, moist air before a big rain.

"There *was* a baking contest, as I recall," Mr. Koski said. "Mama Santoni got first prize. She was my neighbor and often brought over some bread or pastry for me to sample. She said she needed a man's opinion." He smiled at the memory. "I can tell you I was always more than happy to oblige. She was the best baker in town."

Mrs. Dawkins raised her gloved hand. "Oh, now, that's where I'll have to disagree. My dear friend, Mrs. DeVore, God rest her"—she nodded in deference to Ivan—"made the most delicious French cookies. Now, what were they called, Ivan? Those buttery cookies your mother made?"

"Galettes," he replied with humble pride.

"Yes," Mrs. Dawkins said, "the most delicate little waffle cookies. They nearly melted in your mouth with a cup of hot tea. Do you remember the lovely teas we had back then?"

And so it went.

Story upon story. Remembrance upon remembrance. It was as if these memories were contained in a painful wound that had been nursed and ignored in equal measure.

I found myself listening with my eyes as well as my ears, noting the slight movements. Mrs. Dawkins folding her lace handkerchief and placing it on her lap just so. And Mr. Cooper, the barber, stroking his mustache the same way Miss Sadie had described his father, Mr. Keufer, doing.

It was interesting piecing together fragments of stories I'd heard from Miss Sadie. Noting what had changed and what had stayed the same. But for some reason, these stories all made me sad and more than a little rankled. It rankled me that everyone in this town had a story to tell. Everyone owned a piece of this town's history. Yet no one mentioned my daddy. Even when Gideon had been here, he hadn't really been here. I couldn't find much of a sign of his ever even having set foot in Manifest, let alone having left an impression.

I knew I could ask this roomful of people about Gideon. But I'd already asked Shady and Hattie Mae. And of course Miss Sadie. I'd gotten nowhere. I'd be hung if I was going to drag it out of them.

It also bothered me that I didn't have a story. "Telling a story ain't hard," Lettie had said. "All you need is a beginning, middle, and end."

But that was the problem. I was all middle. I'd always been between the last place and the next. How was I supposed to come up with a story for Sister Redempta or even a "Remember when . . ." to reminisce on with somebody else? But then, I wouldn't be here when school started anyway, I reminded myself.

Having gotten a little lost in my own pitiful thoughts, I suddenly realized that the room had grown quiet with that kind of Quaker anticipation—waiting for the next Friend to speak. All eyes were on Mrs. Evans, and her eyes were on me. I felt myself get stony cold inside under her gaze.

"Did you know," she said, quiet but steady, as Hattie Mae took her hand, patting it like a sister, "that my daughter, Margaret, was the president of the 1918 Manifest senior class?"

I didn't know that Mrs. Evans had a daughter. I'd thought of her only as a statue on a porch. Until then, I'd never heard her speak, and I was surprised by her voice. I'd expected it to be sharp and tinny. But it came out quiet and soft, like velvet. And her words carried something sweet and precious.

"She and Dennis Monahan tied, so they drew straws and my Margaret won."

What had happened to her daughter, I wondered. But the way she spoke and the way everyone else listened, I knew better than to ask.

Mrs. Evans looked at me, waiting, expecting me to say something back.

I found I wasn't rankled anymore. "That's real nice," I said. And I meant it.

Miss Sadie's Divining Parlor

JULY 15, 1936

After the Sunday-night service, folks said their good-byes and thank-yous. Shady sat down heavily in one of the pews. It seemed that the evening had taken a toll on him.

I put my hand on his shoulder. "That was a good service, Shady."

"It was," he agreed, but didn't say more.

"Seems like everyone in this town's got a story to tell."

Shady nodded. "I believe you're right about that. The Lord himself knew the power of a good story. How it can reach out and wrap around a person like a warm blanket."

I thought it over. He was right. I just wished my daddy'd wrapped me up in that warm blanket instead of leaving me out in the cold.

I wouldn't ask Shady about Mrs. Evans's daughter.

Not that night, anyway. But I knew how I could settle my mind about it. There was just daylight enough to run the stretch of woods over to the cemetery next to Miss Sadie's house.

I started at one end and worked my way down a row of graves and then another, reading each name carefully, expecting but hoping not to find Margaret Evans. Then I saw big block letters engraved in a heavy granite stone. EVANS— JOHN, DEVOTED HUSBAND AND FATHER. 1868–1926. I knew that it was Mrs. Evans's husband, as her name was on the tombstone next to it with her date of birth, and her date of death left blank. But there was no Margaret.

I was relieved. It didn't solve everything, like why Mrs. Evans spoke the way she did about her daughter, and why Hattie Mae had held her hand, but I could rest easy knowing that there was no Margaret Evans buried in Manifest. She was probably married and living in Joplin or Kansas City with children of her own. Maybe Mrs. Evans just missed her. I hoped so.

It was dark as I turned to go back to Shady's. Miss Sadie's wind chimes jangled in the hot breeze. For some reason, I felt my scar and thought of Miss Sadie's painful, oozing leg. I walked to the welded iron gate and stared down the Path to Perdition, unable to move. Unable to go in and check on Miss Sadie, and unable to turn away. I was paralyzed with the need to tend to her and ignore her in equal measure.

Then, from the shadows on the porch, she spoke to me, beckoning from her darkness to mine.

"It was a dangerous game we played."

I opened the gate. "What? Faking a town quarantine?"

"No, what we did in addition to that."

I sat on the top step, my back against the porch rail. "What could be more dangerous than a fake quarantine and a town-sponsored bootlegging operation?"

"Hope . . ."

Distribution

SEPTEMBER 1, 1918

Word of the miracle elixir had spread well beyond Manifest
before the quarantine began. Mrs. Larkin hadn't been the
only one whose fever and cough had improved because of
the medicine, although most of the folks whose symptoms
had improved were the men who met up with Shady at the
old abandoned mine shaft just outside of town to purchase
their deep shaft. These were the same men who preferred
to drink away their fever and chills. Usually they just woke
up with a whopping headache on top of their other ailments, but one after another was rising from a long night
of cold sweats and raging fevers feeling like he had come
through a rough storm.

If it had been left to the men, the miracle elixir would
probably have gone unnoticed. They would have chalked
it up as just one of the well-known perks of a few stiff drinks.
And since Velma T.'s elixir was something relegated largely

to newspaper advertisements and jokes, people would have been none the wiser. The wives and mothers were the ones who found the brown bottles stashed away under pillow and bed. The women, who had been nursing these men in their infirmity, wondered how they'd suddenly improved while others lingered in the sickness.

The women sniffed the bottles and knew that there were other ingredients at work in that liquor. Menthol, castor oil, and eucalyptus among others. They gave the medicine to sick children and parents and took it themselves when fevers and coughs grew worse. The coughs, fever, and chills went away. The mystery elixir worked. But the bottles emptied. And with more loved ones getting sick and word spreading of an even worse strain of influenza heading west from Chicago, Indianapolis, and Des Moines, those wives and mothers were determined to protect their families.

The directions were simple. Follow the railroad tracks heading west of Manifest. Where the tracks curved south, they were to veer north into the woods. There, between the hackberry tree and the pin oak, hidden by numerous weeds and shrubs, was the entrance to the abandoned mine shaft.

By the beginning of September, Shady and Jinx made their first trip of the quarantine in the dark of night, the elixir bottles resting in the hay of a wheelbarrow. From the in-ground hiding spot, they waited for the sick and weary to come. And they did come. Worn and worried faces; men, women, and children who came with baskets and money. They received their brown bottles in grateful silence and gave what they had. Some dollars, some coins. A few brought only empty bottles for the next person to use.

One woman, pale and thin, handed Jinx a bundled-up

red handkerchief. He felt the rattle of grains inside. "It's mustard seed," she said through the gaps between her teeth. "Good for hot packs to clear the lungs."

Jinx nodded and handed her a bottle. He remembered the pungent smell of the mustard pack his mother had used on him when he was a child. The memory was seared into his chest. A few people in Manifest had succumbed to fatigue and mild flu symptoms. They'd all been working around the clock. Maybe a hot pack would do them good.

"Thank you," Jinx said, looking up, but like a ghost, she was gone.

More came as the night wore on. Jinx nearly fell asleep during a lull. He had hardly slept for days. Perhaps that would explain why he thought he looked into a familiar face as he held out another bottle. It was a man's. There was a coldness to the face, and a smile, but not a friendly one. Then the man was gone. Was it Finn? Was it anyone? It happened so quickly Jinx couldn't be sure, but the bottle was gone.

Jinx retreated into the protective earthen walls of the shaft, waiting for his heart to stop racing. He thought of the last time he had seen that face. How it had looked up from Junior Haskell's lifeless body and said, "You killed him."

"You okay?" Shady asked.

"Yeah. I thought I saw someone I knew once." Jinx shook his head. His mind swirled like a dust devil, conflicting memories chasing each other in circles.

"Someone you'd rather forget?"

Jinx nodded.

Shady moved into the opening, placing himself between Jinx and whatever or whoever might be lurking in the darkness as time crept on.

It had been a while since the last person had passed through. The birds began chirping as they did just before light. Without a word, Shady and Jinx hid the empty bottles and various other gifts of payment in the hay of the wheelbarrow and headed back into town, both tired and on edge. They walked in silence for a time; then they heard a creak.

"Out for your morning constitutional, gentlemen?" It was Sheriff Dean. Leaning against an old picket fence, he whittled casually on a small piece of wood. The sheriff never violated the quarantine by venturing into town, but he apparently did venture from his house once in a while.

"No, sir, Sheriff." Shady took off his hat and patted it nervously against his leg. "A brisk walk would be nice, but we're out, uh . . . you see, we're . . ."

"We're on a mission of mercy," Jinx answered.

"Mission of mercy, you say?" Sheriff Dean eyed the wheelbarrow but kept a safe distance. "That wouldn't involve doling out alkyholic libations, would it?"

"No, sir." Jinx reached into the wheelbarrow and pulled out the red handkerchief the old woman had given him. "Mustard seed." He rattled the grains. "Velma T.'s working on some hot packs to help clear the lungs. She asked us to find some of the herbs she needs. You can look for yourself," Jinx offered. "There's even a couple of mustard packs in here that helped a few people sweat out their fevers and chills."

Sheriff Dean leaned back, apparently not wanting to risk contact with a sweaty mustard pack. He crossed his arms over his belly and narrowed his eyes at Jinx. "You know, there's a fella been seen hanging around these woods, camping down by the river not far from my house. He fits

254

the description of one of those runaways the Joplin authorities are looking for. I saw him myself from a distance but he moved on quick enough. Only thing is, he's supposed to be one of a pair."

Jinx and Shady didn't comment.

"Causes me to wonder why this fella would be coming around Manifest. Maybe he's looking for his better half."

"Maybe," Jinx said.

"If you see a stranger around, you'll let me know." Sheriff Dean stepped to the side, studying Jinx from a different angle. "Course, you're somewhat of a stranger yourself."

Jinx stayed put.

"Truth is," Sheriff Dean continued, his sharp knife peeling away layers of wood, "as I believe I mentioned before, the sheriff from Joplin happens to be my brother-in-law and he's not too bright. If he let some ne'er-do-wells get away, that's his own fault." He stopped whittling and checked the blade against his thumb. Then he looked straight at Jinx. "But this is my town and I make the rules here. I'll be watching you." He paused to let his point sink in. "See that you stick closer to town. We don't need the influenza spreading to the outskirts."

"Yes, sir," Jinx and Shady answered. They waited for the sheriff to leave, but he leaned back against the fence and whittled away at his block of wood. With a nod, Jinx and Shady continued on their way back to town. The sheriff wasn't just keeping watch. It was a downright vigil.

A single candle lit Shady's place, and the mood was equally dark. Small clusters of men huddled around tables, waiting for someone to speak.

"What are we going to do now?" asked Donal Mac-Gregor. "With Sheriff Dean watching our comings and go-ings, you can't just waltz in and out of town unnoticed."

"And Lester Burton's been phoning in twice a day to the switchboard," said Ivan DeVore. "Checking to see if the men are well enough to go back to work. He won't be sat-isfied somebody's not fit to work until they're dead and buried. And even then he'll dock their past wages for not reporting to work."

Jinx thought it strange that Burton was calling in. What news did he expect to find out? Who had he been talking to? And more importantly, who'd been talking to him? Of course not everyone in town had been apprised of the fake influenza before it happened. They just had to hope that the people in town during the quarantine were tired enough of the mine's choke hold on them to go along with the scheme.

"What about the boy?" Hermann Keufer asked, some-what accusingly. "Hasn't he got another rabbit to pull from his bag of tricks?"

Suddenly, all eyes were on Jinx, who sat quietly on a stool behind the bar. Their faces reminded Jinx of Sheriff Dean's warning. He had been identified as a stranger and felt his sense of belonging slipping away.

Shady sheltered Jinx again, this time from the stares of those waiting for yet another miracle. "We'll have to just keep producing the elixir until we figure a way to distribute it again."

There was an uneasy scraping and shifting of chairs on the dusty wooden floor. This time it was Donal MacGregor who came to the rescue.

"Now, come on. I'm sure we've all got better things to do than fuss and fidget around here all day. Let's move along." Like a mother hen, he gathered up his chicks, sometimes nudging, sometimes snapping, and shooed them out the door.

Donal remained in the entryway, as if posting himself sentry.

But Jinx slid quietly from his perch and left Shady's place, letting the door swing shut behind him.

The mood in the town was already somber when the first death of the quarantine was reported a few days later. Mr. Underwood prepared a pine box and was quite put out when Donal said he would take care of the rest. The body would be buried out of town, they said, to keep the smell and germs away.

With shovels in hand, Shady, Jinx, and Donal Mac-Gregor carried the casket out of town. Each sagged under the weight of their heavy task.

They reached the clearing, not far from the abandoned mine shaft, and took turns digging near an old craggy sycamore tree. Six feet down and four feet across. Late-afternoon shadows crept across the clearing as Donal threw out the last shovel of dirt. He wiped his brow and accepted a canteen of cool water Shady offered when Lester Burton emerged from the trees.

"I heard there's been a death."

"You heard that, did you?" Donal said. "Word sure gets around, even in a quarantine."

"Who is it?" His abrupt speech indicated what the men already knew. Burton's primary interest was in discovering if he'd lost a miner. And if so, was there a strong son of thirteen or fourteen left behind to take his place?

"Gourouni," said Donal.

"Gourouni? I don't know him."

"Aye, God rest his soul," Donal said. "He didn't say much. He lived in the little house behind me. Kept to himself mostly." He took in a breath. "No, I didn't know him well, but he could eat, that one. Both of us bachelors, I'd often fix extra. My cooking wasn't the best, mind you, but I never heard a word of complaint out of him."

Shady stood by the open grave and removed his hat. "It's time, Donal."

"All right. Let's lay him down."

"Wait," said Burton. "Let me see him." A note of suspicion rose in his voice, as if this Mr. Gourouni might have a few hours work left in him.

"I don't think you'll want to be doing that," said Donal. "He's been dead more'n a day. Not exactly fresh, if you know what I mean."

"I said let me see."

"Right." Donal nodded at Jinx, who pried open the lid of the coffin.

Immediately, such a stench arose from the casket that Burton covered his nose and nearly retched. Jinx let the half-opened lid drop back down.

"Aye," Donal said. "The smell of rotting flesh is one few can stomach. When Mr. MacTweeg was a lad back in Lochinver, he was on his way home from the pub. He took the shortcut through the Ballyknock Grove when a wild boar charged him, goring his leg, nearly tearing it off before MacTweeg could reach his knife and slice open the

258

boar's throat. Three days he lay there, in the stench of the rotting beast and his own festering flesh still caught on the animal's tusks."

Donal MacGregor took a slow drag from his pipe and let the smoke curl out of his mouth like the story itself. "When some local lads came upon him, MacTweeg lay pinned beneath the bloated, oozing carcass. Clawing and scratching, he was, already fighting his unseen demons. The infection eventually took his leg. But 'twas the stench of death that drove him mad.

"But," Donal said, his mood suddenly brightening, "come have a look if you must." He gave the coffin lid a yank, sending another waft of odor floating up. "He's not at full steam yet."

Burton covered his mouth and gagged again. "Just hurry up and bury him." He whipped out a ragged bandana to cover his nose and stalked away.

The men waited until he was gone; then Shady and Jinx lurched away from the open grave, gasping for air. "Blast it, Donal, did you have to open it a second time?" croaked Shady. "I was barely keeping it in as it was."

"Well, it got rid of him, didn't it? And I don't expect he'll be coming back round to check again." Donal opened the pine box. "Ahh, Stanley, God rest your soul." He hoisted out a smaller, metal box lying within the pine coffin. "A finer pig there never was. He'd been ailing for a time, so I do suppose it was right to put him down."

"Where'd you come up with the name Gourouni?" asked Jinx.

"Matenopoulos told me it's the Greek word for pig. Gourouni." Donal rolled his *r*'s as he said it. Then he wagged a finger at Jinx. "You were right, lad, to come prepared for Burton. But how do you think he knew we'd be here?"

Shady and Jinx were still holding their breath. "Donal, please, just take it in the woods and bury it," said Shady. "No one's going to come around with that smell surrounding us."

Donal was off, carrying the metal box of pig remains, and the smell gradually followed him.

"Looks like you were right," Shady said, sitting down on the coffin like a balloon gone flat. "What did you call it?"

"A mole."

"A mole," Shady repeated, rubbing his whiskers. "So there's someone among us in Manifest who's feeding information to Burton. I wouldn't have believed it."

Both sat for a moment, lost in thought and speculation as to who the mole might be.

Then Shady stood. "Well, we're not going to figure it out sitting here. Give me a hand with this lid."

Shady and Jinx opened the coffin and inspected the dozens of bottles resting in a bed of straw so as not to clank against each other.

"We dug the hole; we might as well use it," Shady said. "That way the stuff'll not be in plain sight, in case someone else happens along."

Jinx climbed into the pit, then helped lower the pine box. Shady eased in after him and the two hunkered down like soldiers in the trenches, their backs up against the wall. Dusk faded to dark.

Jinx broke the silence. "You think folks'll find us here?"

Shady answered with certainty. "They'll find us."

Another few moments passed and Jinx spoke again.

"Shady?"

"Yes."

"D'you think a person can be cursed?"

"How do you mean?"

"Cursed, like when a fellow doesn't mean for bad things to happen, but they just sort of follow him around like his shadow."

"Well, I don't know for sure," Shady answered, speaking as one with a few shadows of his own. "I suppose it's either a matter of outrunning your shadow or staring it down in the light."

"Staring it down, huh? Easy as that."

Shady shook his head and let out a heavy breath. "Nothing easy about it. Don't let nobody tell you otherwise."

The two sat in silence until they noticed a figure emerging from the woods. And then another. And another. They knew to keep away when the sheriff and Burton were around. But now the sick and weary had returned.

Shady and Jinx remained in the open grave, pulling out bottle after bottle. They worked steadily, distributing the elixir. It was an eerie sight—Shady and Jinx, their arms reaching up from the ground, as if the dead could provide some comfort for the living.

PVT. NED GILLEN

Dear Jinx,

Do the Akkersons still have that Shetland sheepdog? The one that could round up a whole herd of cows, practically lining them up single file? That must be how Sarge got his nickname. Fellas in other battalions know him as First Sergeant Daniels, but he's always been Shep to us.

He got hit by a mortar shell yesterday. The guys and me, we're still sitting around like a bunch of scared kids. Oh, we talk all big and cocky, but he was like our dad and we were his boys. We loved him. We'd have walked into a swarm of bees if he'd told us to.

But he's the one who walked into it this time. Way I heard it, the guys were under heavy fire. Hank Turner got shot in the leg and was stranded out in no-man's-land. Shep barked at the men to stay put, then headed out to get him. He carried Hank forty yards and shoved him into a foxhole before the mortar shell got him.

Last I saw Shep, I was leaving to make a run to the Sixty-third Battalion. I didn't salute, of course. This close to the front, you don't salute officers. That only tells Heine who's in charge. But our guys had a sort of vocal salute to show Sarge our respect. Just a little chirpy cricket sound. As I started my trot out yesterday, I gave Shep that quick cricket salute. He conked me in the back of the head with a pinecone for it, but we were his boys. We knew it and he knew it.

I was making my way back last night. Couldn't figure out what was going on in those woods. Sounded like a bunch of crickets were singing to high heaven. I joined in before I realized it was our final salute to old Shep. It sounded pretty. Real pretty.

Ned

P.S. Hey, buddy, can you do me a favor? I'd do it myself, but I'm not there and I want it done in words, out loud. Tell Pop I love him.

A Dying Breath

AUGUST 7, 1936

"School's going to be starting before long and we'll have nothing to show for our summer of spy hunting," Lettie said after we'd clambered up the rickety rope ladder to the tree house, carrying a tin of buttermilk biscuits for our afternoon snack. "In fact, I'd be ready to think the Rattler has been long gone or buried if it wasn't for the note we found on the tree trunk." Lettie's eyes grew wide. "Now, there's an idea. Maybe the Rattler is dead and buried *and* left us that note. Remember Uncle Louver's story about the ghostly figure moving about the woods."

"For gosh sakes, Lettie. We all saw it. We all read it."

"I've still got it right here in the cigar box," I said.

"Are the words still on it? Or have they disappeared?" Lettie asked.

Ruthanne rolled her eyes.

I took the crumpled note from the box and widened my eyes in amazement. "There's nothing here. It's blank!"

"What?" Ruthanne snatched the note away from me. She stared in disbelief at the blank paper. Then she flipped it over. "Oh, very funny. It's on the other side."

Lettie and I laughed. Ruthanne didn't find it funny.

"Don't get your knickers in a knot, Ruthanne. It's too hot for that."

The note lay on the floor in the middle of us and we stared at the four words, each one capitalized. *Leave Well Enough Alone.* The words taunted us. Dared us.

"We've got to come up with a plan," said Ruthanne. "Something clever and resourceful that'll shine a light on the person who wrote this note."

"Yeah, but what if he's somebody really nasty, like James Cagney in *Public Enemy*?" said Lettie. "Remember when he smashed a grapefruit in Mae Clarke's face? Of course, in *"G" Men* he was on the other side of the law as Brick Davis. What do you think he'd do?"

"He'd use his tommy gun, and by the end, the whole town would be dead or in jail," said Ruthanne. "No, it has to be something sneakier, and not so bloody." Ruthanne turned her attention to me. "What would Jinx do, Abilene?"

It was strange. I'd been wondering the same thing. The answer was simple. "He'd come up with some fancy scheme to trick the Rattler into giving himself away. You know, a con."

"Like . . . ?" Lettie and Ruthanne asked in unison.

"Well, let me think." I felt I knew Jinx well enough to put myself in his shoes. What would he do? Then I smiled. "This is kind of like being a diviner. Do you have a bauble?"

I asked in Miss Sadie's Hungarian accent, making my voice thick and husky.

Lettie and Ruthanne just stared at me in confusion.

"A totem or trinket. Something belonging to the person in question." I said the word *question* like it had a *v* in it. *Qvestion.*

Lettie jumped with excitement. "The note. Here, use the note."

I took the paper and made a big show of smoothing out the wrinkles on the tree house floorboards. Then I took a deep breath and pondered the note.

"What is it? What do you see?" asked Lettie.

"She sees a girl who'll believe anything," Ruthanne said, rolling her eyes.

"Oh, for heaven's sake, Ruthanne. I know she's just putting on, but I can play along, can't I?"

"Silence." I held up my hand. "The spirits are thinking."

I looked intently at the note, holding it up to the light as if it would shout an answer at me. And then it darn near did.

"Hey," I said in my regular voice. "The handwriting."

"What about it?" Ruthanne said.

"I knew a lady once, Miss Leeds in Springfield, Illinois. She could tell all manner of things about people just by the way they tapped out their messages on a telegraph machine."

"So you can tell who the Rattler is just by looking at the handwriting?" Lettie asked.

"No, but just like telegraphing is different from one person to another, handwriting is too. See here?" I pointed to the note. "See how these letters are straight up and down, plodding across the page? And at the end of each word, the last letter trails off like it's giving out its dying breath."

"Why, you're right," Lettie said in admiration. "So we should go door to door and ask everyone to write the same words as on this note and we'll see whose matches up." Lettie paused. "But how are we going to get everyone to write it down?"

I answered before Ruthanne could jump on her. "We won't have them write *these* words. They'll write something else." My mind was racing. "Anybody seen Billy Clayton today?"

"He's over at the school yard. Sister Redempta's got him fixing the fence he ran into on his bike." Ruthanne perked up an eyebrow. "Why?"

"Because Hattie Mae's having a contest. She just doesn't know it yet."

HATTIE MAE'S NEWS AUXILIARY

AUGUST 9, 1936

To the faithful readers of "Hattie Mae's News Auxiliary." First an explanation, then an announcement. Many apologies for the mix-up last week. Uncle Henry set out a stack of old newspapers (from 1918 to be exact) to be stored in the shed out back. We all know that man can't part with a penny or a paper.

Anyway, Fred got the papers as far as the back door when his lumbago set in. Of course I had to get him home to bed, even though my knees have been no great shakes lately. Fred's never been a silent sufferer, but "for better or worse," right, ladies?

Well, I guess it's asking too much for Billy Clayton to actually read the papers he delivers. I'm assuming he's got bad eyes, as he hits the bushes and the roof as often as the porch at our house.

For those of you who thought that we were back at war with the Huns, that

Woodrow Wilson was still president, and that you could buy a washing machine for fourteen dollars, wake up and smell the Depression.

Still, it was a hoot seeing the hats that were in fashion at the millinery. Remember the styles for men? Those stiff celluloid collars around their necks and the spats around their ankles. And the lace-up boots we women used to wear. Lord, have mercy.

Remember when Manifest boasted citizens of twenty different nationalities? When you could walk down Main Street and smell Mama Santoni's warm bread instead of dust and wind? Listening to Caruso sing "Eyes of Blue" on the Victrola? When we all bought Liberty Bonds to support our brave soldiers "over there"?

This brings me to the announcement. Due to Fred's "injury" and the fact that his mother is coming in from Springfield to "help," I will be taking a sabbatical from "Hattie Mae's News Auxiliary."

However, some of our younger patrons wanted to know more about our fair town back in the day. So at their suggestion, we are inaugurating the *Manifest Herald*'s Remember When contest. Write up a favorite memory from 1918 in your best handwriting and submit it to the *Manifest Herald* by Friday, August 23. We'll run as many as we can, but the winner will receive a five-dollar cash prize. I asked

Uncle Henry for ten but . . . read the above.

Good luck' and, as always, for all the whos, whats, whys, whens, and wheres you can't find in the rest of this nickel-and-dime paper, turn to

HATTIE MAE MACKE
Reporter About Town

Miss Sadie's Divining Parlor

AUGUST 11, 1936

The town was abuzz about the recent "mix-up" with the newspaper. Billy Clayton loved a good prank and had been happy to deliver the 1918 newspapers that had not made their way to the basement.

He said there wasn't anything worth reading in the current papers anyway. Everyone knew that these days there wasn't much news and most of it was bad. So, for the time being, we waited to see if anyone would respond to the contest announcement.

Hattie Mae was excited about the idea. It was true that we wanted to know more about Manifest back in the day. We just didn't mention, even to Hattie Mae, that we were particularly interested in who might have the same hand writing used in the note telling us to "leave well enough alone."

I stood at the sink in Miss Sadie's tiny kitchen, wrapping

an assortment of exotic tea leaves in a worn piece of cloth. I tied a string around the neck of the cloth and dangled the tea bag into a pot of boiling water on her cookstove. Waiting for the tea to brew, I gazed out the window, watching the clouds churn and roil high above the neat rows of Miss Sadie's garden that in fact had come to feel like my own. Those seeds of all kinds—carrot, pea, squash, pumpkin, onion—rested just beneath the surface. I had touched each one, planted each one in rows. Removed and replaced every bit of dirt just so, in hopes that they might take root in this place.

Those seeds. My seeds. Maybe they were wondering, as I was, if this would be the day rain would come.

I looked at the shed, still locked and dark. As the rich, spicy aroma from the teapot filled the kitchen, I found myself wondering if this would be the day Miss Sadie would tell what she had brewing inside her.

Then I felt her presence behind me. There was less idle talk each time I came. It was as if she had fewer words in her and the ones she had were the story. I pulled a stool over to her and she rested herself on it, leaning an elbow on the cabinet.

There was plenty I wanted to ask her. I wanted a conclusion to the story. I wanted to know about the skeleton key, the last remaining memento from the Lucky Bill cigar box. I wanted to know where Gideon fit into all of this. Why he was never mentioned in any of her stories. But I knew from experience that Miss Sadie told the story in her own way and in her own time. I was afraid that there were parts of it still simmering in her that she might never share.

In the silence of Miss Sadie's kitchen, I thought of Gideon. I wondered about his story and why he had retreated so far into himself, where I couldn't reach him. Why had a cut on my leg been such a big deal? I knew I'd gotten very sick. But I got better. I remembered the way he'd looked at me. I had just turned twelve and he said I was growing up into a young lady. True, "young ladies" were not often found living on the road, traveling from town to town and job to job. But wasn't it more important that we were together? I wondered where Gideon was and when he would come back. *If* he would come back.

Miss Sadie studied me, trying to read my thoughts. But I kept her out. She had her secrets and I had mine.

Suddenly, the kettle whistled, and for the life of me it sounded just like a train whistle blowing in the distance.

Miss Sadie's voice was husky as she began.

"The Santa Fe steamer chugged into town—three days early. . . ."

Day of Reckoning

SEPTEMBER 28, 1918

The people of Manifest emerged cautiously from their homes and headed toward the depot. When Arthur Devlin himself stepped off the first passenger car with Lester Burton and the county medical examiner in tow, they knew the quarantine was over. But how?

Devlin gestured broadly. "You see, Dr. Haskell, they're in fine health, wouldn't you say?"

Dr. Haskell pushed his glasses up on his nose and squinted at the lot before him. Shady, Hadley, Mama Santoni, Mrs. Larkin, and others. "Well, in order to end an official quarantine, I'll need to examine them and—"

"And as soon as you pronounce my miners of sound mind and body, I'll expect them back to work within the hour."

Devlin made a show of brushing off unseen dust from his suit. "Ahh, Eudora. This must have been an awful

274

experience for you. I'm sure you would never have taken part in such a charade if you'd known. Now that it's over, perhaps you would enjoy dining with me this evening in Pittsburg."

Mrs. Larkin was uncharacteristically flustered by the attention of Devlin and the suspicious looks of the people in the crowd. "Well, Arthur, I—"

"Now, Eudora, you turned me down years ago, but I'd hoped you'd learned your lesson. I hate to say it but your husband was a chump. Always working on his books and numbers. What kind of life is that? You know as well as I do, Eudora, that we are both meant for things greater."

"Mother!" Pearl Ann Larkin cried, stepping off the train. She rushed up, throwing her arms around her mother. "Manifest has been all the talk at Kansas University. When I found out they were letting trains back in, I rushed straight home."

Devlin was disgruntled by the interruption but took Mrs. Larkin's hand and kissed it. "I see you are occupied. Perhaps another time."

Devlin ordered double shifts for all the mine workers. No exceptions or you'd be fired. Of course, this meant that production of the elixir stopped. Dozens of full bottles remained in the abandoned mine shaft, because no one could get away to sell them. Sheriff Dean kept one eye on Shady but kept the other on Jinx, like a cat waiting for a mouse to steal a piece of cheese so he could devour both at once.

October 1, the Day of Reckoning, found a ragtag band holed up at Shady's place: Shady, Jinx, Donal MacGregor, and Hadley Gillen, along with Callisto Matenopoulos, Olaf Akkerson, and Casimir Cybulskis. Mrs. Larkin, who liked to have her nose in everything, was conspicuously absent. Those present all stared at the wad of cash splayed out on the bar. "All this for nothing," said Donal. "There's a rat in this town who's been feeding information to Burton and Devlin and I say it's high time we found out who it is."

"We'd all like to know," said Shady, "but right now we've got bigger problems." Hadley counted the money first, then Shady, and finally Donal. No matter who counted, it always added up to $740.

They stared at the money as if they could mentally conjure another $260 before the court hearing at noon. Then they heard a car pull up. In one swift movement, Shady pulled a lever and the portion of the bar with the money sank and was covered by an identical shiny piece of wood, which blended in perfectly with the rest of the bar top. All was quiet when Lester Burton walked in.

Swaggered was a better word. He came in like he owned the place. "You know they'll blame you for it," Burton said. "The double shifts and docked wages, all because of your fancy scheme. And here you are, sitting nice and cozy, probably counting your money."

The others looked up in surprise.

"Oh, you didn't know I knew about all that, the so-called elixir, nighttime rum runs. It took a while, but for the right price, someone's always willing to talk. In fact, get the right rumors started and folks might get the idea that it was one of you who told me what was going on—just so's you could keep the money. I imagine a good tar and feathering wouldn't be out of the question."

"As if anybody's had time to pluck feathers," Jinx muttered to Shady.

"You got something to say, boy?"

Jinx didn't answer.

Just then, a stranger walked in, carrying a briefcase, looking decidedly out of place. Burton regained his composure and leaned on the bar. "While I'm here, Shady, I'll have a shot of your finest. For medicinal purposes, of course."

Shady poured him a glass and slid it across the bar.

The stranger, a young man wearing a black suit, white shirt, and bow tie, set his briefcase on the bar and asked Shady for a glass of water.

"Water?" Burton scoffed. "Why, haven't you heard about the miracle whiskey made right here in Manifest? Drink up, son. What's your pleasure?"

The man wiped his brow with a crisp white handkerchief. "I've heard, but I'm here on business, not pleasure."

As Shady handed him a glass of water, the man looked at it as if he might check to see if the water was up to code. Then the stranger opened his briefcase and pulled out a glass vial of white powder. Under the curious stares of the men and Jinx, he poured the powder into the glass of water and watched it fizz and foam. He raised the glass to the light streaming in through the window, giving it his full attention. He pulled a small notepad from his jacket pocket and jotted down some notations, all the while looking back and forth from the pad to the glass of water.

"Where do you get your water?" he asked Shady with an air of authority.

"Who's asking?" Shady countered with a bootlegger's dose of suspicion.

"From the spring just fifty yards west of here, isn't that correct?"

Now Shady was unnerved. If the stranger had already been to the spring, he'd been uncomfortably close to the whiskey barn. They had planned to take down the stills before the quarantine ended, but hadn't got the chance.

"That's the one."

Burton looked at the man with great interest. "What kind of business might you be in, son?"

"Government." The answer was curt, as if he didn't need to explain himself to the likes of Lester Burton.

"Well, before you go poking around these parts anymore, I think we need a little more information."

"Then perhaps you should take it up with the state board of health. Word has gotten all the way to Topeka that there's something very interesting about this springwater." He poured a small amount of water from the glass into the empty vial and replaced the rubber stopper. Again, he held up the vial to the light, giving it a flick with his finger. He studied the cloudy water and made another notation in his little book. "Hmm," the stranger mused. "Very interesting."

"What's very interesting?" asked Burton.

"Is there a mine near here? A vein of some metal ore?"

"Yes, just a little farther west than the spring."

"That would explain a great deal. I hear you've had a lot of sick folks in this region whose condition improved."

Burton's curiosity was piqued at the mention of the mine. "I happen to be the pit boss of that mine and I have a right to know what's going on. Why would the govern-ment want to know if there's metal in the water?"

"Do you own the spring, Mr. . . . ?"

"Burton. And no, but—"

"Then this is not your concern." He placed the vial in his briefcase and locked it shut.

"I always knew that mine would kill us all, one way or another," Mr. Matenopoulos lamented. "Whether it's black soot in our lungs or contamination in our water, it will get us all in the end."

The room grew quiet as the weight of his words, as dark and cold as a mine shaft, pressed around them. Mr. Matenopoulos and the others were consumed by their gloom and Burton seemed the only one to notice as the young man drank half the glass of cloudy water.

"Now what?" Burton asked.

"Now"—the man tore out a page of his notebook, placed it into a brown envelope, and slid it into an inside pocket of his jacket—"I have some very important infor-mation to deliver at the courthouse." He laid his suit coat over his arm and lifted the glass of water in salute. "Good day."

Burton lowered his voice so the others in the bar couldn't hear. "Now hold on there, son. There's no need to be so standoffish. Smart young fellow like you wouldn't drink that water if there was something wrong with it." He spoke with a smile. "No, my guess is there's something special about this here water. Is this something like those healing springs in Arkansas and Colorado, where people come from all over to buy the stuff? Healing water, they call it."

"Well, I can't speak to that, Mr. Burton. I've never been to any of those places." Then he drank the rest of the cloudy water in one long gulp. "All I can say is I'm feeling better already, and that's a fact." He placed the glass on the bar, winked at Burton, and was gone.

Judge Carlson rapped his gavel. "This court will now come to order." The crowded courtroom grew still. The monthly court date was always a well-attended event, as it provided citizens with a forum to settle disputes, conduct all manner of legal transactions, and hold public auction.

That day's session, however, was jam-packed. The whole local cast of characters was present. Lester Burton sat in the front row, smiling and confident, while Shady and Jinx sat across the aisle. Arthur Devlin sat a few rows back, holding his gold-tipped cane and stretching one leg into the aisle. The man from the state board of health had himself wedged into the second row, briefcase on his lap, with the still pregnant Mrs. Cybulskis on his left and Hattie Mae on his right. Even Sister Redempta slipped in the back door and stood to the left side of the courtroom while the Hungarian woman stood to the right.

Hattie Mae, pen and paper in hand, was prepared to record all the whos, whats, whys, whens, and wheres and so tried not to notice the handsome man sitting beside her. He, on the other hand, made no attempt to avoid noticing her.

"We have a full slate today, ladies and gentlemen, so let's keep things moving." Judge Carlson peered through his half-glasses at the schedule, as if he wasn't fully aware of the item at the top of the list.

"First off, we have—"

"Your Honor," Mrs. Larkin interrupted from the jury box, which was being used for extra seating, "there is a matter of some urgency that I insist be dealt with immediately." She stood. "It has come to my attention that Shady Howard has been producing illegal substances on public property."

Half the courtroom glared at her. As often as she'd been seen making telephone calls from the post office and frequenting the telegraph machine, funneling who-knew-what information to Arthur Devlin, they still couldn't believe she would take this opportunity to knock Shady's legs out from under him.

"Mrs. Larkin." Judge Carlson rubbed his forehead as if this was going to be the beginning of a very long afternoon. "I assure you we will address your grievance, but the first item on the agenda is the settlement of the Widow Cane's property."

Mrs. Larkin sat down, holding her tongue for the time being.

Judge Carlson continued. "As stated, the township of Manifest has the first rights to the land upon payment of back taxes and the land fee in the amount of one thousand dollars."

Shady stood and spoke for the group. "Your Honor, we are a little short of the thousand dollars and are requesting an extension to raise the remaining funds."

The Honorable Judge Carlson was just that. Honorable. He was one of the few authorities around who was not in the back pocket of Arthur Devlin. He would come down on the side of the law, wherever that happened to fall. But his voice couldn't hide the weight of what he was about to say. Judge Carlson shook his head. "I'm sorry, Shady. The statute is clear. As of October first, if the town doesn't buy the land, it becomes available for public sale."

"But, Your Honor, we can pay the portion we have now and—"

Lester Burton stood. "Your Honor. These shysters have been deceiving everyone long enough. Producing illegal alcohol, or their so-called elixir, to raise funds to buy the land. I'd say it's time to put that land up for sale."

Judge Carlson's gavel wavered for a moment. "Very well. Let's get on with it. Since the township cannot make payment in full at this time, then in accordance with public statute, the aforementioned tract of land is now open for public bids."

Lester Burton looked around the room, defying anyone to bid against him. The crowd remained still. "Your Honor, since there is no stipulation that the land be sold in one piece, I'd like to first bid on the section including the spring from the tracks to the stream."

The room ignited with a buzz of murmuring voices. Judge Carlson banged his gavel.

"I thought the mine wanted the whole tract of land."

"The part I want doesn't involve the vein. That pertains to the mine. Right now, I'm not bidding on behalf of the mine. I'm bidding for myself and all I'm interested in is the spring. I'll start the bidding at fifty dollars."

Shady tried to figure what Burton was up to. Jinx snuck a look at the government man sitting in the second row. "Shady, that fellow from Topeka never said the water was contaminated. He just asked if it was near a mine," Jinx whispered.

"So?"

"What if that's a good thing? What if that's why people were getting better?"

"You mean it might be healing water?" Shady pondered the idea. "Like in those spas in Arkansas and Colorado?"

"Yes, and folks come from miles to drink, even bathe in it. Burton will make a fortune."

"Going once. . . ." Judge Carlson looked around the courtroom.

"You can't just let him buy it," Jinx whispered.

"But it's the town's money."

"Then the town will own the spring. You'll all still have a chance to get out from under Burton and the mine," Jinx urged.

"Going twice. . . ." The gavel hovered.

"One hundred dollars," Shady said softly.

"What's that?" Judge Carlson asked, trying to find the source of the bid.

Shady stood. "One hundred dollars."

Burton turned on Shady. "I don't think you want to do that, Shady."

"I think I do."

"Two hundred dollars," Burton counterbid.

"Three hundred."

The bidding went back and forth, a hundred dollars at a time, until it reached seven hundred dollars. That was when Lester Burton knew he was getting close.

It was Shady's bid. "Seven hundred twenty dollars."

"Seven thirty."

Shady's hands were trembling. He looked like he'd have paid seven hundred dollars for one stiff drink, just to take the edge off. "Seven hundred forty dollars."

The courtroom was silent, as if there was not a breath left. Everyone knew he had done all he could. And everyone knew it wasn't enough.

"Seven forty-one." Burton waited for the counterbid that wouldn't come.

Judge Carlson raised his gavel like a man ready to put a dying animal out of its misery. "Going once. Going twice. Sold." He rapped his gavel lightly. "Mr. Burton, if you'll sign the papers with the county clerk, we'll move on to the rest of the Widow Cane's property." Burton whipped out a pen and signed the papers with a smirk.

"Your Honor?" It was Mrs. Larkin again. "About that property . . ."

"Yes, I know, Mrs. Larkin," Judge Carlson said. "I assure you we will address your matter in due time. Now please be seated."

"But, Your Honor . . ." Mrs. Larkin stepped out of the jury box. "As my husband, the late Eugene Larkin, was the county appraiser, I have access to his maps relating to public and private land use in this county. The land just purchased by Mr. Burton . . ." Without asking to approach the bench, Mrs. Larkin whipped out a map and unrolled it on Judge Carlson's desk. "See here? It's this northeast corner."

"Yes, I see. However, where Shady makes his alleged concoctions doesn't change the fact that this land is now up for public sale. So, if you'll return to your seat . . ."

"Oh, but it does, Your Honor," Mrs. Larkin argued. "You see, now that Mr. Burton has purchased that section of land, it reduces the amount of land that has back taxes due. And actually, now Mr. Burton owes an amount in back taxes."

A host of mystified stares focused on Mrs. Larkin. Even Judge Carlson was at first unable to respond.

Lester Burton recovered first. "What difference does that make? They still don't have enough, so let's get on with the sale." He was clearly rattled by his nearly devastating mistake.

Mrs. Larkin continued. "Actually, Your Honor, there's more."

"Of course there is." Judge Carlson sat back and crossed his arms.

"Mr. Burton's property includes a spring, which is considered a public resource, therefore it is required that the taxes on that land go to the nearest township. In this case, the township of Manifest."

"Meaning?" Judge Carlson asked, growing genuinely interested.

"Meaning that if, in fact, the town of Manifest has raised seven hundred and forty dollars—by whatever flagrant and nefarious means"—she looked over her glasses at Shady and Jinx—"due to Mr. Burton's purchase of the spring, they now have the money to buy the rest of the Widow Cane's property, with eight dollars to spare. The county clerk can verify." She handed the map and calculations to the clerk.

"This is preposterous," Burton spluttered. "They had their chance to buy the property. Now it's up for public sale."

Arthur Devlin rose from his seat, his puffy face splotchy with rage. "Sit down, Burton," he roared. "You've done enough to botch this affair. I bid five thousand dollars on the rest of the property, Carlson. Let's get this thing over with."

"Mr. Devlin." Judge Carlson leaned forward, his voice even. "With all this hubbub, I think you may be a bit confused. You see, we are not in your mine. You are in my courtroom and you may refer to me as Judge or Your Honor."

Arthur Devlin's eyes narrowed and he plopped himself back into his seat.

"Now"—Judge Carlson lowered his spectacles—"you should recall that the first step of this process is not an auction. The statute clearly states that the township of Manifest has first right to the land in question as long as they can pay the back taxes and land fee by October first. Then and only then is the land put up for public auction. Mr. Devlin, according to my calendar, it is still October first, and if everything Mrs. Larkin said checks out"—he glanced at the county clerk, who gave a nod—"then, since your own Mr. Burton has graciously provided the township of Manifest with some unexpected money, by law they are still allowed to acquire the remaining land, which includes the vein."

Devlin crushed his cigar to a pulp, but being a businessman through and through, he knew when he was defeated. He mustered three words. "Burton, you're fired."

"Fine with me," Burton said. "You'll all be coming to me for some of that healing springwater. And you can bet it won't be cheap."

The crowd rumbled. What was he talking about? Was that why Shady had bid on the spring?

"That's right, folks," said Burton. "Just ask our friendly government visitor from Topeka. He's got his report all ready about the high metal content in the water and how it has healing properties. Go ahead, son, make your presentation."

All eyes turned to the young man sitting in the second row of the courtroom.

Finally, Hattie could look at him head-on. She held her pen, poised to take note. The man waved his hand. "I don't really think this is the time and—"

Burton fumed. "You came all the way to Manifest to deliver some important information, did you not?"

"I did, but—"

"Then I'm sure the judge won't mind bumping you up on the list."

The man looked at Judge Carlson.

"Go ahead. Let's have all the surprises out at once." Judge Carlson waved him on.

"Very well." He took the manila envelope from his jacket pocket and handed it to the bailiff, who passed it to Judge Carlson.

Judge Carlson opened it and examined the contents with great interest. "This is fascinating material, young man, but I fail to see how recipes for pumpkin pie and raspberry marmalade can have much bearing on the proceedings of this court. Would you mind clearing up what this is all about, Mr. . . ."

"Macke. Fred Macke. Those recipes are for my aunt Eudora."

Hattie Mae, the hardball reporter, dropped her pen, staring up at the man. He grinned at her and winked.

"But," Burton sputtered in disbelief as he realized something had gone terribly wrong. "This is an outrage, Judge. I retract my bid on the grounds that I have been tricked, manipulated, and lied to. This man is a charlatan. He told me he worked for the government."

Mrs. Larkin stepped forward. "He does work for the government, Lester. I've bragged on him a million times. This is my sister's boy. He works in the governor's office . . . the assistant to the assistant." She placed her hand proudly on his shoulder.

"But the water . . . ," Burton continued. "You checked the water, you made it fizz, and then you drank it. It was healing water."

Fred Macke's eyebrows went up. "That powder? Oh, that was just some seltzer powder. I've got a sensitive stomach." He gave a sideways glance at Jinx.

Eudora Larkin spoke up in his defense. "My nephew wouldn't lie. He's honest as the day is long. Perhaps you just misunderstood, Lester." She narrowed her eyes. "Or maybe your greed got in the way of good judgment." She turned her attention back to her nephew. "Now, Fred, you give my best to your mother and tell her thank you for the recipes."

"I'll do that, Aunt Eudora. And thank you for inviting me down for the day." He smiled winningly at Hattie Mae. "I think the sign outside of town is right. Manifest surely does appear to be a town with a bright future."

Hattie Mae had yet to pick up her pen.

Dumbfounded, Burton stared at Eudora Larkin, then sank back into his seat.

Devlin moved into the aisle and spoke directly to Mrs.

Larkin. "Like I said, your husband was a chump in high school. You could have had better."

Mrs. Larkin straightened up tall and proper, narrowed her eyes, and said, "Arthur Devlin, you and my husband may have been in the same grade, but you were never in the same class."

Arthur Devlin stood alone. Judge Carlson reached for his gavel but both Burton and Devlin were gone from the courtroom before it rapped on the desk.

Shady leaned over to Jinx. "Where in the devil did all that come from? You had a hand in this, didn't you?"

Jinx smiled. "It was just a little something Mrs. Larkin and I cooked up while having polite conversation. It really gets her dander up when someone insults the late Eugene Larkin."

"You could have let me in on the secret. It might have made it a little easier on everybody."

Jinx looked a little shamefaced. "Well, Shady, it's just that you don't have the best poker face and we were afraid you might give it away before Burton could bid on the spring."

"What's the matter with my poker face—"

Judge Carlson rapped the gavel again and rubbed his temples. "If we ever get through this day, it will be a miracle. What say you, Shady? Still interested in buying the aforementioned land belonging to the late Widow Cane?"

Shady stood, trying to keep his hat steady in his shaking hands. "Your Honor, I can't say I understand all that just happened here." He stared at Mrs. Larkin as if she had suddenly become someone else. "But if we have enough money, we'd still like the land."

"And do you speak for the township of Manifest?"

Shady looked around the room. One by one, they stood. Donal MacGregor, Hadley Gillen, Mama Santoni. The Akkersons and the Cybulskises. Mr. Matenopoulos and Mr. Keufer. Velma T. and Hattie Mae. Mrs. Larkin and the rest of the courtroom.

Finally, Shady answered. "No, Your Honor. I think the township of Manifest speaks for itself."

HATTIE MAE'S
NEWS AUXILIARY

OCTOBER 2, 1918

What a turn of events we had yesterday at the courthouse. I won't go into detail summing it up, because I think nearly every citizen of Manifest was there to see it for himself.

However, much has taken place since then. This reporter was present at the first meeting of the newly formed Manifest Township Committee, on which a member of each fraternal organization holds a seat. Their first item of business involved Arthur Devlin, hat in hand, negotiating new working codes and payment arrangements for the mine workers in exchange for access to the vein running under the town's land. It was a proud and moving day for all present.

I am also pleased to announce the plans for our First Annual Manifest Homecoming Celebration. The festivities will take place on Sunday three weeks hence, on the newly acquired property formerly belonging to the Widow Cane. Springs and all! Some of you may not know that after Lester Burton realized he'd be paying some hefty taxes on plain old springwater, he accepted an offer from the town to buy his spring at a fraction of the price he paid for it.

The various fraternal organizations are working together to beautify the area around the spring with flower beds and benches and are building a special fountain so that all might come and partake. Even though the water has not been proven to contain any special properties, it *was* used in the elixir that seems to have helped many people overcome the sickness still plaguing so many outside Manifest. Maybe it's healing water after all.

As for news from abroad, I had tea and cookies yesterday at Koski's Diner with Mr. Fred Macke, on a purely professional basis, and he said that at the capitol building in Topeka, where he is the assistant to the assistant, there is much talk of armistice and a possible end to the war in Europe.

Who knows, maybe our young men in arms are closer to the homecoming we have all been praying for.

Remember, for all the whos, whats, whys, whens, and wheres you don't even know you need to know, turn to

HATTIE MAE HARPER
Reporter About Town

PVT. NED GILLEN

MONT BLANC
OCTOBER 4, 1918

Dear Jinx,

What's doins in Manifest, kid? Big orange harvest moon in your piece of sky yet? Rainy here lately, skies cloudy. With the cold that's been settling in on us at night, I'm figuring it's October, though I've lost track of the days.

We've had a rough go of it lately. Our regiment is down to about half strength. Had our share of casualties because of this awful war. But we've had just as many guys taken out with dysentery and influenza. It's like their bodies are so worn out, once a sickness gets hold of them, it just gets worse and worse till they're gone. Heck, Holler, and me aren't sure how we've stayed ahead of it so far. Velma T.'s elixirs ran out a lifetime ago. Guess we just run so much no bugs can catch us. That's what we like to think, anyway.

Right now just being here makes me think of home.

We're stuck in our trenches. Stuck meaning it's so muddy I'm not sure I could get out if I tried. Rain's let up for now, but with wet clothes and wet blankets, it's almost better if it keeps on coming. Better than the wind picking up and chilling our bones.

So, you're wondering why all this makes me think of home. It's the farthest thing from it.

Up to my neck in mud,
Ned

P.S. later in October

Was running back to my regiment today from a rendezvous with command. Still had a couple miles to go. Tearing through trees, trying to stay in the shadows, I had a bag loaded with cans of beans for the fellas. A branch caught the bag and yanked it open. My buddies hadn't eaten in days, and I wasn't leaving without those rations. I had the bag half full when I saw him: a German foot soldier six feet away, eyeballing me through the sights of his gun. Nothing but our own puffs of frosty air between us. I was as good as dead, and for the life of me, all I could think to say was Ich habe widerlich footen. *I knew that wouldn't help. So, with nothing to lose but those beans, I just kept picking them up, slowly, one after another. Old Jerry lowered his gun and said two words before walking away. Two words, Jinx.* "Zuhause gehst." Go home.

Don't I wish, buddy. Don't I wish.

The Jungle

AUGUST 11, 1936

The night air was hot and humid as it hung in my room. The sheets clung to the sweat on my legs, so I threw them off in a crumpled mess at the foot of the bed. Even Ned's letter curled with the damp as I read it for the umpteenth time. I turned off my lamp and moved aside the limp curtains, thinking of Ned and looking for the big orange harvest moon he'd written of. There was only a sliver of moon to be found.

The mementos had added up on the windowsill. I'd studied them so often they had become private treasures to me. Reminders of the stories they'd come from. The cork, the Wiggle King fishing lure, the Liberty Head silver dollar, even little Eva Cybulskis's tiny wooden nesting doll.

I took the only remaining item from the Lucky Bill cigar box. The skeleton key. Miss Sadie had revealed nothing about it. *What lock did it fit into?* I wondered. *Or better yet, what skeletons was it hiding?*

I felt myself drifting off into sleep, the key conjuring up images of things hidden in my mind. Music flowed in and out of those images. Harmonica music.

I sat up as the music seemed to call me, to invite me. I slipped my shoes on and padded outside in my pajamas, following the sweet, soulful sound. It was dark and tree branches and bramble reached for me. The music grew louder, and as I rounded the bend near the train tracks, I felt the warmth radiating from the bonfire, saw the glow on the rough and ragged faces. I knew exactly where I was. People living on the road call it The Jungle.

Gideon says wandering souls tend to walk the same roads. For a lot of folks all over the country, those roads pass through places like this. Places where people who have no home, no money, no hope gather together of an evening to share a fire and maybe some beans and coffee. Where somebody leaves a mirror and a razor behind in a tree so the next fella can catch a quick shave. Where, for a time, they might not feel quite so alone.

Shady sat among them, playing the harmonica, letting the notes drift around these men like a bedtime song. When he stopped, he said, "Anyone for another cup of coffee? There's plenty here, gentlemen." They held out their cups and Shady filled them.

I watched from the bushes for a time, knowing I'd been wrong about Shady and his drinking. He would come back to the house in the morning with bloodshot eyes from the sleepless night and the smoky fire. His whiskers wouldn't be shaved because ten other men had used his razor. He'd take a lie down for a while, then go back to gathering some extra odds and ends that someone might need along his way.

For some reason, I wasn't able to look away. Was this what those men considered home? Eventually, I made my way back to Shady's place and once more looked out at the sliver of moon, thinking again about Ned's letter. His cold nights in the trenches, wet and lonely. His talk of home. I thought of Gideon and wondered where he was tonight. Was he hunkered down with a few men by a fire? Was he eating a warm meal of beans and coffee? Was he thinking of me?

Don't I wish, buddy. Don't I wish.

Remember When

AUGUST 12, 1936

The response to the Remember When contest was better than we'd expected. Folks from all around town turned in their remembrances written out on notepaper, receipts, napkins, even toilet paper. It seemed everyone had a funny anecdote to share or a touching memory of a loved one.

Hattie Mae said that since the contest was our idea, we could help judge the entries. So Lettie, Ruthanne, and I huddled together in the mail room of the *Manifest Herald,* poring over letter after letter, often so caught up in the stories that we'd forget to study the handwriting and have to look over a stack again.

Hattie Mae printed as many as she could in the paper before the winner would be announced.

Remember When . . .

. . . you could watch Mary Pickford, Douglas Fairbanks, or Charlie Chaplin in a moving picture show at the Empire Nickelodeon for a nickel. . . . Mama Santoni played the organ, and during *The Eyes of the Mummy*, she got me so anxious with her scary music, I spilled my lemon fizz and everyone thought I wet my pants.

Rosa (Santoni) McIntyre

. . . Mr. Devlin was the first person in town to buy a Model T Ford, and a week later, Mrs. Devlin, on her way home from the Women's Temperance League tea, drove that tin lizzie into Bonner Lake. That must have been some tea!

Andre Matenopoulos

. . . we kids used to march around town, singing, *"Tramp, tramp, tramp, the boys are marching. I spy Kaiser at the door. We'll get a lemon pie, and we'll squish it in his eye. And there won't be any Kaiser anymore."*

Stucky Cybulskis

. . . the Bone Dry Bill was passed, outlawing all alcohol in Kansas. . . . Most of us didn't remember it then either.

Anonymous

. . . Sister Redempta delivered three babies in one day. I was baby number three. I hope she's ready when my baby comes next March!

Betty Lou (Carlson) Mayes

. . . Mr. Underhill made a tombstone for Proky Nesch, the milkman. He got the date of birth right, which was in 1862, but had to redo the name, because as everyone but Underhill knew, Proky was the son of staunch abolitionists and "Proky" was short for Emancipation Proclamation.

Getty (short for Gettysburg) Nesch

. . . when Otis Akkerson got thrown from his horse and ended up facedown in Mr. Cybulskis's pigsty?

Harry Akkerson

. . . yeah, well, it wouldn't have happened if Harry Akkerson hadn't been riding his bike alongside and spooked my horse with his ding-a-ling bicycle bell. Remember that?

Otis Akkerson

The names especially caught my eye. I knew these people. These names had become familiar to me, like friends, through Miss Sadie's stories. Even Betty Lou Mayes from the beauty shop. I'd recognized her when she'd visited Miss Sadie's house, but didn't realize that her maiden name was Carlson. She must be Heck and Holler's sister. And she's not barren after all!

It was like putting together a big family tree. And even though I wasn't familiar with the tales they told, I felt like I wasn't just reading about them. It was more like remembering them. As if somehow their memories were becoming mine.

"Here, read this one," Lettie said, passing me a prescription slip from the office of Dr. Dennis Monahan.

> Remember when Margaret Evans and I tied for senior class president and we drew straws to decide the winner? I wanted the post but she was the better man.
>
> *Doc Monahan*

The sad mixed with the sweet and set a warm feeling in my stomach. But would there be one about Gideon?

I drew another out of the pile. This one came all the way from Sioux Falls, South Dakota.

> Remember when Ned Gillen won first place in the state track races? That kid could outrun trouble—and he needed to, what with the company he kept.
>
> *Holler Carlson*

A few days went on like this, with more and more memories coming in. Then, the day of the deadline, Mr. DeVore delivered a new stack of envelopes. Lettie, Ruthanne, and I all started in opening a few when Lettie gave a gasp. She turned a little pale and, without a word, handed the paper to Ruthanne.

"Well, I'll be dipped in sugar." Ruthanne handed me the note written in straight up-and-down letters that looked like they were plodding across the page. "We found our match!"

To whom it may concern,
I have read your recent columns regarding past goings-on in this town. I should think you would be more responsible with the information you print in the publication you choose to call a newspaper. I have no such recollection of ever having mistakenly engraved a name on any tombstone, let alone a name as ridiculous as Proky. Furthermore, whoever would name their offspring after the Emancipation Proclamation should blame themselves for any misprint.

Mr. Underhill

"So Mr. Underhill is the Rattler?" I asked in disbelief. "He's creepy enough, but he just doesn't seem the Rattler type."

"Yeah, he seems more like a lizard or a toad," Lettie agreed.

"But it's here in black and white," said Ruthanne. "It's the same handwriting that was on the note at the tree house telling us to leave well enough alone."

We all stared at the notepaper. There was his handwriting, with the last letter trailing off . . . like a dying breath.

Miss Sadie's Divining Parlor

AUGUST 23, 1936

I was so excited to be the bearer of such important news that I ran all the way back to Shady's place. I planned to tell him the whole story of how we'd been searching for the Rattler all summer and we'd found him. So I was disappointed to find him gone. I can't say I was surprised, though, now that I knew what kept him busy at odd hours.

Still, I was itching to tell somebody. So I skedaddled over to Miss Sadie's and tromped up her stairs and into her house.

"Miss Sadie, guess what?" I called. "Miss Sadie?" I said again, looking first in the parlor and then in the kitchen. I saw her through the window, sitting on the back porch. "Miss Sadie," I said, bounding outside, "you'll never guess what happened. We found out who the Rattler is. At least, we think he's the Rattler. It's Mr. Underhill. He left a note at the tree house and we had a contest—"

Miss Sadie hadn't even looked at me. She just sat rocking.

Her hair lay loose on her shoulders, unbrushed. Her face looked dull and ashen. I thought maybe her leg was bothering her, as it seemed to be redder and oozier than ever.

I stepped closer. "Can I get you some cool water and your ointment? Would you like that, Miss Sadie?" I said quietly.

"The ointment does not help. There is too much sickness inside and it festers."

I went ahead and got a glass of water and the balm, even though I knew she was right. When the gash on my leg got bad and I was delirious with fever, the doctor had to lance it open to let out all the infection.

I gently dabbed on the salve, telling her about Mr. Underhill. She nodded but stared off disinterestedly. "Things are not always what they seem."

"What do you mean? You don't think it's him?"

"The line between truth and myth is sometimes difficult to see." As her voice got heavier, and her rocking more rhythmic, I could feel her heading into a story. "As much as we wanted it to be true, it was nothing but a myth."

What was she talking about? What had been a myth? My insides got tight. I wasn't sure I wanted to know.

But she went on. "Who would dare think the outcast and abandoned can find a home? Who would dream that one can love without being crushed under the weight of it? A miracle cure to heal the sick? Pah. What makes us think any of this could be true? And yet all of us, we participate in this myth, we create it, perpetuate it."

Miss Sadie's voice grew deep under the weight of the story.

"But what is worse—we believe it. And in the end, we are crushed by it. . . ."

Homecoming

OCTOBER 27, 1918

Saturday, the day before the homecoming festivities, was cool and overcast, but no one seemed to mind as everyone busied themselves with preparations for the big event.

Along with the changing color of leaves came a vibrant spirit among the people of Manifest. Men set up booths, hung strings of electric lights, and put the final coat of paint on the new gazebo. It was to be a grand affair, complete with a barbershop quartet, pony rides, caramel apples, a pie-baking contest, a bocce tournament, and an evening promenade under the stars. The women were busy baking, rolling, simmering their specialties. Whether they made Greek baklava, French galettes, Italian bread, or German bierochs, all wanted to impress the others.

Word had spread that Mrs. Cybulskis had gone into labor, and everyone saw it as a good sign that their First Annual Homecoming Celebration would also be welcoming a new life. They even dared to believe that their sons at war would soon return.

Jinx walked past the tented booths, through the open field near Shady's place, and watched Paulie Santoni explain the rules of bocce to a group of young men. Paulie held a large hedge apple in his hand.

"Now, the first thing you should know is, the Italians, we invented the game of bocce."

"Is this not just an overgrown game of marbles?" called out a young Frenchman.

Paulie grimaced. "No. Bocce takes true skill and years of practice. Let me explain." He displayed the hedge apple. "Think of this as a bocce ball. You roll the ball and try to get it closest to the jack ball in the circle." He cradled the hedge apple gently in his hands. "The ball, she requires finesse and caressing, you know, like a lady. This is why the Italians are so good at bocce. Watch. You don't want to knock her out. Merely brush her cheek." He curled the hedge apple behind him and let it fly a little harder than planned, knocking the smaller jack out of the circle.

The other young men—Frenchmen, Germans, Swedes, Greeks—all laughed. One boisterous Scot yelled, "Aye, that's *amore.*"

Out of the corner of his eye, Jinx saw Sheriff Dean watching him. As if that wasn't uncomfortable enough, he couldn't shake the feeling that someone else was also watching him. Someone in the shadows.

Just then, Jinx met up with Shady, glancing past him at the sheriff. Shady handed Jinx a pretzel, keeping a sausage for himself. "Compliments of Mrs. Akkerson." He followed Jinx's gaze. "Looks like you have a watchdog."

Jinx took a bite and muttered with his mouth full, "Yeah, he watches every move I make, hoping I'll do something he can arrest me for."

"Word's spread all over Manifest and beyond that you're a con man par excellence," Shady observed. "But the sheriff looks like he's got more on his mind than cons."

Jinx was quiet for a moment. "Shady, you've been real good to me. I think you should know I've got a few skeletons in my closet."

Shady took a knife from his pocket, cut a chunk of sausage, and squinted across the field at Sheriff Dean. "Well"—he popped the bite into his mouth—"what do you say we throw the sheriff a bone?"

Jinx smiled. "What do you have in mind?"

"Just meet me over in the clearing, by that big sycamore tree where we were selling the elixir. Act like you're up to something and make sure the sheriff follows you."

A few minutes later, Jinx pulled his hat down over his eyes and gave a furtive look this way and that, then set off through the trees. He walked slowly and stopped every once in a while to make sure he heard the sheriff's footsteps behind him.

As Jinx came upon the grassy opening, he saw Shady lowering himself into the grave that had never been filled after the quarantine.

"Shady," Jinx whispered in a not-quiet voice.

"Over here," Shady whispered back equally loudly.

"Here." Shady handed Jinx a gallon jug with a cork stopper. "We'd best get rid of these before the sheriff finds out there's still some left."

"Too late for that," the sheriff said, peering down at Shady.

Shady scratched the back of his neck like he'd been caught red-handed. "There's just these two jugs left, Sheriff. How's about one for you and one for us?"

Sheriff Dean shook his head. "Now, Shady. I thought you were swearing off the stuff." He took up one jug and reached for the other. "I think I'd better keep the kit and the caboodle." Sheriff Dean uncorked one jug and gave it a sniff. "So, this is two parts alcohol and one part elixir? Smells a little funny, but after a couple stiff drinks, who'll know the difference?"

He replaced the cork and started to walk away, then called back over his shoulder, "But don't think I won't still have my eye on you, boy."

When the sheriff was gone, Jinx gave Shady a hand up. "I thought I'd moved all the bottles that were left. I put 'em under lock and key, like you said. What was in those jugs?"

"A new elixir." Shady stuck a cigar in his mouth. "One part alcohol. Two parts prune juice."

That evening, everyone was so busy putting on their finishing touches at the homecoming grounds that no one noticed when a beat-up old motor scooter chugged its way into town, spitting out a plume of smoke in front of the jail. A wiry man stepped off the bike as if it was his trusty steed. He removed his goggles from his dusty face, revealing clean white around his eyes that made him look like a raccoon.

Sheriff Dean stood in the doorway of the jail, nursing a mug of Shady's brew. "Why, Sheriff Nagelman, what brings you to our fair state? If I recall, the Kansas side is a little out of your Missouri jurisdiction."

"Knock it off, Ed. I don't have all day. Now, where's the boy?"

"Ah, Leonard, what kind of greeting is that for your brother-in-law?"

Nagelman lit a cigarette, realizing that he wasn't going to be able to rush Sheriff Dean.

"How's life in the big city?" Sheriff Dean asked.

"Just peachy." Nagelman flicked his ashes. "Now, if we're done with the chitchat, I have a cell and maybe even a noose waiting for a certain degenerate you're harboring in this town."

Sheriff Dean took another draw from his mug. "What makes you so sure that kid, Jinx, is your man? Besides, I thought you were looking for a pair."

"One of the church elders came through here last week and said he saw the same boy who was "cured" during the tent revival. If I can catch one, I'll get him to rat out the other. And then Louise Haskell will quit yapping at me about finding the person who killed her nephew, Junior. Besides, I got to string somebody up and he's as good as any."

"Why didn't your church elder report it to me? After all, I am the sheriff here."

"He said there was no sheriff to be found." Nagelman looked at the mug in Sheriff Dean's hand and the jug at his feet. "You must have been otherwise engaged. But who would expect any different from a no-account sheriff of a no-account town?" Sheriff Nagelman took one last puff of his cigarette, then crushed the stub under his foot. "Now, can we go?"

Sheriff Dean thought for a minute, then swallowed the last of his drink. "All right. Follow me."

Jinx had been helping Mama Santoni and little Rosa hoist a big black pot over the fire pit so it would be ready for the simmering tomato sauce the next day, when he caught sight of Sheriff Dean and the goggle-eyed sheriff he recognized from Joplin.

"Now, you come to our house to eat," Mama urged as they finished.

"I can't just now, but thank you. I've got to run." And he did. Jinx ran away from the festival grounds and into the woods, fear rising in him. Maybe if he'd just lie low, Sheriff Nagelman would give up looking and go back to Joplin. As he reached the clearing near the creek, he stopped short.

A man stood in front of him, blocking his way.

"You've been busy, haven't you, boy?"

Jinx stood still, his eyes darting this way and that as he looked for a way to escape.

"What's the matter? Don't you have anything to say to your uncle Finn?"

"I thought we were going our separate ways."

"I bet that's what you thought, now that you're all cozy here. You think you've found a home, don't you?" Finn took a step closer while Jinx inched out of the trees into the clearing. "I seen the sign outside of town. How's it read? 'Manifest—a town with a rich past and a bright future.' I shot a few holes in that theory." Finn pulled a gun from his jacket and admired its gleam. "I've been watching you, the way you latched on to folks around here."

Jinx thought of the night in the abandoned mine shaft when he thought he'd seen Finn. And other times, when he'd felt like someone just out of sight was watching him.

Finn shook his head. "You are something else, boy. I take care of you and your mama—"

"You never lifted a hand to help my mother." Jinx's face flushed with anger. "You just used me and waited for her to die. I'm not going with you, Finn. These folks are my family now."

Finn's smile vanished and his face contorted into an angry scowl. "These people don't even know you. Have you told them that you're nothing but a jinx? That bad luck follows you everywhere and people all around you end up in bad straits or dying? First your daddy, then your mama, then Junior. I'm surprised no one around here has been touched by your curse, but then, it's only a matter of time, ain't that right, Jinx?"

Jinx winced as Finn's words hit their mark.

"That's right," Finn continued. "I'm the only one's free of your hoodoo curse and you're trying to shed me like a snakeskin. Well, let me tell you, boy, blood is thicker than water, and I'm the only blood you got."

Jinx shook his head. He wanted Finn to shut up. "My mother was out of her mind with sickness. She'd never have left me with you. All you wanted was a hired hand. Every con needs a mole, isn't that right? Well, I'm done. You're on your own."

Jinx and Finn were standing in the clearing surrounded by a circle of trees and bushes, cutting them off from the town, from Shady's place, from help. There was a rustle of leaves and a loud snap in the distance, but no one came. It must have been a coon or a badger getting caught in a hunter's trap. Every creature had a basic instinct for survival, but for that poor critter, there was no getting away.

Jinx's own survival instincts were charged. He knew he wasn't going back with Finn. "I'll tell them. I'll turn myself in and tell them it was an accident. And I'll tell them you were there."

Finn nodded. For a second Jinx thought he might actually leave. Then, in one swift movement, Finn grabbed Jinx, twisted him around, and shoved the gun into his back. "Well, now, that'd be a lie. Because it wasn't no accident."

"What do you mean?"

"I mean I killed him on purpose. I just put the knife in your hand so you'd wake up with it. You should have known you didn't do it, boy. You don't have the guts."

Jinx felt a flood of relief, which was quickly followed by anger. "Let me go."

"I can't. Junior threatened me and he had it coming. And now you threatened me. This'll make things real simple. I'll tell the sheriff it was you that killed Junior, and when I said I was going to turn you in, there was a fight and"— Finn cocked the gun—"well, you can see how things will turn out from there. Move into those trees."

Jinx struggled to get away, but Finn held firm. Darkness surrounded them as they entered the thick grove of trees encircling the clearing. Jinx walked forward a few paces, then stopped, not able to see where he was going. Then he sensed a movement just in front of them. He could tell by the way Finn's body tensed behind his that he had heard something.

They both backed up a step, then another, as a dark figure moved toward them. There was a faint rattling sound. The figure moved in an eerie, flowing way as it drove them back toward the clearing.

Jinx felt Finn's grip loosen, then heard a loud snap. He was free. He could get away. But before he could turn around, the gun went off. Jinx felt pain cut through him for only an instant, then he fell and the world went dark.

The following afternoon was warm and aglow with the oranges, reds, and yellows of fall leaves. Most of the Manifest townspeople could be found strolling the grounds of the homecoming celebration, enjoying these days of Indian summer. But everyone knew that an Indian summer could only last so long. A lot of things could only last so long. That afternoon also found three men who stood around an open grave. The same open grave Jinx and Shady had used the day before for their prank on Sheriff Dean. Shady, Donal MacGregor, and Hadley Gillen lowered the casket six feet down.

Sheriff Dean and Sheriff Nagelman approached the grave site just as Shady was finishing his few words of eulogy. "And, Lord, we ask your blessing on this soul, who was with us such a short time. May he rest in peace."

Then Donal lifted a shovel to begin replacing the earth into the grave.

Miss Sadie's Divining Parlor

AUGUST 23, 1936

"What?" I cried. "That can't be right. You've got the story wrong." Hot tears filled my eyes and my words sputtered out all angry and sad, like water sizzling on a hot tin pan. "Jinx didn't die. He grew up and lived a life." *And had a daughter. Me.* I didn't say the last part out loud but that was the thread I'd been weaving throughout the summer. I'd come to know Jinx in a way I didn't even know my own father, who was so far away. It had been such a consolation to me to get wrapped up in Jinx's story. To grow to love him and care about him. To wish and hope that maybe he'd grown up and become my daddy. That he was loyal and faithful and true. And he'd never leave his daughter behind.

But if Jinx was gone, then he couldn't be Gideon. And that meant I'd lost Gideon all over again. I was alone again.

Miss Sadie just kept rocking, waiting for me to sort things through on my own. What was it she'd said earlier?

The line between truth and myth is sometimes difficult to see. Was that all this had been? A myth? Just a tall tale from long ago that didn't have anything to do with me?

I knew the choice in front of me. I could walk out of that divining parlor right then and be done with it all. I could leave Miss Sadie behind and never come back. But I knew these people. Jinx and Ned and Velma T., Shady and Hattie Mae. Even Mrs. Larkin. They'd become part of me. And I loved them. What else had Miss Sadie said? "Who would dream that one can love without being crushed under the weight of it?"

I stiffened my back and sat up straight. The story was about real people who had lived and loved. And in some way I had been allowed into their world. And they had welcomed me. The only way I could give back was to be faithful to the story. To hear it to the end. I would be faithful. Even if it crushed me.

Miss Sadie sensed my resolve and picked up where she'd left off.

"Donal lifted a shovel to begin replacing the earth into the grave. . . ."

St. Dizier

OCTOBER 27, 1918

"Wait," Nagelman said, holding up a hand. He looked at the gravestone that lay flat on the ground. "This isn't his name."

Shady spoke up. "It's his given name. Nobody's born with a name like Jinx."

Sheriff Nagelman looked skeptical. He motioned to Sheriff Dean. "Make sure it's the kid."

The Manifest sheriff took Donal's shovel and lifted the lid of the coffin. He gazed down with intent, looking right into the dead face of Finn Bennett and wondered at his missing foot.

Shady, Donal, and Hadley looked at one another in defeat. They hadn't anticipated anyone's opening the coffin.

Sheriff Dean's jaw clamped tightly onto his toothpick. He rubbed his whiskers and studied the body. Then he closed the lid, handed the shovel back to Donal, and said firmly, "That's him."

"Good enough," said Sheriff Nagelman, brushing his hands as if he'd just taken out the trash. He offered his hand to Sheriff Dean. "I guess things worked out for the best."

"I'd say so," Sheriff Dean answered, arms folded.

"Right." Sheriff Nagelman withdrew his unshaken hand and left.

As soon as Sheriff Nagelman was a fair distance away, Shady, Hadley, and Donal let out a collective breath. Then they all set their uncomprehending eyes on Sheriff Dean.

"Where's the boy?" Sheriff Dean asked.

"He's back at my place, resting," said Shady. "Gunshot went through his shoulder and he blacked out for a time. He's being tended to. Should be fine."

Sheriff Dean motioned to the coffin. "And who's the stiff?"

"He's the one who really killed that fellow in Joplin and tried to blame it on Jinx. He came after the boy and got spooked by something. Stepped into one of Louver Thompson's coon traps, then fell back and hit his head on a rock. I wouldn't wish such an end on anyone, but this man was a bad seed."

Sheriff Dean thought for a moment. "That explains the missing foot. Still in the trap, I expect."

Again, Shady, Hadley, and Donal stared, dumbfounded, at the sheriff.

He seemed to enjoy their confusion and eventually removed the toothpick from his mouth. "I may not be the most straight and narrow sheriff in town, but last I checked

I'm the only sheriff in town. And no cocky city sheriff's going to come in and run the show." He replaced the toothpick in his mouth. "I'd best get going. Shady, that libation you gave me yesterday isn't setting too well with my constitution," he said, and walked off.

After a full minute of the three men watching the sheriff leave and looking back and forth at one another, Donal shook his head and said, "Well, I never."

To which the other two responded, "Never."

Then Donal began shoveling dirt into the open grave while Shady read aloud the verse that had been engraved on the tombstone. "The Lord is my Shepherd, I shall not want."

The First Annual Homecoming Celebration began without a hitch. Most people knew nothing of the nighttime escapade or the unusual burial that had taken place that day. They just milled from one booth to another, sampling each other's fine foods, clapping and cheering for their favorites in the sack races, the egg toss, and the bocce tournament, which ended in a draw between the Italians and the Scots, because the hedge apples kept splitting open.

As day turned into night and soft music began, the gentlemen of Manifest took their ladies' hands and escorted them onto the open-air dance floor lit by a canopy of electric lights.

Jinx sat to the side of the stage, his shoulder in a bandage and sling. Shady brought him a glass of punch. Together they watched children scampering about with glowing faces and eventually nodding off in their mothers' arms. Ivan DeVore stole glances at Velma T. across the dance floor as he worked up the nerve to ask her to dance. Hadley Gillen was on the stage, playing first trumpet in the band. Hattie Mae, with no pen or paper in hand, looked splendid in a pink chiffon dress as she danced a waltz with Mr. Fred Macke.

Pearl Ann, home from college, served punch while Mrs. Larkin held court with a bevy of women. The ladies listened with rapt attention to the story of how Mrs. Larkin and the boy, Jinx, had cooked up the scheme of tricking Lester Burton into buying the springs and how it had been her idea not to tell anyone, including Shady, of their plans. Mrs. Larkin had done some theater work in high school. She had, in fact, played the lead in the senior class production of *All on Account of Polly* and was confident she could pull off her part, but felt they'd get a better performance out of Shady if he was unapprised.

People were smiling. Especially Mrs. Cybulskis, who sat to the side of the dance floor, holding a healthy new baby boy. The whole town was filled with the hope and promise that the hard times were behind them.

Until the army truck pulled in.

At first people thought it was just a latecomer to the dance. But when the young man, dressed in a crisp brown uniform, stepped out of his automobile, they knew otherwise. The music died out with a painful moan. The soldier made his way into the crowd. He showed a paper to Mr. Matenopoulos, who motioned toward the band platform.

Hadley stood, waiting for the news.

"Are you Mr. Hadley Gillen?" the soldier asked.

Hadley nodded.

The man spoke a few quiet words and handed Hadley

an envelope. Hadley held the envelope for a moment, then passed it to Shady. "Read it, Shady. To all of us."

Shady read.

"REGRET TO INFORM YOU, YOUR SON NED GILLEN WAS KILLED IN ACTION OCTOBER EIGHTH STOP HIS BODY RECOVERED IN ARGONNE REGION SOUTH FRANCE STOP LAID TO REST IN ST. DIZIER STOP PERSONAL EFFECTS TO FOLLOW STOP."

A deathly silence became the music that reverberated throughout. The town of Manifest had loved Ned Gillen. And now the town of Manifest was crushed under the weight of that love.

But the boy, Jinx. It buried him.

PVT. NED GILLEN

OCTOBER 6, 1918

Dear Jinx,

Took a piece of shrapnel in the arm yesterday. Didn't even see it coming, but it was just a scratch. So not to worry. Today was a good day. Whenever we quit running or fighting long enough to look around, France turns out to be a beautiful place. Seems like all we've been seeing lately is our own muddy green uniforms, so the bright fall leaves are like a colorful kaleidoscope.

Stopped for a spell today on the roadside. A group of fresh replacements sauntered past. Talk about colors. They were greener than green. Jaunty clean-cut fellas, walking like they had someplace to be. Heck, Holler, and me sat there, all of us thinking those boys reminded us of someone. Could it be someone from home? Was there still such a place? Then we realized it was us *back in June. "Did we ever look like that?" I asked. Heck answered, "Yeah, when we were in the sixth grade." Then, true to his name,*

Holler yelled out, "What's your hurry, ladies? The senior promenade was last week." In a bygone day, we'd have laughed one of those laughs that keeps going on after you forget what was so funny. But that doesn't happen anymore.

We've been on a two-day hike and have had the good fortune to come across trenches already dug. You can tell a lot about a man by the trench he digs for himself. Some are shallow and clumpy. Others are well dug and roomy enough for two. Kind of feels like sleeping in someone else's bed for a spell, but I always feel a debt of gratitude to whoever dug it. Funny thing, it also makes me take a little extra care when I dig one so it might be a place of respite for the next guy to come along.

I'm reminded of a line in a book I read in high school. "It is not down in any map; true places never are." I can guaran-darn-tee you, these foxholes won't be found on any map after the war is over. But for now, my home is wherever me and my buddies lay our heads at night. And where we pray to God we'll wake up in the morning.

There's been some talk of peace. Armistice, they call it. Hope is something most of us have been none too familiar with lately. Some men try to fight it off like a bad cold. Others let it wrap around them like a blanket. Me? It creeps quietly into my dreams and it looks like Pop, and you, and home.

Vive la nuit *(Long live the night),*
Ned

The Shadow of Death

AUGUST 23, 1936

Miss Sadie stared ahead. This time she lingered in the story after she told it, as if she was looking for a different ending.

Even though she had not told me to go, I stood and started out the door. Then, turning back, I took the compass from the hook on which it had hung all summer. My work here was finished. It felt like we'd all done enough.

I can't say I knew where I was heading when I stepped off her porch and walked down the Path to Perdition. I knew when I got to the end of the path that there was no place else for me to go. I wandered around a little but eventually found the tombstone I'd come across the day Lettie, Ruthanne, and I had been frog hunting. The one all by itself in the clearing, near an old craggy sycamore tree.

I studied the letters on the tombstone, letting them tell me their story. Letting them help me make sense of something that made no sense. The letters spelled out my father's name. Gideon Tucker. That was my father. The boy, Jinx. They were one and the same, as I'd wondered about and hoped for all along.

Sitting down with my back against the stone, I took the compass from my pocket and opened the latch. Inside were the words I'd mistaken for the compass maker's name. Now I knew them for what they were. ST. DIZIER. OCTOBER 8, 1918. This was Ned's compass, on which Gideon had engraved Ned's date of death and place of burial. Because for my father, that was the day he began his wanderings in the valley of the shadow of death.

I sat mourning the loss of Ned, a young soldier at arms. Grieving the death of a town. Wishing for my father, who was still wandering.

My tears had been falling for some time when Shady came for me. He stood beside me, stroking my hair.

"He thought it was his fault, didn't he, Shady? Because he helped Ned raise the twenty-five dollars to join the army underage and then Ned was killed. Because he thought he was a jinx."

"I suppose."

"So what happened that night? After the telegram came about Ned?"

Shady sat down beside me. "He left and never came back. With Ned gone, I suppose he felt he'd done the one thing the town couldn't forgive him for. We didn't blame him. No, sir. There was nothing to forgive him for. The problem was we couldn't forgive ourselves."

"For what?"

"For not being able to live up to what we'd convinced

ourselves of. That there was something special about Manifest. That we could overcome our past and start over."

"What about the springwater, the metal ore in the
ground?"

"Some of us started believing our own tale. That it might
be healing water, hallowed ground. But it was just water and
dirt, plain and simple."

"But the elixir. It saved lives."

"It helped people feel better for a while. Until the worst
wave of the influenza hit just a few weeks later. The deadly
one. Then it was beyond what any elixir could cure."

I let his words sink in, then stood up. "Show me."

Shady took my hand and walked no more than twenty
feet from where we'd been sitting. Pushing aside a few
branches, he made an opening in a row of bushes. And there
they were. Dozens of tombstones surrounded by dense
shrubs and weeds. Bodies set apart from the town cemetery
because of the deadly disease that had killed them. This was
no-man's-land.

I walked from stone to stone, feeling the loss of each person. Judge Carlson. Callisto Matenopoulos. Mama Santoni.
Even little Eva Cybulskis. It seemed no family had been left
untouched. Donal MacGregor and Greta Akkerson. And
Margaret Evans, senior class president, class of 1918. Shady
said she'd been the first to die of the influenza in Manifest. All
died in November of 1918.

Then the name that was probably the hardest of all to believe: Mrs. Eudora Larkin. In my mind, she'd been so vigor-
ous, so staunch, that surely if death was to approach her, she
would give it a good tongue-lashing and send it on its way.

But as Miss Sadie had said, "Things are not always what

they seem." It was clear death had come to Manifest and would not be brushed aside.

I felt Shady pull me away. "Come along, Miss Abilene. You've seen enough. Let's go home."

The word struck me as odd. *Home.* That was a word I didn't know the meaning of. "I think I'd like some coffee. Strong coffee."

Shady understood. He took me along the railroad tracks to the bend by the woods. Back to the Jungle, where there were faces familiar to me. People lost and wandering. Like Gideon. Like me.

I sat at the fire and received nods of welcome from the men camped there for the night. Shady handed me a tin cup. The hot coffee scalded me as I sipped.

No wonder Gideon had started closing in on himself. Looking back, I thought it started not when I had been cut, but when I'd turned twelve. I was growing up and he was probably already worrying about the road being a poor place for raising a young lady. Then, when the accident happened and I got so sick, the world came crashing down around him. He thought he was still a jinx and, one way or another, my life could not be good with him. When I'd cut my leg that day, I'd said the same thing as was written in Ned's letter. *It was just a scratch.* Gideon was afraid and he sent me away.

I took another strong swallow, letting the coffee sear my throat. "He's not coming back, is he?" I asked Shady. "He's going to wander in the valley of the shadow of death all by himself."

Shady stared uncomfortably into his coffee cup, as if searching for a way to answer me.

"When we got the telegram from your daddy saying that you were coming, we knew he must be in a bad way. Maybe I should have told you more about when he was here, but it was so long ago. And when Miss Sadie started her story, it seemed like that might be the best way for you to hear what happened."

I drank the last of my coffee, wincing at the bitterness of it. All the weeks of feeling like Gideon had abandoned me. Trying to catch glimpses of who my father was, to find even one footprint in this town that I could recognize as his. Now I realized that through Miss Sadie, I'd witnessed it all. And I did understand. Gideon hadn't sent me away because he didn't want me. Miss Sadie's words came back to me. "Who would dream that one can love without being crushed under the weight of it?" Hot tears burned in my eyes. *Being* loved could be crushing too.

Shady rubbed his whiskers. "The thing is, none of us realized that *we* needed to hear our stories as much as you did. All those Remember Whens in the paper kind of reminded us of who we were and what brought us together." He filled his own cup of coffee, letting the steam warm his face. "Having you here has given us a second chance."

That made me feel warm inside. "Kind of a do-over?"

"Kind of a do-over."

Shady, Miss Sadie, Hattie Mae. They'd all nurtured and cared for me, hoping that I'd take root in this place.

But I couldn't help looking at the rough faces of the men sitting a respectful distance away. The Jungle. The valley of the shadow of death. Manifest. Gideon. Where did I belong? Where was home? I needed to go once again down the Path to Perdition.

The Shed

AUGUST 24, 1936

The sun was just coming up as I made my way back to Miss Sadie's. I cut over the back fence and marched straight to the shed, knowing it would still be locked up tight. But I held the skeleton key. It hadn't ever been mentioned in Miss Sadie's stories, but in my mind, it had worked its way in on its own. I'd wondered before what skeletons this key was hiding. Well, there couldn't be any more skeletons than in Miss Sadie's shed.

The key fit into the door nice and easy, and with hardly a tug, the door swung open wide. The shed was there, waiting for me to come in. Waiting to reveal what had been hidden and festering for so long.

It was a normal garden shed with pruning shears, buckets, watering cans, and the accompanying assortment of cobwebs, dead bugs, and dust. But there were also ten or twelve jugs. This was where Jinx had stashed the extra elixir under lock and key. And he'd kept the key.

Up high on a shelf, there was a box. I took it down and lifted the lid. I pulled out pictures, grade cards, newspaper clippings, childhood drawings, and school papers. All mementos of a boy. A boy named Ned.

I took my time, absorbing the things Miss Sadie couldn't bring herself to tell me. I walked into the house, and in the kitchen I fetched a bottle of rubbing alcohol and some cotton balls. Then I found a sharp knife and heated it on the cookstove. Miss Sadie was sitting on the front porch, rocking, waiting for me.

"Are you ready?" I said.

"I am ready."

Kneeling beside her, I held the hot blade to her wound and pierced it, letting all the pain flow out. I don't recall if Miss Sadie told the rest of the story to me as I cleaned her wound, or if I told it to her through what I'd pieced together on my own. It doesn't matter. All I know is that her story flowed in and out of mine. And you might say I divined the rest.

The Diviner

It is a story of a young Hungarian woman who comes from a family of diviners. And she has a son.

In her young life she has seen much of pain and suffering. She wants a better life for her son. She will go to America.

Her story is like thousands of others and yet her story is just that: her story. The woman and her son set off on a great journey. They cross the Atlantic Ocean on a big steamer and land at Ellis Island. There, with the huddled masses, she and her son are herded through cattle pens to be examined by doctors for sickness or disease.

In the din of different languages echoing in the room, she hears a voice behind her speaking words she understands. It is Gizi Vajda, a girl from her own village. They have not seen each other in years and here they end up together, in America. Or almost in America.

A doctor looks at their papers, then at the boy. Your name is Benedek, the doctor says.

The boy smiles at hearing his name. He holds out four fingers to tell the doctor how old he is. The doctor pats him on the head. A healthy one, he says, even though the boy does not understand. Then the doctor examines the mother. He checks her eyes. One is red and milky. He writes a *T* on her arm for *trachoma*, an eye infection. It is very contagious, so she will not be permitted to stay. She must return to the boat and sail back.

This cannot be. To have come all this way . . . It is just a cold in her eye. Nothing serious.

But her words are not understood. And her son, she cannot take him back on the boat. He is allowed to stay, so he does not get a return ticket, and she does not have enough money to buy one. Gizi says, I will keep him with me. I have a place to stay in New York. I will give you the address. When your eye is better, you will come back.

The young woman hugs her son, kisses him again and again, and, through her tears, says to be a good boy and she will come back. But how will you find me? he asks. She takes a locket from her neck. Inside is a compass. See? she says to him. This needle always points north. But in here, she says, pointing to her heart, I have a compass that always points to you. No matter where you are, I will find you.

She puts the locket around his neck and Gizi holds his hand while they wave goodbye.

The woman takes the long trip back to Europe. Her eye gets better and she works very hard to make enough money to take the boat ride again. This time she is allowed

into America and goes to the place where Gizi is a seam-
stress for a rich family. But the maid who answers the door
shakes her head. Gizi got very sick. She was in a hospital
for three weeks and died.

But little Benedek. The boy who was with her? The
maid shrugs. She doesn't know where they took him.

For a whole year, the young woman walks the streets of
New York. She knocks on doors of churches, orphanages,
hospitals. No one can help her. No one has seen her son.
Until, one day, she knocks on the door of the Orphanage
of the Good Shepherd. Yes, they had a boy there. His name
was Benedek. But he was put on an orphan train and sent
west.

For many more months the woman's search continues.
As she goes farther west into America, she draws attention.
People frown at her thick accent. They raise their eyebrows
at her dark skin. She tells them she is from a family of diviners, a people who read the signs of land and water. But
they do not understand. She is shunned and called a
Gypsy and a fortune-teller. She asks about a boy and they
hold their children behind them. Then she finds a little town
in southeast Kansas called Manifest. And she finds her son.

But now little Benedek is seven years old. He has been
adopted by Hadley Gillen, who owns a hardware store. The
man loves the boy and the boy is happy. The child speaks
their language as if he does not remember the one he heard
as a baby.

If she reveals herself as his mother, she will bring shame
on him. They will shun him the way she has been shunned.
So what does she do? She does what a diviner does. She
watches. She waits. She loves.

As people come to her for their palms to be read or their fortunes told, she puts on a show. She dresses the part. But what she gives them instead is the truth she observes and knows about them. To the young wife who comes in her grief over not being able to have a child, Miss Sadie gives herbs to calm her fears and open her womb. When the aging grandmother who grows forgetful and fears she is losing her mind comes to her, Miss Sadie, the diviner, comforts her. She pats her hand and tells her that the things she does remember, things from long ago, are as real as what happened yesterday.

But mostly, she watches, she waits, she loves.

Only one woman in the town takes note. Sees her pain. Recognizes the look of a mother watching her son, even from a distance. The nun who is also a midwife. She promises to keep the woman's secret. But she provides her with grade cards, childhood drawings, school papers. She does her best to do what a midwife does. She helps the woman realize, in some small way, her motherhood. She helps the mother keep the promise she made in the peekaboo song she once sang to her son. Where is little boy hiding? Where did little boy go? Mama is always watching you. Where you are, Mama will always know.

But the woman, the mother, she watches, she waits, she loves. And she bears the weight of that love. She bears the loss of her son to war. She bears the story of Manifest. When everyone else is crushed by it, by the loss, the pain. When no one else can bear to remember. She is the keeper of the story. Until someone who needs to hear it comes along. When it will be time to make it known. To manifest. That's what a diviner does.

Beginnings, Middles, and Ends

AUGUST 30, 1936

Over the following days, Lettie, Ruthanne, and I took long walks. They listened as I told them the whole story. About Jinx and Ned, and Miss Sadie, and Gideon. And me.

We talked about other things too. About how the town seemed to have come back to life. All the Remember When stories in the paper had folks talking about the way Manifest used to be. And all the fine memories they had. And how people used to take care of each other. There were tears too, but they seemed to be healing tears.

We talked about how Ivan DeVore, the postmaster, had finally worked up the nerve to ask Velma T. to the upcoming Second Annual Homecoming Celebration, being held eighteen years after the first one. She said she knew he'd been sending her those anonymous notes all those years, but it wasn't a woman's place to do the asking.

And the women were piecing together another quilt, only

this time, instead of a victory quilt, it was a friendship quilt, and they asked Miss Sadie to make the center square. After all, it wasn't her fault that a young boy's first and only welding job had been to make her a gate with her family name, Redizon, at the top. Those letters that when poorly welded and a little warped, looked more like Perdition.

Mrs. Dawkins at the drugstore gave Lettie, Ruthanne, and me a dollar apiece for our idea of offering free ice-cold water to folks traveling by on the highway. Once we put up the sign that read COME TO MANIFEST FOR FREE ICE-COLD WATER—IT WON'T CURE YOUR ILLS, BUT IT WILL QUENCH YOUR THIRST, the cars started rolling in. Most folks would drink their free ice water and shop a bit before moving on.

The strangest thing was how we found out that Mr. Underhill wasn't the Rattler after all. Oh, he was the one who'd written the note, all right, and he'd tacked it to our tree. He'd seen us watching him in the cemetery that first day when he was measuring out a burial plot. Turned out he'd been cheating folks for years, shorting their coffins and burial plots by six inches to a foot while charging full price. But when he heard we were on a spy hunt, he got real worried. He had been kind of a spy after all. He thought we'd found out that he was the one who'd fed Devlin and Burton information during the fake quarantine. The past week, Hattie Mae had walked into the Better Days Funeral Parlor and said, "Mr. Underhill, you've got some explaining to do." He must have been on pins and needles for a long time, worried that somebody'd find out, because he broke down right then and there and confessed the whole thing.

He was a bit put out when Hattie Mae said she'd only come in to ask him where he got off calling her a hack reporter and had he or had he not started charging by the letter for engraving tombstones after the incident involving Emancipation Proclamation Nesch.

So the Rattler was still at large.

Remember When entries kept coming in. One surprising entry read

> Remember the waterlogged victory quilt? Most people don't know that it was dried and returned to Mrs. Eudora Larkin with a handwritten apology from Ned Gillen and his friend Jinx. They both signed their names in the middle square, right over President Wilson's washed-out signature. It was a lovely gesture and that quilt has been on my divan all these years. But I'm passing it along to a young lady in the care of Shady Howard who has helped us remember who we are and where we come from.
> *Pearl Ann (Larkin) Hamilton*

But it was Heck Carlson who won the Remember When contest. His entry read

> Remember when Manifest seemed a place too far away to ever get back to? A place too good to be real. A place one was proud to call home. Remember? For those of us who made it home, let us always remember. And for those who didn't come home, let us never forget.

But a question remained: where was *my* home? Lettie finally asked what we'd all been avoiding. "Abilene, what are you going to do?"

I hadn't known for sure until I happened to take a closer look at the book I'd accidentally stolen from the high school and had yet to return. For weeks it had sat on my nightstand, apparently waiting patiently to be noticed. And then I noticed it. It was *Moby Dick*, the book Sister Redempta had mentioned when I'd quoted Gideon's saying about home. The same quote Ned had written in his last letter. *It is not down in any map; true places never are.*

I paged through it for a while, looking for those words. I haven't found them yet, as I've got about six hundred pages still to go. But I did find something else. The checkout card taped in the front of the book. There were names that went way back. There was one date stamp: September 12, 1917. Beside it, in a familiar hand, was the name Ned Gillen. And he must have read the whole thing, as he'd checked it out two more times after that.

But it was the next name that made my eyes well up. March 6, 1918—Gideon Tucker. I had found him. I'd found my daddy. And I would find him again.

The morning of August 30 came. It was overcast as the 9:22 chugged into the depot. Lettie and Ruthanne, one on each side of me, walked me to the train station. I wore a pretty lavender smock that Mrs. Evans had made for me out of an old dress that had belonged to her daughter, Margaret. Mrs. Evans said it complemented my auburn hair and hazel eyes. I didn't even know my hair was auburn.

Lettie squeezed my hand. "Are you sure about this, Abilene?"

"I'm sure," I said as the train hissed a steamy sigh. I held tight to my satchel that held the cigar box of mementos and letters.

"You sent him a telegram, didn't you?" asked Ruthanne.

"I did. It was a little vague."

"Then maybe we should all go back to Shady's place," Lettie pleaded.

One after another, travelers started to get off the train. Charlotte Hamilton, Miss Beauty Parlor, pranced her way down the steps and looked at me a little aghast. "Are you still here?"

I just smiled as her mother called from down the platform. I wasn't too worried about Charlotte Hamilton, daughter of Pearl Ann Larkin Hamilton and granddaughter of Mrs. Eugene Larkin, and likely future president of the Daughters of the American Revolution. She came from good stock and she would come around.

Then it appeared that all who were getting off had gotten off. Ruthanne and Lettie looked at me, apparently not knowing what to say.

"Maybe he didn't get the telegram," said Ruthanne.

"That's right. He'll probably be on tomorrow's train," said Lettie.

"No. He won't be on tomorrow's train," I said, staring off down the tracks in the direction the train had just come from. Then, as if those tracks were calling me, I took off running. I felt on solid ground again, hearing the rhythm of my feet pounding against each railroad tie. I made it clear past the shot-up Manifest town sign before I saw him. Anyone worth his salt knows it's best to get a look at a place before it gets a look at you.

He was walking toward me, one railroad tie after another, as if he'd spent the whole summer getting back to me. He looked thin; his clothes hung a little baggy. I knew he'd gotten my telegram. It was probably not that convincing a con but I guess I was banking on the hope that he missed me. The truth is I wasn't sure he would come. I knew he loved me and he'd only left me because he'd thought it was for the best. But for now he was here. Would he stay?

He walked toward me like a man in a desert, looking afraid that what he saw before him might be a mirage that would vanish when he got closer. I stepped up to him, closing the gap, and at last he knelt down and took me in his arms. He held his face next to mine, and when he looked straight into my eyes with tears in his, I knew. And he knew. We were home.

I took his hand and in it was the crumpled-up telegram Ivan DeVore sent for me at no charge.

Western Union
Telegraph Service

DEAR GIDEON TUCKER STOP REGRET TO INFORM YOU OF
THE GRAVE ILLNESS OF YOUR DAUGHTER ABILENE TUCKER
STOP SHE'S PUTTING UP A BRAVE FIGHT BUT THE LUMBAGO
HAS SET IN AND WE FEAR HER TIME IS NEAR DONE STOP
HER LAST WORDS (SO FAR) ARE: HERMAN MELVILLE SHOULD
STICK TO WRITING ABOUT BIG WHITE WHALES, BECAUSE
TRUE PLACES ARE FOUND IN MANY PLACES, INCLUDING ON
MAPS STOP WE THOUGHT YOU MIGHT LIKE TO KNOW SO
THAT YOU CAN COME TO MANIFEST AND PAY YOUR
RESPECTS IN PERSON STOP WE WILL TRY TO KEEP HER ON
ICE UNTIL YOUR SPEEDY ARRIVAL STOP GOOD LUCK AND
GODSPEED STOP

The Rattler

AUGUST 31, 1936

I've been told that every good story has a beginning, a middle, and an end. As Gideon and I sat for a spell, just the two of us, right there on the train tracks, I told him the story I'd needed to hear. And I knew he needed to hear it too, all the way to the end.

I gave him his box of mementos and watched as he fingered each one: the Wiggle King fishing lure, the silver dollar, the cork, little Eva's nesting doll, and the skeleton key. These treasures that had sparked Miss Sadie's stories and led me back to my daddy. Gideon's eyes filled with tears when I gave him Ned's letters, all in a neat bundle and tied with string. He said he'd like to read them one more time; then we would give them to Miss Sadie. It was what we both wanted.

We pieced together some things in the middle. The fact that the spy map wasn't really a spy map at all. It was just Ned's drawing of home, a place he wanted to remember.

And I'd wondered for some time why Shady kept that bottle of whiskey right out in the open but never touched a drop of it. Gideon said it was because sometimes a man's demons could creep up on him. He figured Shady would rather know where his demon was so he could keep an eye on him.

As for the Rattler? There *had been* a mysterious figure known as the Rattler, who had never really been a spy. Just a ghostly figure some would see walking the woods at night, a faint rattling sound accompanying the movement.

But one night had been different—the night Finn met up with Jinx. "Jinx" would be the way I'd always refer to my young father. There were several people in the woods that night. Jinx and Finn were having their argument. Uncle Louver was out setting his raccoon traps. And there was the mysterious shadowy figure that loomed from nowhere, accidentally frightening Finn into stepping in one of Uncle Louver's traps. The fall landed his head on a rock so hard it killed him dead.

Gideon himself couldn't shed any light on this mystery. But I could think of one person who would have been walking in the woods after being called to the Cybulskis house to help deliver a baby. And who might look a little ghostly at night dressed in her flowing black gown. And who rattles when she walks. Oh, I was sure Miss Sadie had done her part in tending Jinx's wound. But a diviner's jewelry jangles. A nun's rosary beads rattle. It's a universal.

With that, I knew I had my story I would turn in on the first day of school. And I formed the first line in my head as Gideon and I walked into town, past the sign with big blue letters: MANIFEST . . . A TOWN WITH A PAST.

HATTIE MAE'S
NEWS AUXILIARY

SEPTEMBER 6, 1936

Like my aunt Mavis used to say, a whistling girl and a cackling hen had better know when to call it quits. Well, it's time for this girl to hang up her reporter's hat. Yes, this will be the final installment of "Hattie Mae's News Auxiliary," and for your years of readership, I am grateful.

But I am pleased as punch to announce that I will be passing the torch to an up-and-coming writer who, according to Sister Redempta, has an eye for the interesting and a nose for news.

This young writer assures me that she will be truthful and certifiable in giving the honest-to-goodness scoop each and every week.

So for all the whos, whats, whys, whens, and wheres, look at the backside of "Hogs and Cattle" every Sunday to your new auxiliary writer—

ABILENE TUCKER
Reporter About Town

AUTHOR'S NOTE

Like many readers of historical fiction, I find it interesting to know what is fact and what is fiction. Sometimes what I find even more interesting is where the fact or fiction came from.

Manifest, Kansas. *Moon Over Manifest* is a story that came from my family roots. The town of Manifest, although very real and vivid in my mind, is both fact and fiction. Manifest is based on the town of Frontenac, Kansas. Originally, I chose the town of Frontenac as the setting for my story because my grandparents were from that area of southeast Kansas. But in doing so, I stumbled upon a community that was rich in color and history.

I decided to change the name of the town to allow more flexibility in what I could include in it, but other than being a bit smaller and having fictional churches and schools, Manifest is basically the same. Frontenac was a mining town that in 1918 was made up of immigrants from twenty-one countries. In fact, at that time, only 12 percent of the people living in Frontenac had parents born in America. Coal mining was the main industry in Frontenac, and family stories tell of company vouchers and the control of the mine in the town.

The Bone Dry Bill of 1917 made Kansas a "dry state." This meant alcohol was illegal in Kansas well before Prohibition took effect nationwide. However, the two counties in the far southeast corner of Kansas, Cherokee and Crawford, often called the Little Balkans, were known to be the bootlegging capital of the Midwest.

Orphan trains. Ned arrived in Manifest on what was known as an orphan train. Many orphaned children found themselves on trains heading from the East Coast to the Midwest, where they were adopted by families they didn't know. Some children, like Ned, were adopted into loving homes; however, not all were as fortunate. Some children were adopted to be used primarily as hired hands on farms or to help out as domestic servants.

Spanish influenza started out as a highly contagious flu that could infect hundreds of people in a matter of hours. Experts believe that it originated at Camp Funston, a military base near Manhattan, Kansas, in March of 1918. Initially, it was not known to be fatal, but after troop ships carried the illness overseas during World War I, the virus mutated into a much deadlier strain. The same troop ships carried the virus back to the United States, and this began the first wave of a worldwide pandemic that took millions of lives before it ran its course.

Immigrants. In my research into immigrants passing through Ellis Island, I did not come across any story like that of Ned and Miss Sadie. However, Ellis Island has been called both the Island of Hope and the Island of Tears. There are countless tales of heartbreak and hardship that immigrants encountered when making their journey to America, not unlike the one I have imagined in this story.

The rest of the story . . .
Of course most of the story is fiction. But even fiction has to come from somewhere. Many elements in the book were inspired by family stories and newspaper articles from regional papers of both 1918 and 1936.

The boot with Finn's foot still in it came from a story my dad told about his work investigating airplane crashes. Among the wreckage at one crash site, he found a boot "with the foot still in it."

The free ice water Mrs. Dawkins gave out came from the story of the couple who started the famous Wall Drug Store in Wall, South Dakota. They advertised free ice water during the Depression, and cars started streaming into town, bringing new business to their struggling community.

The gate to Perdition is based on a real gate that I came across on my research trip to Frontenac. It didn't say *Perdition,* but it did have an assortment of metal objects welded onto it: horseshoes, a pitchfork, a shovel, a spade, and two wagon wheels. I was there in the fall, so it even had two jack-o'-lanterns propped on top.

Real people. There are four characters named in the book who are real people. On the last day of school, Sister Redempta calls the names of students to give them their grades. Two of those students are my grandparents—Mary Hughes and Noah Rousseau. There are only two other relatives from that area whom I knew personally—my grandfather's cousins Velma and Ivan DeVore. They were brother and sister, and neither ever married. I remember them as simple and good-hearted people. I came across Ivan's name in a newspaper article announcing his new position as the Frontenac postmaster in 1934. So Ivan DeVore is the postmaster in the book, and Velma became Velma T. Harkrader, the chemistry teacher.

Galettes. Finally, galettes are a buttery French cookie that my mother made and her mother before her. My grandmother used a heavy cast iron waffle iron set on an open flame. It is a labor-intensive endeavor to bake one or two cookies at a time, but as anybody who has tasted one can tell you, it is well worth the effort.

SOURCES AND SUGGESTIONS
FOR FURTHER READING

Mackin, Elton E. *Suddenly We Didn't Want to Die.* Novato, CA: Presidio Press, 1993.

Minckley, Loren Stiles. *Americanization Through Education.* Frontenac, KS: 1917.

O'Brien, Patrick G., and Peak, Kenneth J. *Kansas Bootleggers.* Manhattan, KS: Sunflower University Press, 1991.

Sandler, Martin W. *Island of Hope: The Story of Ellis Island and the Journey to America.* New York: Scholastic, 2004.

Uys, Errol Lincoln. *Riding the Rails: Teenagers on the Move During the Great Depression.* New York: Routledge, 2003.

ACKNOWLEDGMENTS

All writers strive to create a good story with colorful characters, a vivid setting, and interesting plot twists and turns. But the elusive element is voice. So first and foremost, I want to acknowledge the four people whose voices I have heard from the time and place in which *Moon Over Manifest* is set: my maternal grandparents, Noah and Mary (Hughes) Rousseau, along with my grandfather's cousins Velma and Ivan DeVore. Their voices and their stories, which I heard as a young girl, are the heart and soul of this book. In the same vein, I thank my parents, Leo and Mary Dean Sander. This book is dedicated to them. You often hear writers thanking the people without whom their books could not have been written. My parents taught me not to waste time trying to figure out if I could do something. Just figure out how to get it done. Without their confidence I would have quit . . . many times over. Eventually, I would have even quit quitting. I guess that means I wouldn't even have started. So I thank them, for giving me the fortitude to keep trying and figure out how to get it done.

Thank you to my wonderful agent, Andrea Cascardi, for your friendship and guidance. You are a trouper. To Michelle Poploff, every writer's dream editor. And to her assistant, Rebecca Short. You both made my first experience in publishing a book pleasant and rewarding.

Special thanks to my group of writing friends, Debra Seely, Dian Curtis Regan, and Lois Ruby, for your many readings of this book, both in and out of sequence, for your comments that improved the book, and for your years of support and encouragement. To my friends at the Milton Center—Essie Sappenfield, Jerome Stueart, Mary Saionz, David and Diane Awbrey, David and Virginia Owens, Naomi Hirahara, Gordon Houser, Christie Breault, Nathan Filbert, Bryan Dietrich—all members of my first critique group, where I cut my teeth writing words on a page and listening to what others had to say about them: Thanks for all you had to say.

To Marcia Leonard for her help in shaping this book.

To Kathy Parisio for the phrase she and her siblings made up as kids, which became Miss Sadie's curse: *"Ava grautz budel nocha mole."* I hope my translation of it was acceptable to all. And to Tim Brady for his often-used admonition to our friend Ned Blick in college: "Ned, you're heading down the path to perdition." Of course, if Ned was going, we all wanted to tag along!

To my group of book club girlfriends, who insisted that someday, they would read one of my books for book club. That meant a lot. I wasn't going to name them, but one recently asked to make sure I knew how to spell all their names. So in no particular order, and hopefully spelled correctly—Annmarie Algya, CY Suellentrop, Dawn Chisholm, Julie Newton, Vicki Kindel, Cara Horn, Chandi Bongers, Gigi Phares, Molly Cyphert, Angie Holladay, and Kathy Kryzer.

And to my little sister, Annmarie—because she's a lot of fun and she would be miffed if she didn't get special mention. But really because I will never be able to write about a spunky young girl without her being two-thirds Annmarie.

Finally, there is a small but important group of people who bring joy to every day of my life. Luke, Paul, Grace, and Lucy Vanderpool. You're the best.

And really finally, to my husband, Mark. For being always true blue.

ABOUT THE AUTHOR

Clare Vanderpool grew up reading books in unusual places: dressing rooms, the bathroom, walking down the sidewalk (sometimes into telephone poles), church, math class. She suspects that some of her teachers knew she had a library book hidden behind her textbook, but the good ones didn't let on.

Clare holds degrees in English and elementary education and teaches a summer writing camp for kids. She loves recommending wonderful books to young readers.

Clare lives in Wichita, Kansas, with her husband and four children.

Clare Vanderpool is available for select readings and lectures. To inquire about a possible appearance, please contact the Random House Speakers Bureau at rhspeakers@randomhouse.com.

MOON OVER MANIFEST

—◆—

CLARE VANDERPOOL

GRADES 4–7

THEMES

Loneliness • Hope/Perseverance • Community
Belonging/Home • Friendship • Prejudice/Bigotry

CURRICULUM CONNECTIONS

Language Arts • Science/Health • Social Studies
Music • Drama • Art

978-0-375-85829-1

ABOUT THE BOOK

Set during the Great Depression, Abilene Tucker is sent to Manifest, Kansas, where she searches to find her father's footprint in the town.

Twelve-year-old Abilene Tucker, the daughter of a drifter, feels abandoned when her father puts her on a train and sends her to live with Shady Howard, part-time preacher and saloon operator, in the small town of Manifest, Kansas. Armed with her most prized possession, a broken compass that belonged to her father, Abilene sets out to discover her father's connection to this worn-out town. What she learns is that Manifest is a town with a history of colorful and eccentric characters, and very deep secrets. As stories are told, and secrets revealed, Abilene starts to understand the meaning of community, the power of friendship, and most importantly, she begins to weave her own story.

Also Available on Audio from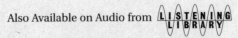

PRE-READING ACTIVITY

Help the class connect to the time period of the novel by having them read about America's Cultural History 1930–1939 on the following website: **kclibrary.lonestar.edu/decade30.html**. Ask students to write a brief essay that discusses the mood of the country during this period.

World War I is also an important aspect of the novel's setting. Share this SchoolTube video to set the time period: **schooltube.com/video/afb90c293f1a40d886fc/World-War-I-Video.** Discuss the hardships faced by the soldiers.

VOCABULARY /
USE OF LANGUAGE

There is some challenging vocabulary in the novel. Ask students to jot down unfamiliar words and try to define those using clues from the context. Such words may include: *vigilant* (p. 5), *perdition* (p. 9), *antiquity* (p. 15), *consolation* (p. 26), *corporal* (p. 31), *revelation* (p. 47), *regalia* (p. 54), *wanton* (p. 55), *enamored* (p. 59), *purveyor* (p. 69), *restitution* (p. 72), *dilapidated* (p. 89), *pyrotectic* (p. 96), *pedigree* (p. 117), *libations* (p. 158), *impasse* (p. 193), *subterfuge* (p. 198), *malady* (p, 216), *depravity* (p. 220), *serendipity* (p. 221), *nefarious* (p. 285), *degenerate* (p. 309), and *bevy* (p. 319).

INTERNET RESOURCES

World War I Propaganda Posters
learnnc.org/lp/editions/ww1posters/5041

**The Woodrow Wilson
Presidential Library and Museum**
woodrowwilson.org/

Great Depression Facts
library.thinkquest.org/07aug/00841/GREAT%20DEPRESSION/facts
%20on%20the%20great%20depression.htm

THEMATIC CONNECTIONS

QUESTIONS FOR GROUP DISCUSSION

LONELINESS—Ask students to discuss how Abilene deals with loneliness. What other characters in the book suffer from loneliness? How do they deal with it? Debate whether Lettie and Ruthanne truly understand Abilene's loneliness. At what point in the novel is it obvious that Abilene and Miss Sadie are a cure for one another's loneliness?

HOPE/PERSEVERANCE—Explain how Gideon's compass is a symbol of hope to Abilene. How does it also become a symbol of perseverance as the story unfolds? Name other symbols of hope in the novel. How does the assignment that Sister Redemta gives to Abilene represent hope and perseverance? In what ways does Miss Sadie represent and offer hope?

COMMUNITY—Ask students to discuss the meaning of community. Describe the town of Manifest. Explain what Miss Sadie means when she says, "The mine whistle was the sound that brought us together. And kept us apart at the same time." (p. 88) Discuss actual occasions in 1917 and in 1936 when Manifest becomes a true community. How does Hattie Mae's News Auxiliary help Abilene connect to the community of Manifest? Explain what Shady means when he tells Abilene, "Having you here has given us a second chance." (p. 327)

BELONGING/HOME—Abilene is constantly searching for Gideon's footprint in Manifest. Explain what Hattie Mae means when she tells Abilene, "Maybe what you're looking for is not so much the mark your daddy made on this town, but the mark the town made on your daddy." (p. 171). Discuss the actual moment when Abilene realizes that she has finally found her home.

FRIENDSHIP—Abilene has ridden the rails with Gideon for so long that she doesn't understand the real meaning of friendship. Debate whether this is why she is reluctant to accept Lettie and Ruthanne's gesture of friendship when they call on her at "Fort Treeconderoga." How do the girls finally become friends? What does Abilene learn about true friendship from Miss Sadie's stories about Jinx and Ned? Discuss how making friends, past and present, changes Abilene's life.

PREJUDICE/BIGOTRY—Ask students to discuss the prejudice and bigotry that exists in the town of Manifest. The entire town of Manifest is made up of immigrants, which makes them prime targets of groups like the KKK. Elroy Knabb and Arthur Devlin are both in the KKK. Cite evidence from the novel that these men don't hide their hatred behind their white masks.

Art © 2010 by Richard Tuschman

CONNECTING TO THE CURRICULUM

LANGUAGE ARTS—Write the story that Abilene turns in to Sister Redempta on September 1. Remember that a story must have a beginning, middle, and an end. Think of an appropriate title. Other than Gideon, to whom might Abilene dedicate her story?

At the end of the novel, Hattie Mae turns her News Auxiliary column over to Abilene. Consider the people that Abilene has met in Manifest during the summer, the many events that she has witnessed and read about, and her reunion with Gideon. Then write Abilene's first column. Remember to include all the whos, whats, whys, whens, and wheres.

SCIENCE/HEALTH—Miss Sadie uses hawthorn root to increase circulation. Ask students to refer to the following website and choose at least 10 common plants and herbs and chart their medicinal use: **herbsguide.net**. Have them include a colored sketch of the plant for identification purposes.

Manifest is a mining town. Among the many health hazards that miners face is Black lung disease. Ask students to find out the causes, symptoms, treatments, and long-term effects of the disease. Then have them write about the disease for a pamphlet called "Health Hazards of Miners" to be presented to workers upon employment in Devlin's mine.

SOCIAL STUDIES—The United States entered World War I in 1917. Woodrow Wilson was president, and in 1919 he was awarded the Nobel Peace Prize. Ask students to visit the following website and find out why Wilson was chosen for this honor: **nobelprize.org/nobel_prizes/peace/laureates/1919**. Then have them write a front-page news story for the *Manifest Herald* on the day the prize was announced.

Have students read about the KKK at the following website: **encyclopedia.kids.net.au/page/ku/Ku_Klux_Klan**. Ask them to write an anonymous story for the *Manifest Herald* called the "Men in the White Masks in Manifest."

MUSIC—Ask students to use sites on the Internet or books and recordings at the public library to locate lyrics of songs from the Great Depression. Such songs may include "Pennies from Heaven," "Brother Can You Spare a Dime," "There's a New Day Comin'," "Headin' for Better Times," and "Dawn of a New Day." Ask them to point out songs that reveal a nation in despair, and ones that reveal hope.

DRAMA—Write and perform a one-act play based on the chapter "Day of Reckoning: September 28, 1918" when the town disperses the Widow Cane's property. Audition class members for the cast of characters, choose a director, and plan period costumes.

ART—The women of Manifest are planning a friendship quilt, and they ask Miss Sadie to make the center square. Consider Miss Sadie's heritage, her role in the town and its history. Then ask them to design the square that Miss Sadie might make. Students may also design a square submitted by Abilene, Lettie, Ruthanne, Hattie Mae, and other women in the novel.

POST-READING ACTIVITY

Ask students to write an essay that compares Abilene's search for "home" to Dorothy's search for home in *The Wizard of Oz*. Who is Abilene's Aunt Em? Which characters might be compared to the Tin Man, the Lion, and the Scare Crow?

Guide prepared by Pat Scales, Children's Literature Consultant, Greenville, South Carolina.

ABOUT THE AUTHOR

Photo © Annmarie Algya

Clare Vanderpool loves reading historical fiction, and conducted the research for *Moon Over Manifest* by reading old newspapers, yearbooks, visiting graveyards, and reading numerous archival records about old mining towns, World War I, and the Great Depression. She based the town of Manifest on the real southeastern Kansas town of Frontenac, home of both of her maternal grandparents. Vanderpool lives in Wichita, Kansas, with her husband and their four children. *Moon Over Manifest* is her first novel, and is the 2011 Newbery Medal winner.

A CONVERSATION WITH
Clare Vanderpool

Q: You stated in your Newbery Medal acceptance speech, "laughter unites us as people." Which character in *Moon Over Manifest* brings the greatest smile to your face?

A: Many characters have shining moments that make me smile, but if I had to choose I'd have to say Abilene and Shady. They both have such a nice mix of funny, sweet, and sometimes sad. But then there's also Hattie Mae. She's a fun character to write with all her news auxiliaries and her take on the whos, whats, whys, whens, and wheres of Manifest. I also enjoyed how her character evolved from the teenage Manifest Huckleberry Queen of 1917 to the wife and mother she became.

Q: Which scene gives you the giggles?

A: I laugh when I re-read certain parts like when Ned and Holler told Heck that *Ich habe wiederlich footen* means *Put down your weapon*. (It really means "I have stinky feet.") And the part where Mr. Matenopolous is telling of his friend Mr. Zoutsaghianopoulous at Ellis Island. He struggles with changing his name and finally agrees, "Take out the H."

Q: The elements of humor in the novel are so layered. What do your young readers say is the funniest part?

A: I get comments about when Ned and Jinx pull the prank with the poison ivy. That actually happened to a friend of mine when he was young, not that it was a prank but he "used" the wrong leaves. He must not have been a boy scout or he would have been taught, "Leaves of three, leave them be." I also hear young readers say they like the part where Jinx's Manchurian Fire Thrower blows up the Manifest water tower, dousing the Victory Quilt. Also, when the girls sneak into the high school and some fireworks go off giving Abilene a chance to escape. I think the consensus is they think Manifest would be an exciting place to live!

Q: Every small town has eccentric characters, gossips, snobs, swindlers, etc. Other than Abilene, which character do your young readers express the most interest? Why?

A: Definitely Shady. I think young readers connect with Shady in much the same way that Abilene does. They trust him, they like him, they see him in his flawed goodness, and I think he provides a sense of security in the way he treats people with kindness and respect. They also seem to think his house would be an interesting place to go to church.

Q: Writing historical fiction requires a lot of research. Which part of the research did you enjoy the most? Reading old newspapers, visiting graveyards, etc.

A: I loved all of the research. For me, poring through old newspapers is the next best thing to time travel. I also read books on the Great Depression, bootlegging, World War I, the

Spanish Influenza, orphan trains. My favorites were anything that had firsthand accounts. I read and listened to many stories of teens on the road during the Great Depression. It was fascinating and very moving to hear people who are now in their later years tell of life on the road when they were young. They spoke with such clarity and there was still a great deal of emotion connected to their experience. There were some heartbreaking stories. The same is true of stories of immigrants and their experiences in coming to America. At Ellis Island, you can pick up phones and listen to actual voices of people who came through Ellis Island tell of their experiences. Very moving.

Q: You believe that story can change us. How did telling Abilene's story change you?

A: I hope Abilene's story has changed me for the better. In accompanying Abilene on her journey to Manifest and her search for home and place, I had a great deal of admiration for the way she pays careful attention to the people around her. She is attentive and open. Everyone has their quirks, their rough edges, their foibles, but everyone has a story to tell. I hope because of Abilene, I am more inclined to listen.

Q: What things were revealed to you along the way?

A: There were some story elements that were revealed to me along the way. I didn't know from the beginning that Ned was an immigrant and an orphan. He seemed like such an all-American kid and in the writing process when I fleshed-out more of his story, I realized that, in fact, he is an all-American kid in the truest sense—someone who came from somewhere else, like most people in this country, with dreams of a good life and a bright future. Of course, not all dreams in Manifest are realized and at one point their world comes crashing down around them. But the people of Manifest are resilient and it is through the town's retelling of their own story that they gain a renewed sense of promise and optimism.

Q: How has winning the Newbery Medal changed you as a writer?

A: There are two answers to that question. The first answer is it has added a little pressure to write another good book. But that is not really a complete change because I wanted to write a good book the first time around as well. The second answer is I hope it hasn't changed me too much as a writer. I have a great deal of respect and appreciation for the award. It is a great honor and one I will always treasure. But when I sit down to write, I have to forget about that incredible gold sticker that is on my book and the medal that sits on my bookshelf. Because those are part of my story and *Moon Over Manifest.* But the characters in my next book have their own story that needs to be told. That is always the great joy and challenge of being a writer.

Q: What is the most insightful question that you have received from a young reader?

A: The most insightful question I've received from a young reader is did I cry when I wrote the chapter called "The Diviner," where we find out that Miss Sadie is Ned's mother and the incredible sacrifice and loss she experienced. I find the question insightful because it tells me that young readers know and have experienced for themselves the incredible connection a reader has with the characters in a book. And the answer to the question is yes. I have four children and it breaks my heart every time I read of Miss Sadie saying goodbye to her little boy, telling him she will find him. It helps a little knowing that she did find him.

Q: What are you writing now?

A: I am writing a story about a Kansas boy who gets uprooted from his home and put in boys' boarding school in Maine. It is historical fiction in that it takes place in 1945, but it is less dependent on historical events. My main characters meets another boy and they go on a quest of sorts. I know that's a little vague, but you know how writers are. They'd rather you read about it than tell you the story up front.

MORE CLASSROOM-FRIENDLY BOOKS IN THE NEWBERY FAMILY

When You Reach Me
Rebecca Stead
978-0-375-85086-8

THEMATIC CONNECTION

SELF-IDENTITY—Describe Miranda at the beginning of the novel. How does she change as the story unfolds? How does working at Jimmy's and being part of a group give Miranda confidence that she didn't have when she only hung out with Sal? The first note that Miranda receives says, "I am coming to save your friend's life and my own." (p. 60) Explain the literal and figurative meaning of this note, and what it has to do with self-identity. Discuss the role of the mysterious notes in boosting Miranda's self-worth.

CURRICULUM CONNECTION

LANGUAGE ARTS—Discuss what the *New York Times* reviewer means when she calls *When You Reach Me* "a hybrid of genres." Ask students to discuss the definition of the following genres: *science fiction, adventure, mystery, historical fiction,* and *realism*. Divide the class into small groups and ask each group to prepare a debate about which genre(s) they think the novel fits. Ask them to cite passages from the novel to support their debate.

Holes
Louis Sachar
978-0-440-41480-3

THEMATIC CONNECTION

BELONGING—Stanley is overweight and considered a misfit by the boys in his school and neighborhood. Ask students to discuss why Stanley is an easy target for bullies. At what point in the novel does Stanley begin feeling that he is a part of the group? Who is the leader? How do the guys view Stanley at the end of the novel? How might Stanley be considered a hero? Involve the class in a discussion about how Stanley's heroic status might change the way his classmates view him when he returns to school in the fall.

CURRICULUM CONNECTION

MATH—Zero cannot read, but he is excellent in math. Have each student survey at least 20 adults asking them whether their strength in school was reading or math. Collect the data gathered by each student and have the class construct a graph that reveals the results of the survey. Study the graph and engage the class in a discussion about the importance of both subjects.

Bud, Not Buddy
Christopher Paul Curtis
978-0-440-41328-8

THEMATIC CONNECTION

HOPE—Ask the class to discuss how the flyers in Bud's suitcase give him hope. Bud's mother once told him, "When one door closes, don't worry, because another door opens." (p. 43) How does this statement give Bud the hope he needs to continue his search for his father? Discuss the moments in the story when a door closes for Bud. At what point does the door open? Cite evidence in the novel that Herman Calloway had hope that his daughter might return.

CURRICULUM CONNECTION

SCIENCE—Lefty Lewis sends Herman Calloway a telegram telling him about Bud. Have students construct an illustrated time line that shows the development of communication from the invention of the telegraph to today's new technologies.

The Watsons Go to Birmingham—1963
Christopher Paul Curtis
978-0-440-41412-4

THEMATIC CONNECTION

FRIENDSHIP—Kenny becomes a real friend of Rufus, but realizes that he has damaged their relationship the moment he joins in laughing at Rufus on the bus. (pp. 43–46). Have students write about a situation in which they slighted someone without just cause, how they felt afterward, and what they did about it. How does Kenny's acknowledgment of his injustice help to correct it?

CURRICULUM CONNECTION

HISTORY (CIVIL RIGHTS)—Life in 1963 was quite different for African Americans than it is today, especially in the South. The '60s were turbulent times in America. After reading the novel, have students find inferences that blacks and whites were treated differently. (pp. 5–6) Check reference books in the school media center for historical details of the Birmingham church bombing and look for the names of the young girls listed on the "In Memory of" page. Probe the question raised by Kenny (p. 199), "Why would they hurt some little kids like that?" Have students create a class book on What America Was Like When the Watsons Went to Birmingham in 1963.

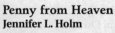

Penny from Heaven
Jennifer L. Holm
978-0-375-83689-3

THEMATIC CONNECTION

DEATH—The death of Penny's father drastically changes the lives of his family members, in part because of the way he died. How is Uncle Dominic's life changed by his brother's death? How does the truth about her father's death alter its emotional impact on Penny's life? How is Penny directly influenced by her mother's loss? On page 233, Penny wants to tell people, "almost dying is awful easy. It's the living that's hard." How has her life reflected this statement?

CURRICULUM CONNECTION

HISTORY—Penny doesn't understand why her father was put in an internment camp, and no one seems to be able to answer her questions. Ask students to research the arrest and internment of non-naturalized Italian Americans during World War II and to write a letter of explanation to Penny. Students should assume the voice of a government official, the arresting officer, the prison warden, one of the family members, or someone else that might have had a role in the arrest.

Turtle in Paradise
Jennifer L. Holm
978-0-375-83690-9

THEMATIC CONNECTION

BETRAYAL—Turtle, Slow Poke, Nana Philly, Aunt Minnie, and Sadiebelle all experience betrayal in one form or another. What does it mean to betray someone? How do these characters each cope with the betrayal? How do their experiences change their view of life and their relationships?

CURRICULUM CONNECTION

SCIENCE—The 1935 hurricane that hit Key West was one of the worst in history. It is a miracle that Turtle and the Diaper Gang escaped death. Ask one group of students to research the weather conditions that cause a hurricane and another group to prepare a hurricane safety brochure. Have two other groups make a time line of hurricanes in the United States: one group should record from the first recorded hurricane to 1950, and the other should record from 1951 to present. The time line groups should also include information such as loss of life, size and strength of the hurricane, location hit, and other details that tell the story. Lastly, have each group can present their findings to the class.

Hattie Big Sky
Kirby Larson
978-0-385-73595-7

THEMATIC CONNECTION

COMING-OF-AGE—Describe how Hattie changes in the year that she spends on the Montana prairie. Debate whether her idea of "home" is different by the end of the novel. Hattie says, "I'd arrived alone, and I wanted to leave that way." (p. 282) Why is this so important to her? How is she a success even though tragedy prevented her from proving the claim?

CURRICULUM CONNECTION

HISTORY—Ask readers to use resources in the library or sites on the Internet to find out about the Homestead Act approved by Congress in the late 1800s. How was the Homestead Act of 1910 different from the original act? Discuss how the rules of the act made it almost impossible for an independent 16-year-old girl to prove up on a claim.

Whittington
Alan Armstrong
978-0-375-82865-2

THEMATIC CONNECTION

LONELINESS—Bernie was especially lonely after his daughter died. How can one be independent and lonely? Ask students to discuss the difference between sadness and loneliness. How do the animals in the barn fill a void in Bernie's life? Cite scenes from Dick Whittington's story where he experienced loneliness. How did he take charge of his loneliness?

CURRICULUM CONNECTION

THEATER—Allow students to work in small groups to select a favorite chapter of the novel and write it as a one-act play. Use appropriate costumes or masks to distinguish the characters. Design a simple scene backdrop, and choose appropriate music to open and close the scene.

Classroom
CAST ▶

RANDOM HOUSE
CHILDREN'S BOOKS

Video Podcasting Program

Visit **RHCBClassroomCast.com** for free videos of authors discussing their work, research, and how they go about writing their books. Participating authors include Candace Fleming, Jennifer and Matthew Holm, Mary Pope Osborne, Louis Sachar, and Eileen and Jerry Spinelli.

ClassroomCast videos are perfect for author studies and are interactive whiteboard-friendly!

Random House Children's Books is now on

Tune in to our channel often to share book trailers, author interviews, and teasers with your students.

SchoolTube.com/user/randomhouse